The Lunar
Codex

Annie O'Connell

Fulton Books
Meadville, PA

Published by Fulton Books 2022

ISBN 978-1-63860-820-2 (paperback)
ISBN 978-1-63985-836-1 (hardcover)
ISBN 978-1-63860-821-9 (digital)

To my boys, Patrick, Michael, Richard, and Kevin,
you are my joy, inspiration, and constant source of entertainment.
To my loving husband, Sean,
thank you for enduring long hours of my
nose being glued to my computer
so I could bring this dream to life.

CONTENTS

PROLOGUE

They say that a person's earliest memories form around the age of two. For me, I was three years old. Things prior come back to me in bits and pieces but are mostly feelings of happiness and love. My most concrete memory in those fragile first years was "the talk" with Aunt Cora and Uncle Roman. I was sitting on my small captain's twin bed, surrounded by my menagerie of stuffies—Ellie, Dog, Bunny, Bobo, and half a dozen others there in place but lacking a name.

Out in the hallway, I could hear Uncle Roman and Aunt Cora talking and knew that something was wrong. Aunt Cora was the epitome of calm and had an amazing way of making everyone feel comfortable and secure. However, as I listened, I could sense the tears in her tone as she discussed the recent phone call with Uncle Roman. I slid off my bed and instinctively took Bunny. He was a well-loved white rabbit my mother had given to me when I was six months old. Bunny was my most trusted confidant, with a faded blue ribbon around his neck and a crooked ear from my insatiable habit of rubbing it on my nose when fatigue or fear was near.

Moving closer to the door, I could feel the soft plush of the baby-blue rug squishing between my toes. As I inched my way closer, I could see them through the small opening in my large wooden door. Although I don't remember the full content of the conversation, the tears in Aunt Cora's eyes and the concerned look on my Uncle Roman's face as he held her close have stuck with me all these years. This was the pivotal night of my life. This was the night that both my parents died, and I became an orphan.

CHAPTER 1

Williston

Twelve years later

"Being on the East Coast will be a pleasant change, don't you think?" Uncle Roman asked as he looked over his shoulder at me in the back seat.

Turning, I gave an attempt at a smile before shifting back to resume my scenery watching. There was an uncomfortable silence as Uncle Roman and Aunt Cora exchanged uncomfortable glances. They were likely trying to think of something to make this move easier than the last ones. In the past nine months, we have moved three times, and I wondered how long we would last at this house.

"The realtor says the complex we're moving into is a real up-and-coming area although most of it is still being built," Aunt Cora added.

"She also said that there are kids your age on our street." Uncle Roman said.

Not wanting to hear how amazing this new house was going to be, I lifted my air pods and drowned out the world to Imagine Dragons. Out of the corner of my eye, I noticed my uncle peer back before dropping his head and turning back to the road.

A few hours later, the feeling of the car shift as it veered off the highway caused me to glance up. I watched as the moving van in front of us followed the exit ramp to the bottom and then turned left onto a minor road. I pulled my AirPods out and sat up in the seat as I looked around. Surrounding the overpass were a few small stores, restaurants, and hotels, on what was otherwise a nondescript area.

"Williston, fourteen miles!" Aunt Cora cheered.

Acknowledging the same sign she saw, I was more horrified by the sight beyond it. Fields and fields and fields of nothing. Nothing, except the occasional cow. My heart sank as I waited to see civilization appear. Uncle Roman must have seen the despair cross my face.

"I know this differs from Scottsdale, but I think you'll like it."

Although we had only been there for four months, I really enjoyed Arizona. We lived in a quaint town, and I could either walk or ride my bike to most places. This was a far cry from that. I put my AirPods in again, dropping my head back against the headrest and turned to stare out at my new companions, the cows. With each one we passed, I tried to ignore the mounting anger. My mind wandered to my parents and tried to imagine what life would have been like had they not gone out that night. Instantly, I felt my back stiffen. Trying to calm myself, I repeated the same thing I had thought a thousand times before—none of us asked for this life. But yet here we are again—moving.

I watched as the moving truck turned right onto a street, aptly named Main Street and felt like I had just turned onto a postcard from the 1950s. Multiple mom-and-pop style stores lined the street. Most of which had a small porch, and of those, many had a set of rocking chairs, some occupied by people fanning themselves. It was late September, and although the temperatures could still be scorching, the meteorologist announced today to be on the milder side, which would make unpacking more bearable. To the right was a large burger-style restaurant just as you entered the town and seemed to be the primary place for everyone to hang out as there was a mass of teens and families surrounding it. Across the street, there was a gas station with a man that was filling the tanks and washing windshields. Up ahead, a large sign was hung across the street, reading *Annual Williston Farmers and Flea Market*. Just past it was a series of tents lining the side streets and under each were small tables with various items on each.

"Oh, look! A real farmer's market!" Aunt Cora cooed.

Her excitement caused the corner of my lip to lift, but I was still mad, so I would not give them the satisfaction of a full smile. At the end of Main Street, there was a large sign noting the Williston Public School. As I searched the area, confusion set in when I realized there were no buildings in sight.

"Do they learn in tents? Where is the school?" I asked.

Uncle Roman glanced back at me, smiling, before reading the sign.

"No. There are buildings back there. Apparently, it is a gigantic complex where all the students go together. The realtor said it is like a giant box with one side each for the elementary school, middle school, high school, and community college."

Momentary intrigue at a school where students ranged from toddlers to twenty was quickly won out by disinterest. Not wanting to delve further into a school that I would not be attending, I resumed my previous position. Curious to see the rest of the town, I was shocked when I realized we had already gone through it!

Again, we passed fields of cows—no, wait, I see a horse out there. We continued for a short distance before spotting a large stucco gateway with *Crystal Shore—Luxury Living* embossed in bronze lettering across a warm-blue background on the right, and its appearance in the middle of nowhere was distressing. The truck turned into the gated area, and we followed. The area surrounding it was wooded with gnarly tall trees that had some sort of gray-colored mesh hanging from it. Watching the long tendrils as they swayed gently in the breeze felt as though they were welcoming me. Hypnotized by the movement, I was abruptly brought back to reality when I heard Aunt Cora say, "It's Spanish moss." I looked up, confused by what she had said.

"The stuff hanging off the trees. It's called Spanish moss."

Nodding, I turned to look out the window again. Up ahead on the right were large construction vehicles on a sizable, cleared area. Closer to the road, a sign in front read *Future site of the Crystal Shore Club House,* with a picture depicting its intended design. It was going to have a gym, gathering area, two pools, and a large waterslide. I guess it would be epic when they finished it. A twinge of regret touched a nerve as I realized I would likely never see the completed project.

Returning my thoughts to the window, I was instantly confused as we passed a multitude of street signs that did not have a corresponding street attached to them.

"Why is there a sign without a street?" I asked.

Uncle Roman, apparently thinking the same thing, answered, "I think it is where the streets are eventually going to be located."

"Kind of gets you in the mood for Halloween," Aunt Cora said in a spooky voice while she wiggled her fingers at me.

"Seriously. Are we the only people living here?" I asked with true concern.

Uncle Roman chuckled. "No. They built from the outer perimeter in so they could build the clubhouse without driving the homeowners crazy."

Content with the response, I returned to my observations. In the distance was a road off to the left with three houses in the middle of a cleared field. Passing by a small street to the right, I saw many more houses and felt my heart lift at the thought that we weren't living in a community of three. Ahead of us, the truck pulled into the small court with the three houses on it. Passing the street sign, I noted we would now live on Crystal Court. Uncle Roman waited at the bottom of the road as we watched the movers skillfully maneuver around the court and back into the driveway of 3501.

"How did they come up with the house numbers? I don't think there are even thirty-five houses in this community, let alone thirty-five hundred," I said.

"The thirty-five refers to the section of the community we are in, and the—oh, one refers to the house number in that section," Uncle Roman explained.

Nodding, I glanced back to the truck and could see that the movers were parked and jumping out of the truck. Pulling up next to them, I grabbed my AirPods, laptop, and a small wooden box with a wolf on it before I stepped out of the car. Stretching, I watched as Aunt Cora walked up to the house to get the key, which was being stored in a key box on the front door. Examining our new home, I noted it was a two-story Mediterranean style with a two-car garage. Before moving, we had decided that I would get the second floor to myself so I could have more privacy. Instinctively, my eyes moved up to where my new quarters would be located and found myself confused by a small balcony over the garage. Uncle Roman, watching my gaze, walked over.

"You can't actually go out onto it. It's more for show. They call it a Juliet balcony."

Dropping one eyebrow while I lifted the other, I stared at him.

"Why would you build something you can't use?"

Before he could answer, Aunt Cora walked back to us and followed our glance.

"Oh, the Juliet balcony. It was what made me want this house! Come on, boys. The door is open."

Uncle Roman and I looked at each other, and he shrugged, pointing to Aunt Cora.

"Does that answer your question?"

I couldn't help but smile as I followed Aunt Cora into the house.

As we approached the front door, I had a strong sense that we were being watched. From the corner of my eye, I noticed the curtains to the house on the right shift. Uncle Roman must have seen it as well.

"We'll unpack today and meet the neighbors tomorrow," he said.

"Let them know the Manson family hasn't moved in, right?" I teased.

"Yes. Something like that."

The entrance of the house had a large foyer with stairs to the right and a tall ceiling going all the way to the second floor. Beyond the foyer was a small hallway that opened to the kitchen and a small breakfast nook to the left. At the far end of the kitchen was a half wall with the sink and extra cabinets, allowing for better access to the main dining area just beyond it. To the right, adjacent to the dining area, was the family room, and just beyond that was Aunt Cora and

Uncle Roman's room. In the backyard, there was a large screened-in patio with a pool and a raised Jacuzzi attached to the pool.

"Go upstairs and check out your area," Aunt Cora suggested.

I nodded as I backtracked to the foyer where the stairs were and made my way up. At the top of the stairs, there was a hallway with an enormous bathroom to the right, a smaller bedroom to the left, and the large bedroom I had seen from the driveway straight ahead. Curious, I headed to the front bedroom and looked out the windows.

Down below, I could see the three movers and my uncle moving back and forth from the truck into the house. Across the street was a smaller house of similar design with a minivan and an old beat-up pickup truck in the driveway. Shifting my attention to the window facing the middle house, I glanced down. There was a small garden-like patio with Edison bulbs strung across the tiled floor and a large outdoor fireplace surrounded by patio furniture. As I was about to turn, I heard the door to the house next door swing open and a girl around my age bounded out with a book in her arm. She was wearing a light-blue sundress that fell just above her knees, a yellow cardigan, and bright yellow sandals. Her hair was down, but short, just above her shoulders. As she walked to the long chaise lounge, her tight curls bounced slightly—the sun seemed to play within each curl, highlighting the occasional gold strands within the brown sugar base. Everything seemed to stop when I saw her, and all I could think was she was the most beautiful girl I had ever seen.

"I think her name is Isabelle." A voice came from the doorway, causing me to jump.

Turning, I could see my aunt smiling at me. She walked across the empty room toward the closet, looking around and nodding in approval.

"I think this will do nicely for you."

Slowly, she sauntered over toward the window I was standing at and looked down to where Isabelle was now sitting before looking back up at me. Smiling, she cupped my cheek in her hand.

"Yes. I think you will do *very* nicely here."

"Aunt Cora, stop."

She let go of my cheek and shrugged.

"I said nothing. I was simply making an observation."

As I was about to continue my argument, I heard a movement in the stairwell and walked over to see the movers carrying up my bed frame.

"It's going in this room." My aunt motioned to the men.

Turning to me, she said, "Looks like your stuff will be unloaded first. Do you need help to get your room together?"

"Thank you, but I want to try by myself this time. If I get stuck, I know where to go look."

"Oh? Where will that be?"

"You'll be in the kitchen making your cookies, brownies, and cakes for our meet and greet with the neighbors tomorrow although it doesn't look like you have to make too much this time." I motioned out the window to our scarcity of neighbors.

Sighing, she said, "I suppose you're right. But I think some brownies are still in order."

As the boxes piled up, I tried to work on clearing them as soon as possible. Fortunately, the movers put the furniture together, leaving me with just the placement of the smaller items around the room. Although we likely won't be here for longer than six months, I really hated living out of boxes, and putting my room together gave at least a small sense of normalcy. By the time Uncle Roman called me down to eat, I only had four boxes left, which contained miscellaneous items. Not sure what to do with them, I carried them to the other room on the second floor that we were going to use as a guest room. We have lived in several houses that have had a guest room, but I don't remember ever actually having a guest over. So when they bought the trundle bed for it, I thought it was a waste of money.

"Jace, dinner is ready," Uncle Roman called.

"I'm coming."

Walking down the stairs, I could see that they adorned the once-barren foyer with a large dresser-style cabinet opposite the front door with a glass bowl and large vase with shells and tall beach grass. Above the cabinet was a large circular mirror with scalloped edges. When I looked in the mirror, I could see family pictures hanging on the wall below the stairs. Continuing through the foyer was the kitchen, which was also fully assembled. The breakfast nook now contained a small table, and a large table was placed in the dining room. The latter could easily feed ten. As I sat at the dining table, I turned to look at the family room, which was completely transformed. A large sectional couch facing the fireplace encompassed most of the room, and my uncle's favorite reclining chair was opposite it. Feeling a bit mischievous, I jokingly asked Aunt Cora, "I thought you said that chair was going to get lost in transition."

Uncle Roman's eyes narrowed as he looked in the living room and then back to us.

"I knew you two were conspiring against my poor La-Z-Boy, so I got the movers to get it on the truck before it could go missing."

Aunt Cora seemed to change the decor of the house every other move, and Uncle Roman's poop-brown La-Z-Boy no longer matched her sea-foam green sectional and white accent tables.

"Don't look at me. She wants to replace it."

"Gee, thanks!" Aunt Cora said, jokingly swatting my arm.

"It's broken in, and it took me years to get it just right."

She sighed heavily. "Maybe I can get a slipcover for it, so it matches."

"How is your unpacking going?" Uncle Roman asked me.

"Great. I just have four boxes left. I put them in the guest room for now."

Aunt Cora frowned.

"Do you need help with it? I don't want boxes out if we don't need to."

"You are probably the only person on the planet that can pack an entire house in less than two days and put one back together just as fast. No one will lift an eye at four boxes eight hours after moving in."

Uncle Roman raised an eyebrow and nodded slightly.

"He has a point, Cora."

She playfully let out a flustered sigh. "I guess you're right. But if someone comments on it, I'm throwing you both under the bus!"

We both laughed at the absurdity of her statement. The house was complete—an art form that Aunt Cora had perfected within the last, ten or so, moves.

"So Jace seems to have noticed a certain neighbor of ours," Aunt Cora said with a coy nod toward my uncle.

He initially stared at her blankly, and then his brows raised as the realization of who she was talking about hit him.

"Aah. Yes, I think you and Marcus are the same age."

One thing I love about my uncle is that he tries not to over-dramatize things. Aunt Cora, conversely, seems to thrive on gossip. I think it is mostly because she never really has anyone she can do it with, so Uncle Roman and I are the unwilling participants.

"Aunt Cora, please, I was looking out the window when she came out. There is nothing more to it."

"So we're not talking about the boy across the way?" Uncle Roman asked.

Aunt Cora smiled sweetly at Uncle Roman as she playfully swatted at him, then looked back at me.

"Okay, okay… I won't say anything further about the way your jaw was on the floor as you were just 'looking out the window.'"

I felt my cheeks flush and looked down at my food.

"Cora, leave the boy alone. Let him get used to being in the house before you get him married off!"

Aunt Cora laughed. "There will be many more adventures before you're hearing wedding bells."

"Oh my god! Please, the two of you," I said, exacerbated.

"Let's watch what we say, Jace."

"Yes, sir. I'm sorry for the outburst."

"Aunt Cora is just teasing you."

He turned to look out the back door before returning his attention to me.

"It's still light outside. Maybe after dinner, you would like to go for a bike ride or a walk?" he asked.

Turning to look in the same direction he just was, I could see that the sky was still bright with the beginnings of warm amber glows in the distance. We likely had roughly an hour left in the day.

"I'd like that."

"Great. Cora, would you like to join us?"

Aunt Cora looked to the table and then around the house again. Although it was clean and appeared to have been lived in for years, she drew her eyebrows in tight.

"I think I still have some stuff that needs attending to here. Next time."

After dinner, Uncle Roman and I went to change into some more comfortable clothes before heading out. He grabbed a few flashlights, and we went out through the open garage door. In the distance, I could hear the loud chirping of the cicadas mixing with the grasshoppers, which made for an interesting mix of melodies. The day was still warm from this afternoon, but a cool breeze was coming through, and I was grateful for the sweatpants and light zip-up sweater I took with me.

As we walked to the edge of the driveway and down the road, we remained silent. In my periphery, I could see him periodically looking toward me, as though he wanted to talk about something but could not find the words. Maybe he wanted to apologize for all the moves. Perhaps he was going to tell me that this was the last one and that I could be a normal tenth grader. But none of that was said or asked, and the tension between us was quickly becoming palpable. I needed to break the silence, but with what? Before I could come up with something, though, he spoke.

"The boy across the street…his name is Marcus, and his mom is going to be your tutor."

I turned to look at him, stunned.

"My teacher will be on the same street as me? Seriously?"

The corner of Uncle Roman's lip turned up as he watched me and then motioned to turn left at the bottom of the road.

"Yes. It is a bit of a win-win. She's two doors away, so there is no reason for her to be late, and she can get home quickly if needed. If you have problems or questions, she'd be right there. Also, she has a boy in tenth grade as well."

I stared at him for a bit, trying to figure if I was happy with this arrangement or not. He looked back at me, and a big smile crossed his face as he put his arm around my shoulders and pulled me close to him.

"How did you get so big? It was only a few years ago you were knee-high to a grasshopper."

I chuckled and said, "A grasshopper? Well, I think you'll fit in fine with the local linguistics."

Looking back at my uncle, I realized that I no longer needed to look up to meet his eyes. I was now eye to eye with him. Feeling a smile creep across my face, I tried to draw an imaginary line from my head to his, and he ducked out of the way.

"Oh no, you don't. There is no way I will have you outgrowing me as a fourteen-year-old. After you are fifteen in two weeks, then we'll talk."

I laughed and tried again for the makeshift measurement. He grabbed me around the neck, so I pulled out and ducked behind him. Smiling, he bent his knees and put his hands up, challenging me to get past him. Standing back, I measured my odds, then I rushed toward him, bobbing and weaving to avoid capture. After successfully evading his grasp twice, I misstepped and ran right into him. Without warning, he quickly threw my head into a tight grip and began rubbing his knuckles across my head vigorously in a noogie. He loved this game as the only way out was for me to say "uncle." I fought to avoid having to say the words, and he grounded slightly harder on my head. Finally, I succumbed to his demands.

"Uncle, uncle, UNCLE!"

Laughing, but somewhat out of breath, he released me.

"I think it will be me on the receiving end of this, in the not-too-distant future."

I smiled as he gently nudged my arm. Soon, we were continuing in silence again.

"I know the moves are rough on you," he finally spoke, interrupting the quiet.

Not knowing what to say, I continued to walk, staring into a field opposite to where he was standing. There was so much I wanted to say but knew it wouldn't change anything. His hand clasped me on the shoulder, turning me to look at him.

"Jace, I love you. I have always loved you and will always love you. Please know that everything your aunt and I do is always with your best interests in mind."

He looked deep into my eyes, and I could see true hurt and concern in them. Not knowing what else to say to ease the situation, I just nodded. He continued to stare at me as he lifted his hands and cupped them around the back of my neck, placing his forehead against mine.

"We only want what is best for you and will do everything to see you are safe and well protected."

I nodded again before he pulled away. As we resumed our walk, his words echoed in my head, and I felt the hair on the back of my neck stand up.

"What do you mean by keeping me safe and well-protected?"

His eyes widened slightly, and his cheeks flushed, which was an odd reaction for a man who was always so strong and reserved.

After a few steps, he answered, "You're a teenager, and by nature of what you are, trouble will be apt to follow you."

I laughed.

"I think I've done a good job of staying out of trouble this far."

He looked at me and smiled.

"Yes, I guess you have. Seeing you get older, though, makes me realize that I'm getting older too. And I'm not ready for it. Like this hair! When did I go gray?"

He ran his hand through his hair, causing it to stand up slightly. He looked like a deranged porcupine, and I chuckled at the sight.

"Oh, this is funny, huh? Get over here for another noogie!"

Seeing him lunge at me, I broke out into a run and started dodging and weaving again, both of us laughing as I did. Suddenly, Uncle Roman stopped short, which caused me to do the same. In the distance, I could hear dogs barking.

"What?" I asked.

He shook his head.

"It's likely nothing, but we're still in a developing community that is mostly open fields. I wouldn't expect to hear dogs."

He continued scanning the field where we had heard them.

"Let's head back home. The sun is almost down, and I'm sure your aunt has a thousand things for me to move, put together, or hang up."

I looked back at the field and then at Uncle Roman. At my nod, we turned and headed back toward the house, but his pace had noticeably increased.

"What is going on? You look as though you saw a ghost."

Clicking on the flashlight, he slowed his stride a bit and smiled at me.

"I guess my inner kid took hold. We're in a new place with no one around and a pack of dogs in the distance that we can't see. My fight-or-flight instinct must have kicked in."

I searched his face and looked back over my shoulder. He had never shown fear like that, and it slightly unnerved me. Turning back toward our block, I could see the lights from the three houses turning on.

"I'll race you back," I said.

He turned to me and smiled.

"You're on!" And he took off running.

"Hey! That's not fair!" I shouted as I ran, quickly catching up to him.

Turning onto Crystal Court, I took the lead as I was on the inside of the turn. He grabbed onto my shirt as we maintained our sprint for home. For the rest of the makeshift race, we continued grabbing at each other and arrived at the driveway at the same time.

"I would have won," I said.

"I beg to differ." He grinned although visibly winded.

I bent down to catch my own breath when I heard a clanking sound, which caused me to stand. Now both of us were looking in the direction it had come from.

Across the court was a boy about my age with a bike flipped over and a series of tools strewn across the floor. He looked frazzled as he picked up tool after tool staring at it before dropping it back on the mat. I glanced at Uncle Roman, who smiled.

"Looks like he needs some help. If you need any tools, I'll keep the garage open."

I nodded and walked across the street.

Chapter 2

Marcus

I grabbed the flashlight from Uncle Roman and made my way across the court to the other teen. To keep from startling him, I purposely swayed my flashlight back and forth so he would notice the movement heading toward him, and when I was within a few feet, he looked up and over his shoulder at me.

"Are you the new kid that just moved in?" he asked.

"That would be me. My name is Jace Northall."

As he stood and turned toward me, I could see that he was slightly shorter than I was—maybe five feet eight. He had auburn hair that appeared in desperate need of a haircut. His chin had the scruff of a five o'clock shadow crossing it, and his attire were comparatively baggy, which made it hard to tell if he was slightly overweight or just hiding in the larger clothes. As he spun around to meet me, he extended a fist. On seeing it, I reciprocated, bumping mine against his.

"My name is Marcus, Marcus Hunter. So what do you know about bike chains?" he asked as he ran his hand through his hair while looking back at the bike.

"I've had to replace a chain or two."

Looking across the tools he had strewn across the towel, I quickly realized he lacked the ones he would need. Since we had just moved in, I was not completely sure where the tools would be, but

Uncle Roman typically tried to keep all our garages set up the same way from house to house.

"You're missing what you'll need, but I know we have them. Do you want to come over to help me look for it?"

He looked back at the house and winced.

"Uh, how many boxes do you have to get through?"

I laughed. "You haven't seen my family move into a house. We unpacked everything already."

"Get the hell out of here! You just moved in at like twelve hours ago. Now I feel that I have to go."

He stood, and we started walking toward my house. Entering the garage, I swung the flashlight back and forth, looking for the light switch. Marcus casually walked to the back wall near the door, running his hands along the wall. After a quick search, I heard a click, and the fluorescent bulbs illuminated the room.

"The same people built all these houses, so I figured yours would be in the same spot as mine."

"Yeah, that makes sense."

He looked around the room and nodded in approval. Although there was not much in the garage, it was neat and organized. The garbage was even in a neat pile in the corner.

"So where do you think this tool will be?"

"Likely in the toolbox, I'm just not sure which drawer."

On the far back wall was a large red toolbox, and as I opened the drawers, Marcus's jaw visibly dropped. My uncle was also a bit of an organization buff and had lined all the drawers in foam, arranging each tool into their respective slots.

"Your dad would have a stroke if he saw my toolbox. It takes just as long to find anything as it does to put it together."

"He's actually my uncle. My parents died when I was three."

Marcus's face flushed red as he looked up from the toolbox to me and then back to the drawer.

"Oh man, I'm sorry. I didn't realize."

"How could you? I just moved here, and you just met me ten minutes ago. It's cool, really."

He looked back at me, his brows knitted as if trying to judge my intention. Realizing that the mistake had not devastated me, his features relaxed, and he smiled. Returning our energy back to the task at hand, we started on the top shelf, then worked our way down. I found the first of the tools I was looking for in the third drawer.

"Got one!"

Marcus took it, visibly perplexed by its appearance. After turning it around and examining it from every angle, he lifted it in the air and pointed to it with his shoulders slightly shrugged, causing me to smile. It definitely looked odd like a cross between pliers and a corkscrew.

"That pops the bad part of the chain out. I need to find the tool to put it back together and the lever to help get it back on the wheel."

I stopped rummaging for a second and looked back at Marcus, who was still examining the chain splitter.

"Thinking about it, do you have links to replace the broken one?"

He stopped and stared at me dumbly, and I couldn't help but smile.

"I'll take that as a no. I'm sure we have some in here."

After a few minutes, I had all the tools we would need to put the bike back in working order. Taking the tools from Marcus, we walked back to his driveway.

"Can you hold the flashlight while I fix it?" I asked him.

Marcus nodded, and I started checking the chain for the broken piece. Once located, I quickly went to work fixing the broken link. Marcus knelt opposite me, diligently keeping the flashlight fixed on where I was working. Out of the corner of my eye, I could see his head shifting to watch what I was doing, nodding periodically as I worked. When I finished, I flipped the bike back over and told him to take it for a quick ride. Handing me the flashlight, he jumped on and rode it around before bringing it back into the driveway.

"Thanks, man. I wasn't sure how I would fix it, and I really didn't want to bring it to Mr. Hendrickson. He owns the bike store in town and charges an arm and a leg to fix stuff. It's almost cheaper to buy a new bike than let him fix it."

"That's crazy. The kit is really cheap, and now you know how to fix it yourself."

He nodded, and we looked around the driveway at the mass of tools, one of which was a hammer. I picked it up and looked at him with a half smile as I raised an eyebrow.

"It's a fix-all," he said with a shrug.

"A fix-all?"

"Yeah. It fixes everything, especially when you need something to take your frustration out on."

I laughed and started picking up the rest of the tools with him. As we walked toward his garage, I could see the colossal mess of stuff everywhere. Marcus looked at me, and his cheeks flushed as he began running his hand through his hair again.

"Yeah, I'm not nearly as organized as your uncle. I have a box over there for the tools."

Just outside the garage on the floor was a small beat-up green metal box stuffed, nearly to capacity. I looked from the box to him and frowned.

"You're gonna need a bigger box."

Marcus smiled. "Great movie reference! I love *Jaws*."

"It's one of my favorites too. Do you have anything bigger we can use? I don't think all this stuff is going to fit in there."

Marcus ran his hands through his hair again as he looked around the room. By now, his hair was standing up on its end from the constant abuse he was giving it.

"I'm sure there is something around here—somewhere."

I cringed as I looked into the hoard.

"How about we grab a box from my house? I can put these away too." I motioned to the tools I borrowed.

Marcus spun on his heels and pointed a finger at me. "That—is a much better idea."

I laughed, and we headed back to my house. As I was trying to put a box together, Uncle Roman opened the door into the garage and jumped a bit when he saw us.

"Oh, boys. I wasn't expecting you to be in here. What are you doing?"

"Uncle Roman, this is Marcus. He needs something to hold his tools in, so I was going to put his excess tools into a box for now."

Uncle Roman frowned at the box I was making.

"You're going to need something sturdier than that."

"I have a box that was my dad's, but it's already filled."

"Let's see what I have over here."

Uncle Roman walked over to a wall adorned with cabinets and shelving and looked around. Smiling, he moved some of the garbage out of the way. Then he rolled out a brand-new toolbox—much like his but only about half as tall. The appearance of the extra box slightly perplexed me as I had not remembered there being a second one when we were just in the garage. Shaking the thought off, I watched as he rolled it out from its hiding spot for Marcus to look at.

"I think this will do nicely."

Marcus's eyes went wide. "Thank you, sir, but I can't possibly…"

"I insist. A man should have a well-organized and functioning toolbox. Now go get your dad's box, and we'll get this put together."

Marcus stood there, stunned and unable to move. I patted him on the back and turned him toward his house.

"He won't take no for an answer, so you may as well go get them."

He nodded as we walked back, but on the way, he kept shaking his head.

"Where am I even going to put it?"

I was thinking the same thing but was unsure of what I should say. As we were picking up the stray tools, I heard footsteps behind us and turned to see Uncle Roman walking up the drive. As he looked past us and into the garage, his eyes widened.

"Wow. That's…quite the space you have in there."

Marcus's cheeks shone red.

"Y-yes, sir."

Uncle Roman stood looking at the area and then back to us.

"Okay, we'll keep the box in our garage while you clear out some room for it in here."

Marcus nodded as he looked back at the garage then began running his hand through his hair again.

"Jace, do you think you can help him clear it?"

I looked at the monstrous mess that was basically from the floor to the ceiling and gulped.

"Uh, yeah, sure. Maybe over the next week or two, we can get it organized."

To Marcus, he said, "Perfect. Then it's settled. Get the tools you can see and bring them by us for now."

Uncle Roman picked up the tattered green box and a few stray tools that surrounded it before turning and heading back to our house. I surveyed the garage, trying to judge how far I could reach before risking an avalanche. Marcus seemed to contemplate the same thing when he finally spoke up, "The easiest stuff to grab was in the front, and he already walked away with it."

"Okay, then let's head back to my house and help him organize it."

As we grew closer, I could see Uncle Roman going through the tools on the bench in the back of our garage.

"You have a good starter set in here."

"They were my dad's...before he left."

Uncle Roman looked up from the tools to Marcus and then to me. As he was about to speak, the door to the garage opened, and Aunt Cora poked her head out.

"There you guys are. And I see we have company."

She quickly exited the house, walked over to Marcus, and took his hand in hers.

"Cora, this is Marcus. Marcus, this is my wife, Cora."

Aunt Cora quickly surveyed the garage and then looked back at Marcus.

"Well, Marcus, do you like brownies?"

Marcus's lip curved, "Yes, ma'am, I do."

"Wonderful! You can test out my first batch in the new house."

With no further hesitation, she slipped her arm into his and walked him into the house.

"We'd better go save him," Uncle Roman said.

Following, I watched as Aunt Cora walked Marcus over to a spot at the table and told him to sit. Then she turned to look at us and motioned that we take a seat as well. She dashed back into the kitchen and returned with a plate piled high with her delicious brownies. Watching the plate as she placed it on the table, Uncle Roman started rubbing his hands together. He playfully eyed Marcus and me as though daring us to take one before him.

"I may be biased, but Cora makes the best brownies I have ever eaten," he said.

Aunt Cora swatted Uncle Roman on the arm. He grabbed her around the waist and pulled her onto his lap and gave her a kiss.

"Seriously, you two!" I moaned.

Aunt Cora giggled as she moved over to the seat between Marcus and Uncle Roman.

"Marcus, you take the first one."

She lifted the plate toward him, and he withdrew a corner piece. She then handed the plate around with each of us pulling a brownie from it. As we each took a bite, Aunt Cora watched us with anticipation in her eyes.

"Ms. Cora, these are the most amazing brownies I ever had," Marcus said.

Her shoulders relaxed slightly as her smile widened. "I am so glad that you like them. Please, have another."

Marcus smiled and grabbed a second helping as he began looking around the house.

"Whoa! You weren't kidding. If I hadn't watched you guys move in this morning, I would have sworn you had been here for years."

"I told you. She has it down to an art," I said.

Aunt Cora smiled as she looked around the room.

"No one likes to live out of boxes. Over the years, we have downsized to the necessities, which really helps."

"The house looks amazing," Marcus said.

As he finished his sentiment, the clock on the wall behind the dining room table chimed, and we all looked at it.

"Oh, man. Nine o'clock! I didn't realize it was so late. My mom's gonna think the stray dogs got me."

Uncle Roman sat up straighter in his chair at Marcus's last statement.

"Stray dogs?"

"Yeah, there was a family that lived just outside the community and moved, but they forgot to take their dogs with them. People around town have been trying to feed them. Even so, it's been a few weeks, and they're getting quite nasty. Animal control has been trying to catch them, but they're a bit too fast."

Uncle Roman shifted uncomfortably in his seat and looked at Aunt Cora.

"Let Jace and I walk you back to your house. If wild dogs are running around, meeting them at night is not the best idea."

Standing, Marcus looked back at Aunt Cora and smiled.

"Thank you for the brownies. They were delicious."

"You're most welcome. Whenever you want more, just let me know."

"Oh, I will!" he announced.

"All right, let's get you back home," Uncle Roman said.

We left through the garage, and Uncle Roman gave each of us a flashlight. Hearing the story of the wild dogs had put us all on edge. Although it was only a few hundred feet between the houses, we all periodically swept the perimeter with the lights.

"Where do you keep your bike?" Uncle Roman asked.

"On the side of the house. It sort of doesn't fit in the garage."

Uncle Roman looked at the garage and nodded in understanding.

"We can take it back with us if you like. Cora is usually home and can let you in whenever you need it."

Marcus thought about it and then nodded.

"Thank you, but I feel like I am taking over your garage."

Uncle Roman chuckled. "Even more incentive to get *your* garage back in order."

Marcus ran his hand through his hair. "Yes, I guess you're right. Besides, my mom will be happy to have a place to put stuff in."

"Let's get the garage closed up," Uncle Roman said.

He hit the button on the door, causing it to creak and come to life, slowly closing. From the front door, we could hear a voice calling.

"Marcus, is that you? Did you fix the bike yet?"

29

"Yes, Mom. Our new neighbors helped."

A small petite woman with shoulder-length auburn hair that matched Marcus's met us by the garage.

"You must be the Northalls. Oh, I am so happy to finally meet you in person."

She looked from Uncle Roman to me, lifting her head as she did.

"What did you feed him in Arizona?" she teased, looking up at me.

"The usual, but I swear Cora is putting some *Miracle Grow* in his food."

Mrs. Hunter laughed as she extended her hand to each of us.

"I am Mary Hunter. Jace, I will be your teacher starting Monday."

She looked back to Uncle Roman, wide-eyed, and asked, "We *are* starting Monday, right?"

"If that is okay with you."

"Absolutely!" she answered, grinning widely.

"Wonderful, I sent you his previous school curriculum and transcripts. Did you get everything?"

"Oh my, yes. Jace is very advanced and way ahead of the schools here. We could likely appeal to advance him to eleventh grade if you wanted."

I looked at Marcus and felt my cheeks flush. Following my eyes, she looked over to her son and then back to me.

"But that is all stuff we can discuss on Monday. I'm thrilled that you two have met and hit it off. Marcus, you have been out here for hours."

It was Uncle Roman who replied, "The boys fixed the bike, and I offered to store it in our garage for the time being."

Mrs. Hunter's eyes widened as she looked at Marcus.

"I can't fit it in the garage. Jace offered to help me organize it, so I can use it to store the bike and a toolbox Mr. Northall just gave me."

"Oh my, I sure missed a lot. Mr. Northall—"

"Please, call me Roman."

"Right…Roman… Thank you for the offer, but you did not have to go through all that trouble, especially with the toolbox."

"It's a spare box I had, and he needed something bigger than what he has. Please. I insist. As a new neighbor."

Mrs. Hunter looked uneasily between Marcus and Uncle Roman.

"I would feel more comfortable if we paid you for the box."

"It's really unnecessary, but if it would make you feel better, we can work something out."

"Yes, please. I genuinely appreciate the gesture, but I would feel more comfortable that way."

"Then it's a deal. Jace and I are going to head home now. We just wanted to make sure Marcus made it here in one piece."

Mrs. Hunter looked confused as her eyes took in our house and then us.

"The dogs, Mom," Marcus muttered.

"Aah, yes. They have been trying for weeks to get them. Thank you."

"We will be by again tomorrow. My wife always bakes treats for our neighbors when we move."

"Sounds delicious. We'll see you tomorrow then."

Marcus turned to me, lifting his fist, and I bumped mine off his.

"Thank you again, sir," Marcus said, shaking Uncle Roman's hand.

"You're most welcome. We'll see you tomorrow."

As we walked away, we gave them both one quick wave. Again, we scanned the perimeter of the yards for anything that could be waiting. Although we saw nothing, the thought of a pack of animal-control-evading dogs made my skin crawl. I felt my pace quicken as we walked to our driveway. Rushing into the garage, Uncle Roman quickly hit the button on the wall, allowing the door to close. I opened the house door and jumped when I nearly walked right into Aunt Cora, causing Uncle Roman to do so as well.

"You two are jumpier than long-tail cats in a room full of rocking chairs."

31

I smiled at the absurdity of the comment and kissed her on the cheek as I walked past.

"I'm going to continue putting some stuff together upstairs before going to bed. I'll see you guys in the morning."

"Good night, kiddo," Aunt Cora said.

"Good work today. Sleep tight!" Uncle Roman hollered from inside the garage.

"Thank you, and good night," I answered.

When I got to my room, I walked over to the window facing the front of the house. My eyes scanned the darkness surrounding our homes, and I wondered if the dogs were nearby. I then looked toward Marcus's house and saw a light was on in the front window. From my vantage point, I could clearly see Marcus, who was wearing a headset and looking at a computer screen, on his desk. Realizing that if I could see him, he could see me, I pulled away from the window and prepared for bed. I pulled the sheets back and lay on the freshly laundered bedding. Then I took a deep breath and imagined my old room. As I closed my eyes, I reviewed my day and couldn't help but smile. Although I hated moving, this move started with a pretty cool friendship. Turning onto my side, I opened my eyes again to look at the side window. As I recalled the girl from this morning, I felt a smile cross my face again. Maybe this move was going to be better than the others.

CHAPTER 3

Meet the Neighbors

The next morning, I woke to the alarm on my phone playing "Let's Get It Started," which I found appropriate, considering the day I had ahead of me. Sliding the bar on the screen to silence the alarm, I lay back on my bed and looked up at the ceiling. Noticing it had the same popcorn pattern as the one in my previous room caused a smile to tug at the corner of my lip. I stretched deep before sitting up, surveying my new surroundings.

The first morning in a new house always seems to be the strangest. When you lie down the night before, it's almost as though it is a dream. Only when you wake up, you realize you did, in fact, move. Walking to my dresser, I looked out the front window to see if there was any movement on our little court. Slowly draping across the ground was the warm glow of the new sunrise, illuminating our little corner of Williston. Standing there, transfixed, I marveled at the variation of colors and reawakening of the world below.

Shifting my attention back to our street for movement, I decided our court does not contain early risers—at least on Saturdays. Grabbing some clothes from the drawer, I headed to the bathroom to prepare for the day. By the time I had finished and was making my way down the stairs, I could smell a small feast being prepared by Aunt Cora.

"Good morning. How did you sleep?" Aunt Cora asked when she saw me.

Uncle Roman looked up from the paper he was reading at hearing Aunt Cora.

"Great. I didn't realize how tired I was when I lay down last night," I answered.

"Yes, the moving usually does a number on me as well. I'm actually surprised you're up so early. We lost two hours in the move here. I figured it would be closer to ten by the time we saw you," Uncle Roman said.

"Well, Black-Eyed Peas woke me up. But if they hadn't, I'm sure the sun would have done the trick!"

Uncle Roman stared at me, visibly confused. Placing a plate of bacon on the table, Aunt Cora shook her head and kissed his cheek.

"It's a band."

Lifting his eyebrows in understanding, he nodded at her statement and returned to his newspaper, which made me smile.

"We're getting the paper already?"

Instantly, I knew it was a stupid question. Aunt Cora and Uncle Roman have everything set up well before we arrive. For instance, we had food delivered yesterday so that Aunt Cora would not have to drive into town. Ultimately, it gave her more time to set up the house and peace of mind knowing we had plenty of food. Following the same logic, I'm sure Uncle Roman set up the delivery weeks ago for it to start today. Seeing he was about to answer, I raised my hand.

"Nope, it was a dumb question."

He looked at Aunt Cora, then back at me, and laughed.

"Am I that predictable?" he asked.

"With moving and a fresh restart? Yes!" I answered.

"I don't know, Cora. It seems we're not very spontaneous in our old age anymore."

"Please don't…," I begged, seeing where he was going with that statement.

As any teen can attest, there must be a rule book somewhere mandating your parents to embarrass you with their overabundant signs of affection toward each other. My aunt and uncle seem to take it to the next level. On the one hand, I hope to have a love like theirs myself. On the other, though, eww!

"Call yourself old, Mr. Northall. I'm still young and spry," Aunt Cora teased.

"Hmm…let's see. I must be about 267, and you're considerably younger at 193?"

Aunt Cora's eyes widened as she looked at me with a smile.

"Don't give away all our secrets!" she exclaimed.

I laughed at the ridiculousness of their theatrics and started filling my plate with waffles, bacon, and fresh fruit.

"It seems the people in this area like their sleep on the weekends. I figure we can head out around lunchtime," Aunt Cora said.

Uncle Roman looked up from his paper as though he had just realized there was food and nodded at her.

"Sounds good to me. First things first, breakfast!"

Folding the paper up, he rubbed his hands vigorously before looking across the table at the food in front of him. Watching my uncle eat is always entertaining since he always rubs his hands together as though he needs to warm them up before he can start. After placing the last of the meal on the table, Aunt Cora finally sat down. Realizing that I had not grabbed myself a drink, I stood to go to the kitchen, which made Aunt Cora jump up from her seat as well.

"What did I forget?"

I laughed. "Nothing. *I* forgot to get myself a drink. Please, sit."

"Good man, Jace," Uncle Roman said.

I walked into the kitchen and opened the fridge. Grabbing the milk, I turned to get a cup when I realized I wasn't entirely sure where they were. Before I could ask, Aunt Cora, who had been watching my every move from the table, was out of her seat to help me.

"Cora, he's going to be fifteen! I'm sure he can handle pouring himself a drink. Just tell him where the cups are," Uncle Roman said sternly.

Stopping in midstride, she sat back down and directed me to the proper cabinet. I glanced back at her and couldn't help but chuckle.

"Am I doing it the right way?" I teased.

"Ha-ha. I'm just not ready to have you all grown up yet."

Uncle Roman tilted his head at her and stared.

"My dear, it is in your nature to be in control, and you don't do well when you are not."

She stopped watching me and turned to look at him. "I am not controlling."

"How long have I known you? You are, and it's one of the many things I love about you. In fact, we would never be as successful in these moves without you and your controlling ways!"

I cringed at the way he phrased it, watching for her reaction. She knitted her brows together and squinted her eyes at him.

"Roman Northall, I'm not sure if that was an insult or a compliment."

Uncle Roman burst out laughing and put his fork down to grab her hand. She continued to stare at him. But her anger was quickly being replaced by a mischievous smile.

"Well, for your sake, I will take it as a compliment. Now let's eat."

As we finished eating, I looked up at the clock on the wall, which showed the time was 10:38 a.m.

"Would it be alright if I went up and played some *Castle Core* until we are ready to head out?" I asked.

"Help clear the table first," Uncle Roman answered.

Completing my assigned chores, I made my way to my room. However, just as I was about to turn onto the stairs, our doorbell rang. Stopping midstep, I backed up and looked at the door where I could see a mass of bodies through the embossed glass. Turning to look back toward the kitchen, I watched as Uncle Roman and Aunt Cora walked to me.

"Maybe they were awake?" Aunt Cora said as she walked to open the door.

On the other side were a man, a woman, and three girls. The man, who was tall and muscular with sandy-blond hair and a full beard, spoke first, "Welcome to Crystal Court. We're your neighbors. My name is Kyle. This is my wife Carolina and our daughters, Alyssa, Zoe, and Isabelle."

As Uncle Roman introduced us, I found myself spellbound. The girl from the porch was standing in my doorway. Seeing my obvious distraction, the only thing to break the trance that I was in was my uncle's pat on my back. Her two older sisters must have caught the gesture and looked at Isabelle and then back at me before snickering to themselves. They only stopped when their mother turned and said something to them in another language—Spanish, I think.

"Please excuse my girls. It's as though they have never met someone new before," Carolina said as she stared at them, causing the girls to drop their heads.

Aunt Cora smiled. "Please come in. Are you hungry?"

"Actually, that is part of what brought us here. Izzie, please give the tray to Mrs. Northall," Carolina said.

"That's an interesting name," Aunt Cora said.

Izzie's cheeks flushed as she explained, "Zoe couldn't say my name right when I was born. So she called me Izzie, and well, it kinda stuck."

Then she walked forward, holding the casserole dish with aluminum foil covering it.

As Aunt Cora took it, she answered, "Thank you. It smells amazing."

"We thought you may be hungry as you just moved in yesterday. I remember a long week of takeout after we had! We wanted to help you out with a home-cooked meal, so I whipped you up some frangollo," Carolina said.

"What is frangollo?" I asked, trying to mimic her accent.

"It's a delicious twist on eggs. She mixes in raisins, honey, and almonds. It's like getting breakfast and dessert together," Kyle explained.

Although I had just eaten, the smell emanating from the dish was making me drool. Looking over, I could see Uncle Roman rubbing his hands together and smiled despite myself.

"Please, come in. I'm sure there is enough here for all of us," Aunt Cora said as she took the plate from Izzie.

"We don't want to be a bother. You probably still need to unpack, and we will only slow you down," Carolina answered.

"Actually, besides the four boxes in Jace's room, we're done," Aunt Cora said.

The group stood there in silence, periodically looking past us as though in disbelief.

"Please, I insist. Come in," Aunt Cora said.

Smiling, Carolina nodded and followed Aunt Cora into the house. Instantly, her face changed, leaving her wide-eyed as she took in the surroundings.

"I have only moved a handful of times in my life, but I could never unpack this quickly!" Carolina said.

Maintaining my post near the door, I prepared to close it once all our guests were inside but was distracted from my duties as Izzie strode by me. She looked in my direction, and for a brief second, our eyes met. Then she turned away to catch up with her sisters. Unable to move, I watched her, feeling a rush run through me as she turned to look back at me again and smiled. In that instant, I felt a pat on my back and jumped a bit.

"Let's not send the air-conditioning to all of Williston, okay?" Uncle Roman whispered.

One of his eyebrows arched as the corner of his lip twitched.

I rolled my eyes at him and shut the door. Then I followed him to the dining room, where everyone was finding a seat around the table. Aunt Cora was in the kitchen, as was Carolina, who was pulling out dishes for everyone. Aunt Cora, looking up as I passed, asked, "Can you grab the milk and juice from the fridge?"

Nodding, I grabbed the items she had requested and proceeded to our guests, who were all seated. Uncle Roman had positioned himself at one end of the table. Kyle was at the other end with the girls to his left. I positioned myself in the middle seat and opposite the girls which would allow Aunt Cora to be closer to Uncle Roman and Carolina to be closer to Kyle. As I looked up, though, I realized I was sitting directly across Izzie and felt my cheeks flush again. She looked across and smiled before looking away.

"So what grade are you in?" Kyle asked.

Words escaped me momentarily as I tried to plan a coherent sentence in response. I opened my mouth and felt my discomfort mounting at not having an answer immediately. Uncle Roman must have seen me floundering and tried to throw me a lifeline.

"Jace is in tenth grade, but he may advance early to the eleventh."

All three girls' eyes went wide as they turned to me. I hated it when he told people how advanced I was in my studies. All I wanted was to feel normal, and here he went, stressing how I was different. Feeling my cheeks flush once more, I glanced at the girls to determine what they could be thinking. Izzie must have seen my reaction and furrowed her brows.

"So you're a prodigy or something?" Zoe asked.

"Good lord, girl! Where are your manners?" Kyle interrupted.

"What? I'm just trying to get more information," Zoe answered.

Kyle dropped his head before lifting it to glare at Zoe. He turned to Uncle Roman and said, "My apologies, Roman. Zoe is my free-spirited one."

Uncle Roman laughed. "There's nothing wrong with a strong sense of curiosity."

Uncle Roman looked back at me, as though trying to judge my ability to communicate, and frowned a bit before continuing.

"We have had Jace homeschooled since he was young. Being able to move at his own pace has allowed him to speed through many of his areas of study. It is also why he could be in eleventh grade."

The girls were staring again while Izzie frowned slightly.

"So you won't be going to Williston High?" she asked.

"No. Mrs. Hunter is my tutor," I answered, grateful my voice had returned.

"Marcus's mom?" Alyssa asked.

I nodded, looking awkwardly around the room. Thankfully, Aunt Cora took that as the ideal time to serve the food. She quickly placed a few spoonfuls onto each plate and began handing them around the table. Unsure of how the flavors would mix, I hesitated a bit. Kyle must have noticed because he said, "It sounds like it won't work, but it's quite tasty, I assure you."

I stabbed my fork into the center of the egg mixture, grabbing up raisins and almonds, and took a bite.

"This is delicious!" I said.

"Told you!" Kyle answered with a grin.

"Oh, Carolina, this is one of the most delicious things I have ever had. You're going to show me how to make this," Aunt Cora raved.

"Absolutely. But it is quite easy. It's one of the first things I taught the girls to make," Carolina beamed.

"So tell us about yourselves?" Uncle Roman asked.

"I'm actually very proud of Carolina. She just opened a café in town, which has been doing rather well," Kyle beamed.

"We opened at the beginning of September. Since then, we have had a steady stream of customers, which is all we can hope for," Carolina added.

"If the food is all like this, you're going to need to set up a permanent table for me!" Uncle Roman teased.

"Absolutely. Just let me know when you're coming in," Carolina said.

"And what about you, Kyle?" Uncle Roman asked, taking another bite of his food.

"Just before we opened the café, I had retired as a corrections officer."

Uncle Roman glanced up across the table and nodded. "Looks like I will know where to go if I have any trouble."

Kyle chuckled and nodded back.

"I'm considering starting a business in personal security, but I desperately need some time off first. I've been waking up at 4:30 a.m. for over twenty-five years and would love to sleep in."

"I can appreciate that," Uncle Roman added.

"How about both of you?" Kyle asked.

"We just moved from Scottsdale, Arizona. Cora is my home base keeper while I am a consultant physician."

"So we have a doctor on the block. Looks like *I* will know where to go if I have any trouble too," Kyle said, earning a grin from Uncle Roman in return.

"What exactly does a consultant physician do?" Carolina asked.

"The title holds many meanings, but for me, I help get new physicians' businesses up and running."

"Are you able to tell us where you are working now?" Izzie asked.

"No. If the doctor wants to let people know, it is up to them."

Izzie nodded thoughtfully.

"If you have a business card, I can put it on the counter in the café to help drum you up more business," Carolina added.

I felt my stomach drop and looked down at my food, slowly picking at it. Uncle Roman glanced at me and shifted slightly in his seat.

"I have a headhunter who typically finds me jobs…but I think having another source of job opportunities would be great."

Not sure I heard him correctly, I looked at Uncle Roman, who smiled at me. Aunt Cora was also looking at him, and she, too, smiled softly as she grabbed his hand.

"This is so nice. Just over twenty-four hours in our new home, and we have friends surrounding us," Aunt Cora said.

The clock chimed, and Kyle looked at Carolina.

"We should probably get back to the house and finish setting up," he said.

She looked over her shoulder, and her eyes widened.

"Oh wow, yes."

Carolina looked back at us.

"We are having a get-together later this afternoon and would love for you to come. It will be a mix of adults and kids from around the area and a great opportunity for you to meet more people."

Aunt Cora looked at us then answered, "Absolutely. What time do you want us there?"

"We're expecting everyone at three."

"Can I bring anything?" Aunt Cora asked.

"Normally, I would say you have enough to do with a new move, but it seems you are finished unpacking. So if you could bring an appetizer, that would be great."

"I can handle an appetizer or two," Aunt Cora answered with a wink.

Everyone stood up then, and the Lewis family made their way to the front door. As they were about to leave, Izzie turned quickly, looking at me.

ANNIE O'CONNELL

"Don't forget your bathing suit!"
I felt my cheeks flush and smiled.
"Definitely," I answered.

CHAPTER 4

Castle Core

We waved as the Lewis family headed back to their house. I spun to head upstairs, hoping to rummage through my clothes and find something nice to wear when Aunt Cora laughed.

"Why, Jace Northall, I believe someone has a small crush."

I froze where I stood and turned around, feeling the blood rushed to my head. Uncle Roman must have seen my look and cringed slightly.

"Cora, leave the boy alone."

"I'm just saying. I know what I was seeing."

Walking closer to me, she whispered, "And it seems to be mutual."

She turned to head into the kitchen, and I felt the corner of my lip lift as I looked up to see Uncle Roman watching me.

"Go on. I'll call up when we're ready to head over."

Nodding, I bounded up the stairs, skipping two or three steps at a time. Quickly, I ran to the window and looked toward Izzie's house, hoping that she would come out. As I stood there, I realized that without curtains, anyone could see me. Stepping back from the window, I made a mental list to purchase some soon. I walked back to my dresser and started working my way through the handful of bathing suits I owned, trying each one on to determine the best look. Feeling overwhelmed, I heard my door open and turned to see Aunt Cora.

"Want some help?"

I looked at the bed, which was covered in clothes, and grimaced. "Is it that obvious?"

She chuckled as she glanced at the bed. Go try some things on so I can give you a female's perspective.

I smiled and grabbed a handful of clothes before heading toward the bathroom. Putting on the first bathing suit, a pair of blue shorts with pink palm trees. I walked out. I lifted my hands, shrugging as I turned around for her to better evaluate my first outfit. She touched her chin, appraising me, and then wrinkled up her face while shaking her head.

"It's like you're trying too hard to be from Florida. How about that one?"

She pointed to a gray suit with green stripes and a drawstring. "Do those still fit you?"

"There's only one way to find out."

I walked into the bathroom and quickly changed into the suit. It posed the same problem I always have with clothes. The waist fits great, but the length is too short. Walking out of the room, I scrunched up one side of my face as I turned for her.

"Nope. Way too short."

I sighed as I looked at the remaining options on the bed.

"The other two are the same size... Maybe I just won't go swimming?"

"Hmm. Give me a second."

She stood up and left the room, only to return a few minutes later. From the door, she tossed a plastic bag to me. Inside was a brand-new bathing suit in gray-and-yellow stripes. I looked up at her with a smile.

"When did you get this?"

"I knew we would have a pool here and was pretty sure you had outgrown all your suits, so I bought a new one before we left Arizona."

As I walked past her, I gave her a kiss on the cheek before heading to the bathroom to try on the new suit. Walking back into the room, Aunt Cora's entire face lit up at the sight. She stood and touched her hand to her mouth.

"It fits perfectly and is an excellent color for you. Now what shirt will you wear?"

"Good question. I don't want to wear anything weird."

"Ha, like taco kitty?" she asked.

"Hey, taco kitty and I are close buds. I just don't know if this crowd is ready to meet him."

I walked back to my drawers and rummaged through, trying to find something that would look good. At the bottom of the drawer was a gray T-shirt with a picture of baby Yoda. The caption "Don't make me use the force" written around him. Lifting it from the drawer, I turned to look at Aunt Cora and gave a slight shrug.

"You can't go wrong with baby Yoda," she agreed.

Looking into the closet, she pulled out my reef sandals and handed them to me.

"Perfect. I think you're ready to make your grand entrance."

Smiling, I walked over and wrapped my arms around her, lifting her slightly from the floor. She giggled and squirmed slightly till her feet touched the ground and I finally let go.

"Thanks, Aunt Cora."

I looked over at the clock, which showed it was 12:42 p.m.

"I think I'll play some *Castle Core* while I wait."

"Sounds good."

Turning to leave, she stopped and looked back into the room.

"I think we need to get you some drapes in here."

"Oh yeah, I was going to ask about that."

As I played, I kept checking the clock, wishing that it would move faster. After realizing that I was aimlessly wandering around *Castle Core*, I sat back and turned toward my new enemy—the clock.

"Only 1:45 p.m.," I let out an exasperated sigh.

Having breakfast with Izzie and her family was amazing, and I couldn't wait to see her again. I found my mind drifting, imagining all the different encounters that we could possibly have and the thought-provoking conversations that I would amaze her with. In that instant, my heart froze. What *would* I say to her? I had no clue what she liked or didn't like. I stood and walked away from the computer, back to the window to look out onto the court. It was quiet again, except for some noises coming from behind the Lewis house. Unsure if I would see anything, I walked to the guest room and glanced out the side window, which overlooked their house and part of their yard. I could see smoke billowing up from the grill and could make out the silhouette of Kyle, cooking something that smelled amazing. Along the pool's perimeter, Zoe and Alyssa were busy setting out tables and chairs and decorating with a tiki theme. I searched the yard to find Izzie, but she was nowhere in sight.

"Maybe she is inside helping Carolina? But what if she went to a friend's house and won't be there?" Panic slightly rising at the thought.

Deciding that I would go insane if I continued to wait up here, I opted to go to Marcus's house till the party started. Hollering to Aunt Cora and Uncle Roman as I left, I ran out the door and to his house. When I knocked on the door, Marcus answered and seemed bewildered by my presence.

"What's up?" he asked.

"Nothing. I just figured I would hang out here till it's time to go next door."

Marcus stood there, dumbstruck. Instantly, I had a pit at the bottom of my stomach, wondering if the Lewis's would have a party and not invite the only other house on the block. I felt my cheeks flush, and my heart quicken its pace as I stood there, looking at him while trying to think of something to fix my mistake. Finally, his face changed into a smile, and he playfully punched me in the arm.

"Your face was priceless! Sure, you can hang out here. Man, what would you have done if they hadn't invited us?"

"I guess I never considered it. There are only three houses on the block, and it would be insane to have two of the three there and not the last."

Inclining his head slightly, he answered, "That makes sense. So what do you want to do?"

"I was playing *Castle Core*—" I started before Marcus cut me off.

"Wait! You play *Castle Core?*"

"Uh, yeah?"

"Okay, come in. *That* is what we are doing!"

Marcus grabbed me by the shirt and bodily pulled me into the house, dragging me to his room. Walking in, I felt my nose being assaulted by an overwhelming aroma of what I can only describe as a gym locker room after the football team had run laps for an hour and dropped their sweaty shirts in the corner.

"Take a seat," Marcus offered, seeming unperturbed by the smell.

"Uh, where?"

As though looking around for the first time, his face shone slightly crimson. Marcus hurried around the room, grabbing clothes off his bed and the floor, and began haphazardly tossing the items in the general direction of the hamper. The room appeared to have undergone an explosion—one that had left food plates, wrappers, clothes, and a general mess strewn across every inch. There was only one spot that was spared from the tidal wave of disarray. In the far corner of the room, positioned under the large bow window, looking out to the front of his house, was an L-shaped desk. A large black high-back chair with green accent striping was parked in front of it. Sitting on the desk was a desktop—a coveted Alienware Aurora R10, which is one of the most powerful gaming machines! Its graphics appear to jump off the screen at you. To intensify this already amazing setup, Marcus had a tri-mount monitor and headset, completing the immersion. I instantly felt inadequate thinking of my repurposed Dell Laptop from two years ago. Marcus's face beamed with pride when he looked in my direction. He noticed my jaw hanging open as I admired the beautiful creation sitting in front of us.

"I've been saving for a few years to put it together. Mom helped with some items. But odd jobs here and there, birthday money, everything I made went into building it."

"It's...amazing!" I said, not taking my eyes off it.

"Here, sit down and log on," Marcus advised as he stood up and motioned for me to sit.

As I sat, the chair enveloped me in memory foam, and it felt as though its designer had molded it for my body alone, and I found it was more comfortable than even my bed. As the game loaded, I felt a vibration run through my back and jumped a bit at the sensation.

"It's a gaming chair that reacts to the game and vibrates to improve the experience."

Quickly, Marcus began running through all the minute details of the machine.

"You'll never want to play the old way after playing with this setup."

Looking back at the screen, I felt as though it had sucked me into a distant world, and I was only on the log-on screen! With there being three monitors, my peripheral vision was now fully engaged. The once-dull-appearing graphics I was used to seeing on my laptop roared to life with brilliant colors and shapes surrounding me.

"Don't forget the headset," Marcus said.

From the small stand in front of the center monitor, I picked up the black headset and placed them over my ears. Marcus pressed a button on the keyboard, and it filled my ears with the fantastic noises of the game and subtle background ambience details that had not been obvious to my computer. As I felt myself being pulled into the game, a tap on my shoulder brought me back to reality.

"They're noise-canceling headphones," Marcus said. "Great when no one is in the room or if you're trying to ignore someone. Not so great when you have someone with you."

"Wow! I didn't even hear you."

"Log on, and let's see where you are. We can form a cohort."

As I moved the mouse to start my log-on sequence, something twinkled outside the window. Lifting my head to see where the beam of light had come from, my pulse picked up, realizing that it was Izzie and Carolina returning. I watched, mesmerized, as she made her way down her driveway toward their mailbox. After rummaging through it and taking the few parcels from inside, she started her way back up toward her house. I had not realized how transfixed I was with her every movement until I heard Marcus snort behind me.

Turning, I looked at him. He was grinning as he looked back and forth from Izzie to me.

"You know she can see you, right?"

"Wait, what? What are you talking about?"

Ice swam rapidly into my belly, and my mouth went dry.

"Well, *I* can see you staring at her out of your window. Obviously, she can see you doing the same thing."

I felt a rush of emotions. It was as though a tidal wave of hot and cold had erupted together and were fighting for dominance in my abdomen.

"I don't..."

"Bro, you so do. Your current approach is super creepy, though. Perhaps, and kinda thinking out loud here, you should...I don't know...talk to her?"

Marcus continued with his teasing, making a sarcastically shocked face as he spoke. As I watched his theatrics and realized the significance of what he was saying, I felt all the heat in my body coalesce around my head. Marcus must have seen it and smiled but continued with a fresh approach.

"Look, Izzie and I have known each other since we were in kindergarten. We moved on the street roughly around the same time too, about five years ago. Although we're not as close as we used to be, I'm sure I can act as your go-between."

Still reeling from his revelation, I found it difficult to form words. So I sat there and stared blankly at him.

"I mean, I *do* enjoy watching it from over here. So it's totally cool if you want to continue at your own creeper pace."

Feeling my senses wake up again, I said, "No. That would be great—a proper introduction, I mean."

Marcus looked up at Izzie's house and then back to me with a wry smile.

"You know she plays *Castle Core* too, right? Are you logged on yet?" Marcus asked.

"Not yet."

"Good, let me log on. I'll find you, and then I'll summon Izzie. I can try to join us all together in a cohort."

Realizing the amazing offer he had just presented, I immediately got out of the chair to allow Marcus access to the computer. With a few quick motions, Marcus logged on and was searching for our avatars.

Once you enter the game, it brings you to Elemental Plaza, an opening scene that acts as a staging point. In this area, a player can purchase any items they may need for the journey, meet other players, form cohorts or create challenges. The larger your cohort and the more challenges you win, the higher you rank. I always felt that they got their inspiration for the Plaza from Disney World as it had the feel of Main Street USA with branch-off points at the end of the road leading to the different lands. Since everyone always started here, it was also the easiest location to meet other players.

"What's your name in the game?"

"Lukariah321."

Marcus stopped and turned to look at me, an eyebrow raised.

"Where did you come up with that?"

I hesitated a moment, considering giving the significance of the name. If I could talk to my eleven-year-old self, I would talk him out of the combination as I hated explaining its significance now.

"Lukariah was my dad. He died when I was three. I lost both parents, and it left me as one."

Marcus's eye grew wide. He showed the typical telltale signs people do when not knowing what to say. Seeing his uneasiness, I tried to allay his concerns and remove the awkwardness that had stemmed from the name, like it always did.

"It's been twelve years since they passed, and I don't really remember them that well. Some memories are stronger than others. But it's more like feelings, sounds, and smells that I remember instead of solid situations. I seriously wish I could rethink the name, but you can't change it without starting over."

Marcus watched but did not answer. Feeling the awkwardness mounting, I did what I always did in those situations and kept talking.

"For instance, I remember my mother's smile and her perfume. Sometimes I smell it and find myself drawn to it, hoping that I will come across her. It's the same with my dad. Like I recall his laugh, and I can vividly remember him swinging me around in our old living room."

Marcus just stood there, and I could feel my cheeks flush brighter. Realizing that I needed to change the topic quickly, I blurted out, "I'm not upset over it, so you shouldn't be. It's why I rarely talk about it."

Seeing Marcus visibly relax a bit, I looked toward the screen and noticed his screen name: Enos12605.

"Your birthday, I assume?"

After a brief pause, he answered, "That would be correct. Apparently, Enos was a popular name."

"So are you a January baby or a December baby?" I asked.

Perplexed, he looked at the name and realized how it might be confusing.

"January 26," he amended.

"Where did you come up with Enos, though?"

The corners of Marcus's lips rose, "He's the god of judgment. It felt appropriate, at the time."

Not sure how to answer, I nodded in approval and watched as he summoned my avatar. After Lukariah321 was visible on screen, he did the same for Izzie.

"Ilaria424. Is that Izzie?"

Marcus nodded. "She's a tree nymph. Not much help in battle, but she comes in handy before and after. She's able to help you gain supplies and heal faster too."

"April 24? Is that her birthday?"

"Yeah, I guess we're all original in our thinking."

I chuckled to myself as Marcus sent the summons. After, he sat back in his chair and looked out the window. He must have sensed me staring at him. Without looking at me, he pointed out the window toward Izzie's house.

"Her room is over there. It's the front room on the second floor. Once she realizes I am calling her, she usually comes to the window to wave. At least she used to."

Instinctively, I stepped out of view of the window. Marcus turned to look at me. "Honestly? Aren't we trying to break that habit?"

Realizing the idiocy of the move, I crept back to the spot and watched the window Marcus had pointed out. Although it seemed to take an eternity, the curtains finally moved, and the frame of a waving girl was visible.

"Sweet! She saw us!"

Within a few minutes, a new creature materialized on the screen. When you summon a player to an area, they appear on the screen, like Mr. Scotty beaming them to your location. As the flickers of light dissipated around her avatar, I could see that her character looked more elfish. She wore dark leather pants with a red sleeveless shirt, which also appeared to be leather, and a patchwork of material that buttoned up and was formfitting. Over her shoulder rested a bow while a green leather pouch hung at her waist. Her hair was long and dark with small braids framing her face at the front, and tied in a plat down her back. Marcus moved to the text box next to her name and began typing, but a text bubble popped up before he could finish.

I could feel my pulse reach a near staccato pace as we stood transfixed, looking at the computer. Marcus swiveled in his chair and looked at me.

"Are you coming, or are you just going to stand there?"

Realizing that I had slowly been backing away from the computer since the message bubble appeared, I inched back in his direction.

"I…I don't know what to say to her."

"She messaged *me,* not you. Remember?"

"Oh yeah. Of course… Well then, what are *you* going to say to her?"

"I'm honestly not sure. I haven't talked to her in almost three years."

I swung my head in his direction and glared at him. "Are you serious?"

Marcus chuckled. "No. I spoke to her yesterday at school."

He then mumbled, "It was three years before that, though."

"What?" I asked, half exasperated.

"Look, just because we live next to each other doesn't mean that we're besties."

I felt a rush of heat start in my core and slowly creep toward my head.

"You kinda said that you two knew each other since forever, and you could put a 'good word' in for me."

Marcus looked contemplative. "I didn't say that… I don't think I said that."

"If you didn't, you sure implied it."

Frustration mounting, I waved it off and looked at the screen.

"What did she say to *you?*"

Watching Marcus move the cursor to the message center was like waiting for the killer to attack the lead character in a horror movie. Before he could click on the message center, the number changed from a blinking red number one to a three.

"She's not messaged me a single message in three years, let alone three."

I watched Marcus, waiting impatiently for him to push the button.

"Are you just going to admire the number, or are you going to check it?" I asked.

I could feel anticipation coloring my voice and tried to calm myself. But as the seconds ticked on, waiting on the contents of the message was driving me nuts. I think Marcus knew it and was dragging it out to torture me. As I had thought, he looked up and gave a crooked smile.

"Okay, Casanova. I'm checking now."

As he clicked on the button, a small window appeared with the avatar of a fairylike creature in the top left corner and the name Ilaria424.

Without realizing it, I had moved closer to the screen and was analyzing her avatar. He sat back in his seat and watched me.

"Would you like to sit?"

Realizing that I was slowly pushing into his space at the computer, I backed up and apologized. I looked at Izzie's name and tried to figure where she came up with Ilaria. Marcus must have realized it and explained.

"Ilaria means happy, plus she thought it 'sang' when she chose it."

I felt a rush of jealousy run through me and stared at Marcus in disbelief.

"*You* helped her set up her account?"

"Yeah. We created the account like three years ago. She was over here all the time, and then…she wasn't."

I felt a sense of guilt as I watched the change in his demeanor.

"What happened?"

"I'm not sure, but I suspect her sister's popularity played a huge part. My mom is not poor, but I don't come from money. I'm not sure if you noticed. I'm not exactly easy on the eyes either. It doesn't really help with the whole cool vibe *they* have going."

Marcus seemed to drift off in his thoughts. Although I had only known him for a short period, I was confident that he was a great friend and hoped that his theory about Izzie's sisters was wrong. Remembering my morning with the trio left me now with more questions than answers, and I wanted to ask him to fill in the missing blanks for me. Unfortunately, I wasn't sure that he would have any more information to give. Besides, asking seemed like it would be dropping acid on an already-open wound. Unsure what else to say, I tried to remain a stoic force for him while he worked through his emotions.

"Your uncle is some fancy doctor, right?" he finally asked.

"He's a doctor. I don't know about the fancy part."

"You stand…well stood…a better chance with her than I could. At least through her sister's eyes."

"Why do you say I 'stood' a better chance?"

"You're a creeper."

Marcus said it so matter-of-factly I wasn't sure if I heard him correctly.

"Thanks?" I grumbled and looked back at the computer.

"You can fix it…I think. Either way, let's see what she said."

> *Hey Marcus, it's been a long time since we joined forces in here.*
> *Need help with a combination lock?*
> *Or are you about to embark on a battle that you need back-up on?*

Felling a twinge of jealousy, I looked quizzically at Marcus, "A combination lock?"

He quickly retorted, "Whoever made those needs to be beaten. They're impossible to open!"

He calmed a bit, after realizing how crazy he sounded.

"I *may* have needed her help to open my locker…more than once yesterday."

Seeing his reaction and imagining him struggling, I had to fight back a laugh. Marcus looked indignantly at me then must have realized how ridiculous he appeared and smiled too.

"Be grateful you don't have to deal with those things. They're seriously evil."

Another chime from the computer brought us back to the task at hand.

"What did she say?" I asked.

Marcus spun in the chair and stared at me.

"Although I am a god in the game, unfortunately, I lack omniscient powers in actual life. Now if you would like, I will check."

I couldn't help but smile and motioned for him to continue. Spinning back to the computer, he clicked on the window, which read, *Are you there?*

Marcus gave me a twisted smile, and I felt a cold chill run down my spine.

"What are you about to do?" My voice rose as the fear mounted.

"Nothing. Just going to answer her." Marcus's smile was growing wider by the second.

"Marcus! What are you about to say?"

Marcus quickly stood up, causing his chair to fly backward, and threw his body in front of mine, blocking my view of what he was typing. Panic began to build, and I briefly contemplated smashing the machine but quickly thought better of it. Before I could read or stop the message, Marcus had sent it to Izzie. Satisfied, he walked away from the computer to collect his chair, which was now on the other side of the room. After blinking in disbelief at his actions, I turned to the computer to read the secret message.

> *No combination locks to defeat over here, but*
> *I am here with our new neighbor.*

Marcus pulled his chair back into its place and resumed his position while I read what he wrote. I turned to him, to see he was sitting back with his arms crossed and a huge Cheshire smile.

"What was *that* all about?" I asked.

"Watching you squirm was all the motivation I needed, and it was worth every moment. Did I make you nervous?"

I contemplated if I wanted to laugh or punch him but was distracted by a small bubble with green dots forming in the chat window. We watched in anticipation as it disappeared, only to return and then disappear again just as quickly.

I looked at Marcus and then nudged him in his chair.

"Well, I wasn't nervous, but now I'm not so sure!" I croaked.

Marcus shoved me back and was about to respond when the telltale chime sounded again. We both looked back at the computer.

> *Hi, Chase. What are you guys doing over*
> *there? I hope you're still coming over. The party is*
> *about to start.*

As I read her response, I felt a rush of annoyance run through me. "It's Jace with a J. Actually, she got the entire name wrong. It's J-A-C-E."

Marcus was just staring at me, one corner of his mouth turned up.

"Now that we have the phonetic spelling of your name established. How should I respond?"

"I have no idea. You two are the ones who are friends. I'm just the new guy, remember?" I retaliated.

"Okay, okay. Calm down."

Marcus started typing as I eagerly looked over his shoulder and tried to regain my composure.

> *J-A-C-E came over to tell me of his undying love for you while we killed time before your party.*

As he was about to hit the Enter button, I grabbed his hand.

"You cannot send that!"

"Why not?"

"Besides sounding like a condescending jerk in it, I am not professing my love over here."

"Wow, strong words, Northall."

Marcus turned back to read what he wrote and grimaced, "Okay, maybe it is a smidge harsh. Let's try it again."

> *Our new neighbor's name is Jace. I got it wrong too.*

> *We're just killing time till your party starts.*

"Better?" Marcus nodded at the screen.

"Much!"

He hit the Enter button, and we waited. A few minutes later, another chime rang, and we looked back to the computer.

> *Oh, no. I'm sorry, Jace. That's a unique name.*

Another text bubble started, causing us to stare at the screen.

> *So what is the mission?*

I looked at Marcus and could see the look of mischief written all over his face.

"I don't know what you are thinking of doing, or saying, but don't do it."

Marcus's smile widened. "What? She wants to know our mission."

As he typed, I jumped at him. We started wrestling for the mouse and keyboard, and all the while, Marcus was laughing. "She just wants to know the mission!"

We were still grappling for control of the computer when there was a knock on the front door. Both of us froze and turned to look in its direction.

"Does your mom have any other impromptu guests she is expecting?"

Marcus shrugged. "Hell, if I know. I just live here."

We listened as Mrs. Hunter walked from the kitchen past the room and opened the front door.

"Izzie! What a wonderful surprise. What brings you by? Aren't you needed at your house for the pool party?"

I let out a noise somewhere between a gasp and a punch in the gut and strained to listen. My heart raced as I tried to surmise what would have brought her here. As the panic began to swell, I felt as though my brain was short-circuiting. Unable to come to a logical conclusion, I stared at Marcus, who appeared just as befuddled as I was.

"Look, just because I live with two women doesn't mean I understand them," he said.

While the two of us were still trying to figure out what motivated Izzie to come to the house, the door opened. A small-framed girl with curly hair was standing there. She was wearing short shorts and a hot pink tankini with a loose-fitting white top over it, which was tied at her waist. I felt my pulse quicken.

"If I'm not interrupting...," she said as the corner of her mouth lifted.

Marcus looked at Izzie, then at me, and down at my hand, which was still gripping his shirt. Without warning, he broke out into a deep belly laugh. Not completely understanding the scene in front of her, but finding Marcus's laughter infectious, she giggled along with him. Realizing what he was laughing at, I released his shirt and began laughing too. Mrs. Hunter looked confused as the three of us were now all laughing, our amusement feeding off each other's and refueling it. Finally, when we quieted, she looked to Izzie and said, "I'm glad you're here to help keep these two under control."

Izzie smiled and then nodded. "I'll do my best."

As Mrs. Hunter left the room, we all slowly regained composure as Izzie still stood in the doorway.

"This explains what was going on. All I could see was the curtains moving back and forth and shapes moving around."

I looked from Izzie to the window, and I felt my cheeks flush again.

"Aww, shucks. You came to save us?" Marcus teased.

"More to find popcorn to watch the show that was unfolding over here."

Smiling at Marcus, she then turned to look at me and walked over, extending a hand.

"Let's start over. I'm Izzie."

Smiling, I extended my hand and shook Izzie's but could not speak again. Marcus was watching us and nudged me in the arm, causing me to shift forward slightly. I turned to stare at him. Marcus stood up and rolled his eyes. He put his arm on my shoulder and looked at Izzie as he said, "This is Jace. His friends call him Jace. At least this one does."

Izzie giggled and looked from Marcus back to me.

"Well, it's very nice to remeet you, Jace."

"It's great to see you again!"

As I spoke, I realized how stupid I sounded and winced as I felt the heat creep up to my face.

Marcus broke into laughter again and fell backward onto his bed. "Best Freudian slip of the *century!*"

Izzie lightly kicked him in the shin, which only seemed to encourage his laughter. But just as quickly as his laughter had started, he stopped just as fast and sat up furrowing his brows.

"Wait a tick, what do you mean remeet?" he asked.

"My family brought them breakfast this morning," she started. "They offered for us to stay and eat with them."

Then she turned to me. Marcus nodding as he watched us talk.

"It must be hard coming to a new neighborhood and not knowing anyone. Where did you move from?" she asked, ignoring Marcus.

Finally, able to find my voice, I considered her question.

"This time? From Arizona."

Izzie's deep green eyes widened, and I realized I had confused her.

"My uncle's job has us moving frequently."

Again, Izzie stood wide-eyed before finally speaking, "Your... uncle?"

I realized the common misconception that people have when they see my small family. I didn't really want to start this friendship with her feeling bad for me. So I tried to explain my family tree as quickly and with as little awkward information as possible.

"I...I didn't know. I just thought—" Izzie said.

"It happens all the time. And by the time most people realize it, we're moving again."

Izzie gasped a little. "How frequently do you move?"

Warmth filled me with her question. *Was she nervous I would leave soon?* Unsure how to answer, I stared at her for a moment. I was contemplating several suitable responses, but all that came out was "It depends."

"You're not moving soon, are you? You just got here."

I felt a smile cross my face, but before I could answer, Izzie's phone went off. She looked down at it and frowned. Then she said, "It's my mom looking for me. The party is starting, and she's freaking out. Let's head over before she sends out a search party for me!"

CHAPTER 5

Pool Party

As we walked over to Izzie's house, I could hear music playing and the aroma of burgers and hot dogs wafted through the air. Marcus held his head up, sniffing, and sighed.

"You're in for a treat. Her dad is a magician at the grill!"

Izzie smiled. "Yeah, he's not so good in the actual kitchen. But at a grill, he's a completely different cook."

Walking around the side of the house, I saw the fireplace and chaise with the Edison bulbs hanging above it and realized we were entering through Izzie's little sanctuary. She glanced over at me and then nodded up toward my window. I followed her eyes and reluctantly looked back at her.

"Is that your room?" she asked.

I gulped and nodded. Marcus broke out laughing and grabbed my shoulders before walking past us and into the pool area.

"Told you she could see you."

I froze in place causing Izzie to turn and look at me, her mouth turned down.

"You coming?" she asked.

I wasn't sure what to say, so I just stared at her.

Seeing my embarrassment, she walked over and whispered in my ear, "I only started coming out here yesterday," smiling as she turned and walked to the backyard.

I felt the corner of my mouth lift as I watched her walk away, and after taking a deep breath, I followed her. Turning the corner, I saw Kyle at the grill, who enthusiastically welcomed me, "Hey! There he is! Burger or dog, Jace?"

"One of each?" I answered more as a question than as a solid statement.

"Now that's what I like to hear! Carolina, let's get this boy fed."

Near the house, Carolina had a large table set up with an assortment of BBQ food. The dishes on it ranged from burgers, fries, sliced steak, shish kebabs to potato and macaroni salad. As I began filling my plate, I heard my aunt and uncle coming around the side of the house. As they came into view, I could see Uncle Roman was carrying about four trays, and I shook my head.

Carolina followed my gaze to where they were standing, "Oh, Cora, that's too much! This is a get-together for you," she exclaimed.

"My wife cannot keep herself contained to one item, especially with desserts," Uncle Roman had answered for her.

Carolina chuckled as she walked over to meet them.

"What did you bring?" she said as she looked over the packages.

"Brownies, apple pie, key lime pie, and churros."

Carolina's eyes went wide as she looked at Aunt Cora in disbelief.

"You seriously made all this since we were last there?"

"I had the ingredients in the house, and now I have a double oven. It wasn't a bother, really."

Still in shock, Carolina motioned them to the table where all the food had been laid out. Uncle Roman placed the trays in their designated slots and then looked back over the assortment. He began rubbing his hands thoughtfully. Shaking my head, I handed him a plate and a napkin before taking my food over to a table where Marcus and Izzie were sitting. As I sat down, Izzie scanned the table and jumped up, rushing to a cooler before hollering back.

"What flavor pop you want?"

"Pop, as in ice pop?" I asked.

She laughed. "No, soda."

"Ohhh. Coke, I guess."

"Marcus, what do you want?"

"Coke too, please."

Grabbing three cokes, she returned to the table and sat between Marcus and me. Before I could take a bite out of the hot dog, there was a loud ruckus coming from the side of the house. Without warning, Zoe squealed at an octave that could have shattered glass, bounced out of her seat, and went running.

"Brian, welcome back. Zoe should tackle you any second now," Kyle teased.

As though on cue, Zoe jumped at a very tall and muscular teen in a dark blue swimsuit and a gray T-shirt that appeared to be one size too small just so it would accentuate his biceps. Behind him were two other guys. While each was muscular, they did not match Brian's size. Although he was not loud or overbearing, Brian's presence was immediately known, and everyone seemed to be drawn to him like a beacon of true north. It was fascinating to watch and a bit awe-inspiring. While watching the three teens enter, I heard Marcus sigh heavily, and I turned to look at him, "What?"

"He brought Ethan Campbell. He's a bit of a jerk and thoroughly enjoys torturing me. It's almost a sport for him. You'll be next on his hit list. He enjoys *fresh blood*."

Izzie was listening to Marcus and shook her head.

"Yeah, he is a bit much, at times. But he's one of the most popular guys at school, and he's Brian's best friend, so he's here."

"I'm assuming Brian is Zoe's boyfriend?" I asked, hoping it did not seem like a stupid question.

Looking back, Zoe was all over him, and it surprised me that Kyle didn't seem bothered by it. Unintentionally, I scrunched my face up as I watched the encounter.

"Tell us how you really feel, Jace." Marcus teased.

I turned to look at him, unsure of what he meant.

"That face. I guess you're not so into PDAs?"

"What is PDAs?" I asked.

Izzie sighed as she pointed to her sister and Brian. "That. Public displays of affection."

"Oh yeah. That doesn't bother me. I was just more shocked by your dad's reaction, or lack of it."

"He puts up with it because he thinks Brian has a strong future ahead of him and likes that Zoe is dating him."

Izzie's eyes suddenly went wide as she looked in the group's direction. She dropped her head and mumbled, "Great. She's bringing them over."

Marcus shifted uncomfortably and seemed to look for an escape route when a voice behind me spoke, "So this is the new kid on the block, huh?"

I turned to see Brian standing behind me and had to strain my neck to see all of him. Up close, he was even bigger and could almost double as a barn door. I stood up and extended a hand to him.

He took it and said, "Brian Mitchell. These are my friends Mike Townsend and Ethan Campbell."

As I turned to Ethan, I saw him staring at Izzie. Out of the corner of my eye, I also saw her turning away from him.

I returned my focus to Brian and said, "My name is Jace Northall."

"So, Jace, when did you move in?" Brian asked.

"Yesterday, actually," I answered.

"Seriously? And you're at a party already? Nice."

He patted me on the back and gave me a toothy grin. Zoe approached us with a plate of food for him and snuggled up under Brian's arm. He took the food in one hand and warmly pulled her close to him. Looking down on her adoringly, he said, "Thanks, babe."

"Gotta keep you fed," she teased.

He leaned down and gave her a quick kiss on the top of her head. Then he turned to the assortment of food on his plate.

"So what manner of deliciousness did your dad cook today?" Brian asked her.

Zoe giggled like a schoolgirl, which was a much different attitude than I had seen her display earlier today.

"You know him. All the usual suspects," she cooed.

Distracted by Zoe's theatrics, I nearly missed Ethan maneuvering around the group to kneel beside Izzie.

"Hey, girl. You're looking amazing today. Want to go for a swim?"

I felt my blood boil as I watched him trying to be all charismatic with her. The only thing holding the reins of my temper was the cold shoulder she was obviously giving him.

"I think I want to eat first. But if you want to go, the pool's right there. I'll be in later," she said.

Marcus dropped his head, trying to hide the smile that was forming at her response. Ethan shot a glare at him, narrowing his eyes slightly. Standing up, he looked back toward Kyle.

"Mr. Lewis. Do you still have the volleyball net?" he asked.

"Yes, we do. It's in the shed on the other side of the house. You'll have to set it up, though."

"Not a problem."

Ethan then turned to look at Marcus with a menacing grin.

"Hey, Hunter. How about you give me a hand getting the net out?"

Marcus slightly choked on the piece of burger he ate.

"As amazing as that offer sounds, and it really does, I think I'm going to sit the game out. So I'm just going to stay here."

Ethan stood up and walked over to stand behind his chair and put his hands on Marcus's shoulders and started massaging.

"Come on, Hunter, you can even be on my team."

Marcus was visibly uncomfortable with the contact and shifted with each squeeze of his shoulders. Izzie seemed upset as well although Mike was giggling behind me. Watching the encounter, I wasn't sure if Ethan was always like this to him or if he was just being exceptionally passive-aggressive today. Regardless, I decided I was going to put an end to it. "I'll go with you," I said.

Marcus's head shot up to look at me, shaking his head slightly and his eyes wide. Ethan slowly looked up and the corner of his lip lifted.

"Great. Let's go get it," Ethan said.

He turned to walk toward the screen door leading to the other side of the house. Marcus became more visible in his earnestness that I did not follow Ethan. I shifted my head and cocked an eyebrow at him while moving my hands in a "slow down" motion. I looked toward the screen door and saw Ethan standing there with an almost-genuine smile on his face. Instantly, I started reevaluating my decision to go with him. Realizing my options were now limited, I made my way toward the door.

As I passed Ethan, he looked up at me and said, "Damn, you're tall."

I half smiled. "That's what I hear."

Laughing, he placed his arm on my back and nudged me forward with more force than was necessary.

"It's around the corner. You would think that someone like Kyle would keep things organized, but that shed is a mess and dark. You need to be careful that you don't get hurt getting stuff out of it."

I narrowed my eyes at him, trying to determine whether he was giving me information or a genuine threat. Standing in front of the shed, he pulled the doors open. I could see that he was telling the truth about how imposing it was. Tools, pool supplies, equipment, chemicals, tiki torches, and every other thing had just thrown in there. It showed a complete disregard for the safe extraction of anything at a later date.

I grabbed the back of my neck and rubbed it, unsure what I was looking for or even where we would find it when Ethan said, "I think it's over there in the back."

He pointed in the farthest corner that appeared to have some netting visible. In front of it, though, was an obstacle course of death. Tiki torches were lying all around with their pointy edges sticking out in every direction. It looked like they were waiting to impale the first unfortunate soul that entered this death trap of a shed.

"Is he serious about this? How many of these things does one person need?" I asked.

"Yeah, he keeps the rest of the house organized, but I think he just gave up on this. You're tall enough. You could probably just reach in and grab it."

I turned to look at him and then back into the mess. I was trying to gauge where I'd find the best footing to get in and out in one piece. Shifting back and forth, I surveyed the surrounding debris.

Then I tried to determine what I would need to move to free the net in the back. Carefully, I positioned myself and took a step into the shed, praying that my sandals would stay on my feet.

As I looked down at my foot, I felt a shiver run up my back. Instinctively, I shifted my body weight to the right and turned just in time to watch Ethan sail past me into the mess. His arrival caused chairs to upend, buckets to flip, and a hoard of tiki torches to roll down onto him. I stood there, stunned, trying to figure out how he wound up flailing on the floor. Still in shock, I barely registered the sound of approaching footsteps coming up from behind me. Turning, I saw Brian, Mike, Marcus, Izzie, and Zoe coming closer and looking into the shed.

"Wow, taken out by the new kid, huh?" Mike teased.

Still stunned, I stared back into the shed. Coming back to my senses, I reached out my hand to help Ethan up, only to have him slap it aside.

"Like I need your help!" he screeched.

"From the looks of it, you do," I answered.

The crowd of teens broke out into laughter, which only seemed to anger him more. He continued to thrash about like a fish out of water. Realizing he was not going to accept my help, I stepped out of the way to allow his friends to pull him out of the debris.

Just as they had finished heaving him out, Kyle turned the corner and frowned.

"You guys all right over here?"

"Dad, this thing is going to kill someone one of these days," Zoe exclaimed.

Walking through the crowd, his "Kiss the Cook" apron shifting as he walked, Kyle looked at Ethan, now covered in dirt and debris. Then he peeked into the shed and grimaced.

"You okay, son?" he asked.

"I'm fine, sir. Just tripped is all."

Kyle nodded and then turned to me.

"How about you?"

"I'm fine, sir. Ethan is the one that fell in."

A rumble of low laughter filtered across the group as Ethan's face turned various shades of red. Kyle patted him on the shoulder and said, "I've got a change of clothes you can use. You won't be able to go swimming in *that*."

Ethan looked down and must have realized how disheveled he now appeared. Kyle pulled a cobweb off his hair and crinkled his face as he tossed it to the side. "Perhaps a quick shower too?"

"Thank you," he answered as he followed Kyle back toward the house.

Brian turned to look at me.

"Fancy footwork, kid. Not sure how *he* ended up in there and not you, but I needed that laugh. Few people get the better of Ethan. But a word of warning, I'd recommend watching your back from here on out."

"What does that mean?" I asked incredulously.

"He's a bit of a sore loser," Mike answered.

"Oh great," I said with a long sigh.

I looked back into the shed. The girls were now standing in front of it, examining the contents.

"Unless we pull half of this out, I can't see us getting to that net," Izzie said.

Brian looked from Mike to me and nodded.

"We can get it. I'm itching for a game now, anyway," he said.

Slowly, we began pulling items out of the shed and lining them up along the side of it, and in short order, we had successfully reached the net. In the corner, just below where it lay, I saw a ball. I picked it up and tossed it back to Izzie, who was helping with moving the items.

Once we had pulled the net and the ball out, we placed the items back into the shed in a more organized way—for easier access next time. Izzie took the ball and net to clean the built-up gunk and grime off them. Just as we were finishing and closing the shed door, Ethan turned the corner to see us.

"Feel better?" Brian teased.

As we walked past, Ethan pretended to punch Brian in the gut. Brian folded over him with an exaggerated groan. I lingered back slightly, wanting to be sure this was not a gift Ethan would hand out to all that passed by him. Fortunately, he seemed to only fixate on Brian and wrapped his arm over Brian's back as they made their way to the pool area.

I let out the breath I had been holding when I felt a hand on my shoulder. It made me jump slightly. When I turned, I saw it had been Izzie. "You okay? I'm glad *he* fell into the shed and not you," she said.

"I think that had been his intention. One minute I was gauging the likelihood of my death, and the next, he was supermanning past me into the shed."

She laughed at my explanation, which left me laughing as well.

"Come on, let's get you a drink while they set up the net," Izzie suggested.

As we turned the corner back into the pool area, Izzie and I were still laughing. Scanning the pool area, I saw Ethan in the pool setting up the net. He was glaring at me through it, flames burning from his gaze. Izzie followed my glance and rolled her eyes.

"Ugh. Testosterone!" She sighed dramatically.

I looked down at her with an eyebrow lifted and a lopsided grin. Seeing my face, she smiled too.

"Okay. It infuses some of you with overwhelming surges of it. You, though, you have just enough."

"I think that's a compliment," I teased.

Marcus walked over to us with his back facing the other guys. With his right hand at chest level, he was pointing at his hand and whispering, "I am not doing this. Ethan is going to kill me."

I glanced over his shoulder and then back to Marcus.

"Good news. I think you're safe today. Fairly sure he has my name on his death list now," I said.

Izzie cringed slightly and looked at me.

"Better to meet it head-on. Want to go swimming?" she teased.

Marcus's eyes went wide as he looked at her.

"Did we not just discuss the mortal danger we are in right now?" he asked.

Behind Marcus, I saw Brian walking toward us. I nodded in his direction so Marcus would turn around and spot him too.

"We're putting together a friendly game. Want in?" Brian asked.

"Depends on your definition of *friendly*," Marcus muttered under his breath.

Not wanting to look like a coward, I nodded before pulling off my T-shirt and flipping my sandals off. It was only at that point that I remembered Izzie was standing next to me, and a sense of self-consciousness washed over me. Trying to be stealthy, I glanced over to her and noticed her looking at me before turning away. Seeing her reaction removed any doubts I had, and I felt a smile grow.

"You in, Hunter?" Brian asked with a smile.

He visibly gulped and looked pleadingly at me.

"Who are the captains?" I asked.

"Ethan and I usually are, but it can be you and Ethan if you prefer," Brian answered.

I looked at Marcus, who was now continually running his hands through his hair.

"Ethan and I can be captains. Is it just us kids or are the adults joining?" I asked.

Marcus seemed to calm as he looked past the pool to the adults that had amassed. He must have realized Ethan would not drown him with that many adults around.

"I'm not sure. We can ask," Brian said as he turned to them.

"Hey, any of you guys want to join in?"

The group looked back and forth to each other before Kyle took his apron off.

"I can't pass up a competition. How about you, Roman?" he asked.

Uncle Roman looked at me, asking with his eyes if it was okay. I nodded with a smile.

"Sounds great! What are the teams?"

"We're about to figure that out now. Jace and Ethan are the captains."

As everyone prepped for the game, Zoe brought a coin over from where Alyssa was sitting with the other women.

"Call it in the air, Jace," she said.

As the coin flipped, I said, "Tails."

She caught the coin in her hand and flipped it over the back of her other hand. Then she stood, holding it there to build suspense.

"Today, Zoe," Izzie said.

"Fiiine," she said.

When she lifted her hand, we looked down to see tails. I felt a rush of relief. Looking back over the faces, I tried to determine my best course of action.

"Your pick, Northall," Ethan said.

I scanned the group again and focused on Marcus, who was standing next to Brian. Again, he had his hand up at waist level and was pointing to Brian vigorously. Next to Brian, I saw Izzie and knew that if I didn't pick her first, Ethan would. Then again, if I didn't pick Brian first, Ethan would nab *him*.

Crap. Which one? I thought.

"We're not picking March Madness brackets, Jace," Kyle added.

"Right. I'll take Brian."

Izzie's face dropped slightly, and I instantly felt that I had made a mistake. The corner of Ethan's lip went up.

"I'll take Izzie."

Damn! I knew he was going to do that, I thought.

I scanned the group again.

"Kyle," I said.

"Mike," Ethan countered.

"Marcus."

"Zoe."

"Uncle Roman."

"Alyssa."

As the teams dispersed, Uncle Roman walked over to me and nudged me a little.

"I was getting nervous you were going to forget about me."

"Sorry. I'm trying to play a balancing act, and I think I'm failing at it right now."

He looked at the pool to Izzie and then back to me.

"I think she'll forgive you."

I was about to say something when he raised his eyebrows at me. I instantly closed my mouth and smiled at him. We all jumped into the pool, assuming our respective sides. Brian motioned for us all to gather in the center. Then he looked at me.

"Are you okay with me giving a play?" he asked.

"You know them better, so I'm all ears," I answered.

"Ethan cannot block a spike, especially mine. Plus, he can't help himself from trying. So every chance you get, bump it to me."

"Izzie and Zoe both play volleyball, so be on your A game with them. They will take your head off and not think twice about it," Kyle added.

"Great," Marcus muttered.

"Don't go easy on them either," Brian said, looking at Kyle.

He laughed. "They would never let me live it down."

"Then we're all in agreement," Brian said.

As we turned, the other side had already assumed their positions and were waiting for us. Scrambling, we each took a corner, leaving Kyle in the middle. Along the net, Brian had positioned himself opposite Mike and slowly began taunting him. Izzie sat in the server's spot. Holding the ball, she bounced gracefully in the water before she tossed it high. Izzie jumped up in the water to send the ball sailing at me like a missile.

Although I had been warned, her speed took me by surprise. All I could do was put my hands up to block it. The ball collided with my knuckles and went flying out of the pool toward the women that were sitting. I heard wails of screams as the ball smashed off the middle of the table, sending food everywhere. On the other side of the net, Ethan laughed as he pulled himself out of the pool. He then walked over and tried to help with the mess.

Kyle looked back at me. "I warned you. At least you got your paws up. Otherwise, that might have gotten your nose."

Uncle Roman swam over to me, a grimace on his face.

"Okay. Maybe she's a little irritated with you." He held his fingers close together to show how *little*.

"You think?"

The ball was tossed back to Izzie by Carolina, who said, "Hija, let's try not to kill our guests today, huh? This isn't a championship game, okay?"

"Yes, Mom."

She turned and assumed a similar position.

Great, she's aiming at me again, I thought.

As she tossed the ball, I steadied myself, anticipating its trajectory. She hit it with *slightly* less force but directed it at me again.

"INCOMING!" Marcus bellowed.

I waited until the ball was near before I jumped up. I bumped the ball high in the air but toward Brian, who was at the ready. Seeing the trajectory, he smiled and prepped for his death spike on Ethan. Brian slunk down in the water and jumped up as the ball approached the net. He slapped it down with his giant fist of a hand. Ethan dived for the ball, but missed, creating a large splash in Izzie's direction. As the water dissipated around her, she splashed violently in response in Ethan's direction.

"I'm sorry. I thought I had it," he answered.

"You were nowhere near it." Mike shook his head.

The ball was tossed back to me, and I scanned the water for my target. Although I intended to hit it toward Mike, I looked intently at Izzie. Seeing me focus on her, Izzie set herself to receive the hit and Ethan looked from me to her. I tossed the ball into the air and hit it, turning, at the last second, toward my actual target, but it careened over the net toward Ethan, who had not been looking, and the ball slapped loudly off the side of his face and back into the water.

"Son, it's always best to keep your eye on the ball. Particularly when it's being served," Kyle said, chuckling.

Ethan grabbed onto the side of his face and refused to move his hand.

"I didn't think he was going to hit it to me," he retorted, still grasping his face.

"I think that was the point," Uncle Roman answered.

Kyle looked back to Uncle Roman. "I think this is a bit too much game for me. Want another beer?"

Uncle Roman eyed me, confirming that it was okay with his departure. When I nodded, he said, "Sounds good," and followed Kyle.

Brian looked at the teams.

"Three against five. Someone needs to come over here. I think it's safer for all of us, particularly Jace, if Izzie is on this side of the net."

Before Ethan could answer, Izzie swam over to our side, positioning herself in front of me along the net. I looked over to Uncle Roman, who grinned and lifted his beer toward me. On the other side of the net, Ethan had let go of his face. An almost opalescent ring of red was quickly forming there. Brian pointed to his face and then said to Ethan.

"You have something, just there."

Mike turned to look and broke out laughing, Brian laughing as well.

"You branded him!" Mike said, swimming toward Ethan.

Right up close to him, Mike went hysterical, laughing hard enough that he splashed everyone around as he fell back into the water. "You can actually see the 'Aqua Sport' logo!" he choked out.

I felt heat infuse in my face as I swam over to Ethan, "Man, I'm really sorry."

Ethan glared at me, his eyes narrowed dangerously.

Brian swam up behind and patted him on the back.

"Come on, man. Let's get you some ice."

Everyone but Izzie, Marcus, and I left the pool.

"Maybe we should take down the net?" I suggested.

"Probably wouldn't be a bad idea," Izzie said.

Just as we finished, Zoe came back out onto the deck. She whispered something to her father, who stood up and walked into the house with her. Izzie saw it as well and looked at me.

"What do you think that was about?" I asked.

"I have no idea, but I think it's better that we just stay out here," she answered.

A few moments later, Kyle came out of the house and sat down. I heard Carolina ask what was going on.

"The boys wanted to go get some ice cream, and the girls asked if they could go."

Carolina examined Kyle's face for a while and then nodded before returning to her conversation with the others at the table. Izzie looked back at Marcus and me. "Want to go for a walk?"

"Uh, sure."

"Yeah, sounds like fun," said Marcus.

We all toweled off and then put our clothes back on.

"Mom, we're going to go for a walk, okay?" Izzie asked.

Carolina looked at the three of us and nodded.

"Don't go too far, okay?"

"We won't," Izzie answered.

We walked around the side of the house and toward the street when Marcus made a shivering motion. "On second thought, I think I'm gonna pop home and take a shower," he said.

Izzie's cheeks flushed as she looked from Marcus back to me.

As he walked back to the house, we made our way down the street. I turned back to see Marcus, who was smiling and giving me a double thumbs-up.

Chapter 6

Dog Days

Walking down the sloping curve of Crystal Court, we kept quiet, periodically glancing at each other and smiling. I had a thousand questions running through my head that I wanted to ask her but was unsure where to start. She, seemingly, was having the same thoughts as I was. Because as we turned left onto the road at the end of the court, Izzie finally broke the silence.

"So where did you live before Arizona?"

I laughed under my breath. "Which time?"

She frowned as she looked up at me.

"What do you mean? How many times have you moved?"

"Not counting the first one after my aunt and uncle adopted me? Seventeen."

She stopped and stared at me, her eyes wide and confused.

"Why would you possibly have to move that much?"

"It's the type of work my uncle does. He's sort of a freelance physician."

"Hasn't he ever heard of the internet? Tele-Doc and all? There's really no reason to move that much."

I smiled as I watched her anger rise, enjoying her protectiveness. She started walking again but kept looking back at me.

Finally, she spoke again, "I guess I now understand what he meant when he said you guys were pros at this moving thing."

I nodded and continued to watch her. A thousand emotions seemed to rush across her face as she processed the last twelve years.

"That's so not fair to you! That's at least one move a year. How do you make or keep friends?"

I chuckled as I looked back at her.

"I really don't. When I was younger, I would try, but it was too weird. I would start school one place in the fall and change locations twice by the time that year was over. That's why we decided on home tutors. It's easier than explaining my dropping in and out of schools every few months."

She stopped and stared intently at me, her brows knitted tight. "So when are they going to move again?"

I shrugged, trying to calm her down, realizing my best estimate of six months might only set her off again.

"I don't know exactly when he will finish with his current client and be ready to move on. You and Marcus are the first real friends I have ever had. So I don't want to ruin my time with you thinking about when and how it will be over. This is the most invested into a community we have ever been, so who knows. Maybe this time *will* be different."

Her lips pursed tight, and her face seemed to be flashing various shades of red before a single tear rolled down her cheek, and she instantly turned her face away from me. I walked closer to her and turned her so I could see her face. I could also see the tears welling more aggressively in her eyes. "Izzie, don't cry. Even if I left next week, you two are not getting rid of me that easy. Even though you tried to take my head off with a volleyball today."

She let out a small laugh between tears and gently shoved me.

"You had *that* coming to you. How could you choose Brian before Marcus or me?"

"I was kinda following Marcus's lead on the picks. My goal was not to be a semistationary target in the pool. Little did I know..."

She laughed again and looked at me. "I am the *captain* of the volleyball team."

"Your dad neglected that tidbit when he warned us you and Zoe would go for the kill if the game were on the line."

She shook her head as she looked down on the road we were walking. For a few minutes, we walked in silence. The sky began its iridescent change from day to night, giving off the tranquil hues of brilliant reds and oranges as the earth seemed to be kissed by its new palate. A slight chill filtered through the air as the sun began its slow descent behind the horizon. I saw a small shudder run down Izzie as she grasped hold of her elbows, trying to warm herself. "Dad always says 'red skies at night, sailor's delight.'"

"What does that mean?"

"Tomorrow will be a warm and beautiful day. It's 'red skies in the morning that sailors take warning.'"

"I'll keep that in mind," I said with a chuckle.

I watched her and realized the netted shirt she was wearing wasn't helping with the chill settling in. "Are you cold? Let's head back," I asked.

She looked at me and then down the street before nodding. As she turned, she seemed to grow even colder, nearly vibrating from the chill. I walked behind her and placed my hands on her arms, rubbing vigorously, trying to warm her.

"That feels better, but maybe heading back is a good idea."

Turning, we made our way back in the direction we had just come from. As we came close to the turn onto Crystal Court, Izzie stopped and looked at me. "Could you want to stay here with your aunt? If he had to move again?"

My eyes went wide at the question, and I could see the color rise in her cheeks.

"You mean, *not* go with him?" I asked.

"I'm sorry, it was stu—"

She stopped talking as she looked past me into the brush on the other side of the street. I turned to look where she had been look-ing and saw a set of eyes staring at us. It was an exceptionally large German shepherd standing with its head slightly lowered and its tail even lower.

Slowly moving my head, I looked past Izzie to see how far we were from the house trying to judge if running would help. Then I looked back at the dog, only to see it was now baring its teeth and emitting a low growl. Grateful that I was between the dog and Izzie, but terrified because we were out here alone, I tried to talk to her and encourage her to move back toward the house.

"I'm going to step completely between you and the dog to block its view of you. You need to walk back to the houses slowly and facing the dog, okay?"

Not hearing a response and not wanting to take my eye off the animal, I felt an adrenaline surge. I wondered if there was another dog nearby and if they now surrounded us.

"Izzie, I need you to answer me. Can you walk back to the houses?"

"Y-Yes."

"There are no other dogs, right?"

Her voice caught when she answered. Apparently, she had not thought of that possibility.

"No, I think that is the only one."

"Okay. I'm going to move, and once you no longer see it, start backing up the hill, okay?"

"Okay. I'm ready," she answered with a tremor in her voice.

I took a slow but large step to block the dog's view of Izzie. Trying to keep my head down, I prayed it would not interpret the move as a threat. From the bushes, the growl seemed to intensify, and I felt my heart start to pound in my chest. Slowly, I extended my arms with my head still lowered as I began backing up the road.

"Nice, doggy. Good, doggy. Stay there, doggy," I said while I continued my retreat up the hill toward safety.

Watching my movement, it seemed to contemplate if crossing the street was worth the effort. Feeling an incline come up as I inched backward left me feeling off-balance, but I didn't dare look behind me to judge my footing.

The dog seemed to judge my actions as well. As I reached the precipice of the hill, the dog stopped growling momentarily and slowly sniffed the air.

Crap, it smells the food, I thought.

While I continued my backpedaling, the dog stopped sniffing and perked up slightly as it watched my backward climb. From its vantage point, I must have appeared to be disappearing over the hill because it rose from its position and loped toward Crystal Court.

Wonderful, I thought.

Not wanting to get closer to the people at the Lewis house, I stopped where I was, looking around for something to help as I waited for the dog to breach the hill. To my left was the Hunter house, and along the side of it was a garbage can with a large white bag inside it. I hurried toward the can, hoping that there would be food to distract the dog long enough for Izzie to get help.

Just as I ripped the bag open, I saw the dog again. Glancing inside, I smiled when I saw meat. I whistled toward the dog, and it turned its head toward me. Spotting me, it growled and lowered its head in a defensive position before sniffing the air again. I reached into the bag and pulled out a chunk of what looked like steak. The dog, seeing the food, moved cautiously toward me. As it neared, I could see that it was very thin and its coat was thick and matted. Even then, I could make out the dog's ribs and hips through it.

"Aw, buddy. You must be so hungry," I whispered.

Kneeling, I extended a hand to the dog and tried to calm it. As I assumed the position, the dog snarled at me. I jumped slightly and repositioned myself lower and tossed a few pieces of meat to it. The dog looked at the food and then back at me, continuing to growl but in a less menacing way. Behind me, I could hear someone slowly approaching. I tried to speak in as soothing a tone as possible, not to upset the dog.

"It's okay. He's hungry. But please don't move any closer. If you can get me more food, though, that will help," I said.

Whoever it was seemed to listen as I heard footsteps heading back to where they came from. Returning my attention to the dog, I ripped off another hunk of meat and tossed it but closer to me. The dog hesitated as it looked from the meat to me but slowly advanced. Again, I extended my hand to the shepherd, being sure to keep my head lowered so as not to appear as a threat.

The dog stopped growling, and I held my position as I heard it eating. Taking the last hunk of food from the bag, I placed it in my extended hand and resumed my previous position. I could hear the ground crunching in front of me as the dog inched closer, but I did not look up. Time seemed to crawl as I tried to keep myself calm. It was only then that I realized the vulnerable state I had just put myself into. Just when I thought I wouldn't be able to take it anymore and was going to look up, I felt the dog sniffing my hand.

I opened my fist, allowing it to take the food from it. Gently, I felt the dog pull the meat off my hand and step back to eat it. Within a few seconds, it came back to me, sniffing my hand again and nudging it. Slowly, I looked up to see the dog within inches of my hand. It tilted its head slightly before growling faintly at me. I realized it was more a warning than a threat, so I lowered my head again to break eye contact.

I began speaking softly, hoping to keep it calm. It seemed to realize that I would not hurt it but was also praying that no one behind me did anything drastic. "It's okay, buddy. I've got more food where that came from. You just need to calm down," I continued in a soft whisper.

My heart was hammering in my chest by then. Contemplating my next move as I felt the dog sniff my hand again, causing me to stop talking. Unfortunately, this also caused it to stop and pull back. Instantly, I relaxed, and the dog began sniffing my hand again and then nudged it.

Deciding to take a chance, I let my hand creep up to scratch the dog's jaw. I felt it relax as I did too. Carefully, I lifted my head to look, watching to be sure that it was still calm. I continued to pet the dog, trying to reassure it.

Over my shoulder, I could hear movement, causing the mongrel to back away and growl again. "I have some food in a bag. I'm tossing it to you," I heard Uncle Roman whisper.

Needing to reestablish my trust, I started talking to the dog once more. I gave my uncle a thumbs-up to let him know I had understood. The dog began smelling the air again as I pulled the bag closer to me. Opening the bag, I tried to call the dog to me again. There were hot dogs and hamburgers inside. I took out three hamburgers and carefully repositioned myself, going from a sitting position to a kneeling one.

I gave Buddy—I'd already named the poor beast in my head—a hamburger, first, and waited for him to finish. With each bite, its behavior was changing from a feral animal to a domesticated partner again. I heard a collective sigh from behind me. It meant the others saw the change in the dog's behavior as well.

Grabbing the bag of goodies, I tossed pieces of hot dog to Buddy and began walking back toward my house. "Let's put him in the pool area," I said to Uncle Roman.

He just stood there, mouth slightly open and eyes wide as he watched the dog follow me as though it had been our pet for years.

"Uncle Roman, I need the gate opened," I reminded him.

"Oh, right! Got it."

He walked to the gate and opened it with my new companion following close behind. As we made our way into the screened-in pool area, Buddy tensed slightly but calmed again as I gave him a piece of burger. After eating his fill, he made his way to a corner and lay down in a compact bundle.

Once I realized he was safe and calm, I was able to finally relax. When I turned, I saw a throng of faces staring at me from the Lewis pool area.

"You good?" Kyle hollered from where he was.

"Yes. He was hungry and scared but seems fine now," I answered.

"I called animal control. They're on their way," Carolina said.

I looked back at the dog and felt a sense of guilt at letting strange people take him. I had just calmed him and regained the trust his previous owner had destroyed. I turned to Uncle Roman and saw his eyebrows rise. He must have deduced what I was thinking because he said, "Jace, we know nothing about its character..."

I knew he was right and tried not to think of the dog as my own, but it was hard not to.

"What will happen to him?" I asked.

"It'll go to the shelter where they will monitor for a while. Once they know it is safe, it'll be put up for adoption," Kyle said from the screen door as he entered.

A small flash of light reflected off something in his hand. Looking in its direction, I saw the gun Kyle had. On seeing me frown, he explained, "If this is one of the dogs that has been causing quite the stir around here for a few weeks, I wasn't taking any chances."

"I think you can put the gun down now. He's resting in the corner," I said with more acidity in my voice than I probably should have.

Kyle eyed the resting, emaciated dog and decided my assessment of the situation was correct.

"So you're an alpha dog, huh?" he asked.

His words caught Uncle Roman by surprise, and seeing his reaction, Kyle laughed.

"Calm down, Roman. I just watched a fifteen-year-old kid calm a dog that has been evading the professionals for weeks. I'm a bit impressed."

"I don't know if I'm an 'alpha dog.' I've never had an animal," I said as I looked back to see Buddy snuggled comfortably in the corner and now snoring slightly.

Aunt Cora came to the living room sliders with a bowl in her hands. Seeing her struggle, I met her at the door to open it.

"It's water. I have blankets on the couch for him," she said, smiling as she looked at the dog.

Nodding, I placed the bowl next to Buddy and walked into the house to get the blankets. Hearing Aunt Cora gasp, I turned to see Buddy walking into the house, following me.

"What's up, Buddy?" I asked.

He lumbered over to me and lay down, resting his snout on my feet. My heart swelled with love at that moment, and I looked up at Aunt Cora, who had a similar reaction. Uncle Roman came to the door, saw the position of the dog, and let out a sigh. "I guess we just adopted a dog."

Unsure if I had heard him correctly, I stared at my uncle in disbelief. Aunt Cora hugged him around the waist as she smiled at me.

Kyle appraised the situation in the house and laughed. "Looks like he's adopted you as much as you just adopted him," he teased.

From the pool area, I could hear Carolina walking closer. Her voice reached us as she said, "Animal control is…"

She looked into the living room and stopped talking. "But it looks like we may not need them after all."

There was a knock on the front door, and Buddy barked as he struggled to get up. Trying to calm him, I encouraged him to lie back down while Aunt Cora made her way past us. A large man stood outside the door, and he was looking over my aunt's shoulder to find the dog he could hear barking. From where we were, I really couldn't hear what was being said. So it startled me when I saw a man and a woman entering the living room.

"Yup, this is one of the mutts that we've been chasing for weeks. I'd know that big one anywhere. Tried to take a bite out of me a few times. I'm not sure he's a safe family pet, ma'am," the man said.

"He *was* a family pet before and will be fine with a bit of love and understanding. He was starving and trying to survive on his own. I'm not sure what exactly happened, but I'm sure you almost getting bit was not *his* fault!" I snapped.

The man glared at me as I spoke. As he opened his mouth to speak, his partner placed her hand on his arm to calm him. "I think what my partner is trying to say is the dog that we see here is definitely not of the same intensity of dog we saw just a few days ago. What did you do to catch him?" she asked.

"Well, I didn't catch him! I earned his trust," I answered.

Her eyebrows shot up. "We could barely get within fifty feet of him before he looked like he'd attack or just bolt. It didn't matter what we did. I'm seriously impressed, kid."

She turned to Aunt Cora and Uncle Roman. "So what are your plans regarding the dog?" she asked.

Uncle Roman looked at me with concern on his face. Under my hand, I felt Buddy shift his head. Reflexively, I began scratching his ear, and Uncle Roman's face softened. He sighed. "Looks like we're keeping him."

I smiled and looked down at my new friend as I continued to scratch Buddy behind the ear.

"If there is a change in plans, call us," the woman said before she handed a business card to Aunt Cora. Then she shook her head and looked back at me with a crooked smile. She said, "Good luck, folks. We can see ourselves out."

They turned to walk out the door, and I knelt next to Buddy to hug him. The room seemed to go still as they waited for the dog's response to my impromptu embrace. Without hesitation, Buddy sat up and allowed it. As I pulled away, he began licking my cheek. There seemed to be a collective sigh as everyone realized that my life was not in mortal danger.

"All right. Seeing that we clearly have a new family member, do you have a name for him?" Aunt Cora asked.

"His name is Buddy," I announced.

"Looks like you'll be needing some supplies. There's a pet store just outside Williston. Roman, you want a ride?" Kyle asked.

Uncle Roman was still standing in the center of the room, watching the action like a spectator. Kyle chuckled as he noticed and patted him on the back. "Come on. I'll drive you out there."

"Yeah, sure. Supplies."

Aunt Cora leaned up and kissed her husband before he walked out the door. Then she turned her attention back to me. "So you're new friend is going to need a bath."

"We have some dog shampoo," Carolina offered.

"Wonderful," Aunt Cora answered.

As Carolina left to collect the necessary items, Aunt Cora and I coaxed Buddy into her room. The bathroom there had a large tub that could support the dog and me so I'd be able to clean him. From the family room, we heard the slider open, and Aunt Cora hollered to alert the guest where we were now located. A second later, Izzie stood in the doorway, holding a plastic bag.

"Mom wasn't exactly sure what you were going to need, so she sent me over with everything," Izzie said.

She seemed to survey the room, trying to assess the danger of the situation before walking over. "Is he...okay?" she asked.

"Yeah, he was simply scared, hungry, and dirty. I remedied two of the three problems, buuut he still stinks!" I teased as I rubbed his ear.

Izzie giggled from the doorway as she approached. "What are you going to name him?" she asked.

"Buddy."

I pet his head, which he had lifted to me, seeming to recognize his new name.

Izzie looked at us. "Have you ever bathed a dog before? They usually fight you on it."

I rubbed the back of my neck. "Actually, no. I haven't, have you?"

"Yes. I bathe Wampa all the time. She's our Labrador and used to fight us all the time but now actually loves the tub, and the pool, and the hose, and well, anything with water."

"What do we have to do?"

She walked over to the tub and began filling it about halfway with warm water and placed the shampoo next to the ledge for easy access. Following close behind to watch what she was doing, I soon noticed Buddy had followed me. Looking into the tub, Buddy leaned his head on the ledge and tried to step in.

"Well, I guess that answers the question about if he will fight us." She laughed.

While sitting on the ledge, she patted her leg and encouraged Buddy to come in the rest of the way. With his legs already in the tub, he leaped the rest of the way in, making a large splash as he did so. All three of us laughed as we started wiping the water away from our faces.

Carefully, she showered his pelt with the warm water and lathered him up. As she washed him down, we watched as the water sluicing down Buddy's body went from a deep brown to almost black. My heart broke as I watched, realizing Izzie was probably washing off weeks of dirt and grime.

"You poor thing. You're going to feel so much better when you get out," Izzie said as she scratched behind his ear.

Draining the water, she washed him twice more before the water running down was clear. Buddy was a model pooch and stood still, seeming to enjoy the bath. After Izzie had turned the water off and was reaching for a towel, Buddy began shaking, tossing water in every direction. Each of us tried to block the sprays as we laughed and squealed. For the first time, Buddy lifted his tail and wagged it.

"You feel better, huh, big guy?" I said, placing my head against his.

His big brown eyes seemed to lighten as he shook himself off again and jumped out of the tub. It was as though everything he had been through the past few weeks was washed down the drain with the dirt, leaving behind the happy-go-lucky pup he had been. After he jumped out of the tub, Buddy began running around enthusiastically and barking, playfully, while we chased him trying to dry him off. It was as if he came to life, realizing that he would have more of these days ahead of him and less of what he had before today.

CHAPTER 7

School Days

Two weeks later

I have been told that I am not the easiest to wake in the morning, and most mornings involve Uncle Roman threatening me with various and creative ways to rouse me from my slumber. We usually end in a stalemate with him, leaving exacerbated while I promise to wake in five more minutes. Today was different, though. Aunt Cora came bearing gifts of turkey bacon and eggs. A delicious aroma wafted into the room as she entered, causing Buddy to come to life on the end of my bed.

"Good morning, boys," she started. "They called your uncle to the clinic early today, so I figured we could try a fresh way to wake you up."

My face was down in the soft plush of my pillow when I rolled my head toward her voice and opened one bright blue eye to meet hers.

"That smells amazing. What made you make breakfast this morning?"

Her face lit up as she smiled, her bronze-colored hair pulled into a loose bun, and small loose trundles framing her face.

"Now that I have your attention, let's try this again. They called your uncle to work early today. And since breakfast is the most important meal of the day, I figured we would try something new."

I chuckled as I rolled over. "Yeah, I guess food is an amazing way to wake a man up."

Cocking her head to the side, she widened her eyes as the corner of her mouth lifted. "Are you telling me you're a man now? When did that occur?"

"Okay, maybe not quite a man but getting pretty close to it, though. I'll be fifteen on Monday. It won't be all that long before I will be out of the house and off to college."

Her smile softened as she reached out to brush a stray hair from my forehead. "Don't go growing up too fast. There's a lot of living out there, and no need to take it on all on at once."

Coming back to her usual lively self, Aunt Cora jumped up from my bed and walked toward the door. Her movement caused Buddy to jump up as well.

"Hurry and eat. Even if Mrs. Hunter will be late, I want you to be on time. Besides, this guy needs to go for a walk and eat too."

"It's not Mrs. Hunter. I told you it's Marcus. He…how can I put it? Moves at his own speed."

"That's one way to put it. I watch them in the morning sometimes. I swear that boy would forget his head if it were not attached to his shoulders!"

As she left the room, I rolled over onto my back and stretched. With a few pops, the stray vertebrae in my spine fell back into alignment. Sitting up, I sat on the edge of my bed and rubbed my face then stood up. Buddy had been on the bed and hopped off when I rose, following me. Before walking to my closet, I stole the largest piece of bacon off the plate and began chewing. I rummaged through the closet for a comfortable and clean outfit for the day. A glance at my alarm clock's bright red numbers showed it was 7:05 a.m. and I felt my heart rate pick up.

I grabbed the plate of food and moved toward the window where I positioned myself just out of sight but having an unrestricted view of the court below. Buddy followed as well and planted himself perfectly at my feet, continually licking his lips and periodically whining.

"Shhh. Here, have a piece, but be quiet!"

Over the past two weeks, I had not really had the chance to talk alone with Izzie again. She took part in several after-school activities and sports, which meant she would be gone for most of the day. By the time she came home, she had to play catch up with schoolwork, which left little time for anything else. Or at least that's what I told myself.

Last weekend, we were all able to meet up and play some *Castle Core* from our houses. But I found I missed seeing her. Now I had resorted to catching sight of her when I knew she'd be leaving or returning to her house. Although I felt like a stalker, I found myself drawn to the window when I knew she'd be outside.

As I was grabbing another piece of bacon, I heard her mother call her name. I suddenly stopped in my tracks and waited. As Izzie came out of the house, I found myself transfixed again. She smiled brightly with perfect teeth that were even more noticeable when emphasized by her cinnamon-colored skin. She was wearing light-colored jeans and a teal tank top with a light-green checkered button-up over it.

"You know you can try to talk to her sometime instead of just staring at her through the window," Aunt Cora said from behind me.

I jumped, causing my curtains to move and Buddy to let out a small yip.

"Aunt Cora, you scared the life out of me. I-I'm just looking at what kind of weather is outside...so I know what to wear," I lied poorly.

Walking toward me, she said, "Mmm-hmm. And I'm the queen of England."

Glancing through the window, in full view, she saw Izzie, her mom, and her sisters and waved to them. Alyssa noticed Aunt Cora first and motioned to the rest of the group. Following her glance, each girl smiled and waved before getting in the car.

"I can't believe you just did that!"

Giving me a coy smile, she said, "I thought you were just looking at the weather?"

I felt my cheeks flush at her question and looked down at my plate.

"Finish getting ready and head downstairs so we can get started. Remember, Mrs. Hunter will be here by 8:00 a.m. At least I hope she will."

"Okay. Let me take a shower first."

As she left the room again, I glanced out the window to watch Izzie's family driving off. Hearing yelling from across the court, I turned my attention to watch the entertainment that was about to ensue from the Hunter house.

Looking to the house opposite mine, I could see Marcus running out the front door with his mother calling from inside. Each morning, it was the same show. He was perpetually running late, which always had his mom running late. Typically, there were at least three attempts to leave the house. He would forget his bag, his lunch, a hat, or a sweater. You name it and Marcus would probably run back and forth a dozen times before he had grabbed everything and could leave for school. Today, it only took four trips.

As he closed the door behind him for the last time, he took a deep breath and counted something on his fingers. Once he seemed satisfied, Marcus then crossed his lawn and headed toward the bus stop, which was a few blocks away. Just before he got to the end of his driveway, he stopped and looked up toward my house. Making eye contact, I froze. He must have sensed my uneasiness and shrugged his shoulders dramatically before giving a simple wave. I felt the tension in my shoulders relax as I waved back.

"Jace, how's that shower going?"

Aunt Cora's question jolted me back to reality, and I headed off to the bathroom to resume where I had left off. After, I put on gray shorts and a blue shirt sporting a kitten wearing pilot goggles and sitting in a taco as though it was flying.

Walking back into my room, I made a quick assessment of everything I would need for school and headed downstairs to the breakfast nook. As I passed Aunt Cora, she put her hand up, which caused me to stop. She looked at my shirt and then lifted an eyebrow. Rolling her eyes, she said, "You can explain that shirt to me all you want. I'll never understand today's teenage fashion."

I laughed. "First, it's taco kitty. Second, I'm sure you had some crazy fashions that left your family scratching their heads when you were younger."

Aunt Cora chuckled. "Feed Buddy and then take him for a walk. I'll put out some juice for you when you get back."

I grabbed the leash and saw Buddy's excitement as he started vigorously wagging his tail and turning in circles. Aunt Cora and I both laughed as I wrestled to get the leash on him. Once secured, we headed out.

After we returned, I fed him before I set myself up for the day. Once Buddy had finished eating, he came and lay down at my feet, which was now part of his routine. I likely could change his name to shadow because he follows me everywhere I go.

I looked at Aunt Cora and said, "Done! With time to spare."

Glancing at the clock, she countered, "Not really. It's 8:08 a.m. You're lucky she's just running late…again."

Compared to the previous home instructors, Mrs. Hunter was my favorite. She always seemed happy, which made the lessons more entertaining. We would spend much of the day laughing while we discussed each topic. For instance, instead of teaching me history, she would essentially reenact it. It made the lessons even more enjoyable. When the doorbell rang, a small rush of excitement ran through me. Buddy jumped up from his position and headed to the door, barking. He only stopped when Aunt Cora shooed him away.

I heard Aunt Cora at the front door. "Good morning, Mary. Sorry for the dog. Jace is all ready for you in the usual spot."

As Mrs. Hunter made her way down the long corridor of our house, I could hear her flip-flops smacking the back of her heels.

"Where's my favorite student? You ready to get this party started?" she called out.

I smiled cheerfully. "Ready as ever."

"Before I leave you two, would you like a drink, Mary?" Aunt Cora asked.

"I would. But the one I have in mind would make it inappropriate to continue teaching."

Aunt Cora looked up from the fridge in alarm. On meeting Mrs. Hunter's playful eyes, she laughed too and said, "Mary, I can totally appreciate that!"

Mrs. Hunter giggled as she sat down with me in the nook. Buddy resumed his previous position.

"Okay, let's get started. What would you like to work on first? We started with math yesterday, so maybe history today?"

"Sounds good to me."

Mrs. Hunter was amazing at her job. She could move from topic to topic with minimal transition, which helped the day fly by. Before I knew it, her last alarm was going off, and Green Day's "Closing Time" signaled the end of the day for us. Whenever it would play, I couldn't help but laugh.

Mrs. Hunter was in the middle of packing up her things and giving me last-minute assignments when we heard the front door open. Buddy lifted his head from his position, looking in its direction.

I heard Aunt Cora mute the TV, and we watched as she made her way to the front door, Buddy close behind her. Mrs. Hunter and I looked at each other and then down the hallway when we heard Aunt Cora speaking to whoever just entered the house.

"You're back early. What happened?"

I could hear my uncle's deep voice. "Well, hello to you too."

"I'm sorry, you just took me by surprise. You're usually home much later. I'll start preparing dinner now."

"No, no. It was a long day, and I really needed a break. Dr. Johnson is very...very...tenacious. I just wanted some time away with my two favorite people." He must have noticed Buddy at Aunt Cora's heels because he added, "And our new four-legged friend."

"Mary is just finishing up with Jace now if you would like to say hello."

Mrs. Hunter had been finishing putting her bag together while my aunt and uncle were talking in the hallway. Both of us trying not to listen in.

"Okay, Jace, I would like a three-page paper on the Civil War. Proper format, including references. Let's say Tuesday, after the holiday?"

"No problem. I'll start working on it after you leave."

Mrs. Hunter frowned and looked at me pensively.

"It's Friday, Jace. Go out and enjoy yourself. You have three days to complete it. Marcus needs to get out of the house too. You should go find him."

As we finished reviewing assignments, I saw the tall form of my uncle walking toward the kitchen. Although he is in his forties, he has a handsome blend of salt-and-pepper hair. He also has a much younger-looking face, chiseled features, and narrow bright blue eyes.

"Ah, there's the most attractive tutor in Florida," my uncle beamed as he saw Mrs. Hunter.

Mrs. Hunter's cheeks went a rosy shade of red as she smiled and playfully swatted the air in his direction.

"Oh, Dr. Northall, stop."

He smiled and put his hand on her shoulder.

"Mary, please, call me Roman. There is no need for formalities here. How is our man Jace doing?"

Aunt Cora chuckled. "Oh great. Another one that thinks he is a man now."

Uncle Roman looked at Aunt Cora and then back at me. Smiling, I just shrugged my shoulders.

"He's doing wonderfully, Roman. Out of all the years I have been teaching, Jace is one of the smartest students I have ever had. He is self-motivated, a fast learner, and absorbs material well."

Mrs. Hunter hesitated somewhat, and he lifted an eyebrow.

"I hear a 'but' coming."

"Don't get me wrong," Mrs. Hunter started. "I love teaching Jace, I just thought... Look, if I have stepped out of my bounds, I'm terribly sorry."

Aunt Cora took Mrs. Hunter's small hand in hers and looked her in the eye. "We appreciate everything that you do for Jace, but the lifestyle we lead... Well, we move. A lot. And sometimes it is just easier when Jace is homeschooled, especially when trying to keep up with different school's curriculum, which can differ from state to state or even region to region. It's not perfect, but it works for us."

Mrs. Hunter gave a half-hearted attempt at a smile and then looked at me somewhere between pity and happiness.

"Okay. Time for me to head home to Marcus. Hopefully, he didn't miss the bus. I swear that boy will make me gray prematurely! So same time Tuesday?"

"Yes, ma'am," I said.

I felt a small tug from deep within at Mrs. Hunter's acknowledgment of my lack of social life. I hoped she would have been able to get through to them. It's a topic we do not touch. In Scottsdale, I had asked to go to the high school near the house. I was told that they would think about it. Three weeks later, we moved.

The memory brought up the anger I had the day they announced our next move. But looking at Mrs. Hunter, I smiled and tried not to change my facial expression. However, the twinges of anger were growing. Buddy must have sensed it because he whined, nudging my leg. I leaned down to pet him, continuing my attempt to calm myself.

While Mrs. Hunter was picking up her bags, there was a tremendous crash from the front hallway. It caused all of us to jump a bit while Buddy seemed really spooked. Immediately, he was whining and began circling and pacing but avoided the place where the noise had just come from.

Each of us was looking around uneasily, but Aunt Cora was the first to speak up, "Maybe the wind blew the door open?"

We all walked to the front hallway. The large table positioned on the wall next to the front door was now on its face. The vase, bowl, and beach glass that had been resting on its surface had shattered with their remnants scattered throughout the hallway.

I nervously smiled and said, "I guess the ghost followed us."

CHAPTER 8

The Ghost

Being a stay-at-home mom, Aunt Cora took care of the house as though it was her job, and our home was always immaculate, with everything in its place. Although she expected it to stay clean, Aunt Cora was still a very easygoing person. So following this one fundamental rule never seemed like a chore to me.

She also took great care and meticulously decorated to fit the style of each house. Sometimes she'd even buy items to fit the new decor of the region we were in. Two years ago, while living in South Dakota, she had found a small vase. Oddly enough, after purchasing that item, *stuff* started happening. A bowl would be on the opposite end of the table, the coffee cups were up instead of down in the cabinets, and doors that we knew had been closed would be open.

The occurrences were few, so we never really gave it much credence. But after a few months of oddities, Uncle Roman was the one who had matter-of-factly said, "We must have a ghost." That prospect would have scared most people. But secretly, the thought gave me hope, and I wished for the oddities to continue.

I liked to think it was one, or both, of my parents letting me know they were close by and watching over me, and had even proposed the idea to Uncle Roman once, although he did not seem to hold the same sentiment. The thought seemed to bother him more than comfort him, so I never brought it up again. My parents were a sore spot for my aunt and uncle. Talking about them usually led to agitation and annoyance, which is why I typically left the topic alone although I was desperate for information and comforting stories of them. To me, they were silhouettes of a past that I longed to give more structure to. I yearned to hear of my father's antics as a young man and if I was like him as well as learning about my mother and her hopes for my future. I wanted to hear the stories of how they met and their reaction to finding out I was coming. How had they chosen my name? The list of questions was never-ending. Unfortunately, this would be a topic that would be left to haunt me for the rest of my days.

Mrs. Hunter was the one to break the stunned silence. "Does this sort of thing happen, uh, often?"

Aunt Cora, still assessing the damage, looked up. "No. It does not. The 'ghost' was a joke we had at one of our previous houses when we would misplace things. But nothing like *this* has ever happened before."

Her words felt like a stab in the belly. Deep down, I did not want to believe that it was a joke. However, I could also see how there may be rational explanations for such occurrences. As I was about to speak, I could see Aunt Cora recompose herself and give me a look of concern. She then shot a glance at my uncle, who seemed to realize the need to ease the tension in the room.

"Well, on that interesting note, let's get Mary back across the street in one piece before the yard tries to swallow her," Uncle Roman mused.

Mrs. Hunter stopped in her tracks and stared blankly at him.

"Mary, I'm joking. This table is an antique and has a weird leg. It must have buckled, and that caused it to turn over."

I was about to say that the table was brand-new, and a "weird leg" couldn't flip something that big with force enough to throw its contents across the room. As I opened my mouth to speak, though, I looked up and saw Aunt Cora shoot me a death stare. Reading between the lines, I offered a hand to Mrs. Hunter as I started walking her to the front door.

"Let me help you over the stuff in here," I said to her.

Once at the door, she turned to me.

"Jace, are you coming over to hang out with Marcus when he gets home?"

I tried to keep the eagerness from my tone.

"That sounds great. Maybe I'll try to come over later."

She frowned. "How about you come over around four? That will allow me time to see how much homework Marcus *really* has."

As though we were two children asking for candy, we looked to Aunt Cora and Uncle Roman for permission. After a moment's hesitation, Aunt Cora finally answered, "I think you have all your chores done, so I don't see why not. Roman?"

Aunt Cora nudged my uncle, who was still engrossed in the scene on the floor. When he looked up, he said, "Oh, of course. And I'm glad that I know his mom." He winked at Mrs. Hunter.

"Perfect! We'll see you at 4:00 p.m. I'll make perogies, so come hungry," Mrs. Hunter said.

Uncle Roman laughed. "With an offer like that, I may show up with him!"

Mrs. Hunter's cheeks shone more red than usual when she said, "Of course, you are all welcome to come by if you would like."

"We'd like that very much. It would be nice to be together for a friendly visit. Roman and I have some more stuff to complete in the house tonight. Perhaps we can join you for dinner later?" Aunt Cora responded.

"Wonderful idea! How about six?" Mrs. Hunter said, clapping her hands together.

"What time is it now?" Uncle Roman asked.

I reached in my back pocket and pulled my phone out: "2:40."

"More than enough time to get everything together. I'll see you all tonight. Be sure to bring your appetites!"

As Mrs. Hunter left, I waved and then closed the front door. A sense of relief washed over me, knowing that I could now fully assess the amount of damage the table toppling had caused. Although there had not been much on it, what was there was mostly glass. Aunt Cora shook her head as she surveyed the room. Then her gaze rested on me.

"Can you go grab a broom, dustpan, and the vacuum, Jace?"

I nodded and walked to the back of the house. Once they thought I was out of earshot, I could hear Aunt Cora and Uncle Roman talking in hushed tones. "It's getting harder to hide. I'm not sure how much longer we can keep this going?" Aunt Cora asked.

I stopped in my tracks just out of their view and continued to listen.

"The entire table flipped over! My favorite vase is in a million pieces on the other side of the foyer. Do you think she bought the 'faulty leg' on the table?" she debated.

My heart froze. Aunt Cora had just said it was one of us being forgetful. That the ghost theory was just something they came up with to make light of the situation. Was there more to it? Did we really have a spirit, or two, in the house?

I grabbed firmly at the hope that it would be one or both of my parents again and felt a weight lift. Returning to the room, I could see that Aunt Cora seemed genuinely unnerved, and Uncle Roman was profoundly serious.

I coughed as I was walking back in their direction to alert my presence, and they both stopped talking. Grabbing the various cleaning supplies, we all set to work cleaning in silence. Uncle Roman and I lifted the table off its face and placed it back against the wall. Instinctively, I looked at the front of the table, trying to find something that could explain what had happened. Uncle Roman seemed to do the same. As though drawn by a magnet, we both knelt to look at the legs, grabbing them and giving a sturdy shake.

I looked at my uncle. "My side is secure. Front and back. How about yours?"

He looked down at his hand, which was still securely around the left front leg, as though contemplating what his next statement should be. Aunt Cora was watching both of us while she slowly swept up the remnants of a vase, dish, and lamp.

Without lifting his head, he said, "This front leg feels loose. I'll tighten it before we put anything else in it or on it."

Then to Aunt Cora, he said, "Do we know where the warranty papers are, Cora? If it is defective, I want to return it before the warranty runs out next month."

Aunt Cora nodded toward the cabinet itself. "It's in the top drawer."

As I stood, I could see that most of the glass had been cleaned, and I just wanted to get upstairs. Besides overhearing their conversation, the fact that Uncle Roman blatantly lied to me left me needing some air.

"Do you guys still need my help?"

Aunt Cora stood up and reassessed her handiwork and said, "No, I think we can finish up from here."

"I'm going to head upstairs then. If that's okay with you?"

Uncle Roman smiled. "Yes, it is. Don't forget you promised to go to the Hunter's at four."

I nodded as I walked upstairs. My thoughts were still fixed on the table, and I felt a hundred questions rush through my head at once. Shaking them off, I headed to my room, where I put my books into the nook in the headboard of my captain's bed and lay back on the pillows. Still reeling from the past twenty minutes, I felt a cold nose rub against my hand. I looked down and saw it was Buddy's head resting on my bed as he looked balefully at me.

"What's up, big guy? Did that scare you too?"

I scratched his ear, and he climbed up onto the bed, snuggling against me. I rolled onto my side to make more room for him, and after he had settled, I draped an arm over him.

Thinking about the occurrences from today, I soon felt an urge to be close with my parents. Sitting up, I slid off my bed, trying not to disturb Buddy, who was now snoring, which caused his lip to flap like a curtain blowing in the wind. Grabbing the drawer under my bed, I pulled it open. Groping blindly within the drawer, I made my way to the back right corner until I had found what I was looking for.

Pulling the object out, I sat back against the side of the bed to look at it. It was a small dark wooden box with a wolf etched on it in midhowl. There was also a full moon on the lid. This was where I keep my most treasured memories safe. Brushing a hand against the grain of the wood where the wolf was, I felt a smile tug at the corner of my lip.

I always felt as though that wolf was there to protect my leftover trinkets from my previous life although there wasn't much to protect. A few pictures of my parents and even less of the three of us together lay inside. My favorite picture was the one from my third birthday party; -the last one I have of us altogether. There were also two pieces of jewelry in the box—my mother's necklace and my father's ring.

The necklace's charm lay in the word "Mom" that was etched across the outer ring of a silver heart. My birthstone, an amethyst, jutted out from its center. My father's titanium ring was adorned with Celtic knots running across the band and three rubies evenly spaced throughout. There was a time when his ring was so large and imposing. Now, though, my ring finger was big enough to comfortably support its weight on my right hand. Although wearing it brings me great joy, I never wore it outside my room for fear of losing it or upsetting Uncle Roman and Aunt Cora. Still wearing the ring now, I walked over to my desk and sat down, trying to reflect on the afternoon.

Sometimes I wish I could freely talk to them about my parents…about that night. Unfortunately, whenever I bring it up, there is a change in their attitude, and tension instantly builds. It is almost as though they feel responsible for my parents' fate. Obviously, that's not possible since they were babysitting me when it happened.

The only information I had was that my parents had gone to the annual Harvest Moon Festival across town, which was like a fancy Halloween party for adults. When they were coming home, my father had somehow lost control of the car and their injuries from that accident had caused their deaths. There had been insinuations over the years from those who heard the story that my father had been drinking and that had caused the accident. But I could never believe that. I remembered little about them, but from what I do, I don't see my father putting them in danger like that.

As I sat at my desk, I heard Izzie's voice coming from outside. I waited a few minutes before I walked to the window and looked down. She was curled up in her usual spot on a curved wicker couch with tiffany-blue cushions next to the large stucco fireplace, a book in her hand.

I wish I knew what she was reading, I thought.

Kyle interrupted my thoughts, calling her in to help with something inside the house.

"I'll be there in a minute. I just want to finish the last page of this chapter," she said.

"Okay, but not too long. Momma is making empanadas to bring to the café, and she wants to show you how to make them."

"Grandma's recipe?"

"Of course!"

"Okay, I'm coming now."

"Thought that might get you."

As she got up from the couch, she turned back to put her book down. Standing up, she suddenly froze and looked up toward my bedroom window. Quickly, I shifted to the left of my window and out of her sight.

Well, if that didn't look suspicious. *God, I must look like such a creep*! I was thinking.

After waiting for what felt like a safe amount of time, I braved a look back out the window. Izzie had disappeared, and so was her book.

Yup. I'd officially become the creepy next-door neighbor.

CHAPTER 9

Carolina's Café

Looking back at the bed, I watched as Buddy stretched out, encompassing most of it.

"You have it easy, big guy! Sometimes, I wish we could change spots," I said with a chuckle.

I could no longer hear Aunt Cora or Uncle Roman in the foyer and assumed that they had moved toward the kitchen. Walking back to my computer, I sat and stared at the screen. In the corner, I could see the icon for *Castle Core* and clicked on it. As I waited for the program to load, I remembered Marcus's computer and frowned at the pathetic graphics mine was emitting.

I wonder if I could head over there now? I thought as I looked at the small clock next to my bed, which read 3:02 p.m. As I was about to leave, I remembered Mrs. Hunter's concern about Marcus's homework. Begrudgingly, I remained seated at my desk, knowing deep down that he would not be finished yet.

I heard Buddy come to life and jump off my bed, which caused me to start a bit. "Where are you heading off to?" I asked.

As Buddy nudged my bedroom door open and headed toward the stairs, I could smell what had risen him from his slumber. With the door now open, I could also hear Aunt Cora feverishly moving around the kitchen. She seemed to be louder than usual, which I assume was related to this morning's furniture fiasco.

A small chime was heard from my computer, and I turned to look at it. Moving the mouse to the blinking red number in the corner, I clicked and watched as a screen opened with an avatar of a strong shirtless male with his arms crossed. Above the avatar was the name Enos12605.

Please tell me you are coming over here soon.

I felt the corner of my lip lift as I began my reply.

Aww, Marcus. Do you miss me?

I watched as the conversation bubble filled and disappeared a few times. Finally, the bubble chimed with a response.

Ha. I need a diversion from my mom. She won't leave me alone about homework.

Sorry, man. Your mom was extremely specific about what time I was to come by.

Boo. You're no fun. But seriously, when are you coming to save me?

Imagining him dodging his mother made me giggle.

She told me to come by at 4. My Aunt and Uncle are coming at 6 for dinner.

The conversation bubble turned on and off a few times, and it was obvious that he was thinking through a proper response.

I guess that means I'm not getting out of my math work tonight. (sigh). Fine. I'll see you in 30 minutes. Don't be late!

We'll be there. My Aunt and Uncle are never late.

I closed the conversation window and stared at my avatar in Elemental Plaza. Hovering over the search tab, I hesitated, thinking through all the possible reasons not to click it. Without allowing myself to think too hard on it, I quickly hit the button and did a search of Izzie's avatar. After a few seconds, I received a message indicating that she was idle. This meant that she was either away from her computer or not logged on. I sat back in my chair and looked at the clock—3:22 p.m. Standing, I walked to the front window and looked out across the court and noticed that Izzie's family car was gone. I wondered if the whole family had left or just her mom. For a moment, I contemplated walking to her house and knocking. The thought of seeing her father, or worse, Zoe helped to quickly change my mind.

Lying back on my bed, I lifted my hand and admired my father's ring again. Shifting it back and forth, I watched as the three stones each took up the light from my window and reflected it in various directions, one of which was on my wall. As I lay there, transfixed by the little light dancing across the wall, I imagined my old life. The images started coming in waves, and I felt myself slipping into the depths of my memory to relive a scene with my parents.

As though watching a movie of my life, I reveled in the smell of my mother's perfume as it emanated through the room. In the distance, I could hear my father laughing as he chased me around the living room. Now feeling the wind as I ran, gleefully giggling, I turned to look at him. His steel-gray eyes, highlighted with small specks of greens and blues, smiled warmly as he reached out to touch my face.

"I love you, Daddy," I said.

A large smile crossed his face as he cupped my cheek. "I love you too, little man."

Across the room, I could make out the form of a female, and I watched as my hands instinctively rise to her, opening and closing my tiny fists. I tried in vain to focus in on her, but she seemed to be lost in a shadow that would not lift. Reaching further, I felt myself fall and woke as my face hit off the floor.

Opening my eyes, I realized that I was no longer on my bed but on the floor. Sitting up, I rubbed my cheek and looked around the room, trying to figure out how I had come to where I was. It was almost as though I had been sleepwalking, but I knew I had not fallen asleep. Feeling its weight on my finger, I looked at the ring, perplexed by what had just occurred.

"Jace! Are you okay?" I heard Uncle Roman holler up the stairs.

I glanced at the door, anticipating how much time I would have to put the ring away before he came up to check on me.

"Uh, yeah. I kinda fell off the bed."

Silence lingered in the air as my uncle was obviously trying to process the insanity of the situation. His fifteen-year-old nephew had fallen off a bed hard enough to make noise that he had heard downstairs. As expected, I heard his footsteps on the stairs, as I raced to put the ring back into the box and place it back in its secret spot under my bed. Just before he entered my room, I positioned myself onto the bed, trying to look natural.

Knocking on the door, Uncle Roman slowly opened it till he saw me.

"Is everything okay?" he asked as he scanned the room.

"Everything is great," I lied.

Uncle Roman narrowed his eyes at me and walked in. As I watched him survey the room, I began to feel the burn on my left cheek from where my face had slid across the carpet. Not wanting to bring attention to it, I lay down on my bed using the pillow to hide the likely red mark. He turned to watch me assume the new position and raised his eyebrows.

"Can you tell me *how* you fell out of the bed?"

"I must have dozed off and rolled off."

"I don't think you have fallen off the bed since you were a toddler. Is anything bothering you?"

His question caused me to laugh to myself. Of course, there were things bothering me and I would love to talk about them, but what would that accomplish? Not wanting to play the charade of questions, I simply shook my head.

"Nothing's wrong. I'm just bored and waiting to head over to Marcus's."

Uncle Roman eyed me warily. "Fortunately, your aunt just finished with her casserole. We can head over now if you would like."

I looked at the clock, noting that it was 3:45 p.m.

"I thought Mrs. Hunter wanted us by later?"

"Your aunt is calling her now. Are you ready to go?"

"Just let me use the bathroom first. I'll meet you downstairs."

Uncle Roman scanned my room once more as though trying to determine what else could have created the noise. Unable to determine an obvious answer, he nodded and walked out.

"Can you be ready in five minutes?" he asked as he went down the stairs.

"Sure," I answered.

After I heard him in the foyer, I jumped off the bed and ran to the bathroom to determine the extent of the injury. Flipping the light on, I turned to look at my left cheek and could see a nice rugburn forming. *Crap. How am I going to hide that?* I thought as I turned my face in the mirror.

From the stairs, I could hear Uncle Roman saying, "Are you ready?"

Panicking, I flushed the toilet and looked at my reflection again. "In a minute."

Turning the faucet on, I started splashing cold water on my face and could feel the relief from the burn that was forming there. Turning to grab the hand towel, I started blotting my face. After I repositioned the hand towel, I looked back in the mirror and did a double take. The once very bright red abrasion to my cheek was fading as though it was being reabsorbed into my skin. Within a few seconds, the angry burn had completely disappeared and I began to wonder if I had hallucinated it.

At the bottom of the stairs, Aunt Cora and Uncle Roman were both looking up at me with a look somewhere between confusion and concern. Neither spoke as I walked down the stairs, and I felt a need to get to Marcus's house grow exponentially.

"It smells good, Aunt Cora. What did you make?"

She stared at me for a moment as though I had just spoken a different language before seeming to comprehend my question and answer.

"Hash brown casserole."

"I don't remember you ever making that before," I answered.

"I haven't. The internet helped come up with this one. It's apparently an old family recipe," she said, now beaming and more like herself.

"Is everyone ready?" Uncle Roman asked.

Nodding, we made our way across the court to Marcus's house in relative silence. Once there, I knocked on the door. Before I could pull my hand away, the door swung open with Mrs. Hunter on the other side, looking frazzled.

"Cora, Roman, Jace. You're…early," she said.

Uncle Roman's eyebrow's raised as he turned to Aunt Cora. "I thought you called her to let her know we were coming over…now?"

Aunt Cora smiled sweetly at Uncle Roman and then turned back to Mrs. Hunter.

"Mary, you help with Jace all week. The least I could do was help you cook. Maybe even catch a new recipe or two. Plus, it will give the boys…all of them…a chance to get to know each other."

Uncle Roman and I exchanged a glance. Unsure what else to do, I shrugged while Uncle Roman rolled his eyes. He then looked back at our host, apologetically. Although it was only a few seconds, the minor break in conversation had created tension. That is until another voice came from within the house. "Mary, where are your manners? Of course, of course. Please come in."

A woman with similar features to Mary Hunter was walking toward us. She appeared to be a few years Mary's senior. But she had the same auburn hair as her kin. A single streak of white flowed down the front of her face, giving it an interesting contrast. Her clothes were more eccentric than Mrs. Hunter's and she appeared more confident. As she scanned our tiny group, she seemed to narrow her eyes slightly before her nose flared. The action left me feeling slightly uncomfortable, as though we were creatures on display, but ignored to feeling as Aunt Cora and Uncle Roman did not appear phased by it.

"My name is Lilly, and I am Mary's sister. You must be the nice family with the boy across the way Mary has been teaching. I believe your name was Jace? I have been out of town for the past few weeks and haven't had the honor of meeting any of you yet."

Around this time, Mrs. Hunter seemed to come back to herself jumping slightly as she tried to continue the introductions unsuccessfully.

Extending his hand, Uncle Roman picked up where she left off. "My name is Roman, and this is my wife, Cora, and our nephew Jace."

Lilly reached forward to Aunt Cora, offering to take the casserole dish. Lifting the corner of the tinfoil, she said, "What do we have in here? It smells and looks delicious."

Cora's face beamed. "Just an old family recipe. Creamy hash brown casserole. I wasn't sure what to make but settled on this. It's a general favorite."

I felt my eyebrows lift as I listened to Aunt Cora's description of her internet find. Uncle Roman must have seen my reaction and put his hand on my shoulder, shaking me a bit saying, "Jace is excited to have some."

Feeling my eyebrows climb a few inches higher, I stared at him before slowly nodding.

Aunt Lilly laughed a deep hearty laugh. "Hunny, you're in the South. We live on food like this!"

Mrs. Hunter smiled politely at the exchange. Then she suddenly jumped again, as though she had remembered something important. It caused most of the group to stop short and look at her. Aunt Lilly spoke up first, "You must forgive my sister. It seems it has been some time since we have entertained people, and she seems to be a bit *jumpy* today."

Mary's cheeks reddened, and she narrowed her eyes at Lilly before ignoring her and saying, "Please, come in."

Aunt Lilly stepped out of the way, allowing us to pass. Just behind her, I noticed Marcus standing in front of his room, smiling at the interaction. Glancing back to Marcus, Aunt Lilly asked, "Boys, what are you two going to be up to?"

I looked to Marcus, unsure what to answer.

"It's beautiful outside. Please tell me you are going to be doing something other than *Castle Core* today," Mrs. Hunter begged.

I laughed and looked back at Marcus. "I'm still a tourist here."

"What if you both head over to the café in town?" Aunt Lilly suggested.

Marcus looked back at me. "Oh yeah, Carolina makes the best food."

"Her frangollo was amazing, so I can only imagine," I answered.

"That settles it. To the bikes!" he proclaimed.

The adults laughed at us as we headed to the door.

"Jace...," my uncle called, causing me to turn around. Pulling out his wallet, he handed me some money. "This is for the both of you."

"Thank you, sir," Marcus said.

"Be back before the sun is down, okay?" Mrs. Hunter said.

"Will do," Marcus said as he kissed her on the cheek and took me by the arm as he ran out the front door, dragging me with him.

Grabbing the bikes, we headed toward the main street.

"I haven't been off the block since I moved in," I said.

"Are you serious? We really have to get you out more often," Marcus started. "It's a pretty straight run from here once we're out of the complex."

"I vaguely remember, so I'll follow you," I answered.

Making our way through the complex, I noted a few changes to the clubhouse as well as the repositioning of the heavy equipment. We turned out onto the main wooded roadway and continued biking until I could see a stoplight in the distance.

"There's main street. The café is about halfway down the street," Marcus pointed out both.

As we pulled up, I remembered the location as being where the farmer's market had been when we had moved in. Although all the businesses were close by, each had a distinct feel to its exterior. Most were drab and looked worn out as though they had not been updated in decades. Compared to them, Carolina's was bright and inviting. It had peach tones on a stucco facade with a bright green sign reading *Carolina's Café* in script across it.

"There it is. You have to try her key lime pie. It's insane!" Marcus gushed.

Nodding, I followed him in. Along the back wall was a counter with various pastries and desserts. Above the counter were blackboards covered in elegant script describing available breakfast, lunch, and dinner items.

Walking through the front of the café, we passed various chairs and benches. In many, people had set themselves up to enjoy their treats along with their company. Looking in the display window, I felt my mouth water as I tried to determine which one I should get. Since I had my head down, I only heard the familiar voice talk to Marcus from behind the counter. On recognizing it, I winced as I contemplated if I should lift my head or not.

"Hey, Marcus. What are you thinking of getting?" Izzie asked.

"I'm not sure yet. We're trying to figure it out now," he answered as he patted me on the back.

"Who are you with?" she asked as she bent down to look through the glass window.

I looked up and met her eyes. My heart froze momentarily at the stupidity of thinking I could hide in front of a window. Wanting to kick myself, I slowly stood up to look at her from over the counter and said, "Oh, hey. I didn't realize that you worked here," trying to keep my composure.

"Well, it *is* my mom's café," she hissed.

"Right. That would make sense."

I trailed off, and an awkward silence grew. All I could think was that I had messed things up with us, which now made it hard to look at her while she stared intensely at me.

Thankfully, Marcus must have sensed the tension as he looked back and forth between the two of us and interjected, "So what do *you* recommend?"

As though surprised by his question, she looked back at him and blinked. "What?"

"Well, I figure this is your mom's store, so you would know what best to have."

"Oh, right," she answered.

Looking down into the display case, she grabbed two red cupcakes with white icing and brought them to the top of the counter. "*This* is the best dessert she has."

"Then I want to buy you one too," I said.

A small smile tickled the corner of her lips as her cheeks slightly flushed.

"Thank you. But Mom won't let me eat behind the counter."

"Can you see if you can take a break and sit with us?" Marcus asked.

Izzie looked over her shoulder toward the back kitchen and frowned.

"I just got here, and I don't know if she'll be okay with it."

Alyssa was walking back and forth behind Izzie. It seemed she had been watching us as we all talked. After pouring a cup of coffee and collecting a few pastries for the man behind us, she squeezed in. Ringing up the man's order, she spoke under her breath, "Go talk to Mom. I'm sure she will say yes to a few minutes to hang out with them. It's not all that busy back here, and Zoe and I can handle it. If it picks up, though, then you can come back."

Izzie looked at Alyssa and then back to me. "Okay, I'll go ask," and turned to leave.

After Izzie was out of hearing range, Alyssa reached over the counter and grabbed my arm with a force I was not expecting and leaned in, whispering in an angry tone, "I don't know why you went all MIA in your house for the past few weeks. I also have no clue what your thoughts are with Izzie. But if you hurt her…let's just say I know where you live!"

I felt my eyes widen at her threat and felt my mouth go dry. I nodded to Alyssa and then looked back to Marcus, who was grinning. As Izzie walked back, she had a smile on her face until she saw mine. Frowning, she asked, "What? You look like you just saw a ghost."

"Nothing's wrong. Everything is great," I blurted, causing Marcus to bust out laughing.

"Can you sit with us?" he asked.

"Yes," she answered with a smile as she dropped her apron behind the counter.

Marcus patted me on the back and said to Izzie, "Those cupcakes look really rich. Do you have something to wash it down with?"

"You're right. You can't have red velvet without milk," she answered.

Grabbing three containers, she exited the counter and walked to a table near the front of the store. Marcus and I followed with the cupcakes in hand. Izzie chose the seat closest to the window so that she could see the counter and run back if needed. Marcus chose the seat to her right, and I sat to her left, also next to the window.

Looking at the cupcake, I felt the warmth of the late summer sun as it washed through the window onto my back. Before I could take a bite, Izzie spun violently in her seat to look at me. I shot up straight in my seat to look at her. "Why are you avoiding me?" she demanded.

"What? I'm not—"

"Yes, you have. Like Wednesday, I tried to take Wampa for a walk with you when you took Buddy out. You were all ready to go. But when you saw me, you bolted back into your house. Then you took him out twenty minutes later."

I remembered that day and cringed slightly. In my head, I had justified that I didn't want to stress Buddy out by being with another dog. In reality, I didn't know what to say to her.

"I-I didn't mean to upset you. I—"

"You just didn't want to hang out with me?"

Marcus was watching us as though he was at an intense tennis match. His head was flipping back and forth. Izzie must have seen it as well and turned to him. "Would you stop that?" she said.

"Stop what?" he asked.

"The whole head thing. It's really distracting!"

Cupping both cheeks, he leaned with his elbows on the table.

"Better?" he asked. We both laughed, looking at the ridiculousness of his posture.

"How are you going to eat your cupcake like that?" I asked.

Marcus furrowed his brows while looking down at his treat. Then his eyes widened.

"Oh, this should be good." Izzie smirked.

With his hands still on his cheeks and elbows on the table, he slightly shifted himself back in the chair to get more leverage. Then tipping his face down, Marcus took a big bite out of the cupcake. As he lifted his head, his face was covered in frosting, but he continued to chew triumphantly.

Izzie shook her head although she was smiling as she handed him a napkin. "You have a little something on your face."

I looked at Marcus and gave him a smile, grateful for his ability to break up a tense situation. Turning toward Izzie, I tried to think of my words carefully. "I swear I'm not avoiding you."

She sat back in her chair, crossed her arms, and lifted an eyebrow. Realizing instantly that I was treading a dangerous path, I backpedaled. "It's not avoiding you. I guess I'm just afraid."

"Afraid? Of me?"

"No. Of getting…too close…"

I trailed off. I saw her face and posture softened before she reached out and put a hand on mine. My heart skipped a beat.

"Because you move and don't know when the next one is coming?" she asked.

"If it makes you feel any better, he avoids me too," Marcus said with his mouth full of cupcake.

I laughed and shook my head.

"No, he doesn't! He goes by your house or you're at his all the time."

That wasn't technically right, but I was at Marcus's more than not. But how did I explain that to her without upsetting her? Marcus and I could hang out with no tension. And I wanted to be with Izzie, all the time. The problem was, I didn't want to do or say something that would embarrass me, so…I avoided her.

As I worked through the logic for myself, I dropped my eyes, realizing that she was right. I looked at Izzie's hand that was still on mine and then up at her. "I'm sorry. I'm not good with this whole friend thing, and it's harder with you..."

Her eyes lit up, and I instantly wanted to eat my words.

"Because he's madly in love with you," Marcus blurted out.

I violently turned my head to look at him, glaring.

Out of the corner of my eye, I saw Izzie drop her head slightly but smile. As I fumbled for the right words to say to her, there was a bang on the window next to us, which made me jump.

Izzie instantly pulled her hand away from mine. I looked up to see Ethan standing on the other side of the window, staring at me. I watched as he turned to walk into the café and to us. Once at our table, he turned the empty seat around so that he was leaning on its back next to me.

Ethan looked at the cupcake on the table and then back at me. "I love those. Her mom makes them the best. Have you tried it yet?"

I kept my head down, trying not to cause a scene when he grabbed my cupcake and opened it. I watched but kept my mouth closed as he bit into it, making annoying sounds of delight as he chewed.

As if suddenly noticing the expression on my face, he pretended to look shocked. "Oh, I'm sorry. Was that yours?"

"You know it was," Marcus said.

Ethan turned to look at Marcus with a small lift at the corner of his lip. "Then we're even. Tell him not to touch what is mine, and I won't touch what is his."

My eyes went wide as I turned to look at Izzie, realizing he was referring to her. She seemed shocked by his answer too as her cheeks reddened, and she opened her mouth in an obvious attempt to explain, although no words came out. I looked at her and then at the half-eaten cupcake and felt my temper rising.

I grabbed my wallet and dropped $20 on the table for the food. Then I walked out with Marcus following behind. Izzie was calling out although I didn't hear what she had said.

"Jace, wait up!" Marcus hollered as I jumped on my bike and rode away.

With the wind blowing in my face, I could feel the sting of tears in my eyes. Turning into the Crystal Shore complex, I finally slowed my pace, allowing Marcus to catch up. "Christ, you're fast when you're mad!" Marcus said, huffing as he came to a stop next to me.

"Did you know about that! About them?" I spun on him with acid in my tone.

Marcus looked up and motioned with his hands for me to calm down. But I was too angry for that. "Did you?"

"Look, I think those two are on different pages. He kinda backed her into a situation where they looked like they were dating although that is *not* what she was thinking," he said.

I looked at him with my face screwed up. "That doesn't even remotely make sense."

Marcus sighed as he tried to recount what he had seen during school. As he gave me a rundown of the day's events, I found my anger reducing to a slow simmer.

"We all know that he likes her, but she has never reciprocated that. Today, he tried another approach. Instead of asking her to be his girlfriend, he kinda just assumed the role for her."

I stared at him dumbly. "How?" I asked.

"He was everywhere she was today, and when he was with her, he was holding her books or her hand. At lunch, he even paid for it."

As I listened, I felt a pit forming in my stomach and wasn't sure if I wanted to hear anymore. "But she didn't tell *him* she wasn't interested?" I countered.

"I think she was more in shock by it. Look, I don't think she likes him. Jace, she likes *you*. But you being so weird likely aided in her not being completely forthright with Ethan."

I leaned back on my bike and looked up to the sky as though looking for divine intervention. "I don't know what to do," I said.

Marcus smiled. "I do."

I looked at him quizzically.

"We're going to a party tomorrow night…with Izzie."

CHAPTER 10

Dinner

As we entered Marcus's house, I could hear Aunt Cora and Mrs. Hunter laughing from the dining room, which was between the kitchen and the den. It had a large ornate wooden table with matching chairs surrounding it and red plaid seat cushions on each. They placed Uncle Roman at the head of the table with Aunt Cora to his left. Opposite Aunt Cora were Mrs. Hunter and Aunt Lilly, strategically placed for easier access to the kitchen. Aunt Lilly stood and motioned for Marcus to sit next to her.

"I keep this one close to me. You never know what he'll get into."

Marcus let out a sigh and rolled his eyes before smiling and sitting. I chuckled as I watched his reaction but was still feeling agitated from the earlier encounter. Aunt Cora was watching me intently, and I tried not to meet her eyes, unsure what type of response she might have if I did.

As I sat there in silence, I tried to fight the tears that were burning my eyes again. Marcus must have seen it too and tried to distract Aunt Cora. "You have to try her perogies, Mrs. Northall," Marcus said.

Aunt Cora playfully choked on her food.

"Oh please, Marcus, no need for Mrs. Northall. You can call me Cora," she said.

117

"I'm not sure how they do it up north, but we're down south. It's not considered good manners for someone to refer to an adult by their first name alone. How about Ms. Cora?" Aunt Lilly asked.

Aunt Cora thought for a second and smiled. "That works for me."

Aunt Lilly stood and gave everyone a quick rundown on the spread in front of us.

"Cora has brought for us a delicious hash brown casserole. I confess, I took a small spoonful earlier and had to fight the urge to keep going."

She smiled and winked at Aunt Cora before continuing, "Over here, we have fried chicken with a side of gravy, buttermilk biscuits, stuffed baked potatoes, jalapeño bread, and of course, some peach cobbler for after the meal."

Uncle Roman sat up in his chair to admire the array of food options.

"Where to start?" he asked, rubbing his hands together.

Aunt Lilly laughed, stretching to grab his plate. "Start closest to you and make your way around the table, of course."

Without giving him an option, Aunt Lilly started loading up Uncle Roman's plate. Soon it was difficult to see where each food item stopped, and the next began. Growing up with Uncle Roman, I had seen him eat, but I had never seen his plate overloaded. Looking at his face, I could see he hadn't either.

"We like our men with meat on their bones down here," Aunt Lilly mused when she saw how large Uncle Roman's eyes became at the site of his plate in front of him.

Marcus laughed. "I don't wear baggy clothes for nothing."

Aunt Cora laughed, and Marcus flushed. Realizing there was no way out of his previous statement, he smiled and raised a drumstick to us before dipping it in gravy and taking a large bite out of it.

The rest of the meal comprised of delicious food, small talk, and laughter. As I sat there listening, I thought back on all our moves. I realized that there had not been a time that we had a sit-down meal with a group of friends like this and it made me want to cherish this dinner even more.

Once we finished, Marcus and I helped clear the table. After, we were quickly told that we did not have to entertain the "old folk" anymore. Our freedom granted, we made our way back to Marcus's room.

Inside, I sat down on his bed as he headed to his computer chair. Instinctively, I looked across the street toward Izzie's house, but it was mostly dark. Marcus followed my gaze.

"She won't be home for another hour or so."

"How do you know?" I asked.

Marcus's face flushed. "The café closes at eight. By the time they finish cleaning and closing, it will be closer to nine."

I narrowed my eyes at him.

"Look, I'm not trying to take your girl," he teased.

I smiled before grabbing a pillow from his bed and lobbing it at him.

"Besides, you have bigger fish to fry than me."

I nodded. "Ethan Campbell."

"Pretty much."

"So tell me more about this party. How do we get there and where is it?"

"Well, funny thing. I'm not *exactly* sure of all the details," he said sheepishly.

I rolled my eyes and fell back onto the bed.

"You're killing me, Smalls!" I teased.

"I thought I would get to talk to her before then to get more information. Ethan kinda threw a monkey wrench in the works. We can try to ask her later when she gets home."

"I seriously doubt she is going to want to talk to me after this afternoon. I didn't even put up a fight. I just sat there and let him make me look like a complete fool."

"So I was watching both sides, and she was *not* on Ethan's side. Plus, when you stormed out, I left after you. She was pretty upset with him."

I felt the corner of my lip twitch at the thought. In the distance, we could see headlights driving up the main road toward Crystal Court.

"This might be them now," Marcus said as we watched the headlights.

I felt my pulse quicken until I saw the lights turn down the side street opposite ours.

"Guess not." He shrugged before turning back to look at me.

As he was about to speak, another set of headlights approached. I felt my pulse quicken again. But once again, the car turned down the opposite street.

"Is there a party over there tonight? There's never this much traffic over here," he joked. "Here, let's clear our minds with a bit of *Castle Core*," he suggested.

"Sounds good."

Playing was definitely a great way to relieve some tension from the day. Vanquish some ghouls, search out a key to a fortress, and add a demon to our cohort—that's what we needed. We had become so invested in the game that we almost missed the approaching headlights. The only thing that alerted us to their presence was when their truck breached the top of the hill of Crystal Court and blinded us momentarily.

We stopped playing and slowly looked up from the computer to see who had pulled into the court. We saw Carolina's SUV pull into the driveway. Marcus looked at me. "Do you want me to invite her over to talk?"

I stood up and stared at him. "Yes… No… I don't know."

Looking back at the car, I watched as the Lewis family made their way into the house. Concern mounted when I didn't see Izzie with them. "Maybe she met up with someone else after work," I said, dejected.

Just then, we heard a knock on the door, causing us both to turn and look.

"I'm just going to say it. If that is her, she has some serious ninja skills," Marcus teased.

We listened as Mrs. Hunter opened the door and invited the newcomer into the house. Within a second, there was a quick knock on Marcus's door before Izzie opened it and entered. I stood there, unsure what to say and could see the same thought running through her mind as well.

"Wasn't sure if we were going to see you again," Marcus said, breaking the silence.

"I am so sorry about that. I gave him a piece of my mind after you stormed out, and he left shortly after you did."

"So where did you leave off with him?" Marcus asked. Although I was grateful it had been him who asked, I wished it had been me.

"I told him how rude he was to you," Izzie answered, meaning me.

My eyebrows went up, but I felt my heart sink. She had told him how rude he had been. Great! But had she told him they were not dating? I waited, hoping to hear her tell us that, but she only stood there staring at us.

"Oh, good. I'm glad you told him *that*," Marcus said.

"What?"

"Did you happen to solidify your status with him?" He asked.

She seemed to think about his question for a minute or two before her eyes went wide. Then she threw her hands over her mouth.

"Oh my god. In my head, I did, but I don't think I actually talked to him about that."

"Just throwing it out there. Senor Crazy thinks you two are dating. He is looking to take Jace's head off because of it. You kinda need to talk to him about this sooner rather than later."

"Of course. You're right. I'll talk to Ethan tomorrow."

Looking around the room, Izzie seemed to make the same initial inspection of the room that I had. "I see some things never really change?"

Marcus turned to look at Izzie, confusion plastered across his face. Shaking her head, she motioned around the room. That was when it seemed to dawn on him that his locker-room motif had made an impression on her as well.

"It adds character to the room. Besides, I know where everything is," he declared.

Izzie shook her head as she moved the sheets on his bed so it was comfortable enough to sit without being impaled on some random item. As there were no other chairs in the room and Marcus was sitting on the gaming chair, I opted to stand.

"There's enough room for both of us to sit." Izzie motioned to a spot on the bed.

I felt a surge of energy run through me as my stomach did flips, but decided it'd be more appropriate to sit on the floor. "I'm fine on the floor, but thank you," I said.

"Suit yourself," she said, throwing me a pillow. Not expecting it, the pillow hit me in the face, causing me to fall back slightly.

"Oh my god, I'm so sorry! I meant to toss it to you, not *at* you."

Looking at the pillow, I exaggerated, rubbing my head.

"Good thing it's the softer variety. A little bit firmer, and I might have needed a doctor."

Izzie laughed, then threw another pillow at me. That one I caught.

"That's twice *you* have tried to take his head off. I don't know, Jace. I think she has a hit out on you," Marcus joked.

Out of the corner of my eye, I could see that Izzie had her hand resting on another pillow. She quickly lifted it and launched it at Marcus. Instinctively, we both jumped to block the projectile as it made its way toward the computer instead of toward its intended target. Realizing her misaim, Izzie gasped and covered her mouth. Fortunately, Marcus's fast reflexes had ensured he caught the pillow, and he placed it next to him on the chair. "Now that we have that out of our system."

Izzie chuckled. "I'm sorry, Marcus. I know that the computer is your baby. Although I don't think I ever got to see the completed project."

Marcus's demeanor softened as he showed off his newly completed toy. "I never see you on *Castle Core* anymore. We used to have a pretty kick-ass team going."

Izzie's smiled and lowered her head. "I've just been busy with school and after-school stuff."

Seeing awkwardness building, I tried to break it up this time. "What level are you in the game?" I asked Izzie.

"Nowhere near where he is, but I can hold my own. I'm not really a combat player. I'm more of the cleanup-the-pieces player, a healer, so to speak."

Marcus laughed. "Yeah, I would foolishly run into a battle unprepared, and she would put me back together afterward."

"Eventually, you started telling me your plans before going rogue. It saved you a lot of healing time after."

"Yeah, yeah." Marcus tossed the pillow back at Izzie, which she caught with ease.

"What about you?" she asked me.

Enjoying the banter between Marcus and Izzie, I didn't initially realize that she was asking me a question. "Oh, sorry. I've been playing for about three years too. I took a wizard path and have done pretty well."

Marcus was looking at the screen and said over his shoulder, "He was a loner before I pulled him into my cohort. He had no connections...at all."

I felt my cheeks flush. "I guess I had never really met anyone that I wanted to form a cohort with."

Izzie stood and walked over to the computer and smiled at him. Batting her eyes and finally putting her hands under her chin, she attempted to make herself even more adorable than she already was. She was succeeding at it too—for me, at least. Marcus, however, sat there staring at her dumbly.

"What?" he asked her.

Shaking my head, I said, "She wants your seat, genius."

He looked from me back to Izzie and scrunched up his face. "You could have just asked. I would have gotten up."

"Thank you, kind sir, for sharing your throne." She bowed low to Marcus before turning to me.

"And thank *you*, kind sir, for informing *this one* of my intensions." She curtsied, and I felt my heart skip a beat.

Turning away from me, she playfully shoved Marcus out of the way and sat in the seat before logging him out and herself in.

"What's your screen name? We're changing your lone-wolf, well, wizard status tonight."

I chuckled and pointed to the character who was standing next to her. "Marcus already summoned me to the area."

Izzie looked at the character and frowned. "You don't look like a wizard."

"Looks can be deceiving. For me, it's better because I don't have to worry about getting stopped by every person who passes me. Most think I'm just a human, a bounty hunter."

Izzie thought about what I said and nodded, a small smile on her face.

"Hiding in plain sight. Kind of ingenious. What happens if they realize you are a wizard?"

"Either they try to form a cohort, try to fight me for my power, or just keep moving on."

Izzie clicked on my avatar and sent the request to form a cohort. Maneuvering around the screen, she located Marcus's character and clicked on it as well, doing the same thing. "Once you both accept, we must create a cohort name. What should it be?" Smiling widely, she said, "How about Arcana?"

"What exactly does that mean?" Marcus asked

"I think it means 'a mystery.'" I looked to Izzie for confirmation.

Izzie nodded, then continued, "It can also refer to having special knowledge and is used with tarot cards. There are major and minor arcana. It is also a remedy."

Izzie sat taller as she spouted out the definitions until she noticed us looking at her curiously.

"I've been working on helping Alyssa with her SAT prep, so it's kinda stuck," she answered defensively.

Marcus thought about the name and the definitions and then nodded. "I guess it describes who we are pretty well. Arcana cohort, it is!"

As Izzie set up the cohort, she grabbed at her pocket to pull out her phone and looked at a message that had come through. The look on her face was hard to read, but she looked agitated. Marcus saw it too and asked first.

"Everything okay?

Izzie looked at us, then back at the phone as she typed. Once she had finished, she placed the phone face down on the computer desk.

Marcus looked at me, then back at Izzie.

"I'm gonna take a shot in the dark. Ethan Campbell?"

Izzie's head shot around to look at Marcus.

"Wow, so that's an affirmative. What did he say?" Marcus asked.

"Nothing. He—it's nothing."

"Izzie, you need to figure out what you want and do it. Ethan is not one to just stand by and wait."

I could feel anger mounting at Marcus's last statement. When I saw that Izzie was visibly upset, I couldn't help myself and blurted out, "Did he hurt you?"

It came out much more forceful than I intended, and they both turned to look at me. Marcus spoke up first, "Whoa. No. He just thinks that he can have whatever he wants. Now that he has his eyes on Izzie, he thinks he made her his girlfriend this afternoon without asking her."

Izzie's eyes went wide, and she quickly stood up.

"I am *not* his girlfriend!" she protested.

Marcus put his hands up in a calming manner. "Okay. According to *you*, you're not his girlfriend. But from everyone else looking in from the outside, it sure looked that way."

Izzie looked at me and put her head in her hands. She dropped back into the seat, demoralized.

Realizing that she was now in a position that she had not intended to be in made my blood boil. "What did he say?" I asked.

With her hands on her face, she looked at me, sheepishly through her fingers. "He wants to find a private spot tomorrow at the party...to get to know me better."

Marcus spoke up before I could, "Oh, I'm sure that is a totally innocent request."

Izzie looked at Marcus, then dropped her head into her hands again. "It could be. It's just moving so fast."

As though struck with inspiration, Marcus smiled. "Is this the same party you were telling me about this afternoon? Where is it?"

Izzie looked up to Marcus, smiling, and said, "It's an open invite. Tomorrow night at the Blue Grotto. I think they said 8:00 p.m. I'm going with my sisters because my mom would allow nothing else."

Marcus's face now sported an impish grin. "Care if we tag along?"

Izzie looked from Marcus to me and smiled. "I think I would really like it if you came."

Outside the window, we could see a flash of light as though someone was waving a flashlight around. Izzie covered her eyes and waved toward it. "That's my dad. He hates technology."

As she stood to leave, she turned to look at us.

"See you guys tomorrow? I'll text you when we're leaving."

As Izzie walked out the door, she hollered back to the adults laughing in the den. "I'm leaving now. Have a good night everyone."

A chorus of voices hollered back.

We watched as Izzie walked across the lawn and to her waiting father. She turned back to wave at us, and we waved back.

"That went well, Casanova," Marcus smiled coyly.

"Har, har."

I moved back into the room and sat on the edge of his bed, "Thanks, man. Really."

Marcus looked up and smiled. "Aww, shucks."

I threw the pillow back at him, and he caught it quickly.

A knock sounded on the door, and Uncle Roman leaned into the room.

"Hey, guys. It's getting late, so we're going to head home." Then to me, he said, "Are you staying or heading back with us?"

I looked at Marcus, who shrugged and said, "If you don't mind the mess, you're more than welcome to stay."

Uncle Roman smiled. "Great. We'll see you tomorrow morning. We already cleared it with your mom, Marcus."

Aunt Cora came in from behind Uncle Roman. "Don't stay up too late."

Pausing for a moment, she then said, "On second thought, stay up late and have fun. Just stay out of too much trouble."

I saw her make her way to me and knew she had one thing on her mind—embarrassing me.

"I'm good, Aunt Cora. Honestly, no need. Uncle Roman!"

I was half laughing and half yelping by then as she chased me to a corner of the room. Once caught, she grabbed hold of my face and gave me a forceful kiss on the cheek while I squirmed to get away from her.

"There's no stopping her once she has her mind set. You should know that." Uncle Roman was laughing at us.

After she had released me and left, I looked at Marcus who was having a hard time not laughing. Seizing the last pillow, I launched it off his bed at him where it bounced off his head and landed behind him, causing us both to break out into laughter.

CHAPTER 11

Burgerporium

The rest of the night was uneventful, and in the morning, the previous night's occurrences seemed to have been something out of a dream. In a state somewhere between fantasy and reality, I woke to the intoxicating smells of bacon, eggs, and pancakes. Feeling my stomach returning to life and voice its desire, I decided to make my way to the kitchen.

As I was about to sit up, I noticed Marcus moving around in his bed above before finally sitting up and looking over to the trundle I was lying on. For a moment, a look of confusion crossed his face, as though he had forgotten that I had been there. Then recollection, followed by the awareness of the multitude of aromas wafting to us from the other room appeared on his face.

He lifted his head, sniffed, then smiled. His shaggy auburn hair standing up on his head, making him look almost like he had been electrocuted in his sleep.

"Ahhhh. One amazing perk of having guests over. She cooks for a small army. Hope you're hungry!"

My stomach growled in response, and I instinctively covered my abdomen.

"Does that answer your question?"

I stretched and instantly felt the stiffness in my back. Marcus eyed me warily when I recoiled in pain.

"Sorry, man. That thing is *not* the most comfortable bed. I'll get you some aspirin if you need it."

Slowly, I relaxed into a fully supine position, waiting for a second or two before I rolled onto my knees and attempted to stand up straight. Marcus, seeing my awkward movements, stared. I looked up at him and could see the furrow forming in his brows and waved him off. "I'm fine. I just need to get moving. I think I have a new appreciation for my mattress, though."

Marcus chuckled as he turned to open his bedroom door and started walking to the kitchen. Over his shoulder, I could see Mrs. Hunter moving rapidly between the kitchen and dining area, much as she had done the night before.

Wondering what time it was, I looked down at my cell phone. When I looked up, I nearly barreled into Marcus, who had unexpectedly stopped short in the hallway.

"I may just cry. It's official. You're moving in, Jace. Or at least sleeping over every few days," Marcus said while wiping away fake tears.

Aunt Lilly looked up from her coffee cup and quickly motioned for us to come into the kitchen.

"Can't get any of this food from the hallway. Get in here, you two."

Marcus gave his mom a kiss on her cheek and then made his way toward his aunt, almost as though he was stalking her. Aunt Lilly let out a laugh and stood up with her hands out in front of her. Marcus's smile grew quickly as he advanced on his petite Aunt.

Grabbing her around the waist, he lifted her off the floor as though she was a rag doll, swinging her back and forth, causing her to snort in delight. Once her legs were securely on the ground, she looked up at him. Patting him on the chest, she winked and said, "You should know better than picking someone my age up. You may break me!"

Her smile and energy were infectious, and I could feel myself smiling. Just before she sat down, she slowed enough to notice me standing in the hallway. Aunt Lilly lowered her head, motioning to me with her fingers playfully.

"Get over here, Jace."

She motioned me toward her with her arms outstretched. When I hesitated, Marcus noticed and chuckled.

"You better come over because she's going to get her hug, one way or another."

Realizing that my options were limited and seeing the smile still radiating from Aunt Lilly's face, I made my way toward her, and I extended my arms to hug her. Her speed was lightning quick as she wrapped me in a tight embrace, pinning my arms to my side as her tiny frame engulfed me.

"Good lord, what are y'all eating down here? This one's even bigger than Marcus." Aunt Lilly teased before finally releasing me to sit and examine the table.

"All right. Mary, you made enough to feed six families. Boys, let's sit and dig in."

Watching Aunt Lilly and the contrast in her personality from last night surprised me.

Mrs. Hunter saw it too and nudged her sister. "I think your energy is intimidating our guest, Lillian."

She looked at her sister, then at me, and laughed. "Normal is overrated," Aunt Lilly said. "And I can only pull it off in small doses."

We each pulled up a chair as Mrs. Hunter handed out plates. The array of food was amazing: thick slices of applewood bacon, eggs—scrambled, fried, and hard-boiled—towers of pancakes, and stacks of waffles made the table groan. There were three different varieties of syrup too, grits, and a bowl of mixed fruit.

"Mrs. Hunter, I don't think I've ever seen so much food in one location in my life," I said enthusiastically. Then I found myself rubbing my hands as I took it all in and immediately put a stop to that.

Mrs. Hunter laughed and shrugged good-heartedly. "I know a pair of growing boys whom I thought would be hungry."

Suddenly, Aunt Lilly said, "Mary, do you remember when Marcus had tried to rearrange the house to make it more suitable for his skating ring? Is the hole in the wall still there from where he tried to leave his facial imprint?"

Marcus's face was red as he looked over at me. "Hey, it wasn't that big. And yes, it's still there."

Aunt Lilly smiled and said, "Don't be embarrassed. A free spirit is always a good thing."

As we continued eating, I sat listening to the trio reminiscing about times gone past. I felt a longing creep over me—for the family that I had never had and for my parents who could never enjoy the endearing stories of their child's antics. As though Aunt Lilly could sense it, she stopped and looked at me. "What's up, Jace?"

Startled, I looked up and gave her the best smile I could muster. "I'm fine. I was just thinking. I should let my aunt and uncle know I'm okay."

"Already ahead of you," Mrs. Hunter said. "I spoke to Cora this morning. She was ecstatic you were enjoying yourself. Actually, she dropped off a bag for you last night. It has some things you might need."

"Really?"

Mrs. Hunter looked concerned. "Yes. It's in the den, by the couch."

"That definitely sounds like Aunt Cora."

"Hey, Mom," Marcus broke in, "can we borrow the car to head into town today? I wanted to show him around Williston."

Aunt Lilly lit up at the prospect. "Get dressed, boys. We're going shopping."

Marcus's eyes widened as he tried to stop his aunt from including herself in our plans, "I was thinking—"

"Don't worry, Marcus. We won't go shopping *with* you, but I would like to do some window shopping myself."

Marcus looked at his aunt and sighed, the defeat obvious. However, a small smile was also apparent on his face.

Finishing up breakfast, I thanked Mrs. Hunter and grabbed the blue duffel bag from the den before returning to Marcus's room to get ready for the day.

Ten minutes later, I could hear Aunt Lilly call out from the front door.

"This train is leaving in five. Move it or catch the next one!"

Marcus rolled his eyes and yelled back, "We're coming, Aunt Lilly!"

He whispered, "Patience isn't a strong suit of hers."

From the other room, we could hear Aunt Lilly. "I heard that, Marcus Anthony Hunter. And I have plenty of patience…when I want it."

Marcus stopped and looked to the sky as though asking a higher being for guidance, and we both chuckled.

I couldn't help but laugh as something occurred to me. "Wait, your name is *Marcus Anthony*? Like *Mark Antony*? From the Roman Empire?"

"Ugh. I know. She loves history. At least she named me Marcus. Otherwise, it would have been really awkward. Let's get going before Aunt Lilly comes in and drags us out."

As I followed Marcus, I nearly collided with him, again, when he stopped suddenly in the doorway of the house.

"You really need to stop doing that," I said.

Not sure what had caused *this* sudden stop, I looked over his shoulder where I could see a showdown occurring between sisters. Mrs. Hunter had positioned herself next to an old gray Honda Odyssey minivan. Aunt Lilly, on the other hand, was half perched inside a beat-up green Ford pickup truck.

Marcus and I stood at the front door, unsure which sister to follow.

"This should get interesting," Marcus muttered.

"Lillian Grace, that truck is far too small for these boys. We need to take the minivan. Besides, it's not legal to have them riding in the flatbed anymore."

"Mary Lynn, I have never been in a minivan, and I do not plan to start now. Besides, there is a bench in the back seat of the cab, so they will *not* be in the flatbed."

The two women glared at each other, each indignantly standing by their prospective vehicle and unwilling to move. After watching the standoff for a few minutes, Marcus decided for them.

"Ladies, let's all be civil. Aunt Lilly, your truck looks as lovely… and comfortable as ever."

Aunt Lilly smiled back at her sister in triumph.

"*However,* the back seat is not designed for two guys with enough leg span to traverse to the town nearly as fast on foot as by car. The minivan *would be* more comfortable."

"Thank you, sweetheart. Ready?" Mrs. Hunter said.

Lifting her keys, she jingled them in Lilly's direction and without warning, the keys flew out of her hand and landed onto the lawn as though someone had yanked them.

"Lilly, don't be a spoiled sport!" Mrs. Hunter cried out.

My eyes were wide and I was sure my mouth was open wide enough to expose most of my teeth. Marcus just stared at me.

"What? Are you coming?" he asked.

Then he walked to the minivan without saying another word. As I watched him, I found it difficult to move my limbs as I tried to process the previous moments. *He didn't see it.* My head was spinning. *Maybe I didn't see that either. Maybe she just dropped the keys?*

By then, Marcus had stopped at his door and was looking over. He waved for me to follow.

"Sorry, just thought I saw—"

The family sat waiting in the car and stared at me as though I had a third arm growing out of my skull. I shook my head before I jumped in the back seat, pulled the door closed and snapped my seat belt into place.

As we drove into town, I had forgotten about the keys and now found myself transfixed by the movement of the greenery we passed. Although most trees do not change colors and drop their leaves as brilliantly as they do in the north, periodically, you will see a tree or two that does. I searched for those hidden gems within the tree line.

I could hear my fellow car mates talking about the town and what there is to do and not do. However, I remained submerged in my thoughts. When we had moved here, we had passed through the town quickly and had seen little of it in the few weeks since. When we needed groceries, we had them delivered. Being homeschooled, there was no genuine need for me to leave the house either, and we hadn't.

Mrs. Hunter pulled up in front of a hardware store, aptly named "Joe's," and we all piled out of the car. Almost instantly, people were waving to us and asking our matrons how their summer had been, who responded with the typical cordial responses.

After entertaining two elderly women, Mrs. Hunter turned to us. "Can you two head into Joe's first? I need some WD-40 for a stubborn handle in the backyard. If he doesn't have it, no one will. Aunt Lilly and I are going to the thrift store down the road if you need us. We'll meet back here at 5:00 p.m., okay?"

I looked at my cell phone, which read 2:20 p.m.

"Sounds good. I'll call you if we're ready sooner," Marcus said.

"Have fun and try not to get into *too much* trouble," Mrs. Hunter implored.

Aunt Lilly made the *I'll-be-watching-you gesture.* Then she lifted her head and smiled.

"Yes, Aunt Lilly," Marcus said.

As the sisters walked toward the thrift store, I stopped to take a better inventory of the area.

"I didn't really get to appreciate it yesterday. This town is so—"

"Small!" Marcus interjected

"I was thinking quaint, but I guess small would work too."

"If you blink too long, you'll pass through and not even realize it!"

Turning toward the store, Marcus bowed slightly and waved his hand in a doorman fashion. I followed his lead and entered.

The store was small but felt welcoming. A small bell rang as the door opened to alert the insiders of our presence. Each of the aisles was narrow, and the floor creaked as you walked across it. A strong smell of soil and metal drifted through the building, which added to the charm.

Behind the counter was a guy, roughly the same age as Marcus and me. Like most teens, he was engrossed with his cell phone. As the bell rang, he looked up momentarily to appraise us. Deeming us not worth his time, he instantly returned to his task at hand, feverishly typing away.

"It should be down this way," Marcus said as he led us.

We walked toward the third aisle out of the five available. Roughly halfway down, we spotted an easily identifiable blue can with a red cap and matching straw attached to it.

"Gotcha."

Marcus grabbed the can and looked back and forth in the aisle.

"Do we need anything else?" I asked.

Marcus pondered my question for a few minutes and then shook his head.

"I think we're good. If she needed anything else, she would have said."

I nodded, and we walked to the front of the store. Marcus put the can on the counter and pulled out one of the two $20 bills his mom had given him. The boy looked at the can and then up at us. It was as though he was not sure what to do next.

"We need to pay...," Marcus said, nudging the can forward.

Signs of realization crossed the clerk's face. He passed the bar code under the machine's reader and punched a few numbers on the pad. "Five thirty-nine," the clerk said with his hand extended for the cash.

Marcus passed him the money and received the change, then looked at the can, which was still sitting on the counter. Realizing that we had not moved, the clerk looked up at us and stared. Continuing to wait patiently, Marcus finally succumbed and asked, "Can I get a bag?"

Rolling his eyes, he placed the can in the bag and handed both to Marcus. As we opened the door, the little bell chimed again, and Marcus waved to the clerk, who did not lift his head to acknowledge us.

"Wow, I thought all small towns were super polite. What was up with him?" I mused.

Marcus checking the bag, stopped to look back at the store, then at me. "Hmm? Oh, that's Jacob. He's always been weird. Never really talks to anyone. He's been in my homeroom since third grade. He's harmless, just quiet."

Marcus took the money out of his pocket and counted it out.

He said, "$34.61. More than enough for some Burgerporium."

"Burger-what-ium?" I asked.

Marcus's eyes went wide.

"You have never had Burgerporium before? That settles it. Now we *have* to get some. It's just up the road and across the street."

We turned and started walking away from the hardware store and toward the famed burger shop. Thinking back, I remembered seeing it as we drove through town when we had moved in. As we walked, I was caught up in the charm of all the small businesses. The town seemed to be stuck in a time warp somewhere in a 1950s sitcom, where people either smiled, waved, or tipped their hats in our direction.

"Is everyone always so friendly? Aside from Jacob?"

"I thought you lived in the South before. You've never heard of Southern hospitality? Well, there really is something to be said about that."

As we passed by the last of the stores, the burger restaurant came into view. It was recessed back off the main road with a large parking lot in the front and a wraparound drive-through.

"Ah, here we are. This place has amazing burgers but also specializes in handmade shakes and chicken sandwiches. My favorite is definitely the cherry bing shake."

Walking into the Burgerporium, I noticed they had set it up like most fast-food chains with the checkout counter in the front and the tables opposite it. "I'm not sure what I'd like. I'll just get the same thing you do," I told him.

"You sure?"

I nodded, and Marcus turned to the cashier.

Across the counter was a small-framed teen girl with blond hair pulled up in pigtails, bright hazel eyes, and an exaggerated smile as she greeted us.

"Welcome to Burgerporium, home of the best burgers since 1972. What would you like to order?"

Her behavior seemed artificial, and it was hard to tell if she was seriously excited about her job or mocking the obese man in the kitchen that was watching her take the order. Marcus hesitated for a second, and I could see the corner of his mouth go up, along with a small lift of the eyebrow as he analyzed the girl in front of us.

"Okay…let me get two number threes with cheese fries and two medium cherry bings."

The girl frowned momentarily as she typed in our order. "I'm not sure if we have everything for the bings. Let me go check."

She turned and talked with the man standing in the window where the food was served from.

I looked at Marcus and asked, "What *is* in this shake?"

"Just the most amazing combination of ingredients. Vanilla and cherry ice cream mixed and topped with whip cream and two bing cherries."

As I imagined the shake, the cashier returned with a bright smile on her face.

"You're in luck. That'll be $14.82, and your number is 84."

After paying, Marcus grabbed the receipt and winked to the cashier before walking toward the "pick up here" counter. Her cheeks flushed, and she smiled back at him. A television that had a series of numbers and a green "ready" or a red "cooking" next to it hung over the counter. Our number was the third down.

Realizing I would have some time, I inspected the famous Burgerporium. As with the town, the restaurant was also stuck in a time somewhere around the late '60s or early '70s. The color scheme revolved around yellows, browns, greens, and oranges. There was an awning over the counter with old wood shaker shingles and wood paneling throughout the restaurant. Over the tables, hung lights with glass coverings in the same color scheme. In the far corner of the establishment was a large white sign that read: "Welcome to the Burgerporium. Proudly serving Williston since 1972."

Fascinated by the nostalgia, I did not realize Marcus had gone up to collect our food. He nudged me slightly on his way past to get my attention.

"Mom and I used to come here all the time. The place is pretty amazing, huh?"

"It's more amazing how they have kept the decor looking so new all these years."

As we sat down, I brought my senses back to the tantalizing smell coming from the tray.

"Okay, what *did* you order us? Besides the shakes?"

"Cowboy burgers. Pretty much your standard fare burger, except for whatever it is they mix in the meat topped with a special sauce. Mom thinks it's A-1. Aunt Lilly thinks it's Peter Luger sauce. I don't know what it is. I just know it's all levels of deliciousness wrapped in a pretty bun."

I lifted the burger and unwrapped it. The appearance left a lot to be desired, but the smell was heavenly, and Marcus was selling it rather well. With only a moment of hesitation, I bit down into one of the most amazing burgers I have ever had. They cooked it to perfection, and the juices exploded in my mouth.

As I was enjoying a second bite, I looked up and saw Marcus's eyes go wide. He nearly choked on his food and scrambled to pull away from the table. Something changed in that instant, and I felt time come to a standstill.

Behind me, on my right, came a fast-moving object although I was unsure exactly what it was. Looking at Marcus's gaze, I shifted my weight to the left. I saw a fist whirl past my face and come into contact with my drink instead. The movement sent it hurdling past Marcus, causing the paper cup and its contents to explode against the window we were sitting next to.

I continued to roll left, circling around the back of my chair, and spotted a well-built guy. He had dark hair in a tight-fitting yellow T-shirt and cutup blue jeans, and his arm was still in midretraction from the punch he just threw. Without hesitation, I grabbed his left arm and pulled it behind him. Using my body weight and his momentum, I threw his body onto the table with a tremendous crash.

As my would-be assailant contacted our table, time seemed to return to normal. I had his left arm pulled up tight against his back as close to his head as I could come without breaking it while the weight of my arm was spread across his torso. Once Marcus could see that our human torpedo had been apprehended, he also came back to life. Once he found his voice, he said, "Holy hell! What was that? I mean, both of you? What the—why—how?"

Looking down, I could see Ethan Campbell fighting to release his arm from my grip. Behind us were Mike and another guy that I had never seen before. I assumed that was Ethan's backup, but as they looked from me to Ethan, they raised their hands in defeat as they backed out of the restaurant seeing their companion would not be taking part in the chaos as expected.

Realizing that he was alone but not willing to surrender, Ethan started pushing up, trying to break free from my grip.

"Son, I'd stay still if I were you. He's got you wound up tighter than a $2 watch. Seems to me, you'll break your *own* arm if you keep wrestling him like that," I heard a slow drawl from behind us.

Without looking over my shoulder to see who had just spoken, I said in Ethan's ear, "I'm going to let you go. But before I do, you need to let me know you will not try something stupid again."

He laughed. "As though I'm going to listen to you!"

The voice behind us answered again, "Boy, I don't think you're in much of a position to debate."

I could feel him tense under me and heard him growl in frustration. "Get the hell off me!"

"Not until you calm down. Remember, *you* came after me."

The man from behind walked around to stand in front of us. I could see he was who the cashier had been talking to. He appeared to be in his midfifties with salt-and-pepper hair. The tight-fitting button-up shirt had buttons that were seriously being tested by his bulging midsection. Across the left of the shirt was a name tag that read "Mike" with "Manager" below it.

"I see you got this all under control, young man," he said, looking at me. "But do ya think you could let him up long enough for us to get this cleaned up?"

As a sense of relaxation made its way through me, I finally looked around the room. Marcus was now sitting wide-eyed at the table next to us. He was still sipping on his shake, which he apparently had saved in the melee. A sea of faces was looking at the remains of our lunch. Out of the corner of my eye, I noticed the remnants of the bright pink drink still slowly making its way down the window.

Below me, I could see that Ethan was now lying across the table like a dead fish, waiting for me to release him. I looked back to the manager, who was standing with his thumbs in his front pockets. His head remained lowered as he rocked on his heels, looking at me for my decision. I released my grip slowly, testing my captive to see how he would respond. When I didn't feel him tense up, I loosened my grip completely and backed away.

As Ethan stood up, I could see that his yellow shirt now sported various colors from the sauces that had detonated on impact. Behind Ethan, I saw Marcus rocking back on his chair, smiling as he happily sipped away on his shake. Then I saw it—a lone french fry plastered to Ethan's left cheek—one which he was not aware of. The rest of the restaurant noticed, though.

Small bouts of laughter arose, and Mike, the manager, motioned to his face. "You have a little something there."

Ethan swiped at his face, and the fry fell. As he saw it hit the table, he turned to look at me. Flames of fury danced in his eyes as his breath began to quicken.

Mike spoke up again, "I think it's time you headed home, Mr. Campbell. I'm not sure your uncle would be too happy about what happened here today. Oh, and perhaps leave some money to pay for our guests?"

"Yeah, really! Poor Jace only got one bite of his burger and never tried the drink," Marcus chimed in.

Ethan shot him a disgusted look and turned to walk away. Mike cleared his throat, making Ethan turn back toward the table. He reached into his pocket and pulled out his wallet. After rummaging through it, Ethan dropped a $20 bill on the table and then turned and walked away.

"Well, now. Been a while since we've had quite that much excitement in here. Maybe we'll get you both a *to-go* order?" Manager Mike said as though nothing had occurred.

Marcus smiled awkwardly and asked, "Do you want us to wait here or outside?"

Mike looked at the table and seemed to deduce what we had ordered. He looked back at us. "We'll bring it out to you."

Walking past the other patrons in the restaurant, I could hear the inaudible whispers from some while others just watched as we left. Marcus looked like a little kid as he happily slurped away on his shake. I looked back over my shoulder at him and couldn't help but smile at the jovial expression on his face and the light bounce he had in his step.

When we were outside, we moved to the outdoor seating area while we waited for Mike to appear with our new order. I sat and stared at Marcus, anxiously anticipating some answer as to what had just happened. Reveling in the earlier events, he made me wait until he had downed his beloved shake.

He finished the last of it, placed it down on the table, and sat back, rubbing his stomach in pleasure. "*That* was the best thing I've seen all year. What are you? A black belt or something?"

I laughed. "Actually, I've never had a fight or received training before. I'm just as stunned by that as everyone else was."

Marcus eyed me warily. "Now I know you're joking. There is no way that you just pulled that out of the air. That was definitely some black belt level stuff."

"I swear it! I saw your reaction, and before I knew it, Ethan was on the table."

Marcus narrowed his eyes at me. "Okay… We all have our secrets. I'm only glad you're on my side."

We saw the door open and saw the bubbly blond from earlier come out with a bag of food and two drinks.

"Sweet! Refills!" Marcus declared.

The cashier smiled as she handed him the bag. "That was pretty amazing. I don't think I've ever seen someone pin Ethan before." The cashier's smile was bright and genuine as she looked at me. "I'm Lyndsay."

Marcus looked up and noticed Lyndsay staring. "Thanks for the food. We can add you to his fan club if you like," he said.

Lyndsay looked at Marcus, slightly perplexed, then asked, "Are you guys going to the party tonight?"

"If you're talking about the Grotto, then yeah. We'll be there," I said and noticed her brighten up before she turned to jog back into the restaurant.

"Awesome! I'll see you tonight."

Marcus watched as she left, then looked back at me. "Speaking of parties. We'd better get back if we're going to be ready when Izzie leaves."

Grabbing up our bag of food and drinks, we headed back toward Joe's. As we walked, I felt myself suddenly tense when I mentally reviewed the earlier events. Marcus, on the other hand, was drinking his second cherry bing shake with no signs of distress. "Hopefully, he has learned to leave you alone at this point," Marcus started.

"What do you mean?"

"Well, first, he ended up on his face in the shed. Now you pinned him with almost no effort at all."

I thought about that for a minute and then frowned. "But he also made me look like a fool in front of Izzie yesterday."

"I don't know about that. Where did Izzie end up last night after work?"

Seeing what he was saying, I felt a smile cross my face.

"There you go. Ethan has never had someone best him, and you have made him look like a moron twice now…in public."

As we walked up to the minivan, I looked at my phone, which read 4:10 p.m.

"Should we call your mom?"

Marcus pondered for a moment. "Nah, let's eat our food in peace."

Perching ourselves on the front fender of the van, we opened the bag and ate. As we finished the last of our meals, we saw Aunt Lilly walking up to us. Her eyes narrowed. "You know they have seating at the restaurant, right?"

Marcus beamed at her. "We took in the fresh air down here. It's a beautiful October day."

And Lilly's eyebrows lifted as she glared at her nephew. Then looking at me, she asked, "Is that true?"

Using the mouth full of food to my advantage, I smiled and nodded. No need to give more information than what she had asked for.

Mrs. Hunter saw the three of us standing by the car and then looked at the bag of food.

"What happened?" she said in a mom tone as though realizing there had been a problem.

Marcus laughed as he was still trying to finish the last of a cheese fry and nearly choked. "Mom, seriously?"

"Marcus Anthony Hunter, you would never just eat outside. What happened?"

Marcus opened his mouth to speak, but his mom stopped him. "I want the truth. I won't be mad, but I don't like surprises."

Marcus closed his mouth and dropped his head. "Ethan Campbell," he said summarily.

Mrs. Hunter's green eyes went wide as she grabbed Marcus by the arms and started moving him around, fervently looking for damage. "Mom, Mom! Stop. I swear. We're fine. He tried to cause trouble, but Jace put him in his place. Literally, before anything could happen to us."

She stopped examining Marcus and stared at me. Not knowing what else to do, I shrugged and smiled at her.

"We *may* or *may not* be allowed back for some time, but *we* didn't cause the trouble, so I'm sure we'll be fine," Marcus said.

At this, Aunt Lilly broke out into laughter. "Come on, you two. Let's get back to the house."

CHAPTER 12

Blue Grotto

By the time we arrived back at Marcus's house, it was getting dark. Looking at my phone, I noticed a missed call from Uncle Roman.

"I think I should head back home for a bit. They called and left a message."

Marcus nodded. "We're still on for tonight?"

"I don't see why not, but I'll text you after I talk to them."

Turning to walk away, I realized I didn't have Marcus's number. He must have realized it at the same time because he turned to look at me as well. Realizing what we both needed, we chuckled. After exchanging numbers, I turned to walk back home.

Passing Izzie's house, I felt compelled to look toward her room and saw her frame outlined by the lights from inside. As I watched, the curtain moved slightly, allowing me a better view. She was in a teal tank top with a towel wrapped around her head. Just as I was about to look away, I saw her lean forward and wave. Unsure if she was waving to me, I looked back over my shoulder, but Marcus had already gone in with his family. A warmth grew within me, and I felt my face lighten as a smile grew. I lifted my hand to her and waved back. She smiled and then turned as though to answer someone who was talking to her.

Entering my house, I could hear Aunt Cora and Uncle Roman talking in the family room. Passing through the kitchen, I opened the refrigerator and grabbed a can of sprite. I popped the top as I continued my trek to the back of the house.

Aunt Cora was sitting with her legs tucked up under her on the leather sectional's corner. An oversize blanket was draped across her lap. Uncle Roman was in his recliner, just opposite her. Aunt Cora saw me first, and her face lit up.

"I don't think we've ever gone this long without seeing you. Tell me everything!"

Uncle Roman looked over his shoulder. I saw a genuine look of pleasure on his face as he turned back to Aunt Cora.

"Let the boy sit down and relax a bit before you jump all over him."

Sitting in the couch's corner closest to Uncle Roman, I looked at them both and took a sip of my drink.

"I have to admit, we really had a great time. Mrs. Hunter is awesome, but you already knew that. I really enjoy hanging out with Marcus. And his aunt is hilarious too."

Aunt Cora sat up, in almost a kneeling position, and faced me. "And what about Izzie? It shocked me when she came over last night."

I felt my cheeks heat up as I looked at Uncle Roman. He shrugged wide and laughed. Realizing there was no way to avoid answering, I explained, "We had seen her at Carolina's Café. She just came by after the store closed."

Aunt Cora smiled and sat back. "I really like her. She's very polite...and pretty."

"Cora!" Uncle Roman chimed in.

"Well, she is."

I smiled and shook my head. Sometimes talking with Aunt Cora was like talking to someone my age. Looking at Uncle Roman, I remembered the missed call.

"I was already in the driveway when I saw you had called. So I didn't listen to the message. Is everything okay?"

Uncle Roman looked to Aunt Cora, then to me, and lowered his eyes.

"I'm not sure what you do with that phone if you never look at it."

"Yes, sir. I'm sorry."

"Fortunately, everything was fine over here. Mary kept us abreast of everything happening over there, but we wanted to hear from *you* that everything was going okay. Contrary to popular belief, we're pretty fond of you and want to make sure you're okay."

I felt the flush rush to my cheeks again, "Yes, sir."

"Oh, Roman, leave him alone. Jace, Mrs. Hunter says that there is a get-together that you and Marcus are looking to go to?"

My eyes instantly rose to meet hers. "Yes, at the…Grotto. Yeah, Blue Grotto, I think they called it. There are a bunch of people going there."

"Yes, that's the place. Mary said that the Lewis girls were going to take you?"

"Izzie was going to confirm that and get back to us. I haven't talked to them yet, so I'm not sure, but I can text Marcus now," I answered enthusiastically.

As I was about to pull the phone out of my pocket, I heard the *Crazy Frog* theme song go off, and I nearly dropped my phone. Uncle Roman raised his eyebrows. "Well, that's a…unique ring tone."

I realized I had not added ringtones to my phone. Then I remembered I had given it to Marcus to add his contact information. I chuckled to myself and shook my head. On my phone's screen was a text from "Enos." I opened it.

Enos: 😊
Enos: I wish I could have seen your face when the ringer went off
Enos: Izzie and her sisters will drive us, but we're leaving in 30 minutes. Are you still coming?

I looked up from the screen and smiled.

"The ringtone is with compliments from Marcus. I have a ride with Izzie and her sisters, but they are leaving in thirty minutes, and I would like to take a shower. That is if I'm allowed to go."

Aunt Cora and Uncle Roman exchanged looks for what seemed to be an eternity. Then Uncle Roman spoke up.

"You're allowed you to go. But I want a phone number of who you will be with and an exact location. I also want you home no later than midnight. Can these stipulations be met?"

"Yes, sir. I'm sure there will be no problem with any of those."

"Then you better get moving before they leave without you."

I got up off the couch to run for the hallway and stopped. Turning, I ran back to my aunt and gave her a kiss on the cheek. Then I walked to Uncle Roman and extended my hand. He looked at my hand and stood up, pulling me into a tight embrace instead, and said, "Go, get ready. We'll be here when you get home."

Smiling, I ran upstairs. After taking my fastest shower ever, I sprinted back into my room. I began rummaging through my clothes and was at a loss of what to wear. Pulling out my phone, I prayed that the god of judgment would be able to help me pull an outfit together.

> *Jace: Do I need a swimsuit or anything? A grotto is a body of water, right?*

As I waited for his response, I continued to peruse my clothes again when I heard his stupid ringtone. *I really need to change that!* I thought and read the message.

> *Enos: Get a step on it. Everyone is ready to go. We're waiting on you!*

I looked out my window and could see the group by a Maroon GMC Acadia. Looking back into my room, I cringed slightly as I realized that it now closely resembled Marcus's. Luckily, in the corner, I saw a pullover sweater with large blue-and-white horizontal stripes. I paired it with jeans containing a designer-laid hole in the left thigh that Aunt Cora assured me was in fashion. I grabbed the outfit and quickly got dressed. I ran down the stairs, hollering to my aunt and uncle, "I'm leaving. I'll text you later. Love you!"

Realizing that I did not want to run at the car in a full sprint, I slowed and tried to regain my composure. The group turned as I was approaching.

"Glad you could make it. Let's get moving," Alyssa said.

Izzie smiled as her two older sisters got into the front seat of the truck. I turned and opened the door and motioned for Izzie to get in. Marcus stepped in front of her and kissed me on the cheek.

"Oh, you're such a gentleman, Jace Northall!" he said in a high voice.

Before I could react, Izzie laughed and walked up to the door.

"Thank you," she said.

I looked in the truck and saw there were three rows and the second row had two bucket seats. Marcus had already jumped to the third row and was lounging across it, making it impossible to sit with him. Izzie had moved to the far seat in the second row, giving me room to sit in the seat next to her. After buckling myself in, I turned to look over my shoulder at Marcus. Sitting behind Izzie, he waved to me flirtatiously. I glared at him and he laughed.

Izzie turned around in her seat to see what antics he was up to now.

"You're impossible sometimes, Marcus!"

From the front seat, Zoe announced, "Okay, what kind of music do we all like? Your options are The Highway, Y2Kountry, Prime Country, or Garth," Zoe announced.

I looked to Izzie, who was staring at Zoe with her mouth slightly agape. She regained her composure and looked at me but was talking to her sister.

"Zoe is allowing you to feel as though you have a choice. You obviously don't. Those are all country stations. If I had to guess, we're going to be listening to Prime Country, but she will flip around regardless of whether you are listening."

Zoe turned to look at Izzie. "That is so not—"

"That is such a true statement," said Alyssa.

"Fine. What would *you* have us listen to?" Zoe asked.

Alyssa laughed. "Prime Country. We just love teasing you. You're okay with that, Jace, right?"

Not wanting to get caught in the middle of sisters, I just nodded.

"I like heavy metal if you have it?" Marcus chimed in from the back.

In unison, the three girls shouted, "What?"

Izzie turned around. "Since when?"

Marcus laughed. "I figured I would liven things up a bit."

"You really are impossible!" Zoe shouted from the front seat.

The drive took roughly thirty minutes, and we seemed to get further and further from civilization the more we drove. Turning onto an old country road, I noticed a sign on the gate that read "No trespassing." I glanced at Izzie, who shrugged, also having seen the sign.

"So not to be the party pooper of the group, but what about the sign back there?" Izzie asked Zoe.

"Stop it, Izzie. Let's not do this tonight. Everything will be fine. There are tons of people going. Also, we have been here a million times in the past."

Marcus mumbled from the back seat just loud enough for Izzie and me to hear him.

"Isn't this how every horror film starts? I'm the goofy, lovable character, though. So I should make it through enough of the night to realize when it's time to run."

Izzie giggled and playfully swung back to hit Marcus's knee. I sat up straighter in my seat when I saw cars lined up by a rotted-out piece of wood, which likely acted as a barricade in its more useful days.

Zoe was correct in her assumption about the number of people here tonight. Far in the distance was a large fire with a decent number of figures positioned around it. Scanning the parking lot, Zoe pointed out a spot near a red mustang.

"Oh, there. That's Ethan's car. He said he was driving Mike and Brian."

My heart sank in my chest. Immediately, I breathed a sigh of relief when I realized it was empty. *What are the chances it's the same Ethan?* I thought. As though divine intervention needed to kick me at that exact moment in time, Zoe squealed from the front seat.

"Oooooooh! They're coming here. Get your game face on, Izzie!"

Looking out the front window, I saw three large males heading toward the car. Ethan was in the lead, and Izzie instantly seemed anxious at his appearance. I glanced back to Marcus, who smiled and said, "I'd say I have your back, but you held your own just fine earlier."

The whole car seemed to stop and turn to look at me. As I was about to explain Marcus's cryptic statement, the car door opened. Ethan's face went from happy to enrage in a matter of seconds when he looked past Izzie and saw me.

"Oh, hey, Ethan," Marcus chimed from the back seat. "You're looking better than you did this afternoon. Hey! I see you have a fresh shirt."

Both Ethan and I looked at Marcus, but it was Ethan who spoke next, "Can it, Hunter! Big words coming from the back seat."

Izzie, being stuck, literally, in the middle, put her hands up.

"I have *no clue* what y'all are talking about, but these two are with us. So let's all play nice."

Ethan's shoulder's relaxed as he switched his focus to Izzie.

"I will, for you. Why didn't you tell me they were coming?"

Izzie made her way out of the truck with Ethan supporting her arm as she did so. Not wanting to follow in *that* direction, I opened my door. Turning to exit, I came face to chest with what could only be described as a silo with arms and legs. *I'm dead*, was the only thought that went through my head.

"Let me help you out of the truck," The silo mused.

I looked back to Marcus, who was pondering his options—follow Izzie, follow me, or just stay in the truck. Eventually, he turned to exit through Izzie's door but was thwarted when Ethan unceremoniously slammed it shut in his face.

Through the window, I watched as Ethan quickly ushered Izzie away. I could see her looking over her shoulder at us and seemed to be saying something to Ethan. He, however, had his left hand around her waist and was holding her right arm with his other hand. I could feel a burning sensation in my own hands as I watched him practically drag her off. Looking down, I saw the fingernail imprints on my palms.

Marcus saw them too and motioned to the mass behind me.

"Um, I think you'll need to deal with *this* one before you deal with *that* one."

I turned to look back at my current obstacle. He was wearing a flannel button-up shirt with a gray zip-up vest, jeans, and a camouflage baseball cap with *Cabella's* written across it. He was looking me in the eye as he leaned in. His arms were resting on the top of the door opening and they bulged, stretching the flannel shirt. *Does anyone buy appropriately sized shirts in this town?* I thought. Shifting my gaze up, I could see his coffee-colored eyes sizing me up.

"Don't worry, Hunter, we've got enough to go around."

I looked past Marcus once more, trying to find Izzie. Then I felt someone grab me by the collar and start dragging me out of the truck. Not expecting the move, I swung my arm up instinctively and made contact with the behemoth. I cringed at the realization of what I had done although it was more like a backhand as opposed to a punch. My head swiveled, and I could see more of the whites of my future assailant's eyes than color, and I knew a punch was coming my way.

As I braced for impact, I heard a voice coming from the front of the car.

"Eric! What the hell are you doing? They came *with us*!"

I could hear Marcus mumble from the back seat, "I love you, Zoe," followed by an audible sigh as he slumped back in his seat.

Behind Zoe, I could see Brian walking over, which caused Eric to let go of my sweater and drop his arm. My legs felt like Jell-O, and I hadn't even fully left the truck yet.

Zoe shoved Eric with force to get out of the way and came to look at us.

"Are you two okay?"

Feeling air entering my lungs more freely now, I just nodded to her.

"I'm really sorry about that. I have no idea what got into him."

Zoe stepped back and motioned for the two of us to get out of the car. She stayed and made sure we did so without further incident. Having Brian hovering in the background likely helped.

"Hey, Jace. Been a while since we last saw you," Brian said.

Unsure what to say, I just nodded as I followed Zoe, who was now moving as though on a mission from God. She finally stopped at a table roughly twenty feet in front of the truck. Around it was ten other teens, and I quickly scanned the table to see if Izzie was one of them. My heart sank when I realized she wasn't.

Frantically, I searched the area, trying to find her. I could feel the panic growing inside, and I knew I wouldn't be able to relax until I saw that she was all right. Marcus must have picked up on my thoughts because he was looking around as well.

Just when I thought my anxiety would hit its peak, in the distance, we heard a shrill scream. Instantly, I felt the hair on the back of my neck stand up as I prepared to run in its direction. Looking that way, all I saw was a blond girl with pigtails pointing at me.

Marcus started tugging on my shirt feverishly.

"That's the Burgerporium, girl! Crap, what was her name?"

I spoke under my breath, "Lyndsay."

"Yes! Thank you, man. I couldn't remember her name."

She quickly made her way toward me, gathering everyone that she passed.

"*This* is the kid that kicked Ethan's ass this afternoon," she exclaimed.

I felt the heat in my cheeks as a dozen or more sets of eyes landed on me, and the area went quiet for a few seconds. Then Eric let out a guttural belly laugh, which set off a chain reaction.

Lyndsay's face turned to a grimace as she turned to walk toward him and, with her finger pointed at his chest, said, "Are you callin' me a liar?"

Eric tried to regain his composure as he spoke to Lyndsay.

"No. Just wonderin' how this can be that same kid. You know, seein' that he almost wet himself not ten minutes ago."

Lyndsay stepped back, and her eyes narrowed. "Fine, maybe this'll prove it."

She pulled out her cell phone and flipped through a few screens before she landed on a video of what had to be this afternoon's festivities.

I looked at Marcus. "Wonderful. She has a video."

Eric stared at the phone in disbelief, shifting his gaze periodically between me and the phone.

"Holy shit! Is this real?" he asked.

He then broke out in another belly laugh, nearly dropping the phone as he dramatically fell to the floor. Two other guys picked up the frenzy of laughter. They were so amused that they had to lean on each other to keep standing.

Eric eventually pulled himself up and stared at me.

"This kid, right here? *He* pinned Ethan? Where the hell is Ethan?"

The group started looking around for him, and I felt relief wash over me. At least everyone was looking for him now. Zoe walked over to Lyndsay and took the phone. Brian, looking over her shoulder, watched it too.

"That's really weird," Zoe said.

Lyndsay turned to look at Zoe. "What's weird?"

Zoe turned her gaze toward us. "Did you guys plan to go there, or was it a game-time decision?"

Marcus and I exchanged glances, but I picked up on where Zoe was going with her questioning.

"It was a spur of the moment," I said.

Zoe turned to look at Lyndsay, who was now looking suspiciously guilty of *something*.

"It's weird that Ethan would just show up. And more interestingly, why did you have your phone out and ready?"

Lyndsay's face flushed. She looked to another guy in the crowd who was standing at the perimeter. Zoe's eyes narrowed as she focused on her prey. Then, just as quickly, a look of realization registered on Zoe's face.

"Oh my god, *you* called him… *You* told them Marcus and Jace were there, didn't you, Lyndsay?"

Lyndsay looked guiltily around the group of teens but did not answer.

"Why would you do that?" Zoe questioned.

Zoe was talking with her teeth clenched as she slowly moved toward Lyndsay. By that point, Lyndsay was no longer smiling. She was desperately searching for someone to help her, but the crowd parted, leaving her nowhere to hide.

"It's not like that. Ethan is her boyfriend. He should know when his girlfriend's stalker is nearby."

I felt as though I had been sucker punched. When I turned to Zoe for confirmation, she did not meet my eyes.

Lyndsay seemed to take that as leverage as she tried to gain sympathy by appealing to the crowd.

"We all saw Izzie and Ethan. We all know that they are dating. This kid just moved in and is already trying to take her from Ethan."

Eric seemed to take a renewed interest in me, shifting his shoulders as though limbering up. Zoe saw this and turned to him with Brian standing close behind. Reevaluating his current options, Eric decided to back down.

With him effectively neutralized, Zoe returned her attention to Lyndsay.

"Should we tell everyone how you have a crush on Ethan? I mean, *that* is the reason you told him."

To the left of Lyndsay stood Mike, who stared at her. His eyes were showing an emotion somewhere between accusatory and hurt.

"Is it true?" he asked.

Lyndsay seemed to notice him for the first time and reached for his hand.

"Mike, she's trying to cause trouble. I called *you*, not him."

"I know you did, but I also know that you always want to hang out when he'd be there too."

Lyndsay looked around the crowd and began sobbing. Her tears were the fake crocodile ones that a well-trained actress can pull out without hesitation. I felt my eyes roll as I looked away from the insanity. I scanned the perimeter again, then tugged on Marcus's arm to indicate let's go. We walked in the direction Ethan had pulled Izzie.

As we meandered through the bodies of teens fixated on the theatrics behind us, my senses seemed to become more alert. Just like they had earlier in the day when Ethan had attacked. Although the light had not changed, it appeared brighter to me. In the distance, I was more aware of minute noises that I had not been to a few moments ago. It was as though my need to find her had made me acutely aware of everything around me. My heart ached and a wave of something ran up my spine as I imagined all the worst possible scenarios in my head. With each passing minute, I became more acutely aware that I needed to find her as though she was calling out for me to do so.

"It's like they vanished," I said, trying to keep my voice composed.

Marcus nodded as he squinted in the darkness. "I can barely see my hand in front of my face out here!"

Walking across the party area, I could now see that the floor consisted mostly of sand. To the left of where we were walking was a high wall of stone. From our vantage point, I could not see its top, and I assumed we were at the base of a cliff of some sort.

"The grotto is on the other side…well, inside, actually." Marcus motioned toward the wall.

"There's an opening in the wall that lets you into it. After walking through a small tunnel, you enter an enormous cavern. During the summer, it's a great place to swim and cool off, but you would probably freeze your ass off this time of year."

We walked along the edge of the wall, looking for Izzie. I could feel my stomach tying itself in knots, not knowing where she was and if she was okay. At my core, I felt as though I was willing her to send me a signal to direct me, guide me to her. I trusted Ethan as far as I could throw him and hated the thought of her being alone with him in the dark. My frustration was also mounting for her sisters, who did not seem to be phased by Izzie's apparent vanishing act. Were they that blind to Ethan's obvious malice?

"Ahhh! Where are they?" I bellowed, throwing my hands up in frustration.

"They can't be that far. This place isn't that big," Marcus said, trying to reassure me.

Scanning the perimeter of the wall again, I felt the despair setting in. As I was preparing to give up on this direction and head back toward the parking lot, I finally saw what I hoped was the opening. I looked to Marcus for reassurance that he saw it too.

"Sweet! You found it. I can't see anything out here except shadows. Good eye."

Having an overwhelming urge to rush into the opening, I grabbed Marcus by the arm and made our way toward the cavity but stopped before entering. Not wanting to waste time going the wrong way, I tried to listen closely. Was I hearing voices? Again, I looked to Marcus, hoping his hearing was better than his vision.

"Yeah, I hear it too, but I can't make out if it's her," he said as though reading my mind.

Walking through the door was like walking into a blackout room—a freezing-cold blackout room. Marcus grabbed my arm, almost tripping me on the way in. In the distance, I could hear a female voice and a male voice.

"No one is here. No one will know. Come on."

"Stop. I want to go back."

"Just try—"

In an instant, I recognized the voices and could also hear the panic in Izzie's. She was begging to go back. Without hesitation, I let go of Marcus's arm and followed the voices. Within a few steps, my vision had improved tenfold, and it was as though a light had been turned on although none were present. Meandering through the long corridor, my heart rate increased as I heard the fear and panic in Izzie's voice getting louder with each step. "How long is this stupid tunnel?" I asked myself in frustration. Aggravation mounting, I picked up my speed, trying to get to her as fast as I could. In the distance, I could see a glow and knew that my destination was close.

As I entered the cavern, I could see they were on the opposite side of a body of water that seemed to glow. Above it was a large opening that gave access to the night air, allowing the moonlight to reflect off the water. Thankfully, its illumination helped to light most of the grotto, and I could easily see the pair.

Ethan had Izzie backed against a wall in a corner, making it impossible for her to get away from him without swimming. They were standing on a ledge large enough for them. There was a wall to her back, which wrapped around to her left and the pool of water on her right.

I saw Izzie look around anxiously and push Ethan away from her. As her head turned toward me, I could see the dampness on her face and could tell she was crying. Anger raged through my veins like a locomotive. Without realizing I had made a move, I was across the grotto, just behind them. Grabbing Ethan by the shirt, I ripped him away from Izzie. When he turned to see what had pulled him, I threw a punch. It landed squarely on his chin, sending him whirling back into the water.

I looked at Izzie, who initially backed away from me into the corner. Realizing that she was likely still nervous, I extended my hand to her.

"It's okay. I've got you. Let's go."

She hesitated a moment more, glancing at Ethan, who was feverishly swimming to the other side. Apparently, she did not want to meet up with him because she grabbed my hand. Quickly, we made our way along the edge of the pool. Ethan, seeing us, was now moving with purpose through the water, cursing as he screamed my name.

Anger seemed to fuel him now as it had for me earlier. He appeared to pick up speed as he neared the stairway built from the stony ledge into the water. When I first entered the room, I had not initially seen it. At that moment, I knew I needed to get Izzie past that point before Ethan departed the water. As we made the last turn around the pool and to the exit, I looked back. Ethan was at the staircase and actively climbing it. Rage in his eyes.

I pulled Izzie in front of me, realizing I couldn't handle both her and Ethan.

"Izzie, walk straight along the corridor. Hold the wall on the right. Marcus is on the other side at the opening to the cave."

She looked over my shoulder before her eyes went wide and screamed. I somehow already knew where Ethan was before she had reacted. Releasing her hand, I turned on my left foot and spun around. Ducking slightly and pulling my arm back, I was ready to strike when I fully faced Ethan. Once I saw him, I released my arm and allowed physics to take over.

My fist contacted the soft part of his abdomen, and he collapsed around it. His body lifted slightly, and his arms and fists came down hard on my back. Bracing for the impact, I did not drop but pushed up with all my force, throwing him off-balance and causing him to stumble backward. He was only a step or two away from the grotto stairs and my push caused him to hit the top step, and fall back into the water with a large splash. A moment later, Ethan flew up out of the water in a move that could have rivaled Jason surfacing from Camp Crystal Lake on Friday the 13th.

Standing my ground and blocking the stairs, I glared down at him.

"She's not interested in you, so stay away from her, or you'll be dealing with me…again!"

Hearing heavy breathing behind me, I realized Izzie had not left the cavern and was still by the exit. As I turned, she was curled in a ball, leaning against the wall, and wide-eyed as she watched us.

Ignoring Ethan, I rushed to her side and quickly looked her over.

"Are you okay? Did he hurt you?"

She stared at me and then answered.

"No…I'm fine. I just—are *you* okay?"

Confused by her question, I leaned back on my heels.

"I'm fine. Izzie, please. Go back to Marcus. I'm going to get Ethan out of the water."

She peered around me and scrambled to a standing position. "He's already coming out," she said.

I turned to see Ethan, slowly making his way out of the water. "I won't hurt him. Wait here if you feel more comfortable."

She nodded, and I felt a pang of guilt. *I had scared her too.* Turning toward Ethan, I extended my hand out to help him the rest of the way. He looked at it, and his face contorted.

"I got it!"

As he stepped out of the water, he shoved me as he passed, but I didn't react. He made his way toward the exit and stopped momentarily to look down at Izzie, who was still holding onto the edge of the wall, cowering from him slightly.

From somewhere within the cave, we heard a guttural growl. Ethan turned to look back, his eyes wide. This caused me to do the same.

"I think it's time we all leave," I said.

Izzie nodded and grabbed hold of the right side of the wall, quickly disappearing into the opening. Ethan turned back to look at me before he followed her. I looked over my shoulder again to determine where the noise had come from. If I were going to be walking in the dark, I'd like to know that something from behind won't attack me. I strained but saw nothing.

Feeling somewhat reassured to make the trek back to the opening, I grabbed hold of the wall on the right to follow Izzie and Ethan. Within a few dozen feet, I could see the glow of light, and I realized someone had illuminated the opening with a flashlight from their phone. As I got closer, I could see it was Marcus, waiting for all of us to return. Passing him, I saw he was fighting back laughter, so I stopped to look at him more closely.

"Should I ask why Ethan is soaked to the bone?" he asked.

"Use your imagination," I said in a semi-irritated tone.

"Is she outside?" I continued.

Marcus nodded. "Yeah. Not sure where, but she's out. Heads up, he may or may not want to kill you when *you* get outside."

"I think I'll be fine. He's got to be freezing."

As I emerged, I could see Izzie with Zoe and Alyssa. Apparently, she was explaining what had happened. Zoe's eyes flashed lava as her gaze shot up toward Ethan.

Still dripping, he looked over to see them and laughed. "Oh, please. Get a life, all three of you."

The anger building again, I moved toward him but was intercepted. Brian came out of nowhere and punched Ethan, causing him to drop on the sandy floor like a ton of bricks.

Brian looked up from Ethan, who was now resting just a few inches from my shoes. He considered me, then the Lewis sisters.

After his assessment of the situation, he turned back to me and made eye contact before nodding.

Alyssa rushed to me, stepping over Ethan in the process. Unsure if I was about to get slapped or not, I felt myself flinch as she threw herself forward, wrapped me in a hug, and whispered in my ear, "Thank you."

At her words, I felt myself let go and hugged her back. Pulling away, she looked around at the teens who were amassed in the small area. "What's everyone standing around for? It's a party, isn't it?" While walking toward her sisters, she looked back at Ethan. Her eyes scanned the group surrounding them until she saw who she was looking for.

"Hey, Mike? You may need to drive Ethan home tonight. Maybe sooner rather than later."

Mike sheepishly walked over to Ethan. Lyndsay was close behind, her head low as she passed us. Alyssa looked at Izzie. "It's up to you. Do you want to stay, or do you want to go?"

Izzie looked around as all the eyes of the party landed on her.

"If it's all right with you, I think I'm ready to go home."

Alyssa smiled. "Of course it is. Come on, boys."

As we made our way toward the car, I saw Brian walking with Zoe. After a long kiss, he turned to me and extended his fist. "You like to liven things up, huh? Glad my girl has *you* next door."

I met his fist pump and smiled back.

"See you around," I said.

"Unless she tires of me, I'm sure you will," Brian answered.

We piled in the car, taking the same seats we had when we drove there. This time, though, there was mostly silence. I looked back at Marcus, who had fallen asleep in the back seat and was snoring softly, causing me to chuckle. Looking back, my eyes met Izzie's before she quickly looked away. I felt my heart drop. Unsure of what else to do, I turned to look out the window and allowed myself to dose off as well.

I woke with a start when Alyssa pulled into the driveway. She giggled at me through the rearview mirror and said, "We're back, sleeping beauty."

Smiling, I looked over to Izzie, who was also smiling. Seeing this change in her caused me to wake more quickly and sit up in my seat. What had happened while I was out. She looked as though she wanted nothing to do with me when I closed my eyes. Not wanting to jinx anything, I was anxious to head inside as quickly as possible. "I guess this is my stop. Thanks for the invite tonight," I said.

In the back seat, Marcus still had not stirred, so I gently nudged his leg. He sat up with a jerk and slurped the small trail of drool that had made its way down his chin. I chuckled. "You okay, big guy? We're home."

He stretched and extended his arm past his mouth in a subtle but effective attempt to cover up the drool faux pas. Stepping out of the truck on the passenger side, he looked at the girls.

"Yeah, but my bed is calling my name. Okay, ladies. Until the next time, you need rescuing."

Zoe laughed. "We'll be sure to call Jace."

He laughed. "Yeah. That may be a better idea."

I turned to walk to my house, waving good night to everyone over my shoulder. That was when someone grabbed my arm. Turning to see who it was, I felt soft lips meet mine. As they pulled away, I opened my eyes and saw Izzie smiling at me. "Good night, Jace."

"Uh, yeah, good night."

Still in shock, I began walking back to my house and nearly tripped over the hose in my yard. I quickly caught myself and looked up to see all three Lewis girls giggling as they made their way back into their own home.

"I'm okay…"

The only voice I heard was Marcus's as he walked back to his house. "Go to bed, Casanova!"

CHAPTER 13

The Sheriff of Williston

As the door opened, Buddy lifted his head from Aunt Cora's feet and gave a very half-hearted bark. Once the realization of who had entered registered, he quickly jumped up from his spot and ran to meet me. Aunt Cora had been waiting in the kitchen and smiled as I walked toward her.

"Casanova, huh?"

I couldn't even hide my smile as I walked over to kiss her on the cheek. "Good night, Aunt Cora."

"Really? You're going to leave me hanging like that?"

My smile widened.

"Let's just say it was an excellent night, especially the last five minutes."

Her smile widened as she stroked the side of my face.

"Then I'm glad to hear it. Maybe you can give me the details tomorrow?"

"Definitely."

"Good night, Jace."

"Good night, Aunt Cora."

I walked up to my room with Buddy at my heels and closed the door before I dropped face-first onto my bed. I rolled over and switched on my nightstand light when my phone lit up.

I saw it was a message from an unknown number, so I hesitated for a moment before opening it. Eventually, curiosity won out, and I read it.

> *Unknown: Thank you again for helping me tonight*
> *Unknown: It's Izzie BTW*
> *Unknown: Marcus gave me your number. I hope that was ok?*

A smile crept across my face as I thought about what to say. After I wasted time, starting and stopping many times, the phone chimed again.

> *Izzie: Goodnight, Jace.*

Speak stupid! I thought as I fought to think of a suitable response.

> *Jace: It was my pleasure.*

It was my pleasure… Seriously, that was the best I could think of?

> *Jace: All things considered, I had a great time.*

Ugh, that's not much better. What *all things*? Way to bring up her being attacked. God, I'm an idiot!

> *Izzie: My knight in shining armor.*

I felt my face flush, and my heart skipped a beat. The sensation felt as though a jolt of electricity had run through my body, which caused me to jump off the bed. Not expecting my quick movement, Buddy jumped off the bed, alert as though something was about to happen. As he watched me walk to the side window and realized there was no imminent danger, he snorted. Moving back to the bed, he resumed his previous position.

"Sorry, boy. I just—I wasn't expecting that."

Jace: Goodnight, Izzie.
Izzie: 😊

Putting my phone on my nightstand, I grabbed clothes to wear for the night. As I pulled my shirt off, I caught a whiff of the night's endeavors—sweat, wood smoke, and *fear?* Can you *smell* an emotion? I wondered.

I looked toward my bedroom door. The bathroom was only a few feet away, and I knew a shower would be a good option before calling it a night. I turned back toward my bed and weighed the options, finally deciding the smells were not strong enough to justify the need for a shower tonight. Pulling on a pair of blue plaid flannel pants and a green T-shirt, I climbed into bed and flipped off the light.

Lying in bed, I went through a recap of the night, reliving the roller coaster of emotions that went with it. As I thought about Izzie, I felt a plethora of emotions as I remembered the kiss at the end of the night. *My first kiss.* I was reveling in the feeling, but I soon felt a twinge of uneasiness build in my belly. My thoughts drifted back to the cave. She had been cowering…*from me?* Why had she looked so scared? I tossed uncomfortably in the bed, weighing the possibilities. Buddy lifted his head and whined at the movement. "Sorry, boy."

Trying to lie still, I recounted the evening. *Ethan* had her cornered and was about to do God knows what. That was what had frightened her…right? It seemed like a logical conclusion, but something was still gnawing at me. Her face. Did *I* scare her? I couldn't have! She had kissed me.

I rolled over in frustration to look at the window that faced her house. If I had scared her, she would have never kissed me, I told myself firmly. Rolling over onto my back, I stared at the ceiling. Buddy was becoming increasingly agitated with my movement. He let out a low grumble of disapproval, which caused me to chuckle as I pet his head.

My final thought was, *Go to sleep, Jace. You're overthinking things.*

The next morning, I woke to the sounds of voices coming from downstairs. I opened my eyes and looked at my nightstand, where my phone was charging. It told me it was 10:38 a.m. Placing my phone back down, I stretched deeply and enjoyed the feel of the few stray pops from my back. But when I tried to listen to the voices coming from downstairs, I realized they sounded tense.

I could see that Buddy was already up and by the door, emitting a low whimper. He seemed to be aware of the conversation happening downstairs and was equally bothered by it. I sat up and listened closer. Soon, I had picked up a third voice... It belonged to a man.

I threw my legs over the side of my bed and leaned closer, trying to hear what was being discussed. The smell of burning wood instantly assaulted my nose, causing me to recoil. *I really should have showered last night.* I was thinking when I heard Uncle Roman raising his voice. I stood up because I know it took a near-Herculean effort to push him to that point. Whoever was down there with him had succeeded at it.

I made my way to the door, trying not to alert anyone to me being awake yet. I looked at Buddy, who was now eager to get downstairs to investigate. I placed my finger over my mouth, willing him to be quiet. Not knowing the universal symbol for "be quiet," Buddy simply cocked his head to the side before looking back at the door. Slowly, I lifted the door handle. It made a very soft *click* as the handle released from the strike plate, and I froze.

Shhh! I muttered under my breath. The voices did not seem to stop, though. So I cautiously pulled the door open enough to hear better. As I did that, the room went silent.

"*Crap!*" I muttered under my breath.

From down below, I could hear the other man speak.

"Ah, he's finally up. How about we have him come down now to discuss this further?"

"I don't walk into your house and make demands on how you should raise your family. I would expect the same courtesy," Uncle Roman retorted.

What is going on down there? I thought.

Realizing they had caught me, I sighed and opened the door the rest of the way. I made my way toward the stairs, with Buddy close behind. As I passed the bathroom, I opted to take the opportunity and take care of pressing needs, right then. I had a feeling it was going to be harder to do so after I was downstairs.

Bladder empty, hands washed, and teeth brushed, I made my way for the stairs. At the bottom, I turned to head toward the family room.

Aunt Cora was, again, in the sectional's corner while Uncle Roman was standing next to the built-in fireplace. His arm was resting on the hearth, and he was keeping his head down. The other guy was sitting in Uncle Roman's recliner. I stopped short and stared. No one ever sat there, but my uncle.

I felt my back stiffen at the sight, and Buddy let out a low growl in response to the change in my posture. Hearing his response, I was finally able to move again, and I put my hand on his head and petted him. Not knowing what Buddy may do to an actual stranger in the house, I pulled him closer to my leg and tried to calm him.

When I had walked into the room, Aunt Cora had sat up a bit without moving too much. Buddy's growl and her movement, however, were enough to make Uncle Roman look up, and he met my eyes.

The other man did not move and waited for me to enter and sit down on the couch. Looking at our guest, I could see that he was a middle-aged man with dark hair. His tanned skin looked to be approaching a leathery consistency, probably due to constant sun exposure. He was wearing a dark green uniform and a silver star on his left arm with the words Williston PD surrounding it.

His left leg was loosely crossed over his right. Leaning back in the chair, slightly rocking it, he was flipping through a small pad of paper. This man exuded power and an air of superiority. He seemed used to getting whatever he wanted. My uncle was also used to getting what he wanted. But Uncle Roman used a much better approach toward people than whoever this person was.

"I'm glad to see you could finally join us, son. My host felt it unnecessary to wake you up earlier to talk."

I looked to Uncle Roman and could see the contempt he had on his face.

"Jace this is—" he began.

Raising a hand to my uncle, the man interjected, "My name is Wesley Powell, and I am the sheriff of Williston. I have a few questions for you regarding an *incident* last night."

I looked to Uncle Roman, and he nodded for me to continue.

"Were you at a party last night?" asked the sheriff.

"Yes…I mean, yes, sir."

Sheriff Powell raised an eyebrow and nodded approvingly. "I wasn't expecting manners, but I'm glad you proved me wrong. I'm also glad to see you're not a liar."

My uncle's eyes widened to the point of showing nearly all the whites of them.

"Do you make it a habit of insulting people when you enter their homes?" Uncle Roman retorted.

Sheriff Powell looked up briefly at Uncle Roman, the corner of his mouth rose, but he didn't say anything before looking back at me.

"I can still smell the wood smoke on him."

Uncle Roman stood up tall at the accusation. "He would not lie—"

Sheriff Powell lifted his hand and my uncle stopped talking.

"Where were you last night?" the sheriff asked.

"I-I'm not sure. We just moved here, and I don't know all the locations."

"Interesting. Didn't your parents teach you to familiarize yourself with a location before going there?"

Sheriff Powell looked over to Aunt Cora. "You wouldn't want your momma to worry her pretty little head over you."

He winked at her after he said it. Aunt Cora shifted her face, showing the barest hint of disgust.

Seeing her discomfort, I tried to bring his attention back onto me.

"We were at the grotto last night."

The sheriff shifted his gaze back to me. He raised an eyebrow and nodded his head slightly.

"Who else was with you?"

"I don't really know all the people because I don't attend the school here. But I went with my neighbors. The Lewis girls from next door, and Marcus Hunter from across the street."

The sheriff made a few notes on his pad, stopping momentarily to continue asking questions, purposely not looking in my direction.

"Were you in an altercation of any sort last night?"

Uncle Roman's back straightened, which caused me to do the same. Buddy, again, picked up on it and began growling once more and I attempted to reshift my energy to calm him. The sheriff stopped writing to look at me, then at Buddy.

"That dog won't be a problem, will it?"

"No, sir. He just doesn't know who you are and is being protective."

"I'm not stupid, son. I know what it is doing. I just want to know if I'm going to be putting a dog down today."

My heart stopped at his words, and I stared blankly at him. Then I saw Uncle Roman, whose eyes had gone wide again.

"Cora, why don't you put Buddy in our room for now," he said in a quiet voice.

"Yes, that may be best," Aunt Cora agreed.

Standing up, she called Buddy to her and walked him toward her room.

Initially, he hesitated, but eventually, he walked to the room without further incident. Only whining and barking could be heard once he was on the other side of the door.

"Now where were we? Ah, yes. Were you in an altercation of any sort last night?"

I looked back to Uncle Roman.

"Son, he's not going to give you the answers. It is a simple yes or no," the sheriff said.

Anger flared in Uncle Roman's face. He closed his eyes and squeezed his hands into tight fists at his sides, and within a few breaths, the stress seemed to leak from him. After he opened his eyes, he nodded at me to continue talking.

"I'm not sure what you would call an altercation, but I did have to step in to help someone in trouble."

"You're gonna have to be a bit more specific. You see, funny enough, I wasn't there."

By this point, every law-and-order episode was running through my head. Why had he not brought me "in for questioning?" I didn't know how long he had been here this morning. So I was unsure if they had discussed something to keep me out of the local jail. As I considered this, the more agitated I became. I did nothing wrong! Why wasn't he talking to Ethan? *He* was the villain last night. I was the "knight in shining armor," according to Izzie. Thinking of her helped to calm me momentarily, allowing me to think more coherently through his questions.

"There was a girl whom another guy had cornered. She seemed scared, and this guy was *not* taking the hint. So I pulled him away from her and helped her to get out of the situation."

"And that is *all* that happened?"

"Well, he wasn't happy that I had stepped in. After I got the girl away from him, he tried to hit me. I hit him first, which caused him to fall in the grotto."

"Was this the only altercation you had with this other youth?"

"No. He had attacked me earlier in the day when I was eating at the Burgerporium."

My uncle's eyebrows rose. When he looked at me, I half shrugged at him with a weak attempt at a smile.

The sheriff's eyebrow lifted as he tilted his head forward.

"That's interesting. You had a fight with this youth in the afternoon and then another fight on the same day. Son, you either have bad luck, or there is more to this story."

My uncle is one of the calmest people I have ever met. However, I could see that even he was seriously losing his patience. As though it was contagious, I could also feel the anger rising in me. Sheriff Powell seemed to notice the change and swiveled slowly in his chair to look at me more closely. Aunt Cora saw the sheriff's glance and turned in my direction. Her eyes widened, and she gasped slightly, causing me to break my stare down with the sheriff. I turned to her to determine what had caused her distress.

"Interesting," Sheriff Powell mused, letting the word roll off his tongue. "Very interesting."

Uncle Roman looking at me, quickly turned and stared at our guest. "Is my nephew in trouble at this point?"

Sheriff Powell turned to look at Uncle Roman.

"No trouble…yet. Just getting information at this point."

Fury ran through my veins as I said, "Maybe you should ask Ethan Campbell for more information!"

Sheriff Powell smiled half-heartedly at me and finally stood. He put his hat back on and tipped it at Uncle Roman and Aunt Cora.

"I think I have enough information. I'll be in touch if I need anything further."

Uncle Roman looked relieved that the sheriff was finally leaving and escorted the officer to the front door. As they neared the kitchen, Sheriff Powell halted and turned to look at the three of us.

"Your nephew, huh? Funny, I thought he was your son."

Taken aback by the comment, I watched Uncle Roman swallow visibly. However, he stood his ground, staring with the same intensity as the sheriff.

"Jace's parents died in a car accident when he was three. We have been his family since then."

Sheriff Powell seemed to weigh the information in his head, nodding slightly. He smiled at Uncle Roman and asked, "Three years old, you say. They died around, what, 2008 to 2009?"

Uncle Roman shifted slightly at the question. "Yes, 2008. But seeing that Jace's parentage is not in question, we would like to enjoy the rest of our Sunday. So if you wouldn't mind."

Uncle Roman motioned toward the front door.

Sheriff Powell looked back at us and tipped his hat at Aunt Cora and me, again. Then smiling at Uncle Roman as he passed, he said, "I'm sure we'll be in touch."

"We will help with questions relating to your current investigation if we can. Have a good day, Sheriff."

As he disappeared with Uncle Roman down the hallway, I turned to look at Aunt Cora.

"What? Why did you gasp?"

She smiled. "I'm sorry, sweetie. I-I could see you were getting angry. I was nervous you were going to say or do something."

By this time, Buddy was scratching feverishly, and barking so loudly I thought he was going to come through the door. Aunt Cora frowned. "I think you can let Buddy out now," she said.

I looked back, and Uncle Roman was now standing in the kitchen. He had his hands on either door of the refrigerator while he hung his head between them.

"Is it safe to ask what is going on?" I asked.

Uncle Roman sighed before turning to me.

"Jace, is that all that happened last night?"

I felt knots raveling and unraveling in my belly as I tried to go back through the night's events in my mind. *I did nothing wrong! I protected Izzie!* was all I could think.

No longer distracted by the sheriff, I could now see that Aunt Cora's eyes were swollen and red. She had been crying.

"What did *he* tell you happened?"

I felt my eyes burning as I realized this man had upset her so much.

"Aunt Cora, you saw me come in last night. If there had been something wrong, don't you think you would have known?"

The corner of her lips raised slightly as she looked at me. "I know, Jace."

"He said *you* attacked someone last night, a girl," Uncle Roman said.

"What?" I jumped off the couch and stared at them both in disbelief. Buddy began jumping up and barking next to me.

"That is *not* what happened! You heard what I said. There were a ton of people there who could vouch for me. Aunt Cora, Uncle Roman, please!"

I looked pleadingly back and forth between the two of them. I could only see the concern mounting in their faces.

"Okay, fine. Who did he say I attacked?"

"A girl named Lyndsay."

"WHAT?" Again, my voice sounded strained under the insanity of the accusation.

Uncle Roman walked toward me. Stopping a few inches from me, he placed his hands on my shoulders. He still had an inch or two on me, so he could easily look me in the eye as he spoke.

"You are as much my son as if had you been born biologically to us. We promised your parents that we would protect you and help you grow into a strong and competent man. With that promise and our love for you, I *will* protect you with every ounce of strength and power I have. But to do so, I need to know *everything* that happened yesterday."

His eyes were heavy with concern, and I could feel the burn of tears fighting their way to the surface in mine again. I looked back at Aunt Cora, who sat with her hand covering her mouth. She rose from the couch and reached forward for me...for us.

Within two strides, she had met us and pulled us both into an embrace. Feeling the warmth of their love, I felt a single tear I had been fighting defiantly drop, and I quickly tried to wipe it away. As I pulled back, I looked at both and nodded. Then I gave them as best a recount of the day, and night, as I could.

By the end of the story, Uncle Roman was sitting in his chair, rocking in contemplation. Aunt Cora was on the couch. Feeling the anger and frustration of the morning's events hit me anew, I found it difficult to sit still. So I was pacing the room.

At the completion of the story, Aunt Cora smiled and spoke softly, "Your first kiss!"

Uncle Roman looked over to her. "Cora, please. We have bigger things going on right now."

He looked back at me and must have seen my smile that had started by Aunt Cora's words fade to a frown. Without further hesitation, he stood and walked over. He put his arm around me, patting me on the shoulder, and said, "No, she's right. It *is* a big deal. You were a gentleman?"

I felt a flush of heat rise in my cheeks. But I smiled, even while finding it hard to meet his eyes.

"Yes, sir."

Aunt Cora playfully hit Uncle Roman in the chest. "Of course he was!"

Smiling, he pulled me into a hug. "That's my boy."

From the middle of our impromptu embrace, I could hear "Crazy Frog" playing from inside my pocket.

Uncle Roman pulled back and raised an eyebrow. "Marcus really has an interesting sense of humor."

I laughed. "Do you mind if I take this to the other room?"

Uncle Roman smiled and nodded toward the kitchen.

I answered the phone as I walked. "Hey, man, what's up?"

"Dude, you ready for the party tonight?"

I stopped short of the kitchen, unsure what party Marcus had gotten us invited to now.

"Ha-ha. Don't tell me. It's at the Blue Grotto."

After a brief pause, he said, "Yeah…that's where Izzie said, right?" Marcus answered, confusion in his tone.

Once again, my momentum seized. This time, I looked back, meeting Aunt Cora's eyes. She was still hugging my uncle but gently pulled away from him to look more closely at me. Her eyes narrowed as she tried to interpret what was being said. Uncle Roman, seeing Aunt Cora's face, turned to look at me.

"Are you serious, Marcus?"

There was silence on the other end of the phone.

"Marcus, we were at that party last night."

"I mean, last night was kind of like a party, but it was just dinner with our families."

I pulled the phone away to look at it before I put it back to my ear.

"I feel like I'm in an episode of the *Twilight Zone*. *That party* was two nights ago. Last night was at the grotto. The fight with Ethan? The ride home? Izzie?"

Silence fell on the other line, and I looked back at Aunt Cora and Uncle Roman. Finally, Marcus said, "That sounds like an epic party. Hopefully, tonight's is just as amazing."

Unsure if Marcus was playing with me, if I had dreamed it, or if I had, in fact, stepped into the twilight zone, I tried to play along.

"Okay…what time is the party?"

"Izzie said 8:00 p.m. You want to go into town today before the party? There's that great burger joint I want to take you to."

I felt my legs getting weak, and I had to sit on one of the stools positioned next to the island in the kitchen. Around this time, my aunt and uncle had come around too.

"Uh, sure. Let me check with my family first. I'll call you back."

"Sweet! I'll talk to you later. I want to head over there around 1:30 p.m., okay?"

"Sure thing."

As I hung up with Marcus, I stared at my phone in disbelief. I could feel two sets of eyes on me, and I looked up to meet them. Unsure what was real and what was not real, I needed reassurance from the only two people I would trust with my life.

"What happened last night?" I asked in a near whisper.

Aunt Cora's eyes widened. "You went to a party with Izzie, her sisters, and Marcus."

I was unsure if I wanted to laugh or cry at her response. What escaped sounded like a mixture of both.

"So I'm not losing my mind. I'm not sure if Marcus is playing with me or not. He just reinvited me to that party again. Actually, to the same *day* again!"

Looking back at my phone, I remembered the texts I had received from Izzie last night. As I frantically flipped through the text messages, I felt my heart sinking.

"They're not here!"

"What's not there?" Aunt Cora asked.

"Izzie texted me last night. I didn't delete her texts, but they're not here!"

My heart was pounding in my chest, and I began to second-guess everything that had happened up until now. Fear thundering through my being, I looked to my aunt and uncle for balance.

Aunt Cora closed her eyes and looked at the ceiling. When she opened them again, she looked to Uncle Roman.

"We can't hide from this anymore."

"Hide from *what* anymore?" I asked, feeling as though the room was spinning slightly.

Uncle Roman drew his eyebrows in and opened his mouth to speak. That was when we heard a loud bang from the front door, which caused us all to look in its direction. Raising a finger to his lips, Uncle Roman walked toward the front door, looking through the glass before he opened it.

"Lill—" he started when she cut him off.

"Sorry, Roman. Where's Jace?"

He turned to look down the hall back at Aunt Cora and me, as Aunt Lilly barreled past him.

"There you are! Mister, you have been up to some mischief!"

CHAPTER 14

The Truth Revealed

Uncle Roman looked shocked by Aunt Lilly's accusation. Then willing to play the game, he didn't stop her as she blew past him and into the house.

"Please, come in, Lilly," he said belatedly.

"Are you aware of what is going on outside?" Aunt Lilly retorted.

Now back in the kitchen behind Aunt Lilly, Uncle Roman shrugged and said, "We have been inside all morning, so no."

Aunt Lilly walked over to me and took my face in her hands. She turned it this way and that as though examining it for some dirt that needed scrubbing.

I jokingly said, "I did wash this morning."

She stopped moving my face to look me in the eye with obvious irritation in hers.

"I'm trying to see if *you* caused this or if someone caused this *through* you."

I grabbed her gently by the arms and pulled her hands off my face.

"I think I missed something. Can you try to start from the beginning?" I asked.

"Marcus just came in to tell me about the 'weird phone call' you two just had. When he told me its context, I knew that there was an issue. So I came over right away."

I wasn't sure whether I should have felt better or more freaked out, so I settled for watching her pace back and forth, rubbing her forehead as she did.

"*The Twilight Zone*?" I asked.

"Hmm?" She stopped momentarily to look at me before realization crossed her face.

"Oh, yes. I guess that analogy would work," Aunt Lilly answered.

"So then *you* remember everything that had happened yesterday?" I asked.

"Of course, I do," she answered.

Uncle Roman lifted his eyebrows as he stared at her.

She looked at the other adults. "How about you two?"

They nodded simultaneously.

Confused, I asked, "Why are *we* the only four who seem to remember?"

Aunt Lilly turned to regard me, and her gaze seemed to bore through to my soul. After that intense stare-down, she asked, "Jace, when is your birthday?"

"Tomorrow, why?"

"You're going to be fifteen, right?"

"Yes…"

The room fell silent, as though everyone was contemplating the same thing.

"Can someone please explain what is going on!" I exclaimed.

Aunt Lilly smiled and looked at Aunt Cora and Uncle Roman.

"He has no idea about who he is? What he is?" she asked in an accusatory tone. Then seeming to rethink her approach, she asked, "Do either of you know?"

Confused, I turned to look at my guardians.

"What is going on? Someone speak. Now!" I demanded.

Uncle Roman closed his eyes and nodded slightly to Aunt Lilly. My aunt grabbed my hands, causing me to turn to look at her.

"Jace, *we* remember what happened yesterday because magic doesn't affect us. At least this kind of magic."

I pulled my hands out of hers and stood up from my bench so forcefully that I toppled it. Uncle Roman stepped back to avoid a direct collision. Buddy, who had been at my feet, jumped up and barked when the chair barely missed hitting him. I continued to back away from the trio until I was standing in the center of the family room.

Aunt Cora slowly approached me, but Buddy blocked her from getting any closer. As she turned to look back at Uncle Roman, a small twinkle of light at her throat caught my eye. It was the small half-moon, half-sun pendant she wore around her neck. Uncle Roman had bought it for her when they had married. He had promised to "give her the best of both worlds" if she would have him.

For as long as I could remember, she had always worn that charm. She noticed me looking and clasped it in her hand. Then she gave me a pleading look, prompting me to say, "What is going on? You two have never given off a creepy vibe before, but you're thoroughly freaking me out now."

Uncle Roman made his way to me and lightly touched Aunt Cora's shoulder as he passed her. Buddy growled, and my uncle stopped moving, glancing down at the dog. I petted Buddy to calm him but allowed him to maintain his position between us.

Standing opposite me, Uncle Roman had an intense look in his eyes. He looked as though he believed he would never see me—as if he wanted to take in all the features of my face and memorize them.

"You have brought Cora and me more joy than you could ever imagine. I want you to remember that everything we have ever done has always been for you."

He reached out cautiously and grabbed my hand, giving it a reassuring squeeze. I felt as though the air was becoming scarce, and it seemed the floor was about to fall out from underneath me. Aunt Cora must have guessed how I was feeling and leaned toward me, placing her hand on my back encouragingly.

Still pacing, Aunt Lilly asked from the kitchen, "What exactly happened this morning?"

Uncle Roman spoke without taking his gaze off me.

"Sheriff Powell came by to question Jace about a fight from last night with another boy. I think you said his name was Ethan?"

I nodded, and Aunt Lilly let out a forced sigh. With a dramatic nod of her head, she said, "*Now* it makes sense. It's a protection spell!" she said.

We all looked at Aunt Lilly.

"I take it none of you know who Sheriff Powell *really* is?"

Without an answer, verbal or otherwise, she continued, "Our friendly neighborhood sheriff is both the uncle of Ethan Campbell and the alpha of the Devil's Den Pack."

It was now my turn to laugh. Even as I did, I looked around the room and saw no one else was doing the same.

"Wait, are you serious?"

Again, there was silence as the three adults stared at me.

"You're telling me that there are werewolves? That's what an alpha is, right?"

Aunt Lilly nodded. "Jace, there are many things that are real and hide out in the open. Werewolves are just *one* of them."

The color in Aunt Cora's face drained as she covered her mouth and touched Uncle Roman's arm.

"Oh my god! He knows. He'll tell," Aunt Cora said in a near whisper.

"We can't keep doing this, Cora. It's obviously time."

Turning, Uncle Roman moved to sit on the edge of his chair. For the first time, he looked defeated. He dropped his head into his hands and ran his fingers back and forth through his hair and after a few moments looked up.

"When he came this morning, he told us there was an altercation last night. That Jace was being accused of attacking a girl named Lyndsay. We knew there was no way he would ever—could ever hurt someone. We also needed to get more information before we woke him up. As far as the sheriff was concerned, however, Jace was as good as guilty. He actually seemed ready to take Jace away in cuffs!"

Uncle Roman gritted his teeth together as he punched his leg.

"He definitely neglected that small piece of information about his nephew."

I watched, unsure what to say or do. I could feel my mouth go dry and my head began to spin again. I sat back on the couch and closed my eyes.

At that same time, the clock on the opposite wall began spinning and chiming wildly. Aunt Lilly saw it and rushed over to kneel in front of me.

"Oh no. You're like a loose cannon right now. Come back to me, Jace. Look at me."

Aunt Lilly forcefully grabbed my face again.

"Open your eyes, NOW. Look at me," she demanded.

I cautiously opened them and saw the sternness in what was usually a jovial face. The stark contrast forced me to find my balance. As I did, the clock also slowed.

Aunt Lilly's features softened as she sat back on her heels.

"Yeah, kiddo. You did that. I'd venture a guess you've been creating quite a bit of chaos for years."

Aunt Cora chuckled, "Yeah, *the ghost.*"

I numbly looked at Aunt Cora. It felt as though a chasm was opening in my chest and I was going to be sucked into myself. Aunt Lilly frowned as she watched me.

"What's wrong?" she asked.

"I just—I just always thought…" My words trailed off as a tear dropped.

"That it was them?" Uncle Roman asked.

I nodded but wouldn't look up to see his face. My eyes were fixated on the intricate pattern of the rug in front of me.

"How did *you* know?" I asked Aunt Lilly.

"Mary tipped me off, initially, when she told me about the table. But you confirmed it when I met you. You have an aura that others like us can see."

I lifted my head to look at her, unsure if I heard her right.

"What do you mean, others like *us?*"

She smiled softly. "Witches. You haven't been receiving preparation training, so you likely can't see with your witch's eye, but we can fix that!"

The silence between us was deafening. The longer it lasted, the more I wanted to run out of the house. Buddy, who was now curled up next to me on the couch, laid his head on my lap, licking my hand till I pet him.

"So are you ready to talk about all this?" Aunt Lilly asked Aunt Cora and Uncle Roman.

"I had hoped for a less dramatic way to help him, but here we are. To fix this, I think we will all need to be on the same page. Don't you agree?" Aunt Lilly urged.

Uncle Roman seemed to consider her question and nodded in agreement.

"How much do you remember of your life…before?" He looked at me, his words trailing off.

"My life before? Before what?" I asked.

"Before you came to live with us?" he continued.

I stared at him, feeling anger building at the question. Then came more anger at the way he had phrased the question.

"Why? You never want to talk about that. Why now?" I asked, the fierceness in my voice clear to all around.

Aunt Cora looked at her husband before she answered, "Because we were unsure what would happen if you lingered on it for too long."

I stared at her for a while, unsure what to say or think, but remembered a few days earlier when I had fallen off the bed in a trancelike state when I focused on my parents for too long. Hoping for more help, I turned to Aunt Lilly. She was still kneeling in front of me with her hands folded on her lap, listening intently and analyzed them as much as I was.

"Which parent had the powers?" she asked my guardians.

Aunt Cora laughed and walked to the kitchen.

"I'm not sure that was a funny question, Cora," Aunt Lilly argued.

Opening a bottle of water and taking a long drink, my aunt said, "They both did. But each had *unique* abilities."

Aunt Lilly frowned before turning to look at Uncle Roman for clarification.

He stood and walked over to the fireplace before he turned toward us.

"I think we need to explain what is going on from the beginning."

He sighed heavily as he contemplated his words carefully.

"Jace, I need you to hear me out before you ask too many questions, okay?" he asked.

I stared nonplussed at him before nodding, still not sure what I was about to hear.

He seemed to stare off as he began to speak. "There are many species of beings in the world. Witches, goblins, trolls, fairies, demons, werewolves, you name it. To be honest, they base most fairy tales on real beings."

He stopped to let me digest that deluge of information. Believing that I was ready to take in more, he continued, "Most species stayed within the same species, but occasionally, there would be an inter-species relationship. The majority of such cases escaped notice. It was the same with your mom and dad…at first. If those couples didn't draw any attention to themselves, no one particularly cared what they did. An important thing to note is that most species cannot have children of their own. If they wanted one, they would either steal one or conceive one with a human, then steal the baby. For centuries this held true. The only ones that seemed capable of having children were the witches."

He took another pause before he continued.

"A long time ago, there was a child born of a witch and were-wolf. The offspring became extremely dangerous with the amount of power it had, both physical and metaphysical. It terrorized the countryside for decades and was, eventually, killed. After that, a council of supernatural beings was set up to ensure no fae would conceive such a supernatural child ever again. To make certain of this, an extremely powerful group of fae created a spell that made the conception of children between a witch and any other supernatural being impossible."

Uncle Roman paused, and Aunt Cora picked up where he had left off.

"Your mom and dad, however, pulled off the impossible with you. As soon as they realized your mom was pregnant, they went into hiding. We had known your parents for a very long time and followed them. They successfully kept the pregnancy and the first three years of your life hidden with the help of a cloaking spell your mom used. It was around that time your dad's people called him back. The fear of how they would explain you became more and more real."

Confused, I held up a hand.

"Are you telling me I am part witch, part werewolf?"

Aunt Cora and Uncle Roman exchanged glances before he answered, "In a word, yes. But you are so much more than that."

His words hit me like a sledgehammer, and I had to walk to keep my mind from short-circuiting on what they were trying to tell me. If this is how they would keep me from asking questions about my parents, then so be it—I don't need to know. But why are they being so cruel and taunting me with such a fantastical story? Seeing no other option but to hear them out, I decided to try to follow them through their fairy tale.

"But she was using a cloaking spell. Wouldn't that have hidden me?"

Aunt Cora's smile grew but never quite hit her eyes.

"Magical beings *know* other magical beings. Some sense it like a sixth sense. Others can smell it. But we all know when one is near."

"Wait, *we*?" I asked.

Aunt Cora looked at Uncle Roman as though asking for permission. He took a deep breath and motioned for her to continue.

"Yes, *we* are fairies, or fae for short. Over the years, fae has grown to cover all supernatural beings, though. My people are Astrial, and your uncle is a Solarian. People commonly refer to us as sun and moon fairies. An unlikely pair, but we have been balancing each other for almost 150 years."

I stared at her for what seemed to be an eternity before turning back to Aunt Lilly for confirmation.

"I think it is safe to say, we all knew we were not your run-of-the-mill humans when we first met. My sister knows what I am, but Marcus does not. Mary is afraid of what other people's reactions might be if they knew. I think her ex-husband's reaction has skewed her thinking. Now she hides it and wants me to hide it as well."

"What about Marcus? Is he—?"

She smiled as she looked down before she answered.

"He's an intuitive lad. I think he knows something is afoot with me but can't quite put his finger on it. Is he…gifted? Yes. That boy is gifted in many ways, but not magically. But I think we are getting off track. Roman."

Uncle Roman continued his story, "Your dad was not high-ranking in his pack, which meant he had to follow orders. The important thing to understand is that he could not lie to them. His particular breed can smell out a lie from a mile away, and your dad knew it. So if someone realized that there was a child and asked him directly, he would have to tell the truth. That was when we devised a plan that we ultimately acted upon.

If your dad felt he was in danger of revealing you, he would let us know. We were to disappear with you and not let either of your parents know where we had gone. As I said, he cannot lie and would have had to tell his leader. So not knowing where you were was the only way to make this work."

His words struck me in the core of my being at the realization of what he was saying. I felt as though the air had been sucked out of the room as I looked at him. I prayed that he was not about to tell me my life had been a lie. That my parents were alive and well. My breathing became erratic as I tried to process the possibility, wondering if I wanted to hear the remainder of the story or not. How many nights had I lain in my bed wondering about them, imagining their faces, their voices…them! No, I needed to know. My fear was now for my potential kidnappers and their fate after this revelation. Attempting to stay calm, I slowed my breathing and looked to Uncle Roman.

"The plan was acted on, then? That means that he told you that they knew, and I was in danger?"

Uncle Roman and Aunt Cora both glanced at each other before turning back to me, concern apparent in their eyes.

Aunt Lilly, sensing my question, held my hand.

"Let's hear them out before we jump to conclusions."

Uncle Roman took a deep breath before he continued talking.

"Your mom created a link with you that would activate if, and when, you needed it. She said it would energize when you are around the coven age of fifteen. That it would show you how to use your powers when the time was right. Fortunately, she gave us a starting point. She said remembering *them* would help."

Uncle Roman stopped and watched me. Thoughts and emotions were racing through my head, and I was having trouble focusing on one. Aunt Cora must have sensed the inner monologue running laps through my head as I tried to process the unbelievable story they were giving me. She sat on the arm of the couch and grasped my hand in hers.

"They loved you so much that they let you go so you could live. We are not sure what exactly would have happened, but we all feared someone would try to kill you."

My head calmed, and I took a deep breath, finally realizing that they had left out an important detail. I turned and looked at Uncle Roman, who stood stoically with one arm resting on the fireplace. His head was slightly lowered, as though he was unable to look me directly in the face.

Our eyes met, and I took another deep breath as I asked the question that was hanging heavily in the room.

"Where are they? Where are my parents?"

The corner of his lips went up, and he chuckled. "The million-dollar question, huh?"

I waited for his response, never dropping my gaze. I was half hoping that he would tell me the cemetery they were buried in and fearing that he wouldn't.

Aunt Cora walked over to where Uncle Roman was. He pulled her close to him as he answered.

"We don't know, Jace."

His words hit me like a semi. Instantly, it felt as though I was sinking in quicksand, my chest being compressed, not allowing the air to pass freely through my lungs. He watched my reaction, not

185

changing his position. I waited for four heartbeats, allowing the panic to subdue before I spoke again.

"They're alive?" I whispered, unable to pull anything stronger from my vocal cords.

Aunt Lilly's eyes were like saucers as she took in Uncle Roman and me.

"As far as we know, yes," Uncle Roman said.

In those six words, my entire world shattered into a thousand pieces. Everything I thought to be true became a lie. I looked to the people whom I had thought of as my safe havens, my rocks. Everything had changed, and I felt nothing but betrayed.

Instantly, I wanted to get away from them and run as far and as fast as I could. My parents were out there! I had twelve years' worth of life to tell them about. Twelve years of hugs and kisses, stories, catches, and running to do. My eyes burned from the tears that fell like rain as I felt the loss of my parents all over again.

"How could you?" I said through gritted teeth.

The same clock flew across the room and shattered against the wall behind Aunt Lilly. Its sudden movement caused all of us to jump. She turned to see it and slowly nodded. "Appropriate thing to break, Jace."

Clearing her throat, she looked back at me.

"This is a lot of information to take in. I know it is upsetting you, but listen to what is being said. All four of them devised this plan with the intention of you rejoining with your parents in the future. They did it to protect you."

Aunt Cora reached out briefly from Uncle Roman but did not move from her position. Tears were running down her cheeks. I turned away from her and looked at the broken clock on the floor instead.

While I tried to process the torrent of information they had given me, something new stood out.

"Didn't you say that the 'abomination' was a witch-werewolf combination?"

Aunt Cora sensed the agitation rising in me. She began walking toward me but halted suddenly. Then slowly backed up toward

Uncle Roman. The oddity of her reaction caused Aunt Lilly to look at me. As I turned around, her eyes went wide, and she sat back.

"What?"

Aunt Lilly answered, "Your eyes... They're red."

I turned to Aunt Cora and Uncle Roman.

"Has it ever happened before?" Aunt Lilly asked.

"When Sheriff Powell was here, I think he saw it too because he seemed to have a newfound interest in you after," Aunt Cora said.

Aunt Lilly seemed to ponder it a few minutes.

"It wouldn't surprise me if there are other colors that come through. But red is a shocking color to see because it is not common."

My heart sank as I thought back to the story again, and I dropped my head.

"*You* are not an abomination," Uncle Roman said in a quiet but certain voice.

Silence swept the room, and everyone focused on me.

"So what happened to them? My mom and dad. Where were they?"

"We're not entirely sure. Your dad called me the night we left. He said Daegen, his pack leader, knew and was heading to your house. We didn't know how much time we had. We just knew we had to leave. So we grabbed you and anything we could, and...we left," Uncle Roman said.

"All the moving?" I asked.

"Whenever we felt someone was figuring things out," he answered.

I stared at the three of them for a long while. Then I thought back to all the times I had wanted to talk about my parents. I'd want to learn more about them, only to get no answers. But now I had them and a way to see them again.

Unsure what other options I had, I agreed to play their weird game.

"What do I have to do?" I asked.

"We're not entirely sure. Your mom said that you would have help when the time came. She also said thinking about them would get you started."

I looked to Aunt Lilly, who lifted the corner of her lip in a lop-sided smile.

"I guess your mom meant me. Memories hold tremendous power, so remembering would make sense," Aunt Lilly said.

"I remember most of it in bits and pieces. Nothing specific. It's like trying to remember a movie you saw years ago. You have the essence of the plot but can't remember the exact order or all the characters in it."

Aunt Lilly moved closer to me again. "Jace, I want you to remember *them*."

"I don't know how!" I said, aggravated.

Understanding in her face, she nodded.

"Let's start with the last night you saw them and go back from there. What do you remember?"

I felt a lump forming in my throat and struggled to find the strength to create words.

"Pain."

"Okay. That's a start. Do you remember anything else?" Uncle Roman asked encouragingly.

I closed my eyes and said through gritted teeth, "For twelve years, this has been off-limits in this house and *now* you want me to remember everything!"

Uncle Roman's eyes dropped with a flush to his cheeks.

"You're right to be mad with us, but we need your help right now. Sheriff Powell will figure out who you are if he hasn't already. He will tell Daegen. They will come for you," Aunt Cora said.

"There is also the minor problem with the *amnesia* spell, which we think you cast. If you did, it means that your powers are emerging. It's just that we don't know how to help you with them. Lilly is a close second, being a witch herself. Even so, we need to find your parents, in particular, your mom right now. Startup the link she created. Once we get you to them, they will know what to do," Uncle Roman added.

The familiar burn of tears formed, and I fought to keep them from falling. As I struggled to center myself, I opened my eyes and turned toward the two people who had been my parents for the past twelve years. They were who I had come to when I had had night-mares. My aunt and uncle were also the ones who taught me how to read and write and to ride a bike.

I felt the lump in my throat growing again and dread growing in my belly. It was as though I had somehow known this conversation was coming. Aunt Cora had a steady stream of tears actively flowing from her eyes. Uncle Roman stood like an unflappable force of nature.

"Jace, we still love you. We are still the same people and family you have always known. Just as I told you before, we are helping you grow into the man you are to become," he said.

Through tears, Aunt Cora added, "Please, Jace, trust us."

After a pause that seemed to last years, I finally answered them.

"I remember hearing the phone ring. Seeing you both in the hallway. Aunt Cora was crying. At the time, I didn't know what was happening. I just knew it was bad."

Uncle Roman made a small noise of affirmation.

"What about before that?" Aunt Lilly asked.

Initially, I had closed my eyes to keep the tears from falling, but eventually I opened them to focus on my aunt and uncle. Without warning, my vision narrowed, and I felt myself drift like I was entering a dream while still awake.

As I thought more about that night, I could feel a pull. It was as though something was trying to release a lock to a chamber that had been sealed shut. Trying to open this part of my memory met resistance. Something kept dragging me away from viewing my thoughts and memories fully.

Time seemed to lapse. As I focused harder on the locked memory, I felt like I was being wrapped up in a canvas of white. Immediately, my senses sharpened, and I began seeing a figure taking shape. Aunt Cora's gasp in the distance ripped my senses back to our family room, and I lost the image in my head.

All I could see was my aunt looking at me with her hands over her mouth.

"For Christ's sake, Cora!" Uncle Roman roared.

"I'm sorry—I just…"

His face relaxed as he pulled her into an embrace.

"No, I'm sorry. We're all on edge right now. I should not have yelled at you. There is no excuse. But we need to keep our feelings and emotions in check if we're going to help him."

Aunt Cora nodded. He leaned down and gently kissed her forehead, then came and sat next to me on the arm of the chair and patted me on my shoulder.

Aunt Lilly held my hands.

"Use my strength if you need it. You'll know how to do it if the need arises."

"It's okay, Jace. You saw something, right?" Uncle Roman asked.

"I-I'm not sure. I *think* I did."

"Okay, good. Let's try to work off that," Aunt Lilly said.

I tried to relax by slowing my breathing. With the strength and support of Aunt Lilly, I could feel my shoulders relaxing as the energy within me shifted, and I finally closed my eyes again.

Once the swaying of the room seemed to still, I felt more in control. I tried to remember that night again. As though on cue, I could feel the blanket of white engulfing me once more. This time, it came as a sensation, which started at my feet and worked its way up and around me. It was like a vine, advancing to anchor me inside it this time as opposed to suffocating me.

Shaking off the initial panic, I allowed myself to calm. Soon, I could see small fragments of something, perhaps colors which became clearer as pictures rose to the surface.

Relaxing into the scenes unfolding in front of me, I spoke, "I remember you both talking and seeing Aunt Cora crying. I cannot remember the content of the conversation."

Suddenly it felt as though someone hit the rewind button causing the scene to rapidly change. I gripped Aunt Lilly's hands hard for fear I would fly away if I let go.

"I see you both in the living room snuggled on the couch and talking to each other while you watch the fire. The phone is ringing. Uncle Roman is answering it. His face is changing from content to contempt. He is turning and is looking at Aunt Cora. Her eyes are wide, and she appears concerned."

Once more, the scene shifted violently, and it felt as though I was being yanked forward, causing me to grip Aunt Lilly again. Examining this scene, though, I caught my breath.

"I-I see my dad. He's lying on the floor with me. I think we're playing a game."

I tried to focus on the picture and could see my dad had on an ill-formed paper hat and he was wearing an eye patch.

"We were playing pirates, I think."

A warmth washed over me and I could feel the tears forming as I watched the scene.

Captain, we need to secure the boats to bring the treasure back aboard.

Argh! We go now.

Okay, Captain!

A feeling of joy and laughter filled me as I watched him lift me in the air and spin me around. Looking to the left, I could see another figure walking toward the room.

"It's...my mom."

As she entered the room, my father stopped spinning me, and we dropped to the floor again. She was wearing a beautiful blue gown with pearl earrings and a matching necklace. Her golden hair was tied back with small curls framing her face. She bent down and cupped my face in her hands, nuzzling her nose against mine.

My handsome little man.

I no man! I a pirate, Mommy!

Oh no. My mistake. Can I give this pirate a big hug?

Okay, Mommy.

I could feel the tears trailing down my cheek at the sight of my parents and the feel of my mother's embrace. I could also feel Aunt Lilly give my hand a reassuring squeeze. Without warning, I felt another pull. In that instant, I was three years old and in the living room with my parents. I was playing pirate with my father and snuggling with my mother.

Feeling the warmth of my mother as she supported my small body against hers, cradling my head, I could hear her humming something. *Twinkle, twinkle little star.* As she hummed, her body rocked slowly. Soon, I felt the tenderness of my father hugging us both. I lay nestled securely between them. While I relished the comfort of their embrace, my mother whispered into my ear.

You're our special little man, and you will do great things. When you are ready, we will be here to guide you. You need to wear your dad's ring now. I love you.

"She's talking to me now but through a memory. How is she doing that?"

Again, a small squeeze of my hand was all I got in reassurance. I began to panic as the scene with my parents faded from my view. My head felt as though it was on a Tilt-a-Whirl. I found I was becoming more aware of everything happening within my body. Each heartbeat echoed within my ears and I was hyperaware of every movement in my hands and legs. A gentle swaying sensation started in my feet and traveled up my legs and through to my head.

I was floating in space somewhere that I can only describe as the in-between. Within seconds, everything around me was white. A hypnotic rhythm of a swirling sound grew with intensity. I could feel a strong sense of relaxation washing over me in waves. It was like finding peace in a hurricane of wind, color, and light. *So this is what Zen feels like?* I thought.

In the distance, the kaleidoscopic movement of color mixed with something else—a female voice. I turned to and from to pinpoint where it was coming from. My uneasiness mounted as I strained and could not find it. As that feeling swelled nearly to anxiety, the sensation came forth stronger and faster, my heart quickening to match it.

When I thought I could take it no longer, I finally heard the voice come in clear and extremely loud. "Christian!" My head immediately swung right, and I strained to look. She was there. In the distance, I saw her holding her hand out to me, calling me to her. She was wearing a long green dress that billowed, caught in a whirlwind of light. Her golden hair flowed around her face and tears were flowing from her eyes.

I felt as though my heart would split in two as she came closer, only to find the distance between us would grow with each step she took. When I felt I could no longer take it, I reached out to her and screamed, "Mom!"

Instantly, I felt a sharp pain as though someone had smashed my face into a concrete wall, and I grabbed at my head. When I opened my eyes again, I was on the tile floor. Aunt Lilly was still crouched in front of me, holding my elbows. I felt a surge of emotion run through me as the tears flowed uncontrollably. Aunt Lilly just held me, letting me exhaust them. Once I was more in control of myself, I lifted my head and looked into her eyes.

"I saw her. I saw my mom."

CHAPTER 15

The Fix Is In

As I sat there, still reeling from what I had just experienced, a flood of questions rushed to the forefront of my mind. Aunt Lilly was still grasping my forearms while my aunt and uncle held each other behind her. Meeting my eyes, Uncle Roman breathed a long sigh, tension draining from his shoulders.

"Oh, thank God!" he said.

Aunt Cora let go of Uncle Roman and rushed to my side but stopped just before she made contact. Cautiously, she moved to hug me. Seeing her hesitation, I pulled her to me, needing the hug as much as she did. As though a floodgate had opened, she let loose years of pent-up tears on my shoulder. Unsure of what else to do, I held her there and let her cry to completion.

When she settled, Uncle Roman moved closer to us. Gently, he touched her, and she pulled away, still wiping tears and sniffling as she did. Aunt Lilly offered her a tissue from a pack she had in her pants pocket.

Sitting back on the couch, I surveyed the room. The once-pristine room was in complete disarray. Potted plants had toppled, and the curtains were hanging askew. Some pictures were off-center while others had completely fallen off the walls. Even the people in the room showed signs of wear.

"Wha-what happened?" I asked, motioning to the wreckage around the room.

"You did, kiddo." Aunt Lilly chuckled.

"You've got *some* power pumping through you. I'm not sure what kind of witch your mom is, but she passed on some serious genes. No wonder they had to hide you."

My mom! As she spoke, I recalled my mother's words. and I jumped up off the couch, which visibly startled everyone in the room when I did. Realizing that, I stopped midrun and turned back to see three wide-eyed adults staring blankly at me.

"I promise, I'm not running away," I said. "But I'll be right back."

I ran through the kitchen, into the foyer, up the stairs, and into my room with Buddy chasing behind. I knelt next to my bed and pulled out the drawer, fishing for my sacred box in the back. Finding it tucked in its usual corner, I pulled it out and opened it. The first thing I saw staring back at me was the picture of the three of us from my last birthday. After today, I had a newfound appreciation for that picture. They were no longer static figures from a forgotten, long-ago day. They were real, and alive, somewhere. I held the photo close to me and drew warmth from that thought.

Putting it on the bed next to me, I saw my dad's ring and my mother's necklace. I immediately placed the ring on my right ring finger. I remembered that was where he had worn it in my memory. Glancing back in the box, I saw my mother's necklace by itself and felt compelled to take it with me. Would it be weird for a teenage boy to be wearing a charm that says "Mom" on it? Probably, but I didn't care.

I needed to be close to both my parents, and this was the best way I knew how. Before putting the picture back into the box, I held it close to my heart again and then stared at it. I decided it would stay with me from now on, so I folded it and put it in my back pocket.

Looking around my room, I felt as though I wasn't going to see it again. I took in the sights and smells, reveling in them. Had we only been here for two weeks? How had so much changed in such a short time? I wondered.

I took my time walking back to the family room. As I entered, I could see they were trying to put the room back in some order. My presence caused them to stop.

"Did you find it?" Aunt Lilly asked.

Uncle Roman frowned. "Find what?"

Without looking at him, she said, "His father's ring."

I smiled and held my hand up to show the artifact in question.

"How did you know I was going up to get it?" I asked.

"You allowed me to join in your visions while we held hands," Aunt Lilly answered.

She walked over to look at the ring and nodded. She went back to rearranging the couch cushions when she stopped and slowly turned to look at me.

"You have something else," she said with a hint of questioning in her tone.

Her reaction left me uneasy, but I felt I could answer her truthfully.

"I'm-I'm wearing my mom's necklace too. It didn't feel right to take my dad and leave her behind."

Both Aunt Lilly and Aunt Cora walked over to examine the necklace, but only Aunt Cora spoke up.

"Oh, Jace. I remember when your dad gave that to your mom. She had just delivered you. She wore it every day."

Aunt Lilly looked at it and smiled.

"It's not what she told you to grab, but I think it will help us with our current predicament. We still need to fix your accidental spell before it causes long-term problems. It's likely only focused just on this area, possibly the entire town's under it. Even so, I really don't want to wait and find out. It might attract attention if a town full of people lost a day."

"How can this help?" I asked.

"It will ground you and draw on her powers to help reverse what you did."

"How do I fix it, though?"

"Concentration," Aunt Lilly said with a grin.

She glanced back over her shoulder and saw Uncle Roman was still tidying up the room.

"On second thought, Roman, let's wait to clean up. I have a feeling we'll be doing it again soon enough."

Realizing what she was saying, he looked around the room and changed tactics, pulling pictures off the walls and laying them gently on the floor. He tied loose drapes and removed any projectiles to the foyer. I wanted to complain that they were overreacting. However, I had seen the mess afterward and knew this was likely a wise course of action.

After the room had been magic-proofed, I resumed my position on the couch. Aunt Lilly knelt in front of me again, this time on a towel.

She grinned as I looked at it.

"This body may act twenty-five, but these knees feel all fifty-six years they have on them. The tile ain't helping!"

I laughed and nodded. Aunt Lilly then motioned for my aunt and uncle to come near.

"Cora, please sit on Christian's left, and, Roman, please sit on Christian's right to match the masculine and feminine sides of his body."

As my aunt and uncle approached, I put a hand out to stop all of them.

"Wait," I said.

The adults all stopped and looked at me, unsure what to do next.

"Many, *many*, questions, but first, who is Christian?" I asked.

Aunt Lilly laughed. "Ma boy, that's your *actual* name. Cora and Roman created Jace Northall."

I was shocked, but when I looked to them for confirmation, Aunt Cora's cheeks flushed. Uncle Roman nodded before speaking up, "We were hiding you. We changed all our names."

My eyes opened wide as I tried to comprehend what he was saying.

"Okay. What are our names? Our *actual* names?

Uncle Roman briefly looked at Aunt Cora and answered, "We are Nicholas and Sophia Tucker. *You* are Christian Michael Volk."

"Christian Michael Volk," I let it roll off my tongue a few times, feeling foreign and wrong.

"To fix what you have done, we need to create balance. A part of that is speaking your original given name," Aunt Lilly said.

Not in a place to argue with her, I nodded. My aunt and uncle sat next to me in their assigned locations.

"Christian, I need you to focus on something that brings you joy and peace. It is an anchor for you in life and always has been. It should not be a person but an item."

I mentally flipped through my belongings, taking inventory of what had always been there.

"Does my dad's ring count? It was the thing I always seemed to pull out when I needed comfort."

Aunt Lilly sat back on her heels and considered the question for a long time.

"I think it should. It's not a person although it connects to one." Then she shrugged and said, "What's the worst that could happen?"

Uncle Roman cleared his throat. "If I may, Lillian, there seems to be quite a bit that can go wrong based on what we already witnessed."

Aunt Lilly laughed as she looked around the room. "I guess you have a point."

Aunt Cora walked over and touched my face lightly as she assumed the position Aunt Lilly assigned us earlier.

"All right, folks. We have a memory spell to reverse," said Aunt Lilly.

She looked at each of us before turning to me.

"Okay, kiddo. Here's where we need you to take over," Aunt Lilly started.

"You have opened the gate with your mom. Although she is not with us, she should be able to help lend her strength because we need three witches for this. Five would be better, but three will work."

I just sat there, amazed how this no longer seemed *as* strange to me as it would have this morning. A nagging question remained, though.

The corner of Aunt Lilly's mouth went up and as if she were reading my mind.

"She'll know you need help, and she'll join. She may not know *what* you need help with, but she will figure it out as we continue. Your mom will begin lending her support and power once we start."

The thought sent a wave of emotions over me. I felt a warmth begin in my core and spread out across my body as though I was thawing after a long deep freeze. My mom was out there, and she was going to help me.

"What do I need to do?" I asked.

"You need to remember what you were thinking when the spell likely started."

I thought back to the encounter with Sheriff Powell. Immediately, a flood of rage rose within me. I turned to my aunt and uncle and said, "Just as he was leaving, he questioned you guys about when Mom and Dad had died. There was something in that question that really bothered you. In turn, it really bothered me."

"Jace, I think it started before that," Aunt Cora said.

Aunt Lilly's eyebrows went up as she looked to Aunt Cora for clarification.

"When he insinuated you had bad luck because you had been in two fights in one day, and I gasped," Aunt Cora said.

"Oh yeah, I forgot about that. What did you do that for any-way?" I asked.

Aunt Cora's face softened as though she was trying to work through a monologue in her head. Finally, she said, "Your eyes. Your eyes shocked me."

"What color were they?" Aunt Lilly asked.

"Red," Uncle Roman answered with a slight growl in his tone.

Aunt Lilly sat back on her heels again and pondered this new piece of information.

"What were you feeling?" she asked me.

I thought back to the smug man sitting in my uncle's chair, silencing him. I recalled him trying to intimidate us in our own house. I remembered seeing the anger swell in my uncle, knowing he was holding it back to protect me.

"Anger. No, rage!" I answered.

Uncle Roman nodded in approval.

"Yes, that would about sum it up," he said.

"If I could have attacked him right there, I would have!"

"Sheriff Powell saw it too, if only for a second," Uncle Roman said.

"I've never seen red in, well, any fae. It shocked me," Aunt Cora said.

Aunt Lilly pondered this information and then finally answered.

"Powerful emotions, either good or bad, can release bonds on things and open a person's magic. You likely caused it without realizing it at that moment. You are so close to your coven age. One day would not have changed much."

She stopped and appeared to be thinking through the next steps.

"Okay. We will need to have you in a state of peace and relaxation. We are trying to reverse what you did, so the opposite must be done. Once we start, I will say an incantation. I want you to say it with me. I will try to keep it as simple as possible. Do you think you can do that?"

I nodded.

"Roman, place a hand on Christian's right shoulder, and Cora, your hand on his left shoulder. Christian, take out the picture you have and hold it in your right hand. I will hold it as well. You and I will join our other hands to create a circle. This will connect your mom to us. Your aunt and uncle will act to balance the magic. Are you ready?"

Realizing that I had not mentioned the picture, I hesitated for a moment before I spoke. "How did you know I had the picture?"

"I have a few tricks up my sleeve as well," Aunt Lilly said and winked at me.

A sense of awe hit me as I tried to figure what else she was capable of. Aunt Lilly seemed to be reading my face, and relenting, she added, "I saw the corner sticking out of your pants and figured it out."

I chuckled as I pulled the picture out and unfolded it. I placed it in my right hand. My aunt and uncle put their hands on my shoulders. As they made contact, I reached out for Aunt Lilly to join.

Seriousness crossing Aunt Lilly's face as she said, "No matter what happens, do not let go till I say to let go. Does everyone understand and agree?"

We all nodded and watched Aunt Lilly as she positioned herself more comfortably on her towel. Seeing me looking at her knees, she smiled and squeezed my hands.

"Christian, I need you to bring yourself to peace. Imagine something that is calming and focus on it."

As I closed my eyes, I thought back to the in-between I had been in prior to seeing my mom. I tried to focus my attention there. Again, I could feel the blanket of white rushing up my body and engulfing me in its anchor. This time, anticipating it, I relaxed and waited for Aunt Lilly who began chanting.

> *Retro revolvatur,*
> *Ad normalem,*
> *Ad summum finem,*
> *Reversus ad normalis*
> *NUNC!*

I listened to each line and repeated it as best I could, not knowing what language it was. My best guess was Latin, but it didn't make much difference if I believed in it. As we repeated the words, images formed. In the distance, I could make out a clock. It was initially tiny—no bigger than a grain of salt. As we repeated our lines, it grew until it was as large as a house. The hands were brass and were moving in a clockwise direction.

Realizing it was moving the wrong way, I focused my energy on reversing it. Although I was willing it, the clock did not move in my desired direction. I slowed my breathing and changed my tactics. With my mind's eye, I looked at my right hand and the picture of my parents. I could see energy emanating from it. Soon, it glowed with a ball of light that continued to grow in intensity. Then a figure was next to me, holding my hand where the picture had been.

In my left hand, I could see the shape of Aunt Lilly although it was not as sharp in appearance as that other figures. Where my picture had been stood my mother. She was holding my hand and looked at me with a smile in her eyes. As though understanding what needed to be done, she joined in the incantation.

As we continued, the clock's hands slowed their movement in the forward direction until they completely stopped. Trying to maintain my calm, I watched and waited for it to move again. Although it felt like an eternity, within a few seconds, they began moving backward. Initially, the movement staggered. Then it picked up in intensity, and the hands were soon swinging counterclockwise wildly. They made a whirling sound reminiscent of a locomotive whistle.

I could feel the warmth building between the three of us. When it looked as though the clock might burst, my mom squeezed my hand. Understanding her message, I yelled out, "Nunc!"

When I opened my eyes, I was back in our family room. We were all still in our seats, but the house looked like someone had lifted it off its foundation and dropped it back. Buddy returned from the foyer where he must have been hiding. Cautiously, he loped to where I was and allowed me to pet his head and hug him around the flank.

This time, furniture was strewn everywhere. Even the carefully placed items were now in various spots throughout the house. Looking to my protectors, I realized their clothes were in complete disarray, and their hair had blown wild.

"Do you think it worked?" I asked.

Uncle Roman laughed. "I sure hope so because I don't think the house, or me, can do that again!"

Standing up first, Uncle Roman helped Aunt Lilly off the ground. She was looking around as she was brushing her clothes off and straightening them when she looked out the back window and her eyes went wide. Turning to see what had caught her attention, I looked out the large sliding doors to our pool area and saw Marcus.

CHAPTER 16

Testing Friendships

Aunt Lilly made the first move toward her nephew. I was still processing the previous hour and having a hard time comprehending much of anything. Thinking about his being in my backyard or what he may have just seen was beyond my mental capacity at the moment. I watched as Aunt Lilly walked around the couch and opened the door. She headed to Marcus, who did not move, even as she approached. Through the doors, I could see her talking to him, but I didn't know what was being said.

Although he answered her, Marcus never broke eye contact with me which sent a chill down my spine. Standing up, I walked around the couch and through the open door. Closing it behind me, I made my way to where they were standing.

"Hey, man, are you okay?" I asked hesitantly.

He stared at me, dumbfounded. Then he seemed to shake off what had been holding him back from talking.

"Am *I* okay? Uh, yeah, I'm surprisingly good. Considering that we just watched your living room erupt into a hurricane with all of you sitting there as though you were at a leisurely brunch."

"We?" I asked.

Marcus motioned to the screen door, where Izzie stood. She looked at me sheepishly as she began walking toward us. I glanced back over my shoulder and could see the wreckage looked worse from the pool's decking. I felt a wave of disbelief wash over me. The room was in even more of a shamble than it had been after the first go-round.

Stunned into silence, I could feel Marcus's eyes boring into the back of my head. My shoulders dropped, and I slowly turned back toward him, trying to determine what to say. Aunt Lilly seemed okay letting me guide the interaction although I wished she hadn't been.

Remembering the phone call with Marcus that had started all this, I thought of how best to ask about last night. I needed to do so without making this scene any odder than it already was.

I opted for an open-ended question.

"So about the party…," I trailed off and waited to see what he would say.

He stared at me for a few seconds, his eyes furrowed, then answered, "That was why we came over. Izzie saw Sheriff Powell here and called me to let me know. We wanted to see what Ethan was feeding him."

I looked back at Aunt Lilly. We both smiled as she patted me on the back and gave me a wink before heading back into the house.

"But seriously, what happened in there? It looked like a scene out of *Wizard of Oz*, only the tornado was in the house. I was waiting for a cow to fly by the window…everything else was!"

Unsure what to say, I just laughed as I rubbed the back of my neck.

"It's been a *really* long morning. Let's just leave it at that for now," I said.

Marcus's eyes grew twice their size as he looked at the house and then me.

"Are you seriously *not* going to tell me what happened in there?"

I looked back at Aunt Lilly, who had stopped at the door, and was now watching our exchange. She smiled and then shrugged as she walked into the house. She was leaving the decision up to me.

Marcus saw the exchange and spoke up before I could.

"My aunt's a witch, isn't she?"

Izzie's head whipped up to stare at Marcus, and I let out an unexpected laugh. The bluntness of his question took me so off guard, I didn't know what else to say or do. Aunt Lilly had said that she was quite sure Marcus knew what she was and did not seem upset about it. His mom knew what she was, but was it my place to tell him?

As I was about to speak, I noticed movement on the house's side. Instinctively, I stepped in front of Marcus and Izzie. Without argument, he stepped further behind Izzie and me, nudging me forward.

I glanced over my shoulder at him.

"By all means, you've got this," he said, motioning toward the noise.

The thought made me chuckle slightly, but I quickly regained my composure. I strained, trying to anticipate what was coming around the side of the house. With my newfound knowledge, it could be anything from a chipmunk to a werewolf. No matter, I wasn't taking any chances.

"What is it?" Marcus asked.

"I'm not sure. But be quiet!" I answered in a whisper.

Just when I felt I couldn't take it any longer, I saw a face poke out from the house's side. My shoulders relaxed instantly.

"Zoe?" Izzie said as she saw her sister.

"Jesus, Zoe! You gave Jace a heart attack!" Marcus said as he hit me on the back.

I shot around to stare at him in disbelief.

"A heart attack? Really? Me?"

"What? I'm just relaying it, as I see it."

I let go of a small chuckle as I watched Zoe and Alyssa cautiously make their way around the corner, shoving each other and arguing in loud whispers.

"I'm glad you two aren't trying to sneak up on someone," Izzie teased.

"Shut up, Izzie! We came over when we saw *you* running back here," Zoe said.

Realizing they would see the house, I felt numb, and my mouth went dry. I instantly wanted to stop them from coming any further.

"STOP!" I yelled, and both girls froze where they stood. Alyssa emitted a small yelp as she did. Zoe regained her composure first and looked around.

"What? Is there a snake, a trap, what?"

ANNIE O'CONNELL

Izzie turned to stare at me, and I quickly realized what I had done. I felt the corner of my mouth lift slightly on seeing their faces.

"No, there's nothing over there. I…"

I looked over to the house and felt a sense of dread come over me again. How was I going to explain this to them? I could barely understand it myself.

"What are you guys doing over here anyway?" I asked.

"We saw the sheriff and then Izzie and Marcus running. We thought you were in trouble and needed help. Are you okay?" Alyssa asked.

By then, Zoe had opened the screen door to my pool patio. She looked from us then into the family room, Alyssa's gaze following hers.

"Whoa! I guess it's what I expected, but…wow!" Zoe said.

"What do you mean, you expected?" I asked.

Zoe was about to speak when Alyssa touched her arm and answered.

"I was in my room reading when I saw flashes coming from outside my window. Considering it's the middle of the day, flashes of light from anywhere would be weird. So I got up to see what was causing them. When I looked over toward your house, every window was flashing light, and the curtains were swaying back and forth. It was the most bizarre thing I have ever seen!"

Zoe, seeing a lull in Alyssa's explanation, continued with her side of events.

"She called me into the room so I could see it too. It was around that time we saw Marcus running like his life depended on it. A few moments later, we heard our door slam downstairs and saw Izzie following him. We watched the light show in your house until it stopped. Then we decided we would try to come over and see if you were okay. I'm glad to see all of you survived…whatever that was. Although I would really like to know what happened?"

As Zoe spoke, I looked over to Izzie, who was standing slightly behind Marcus. A pang of guilt hit me again as her face took on the same look it had the night in the grotto. I glanced at the house and then back at my friends. How could I possibly explain the morning's events without looking insane? I scanned the group, trying to determine if telling them the truth was a logical choice. Deciding there was no other way around it, I took a deep breath and sent a prayer up. Then I relayed the morning's events as I remembered them.

The four of them stood there in disbelief, periodically looking back and forth to the house and me while listening to my recount of the morning. When I had finished, I waited for what seemed like an eternity. I wished for one of them to speak and felt my heart drop when none did. *Well, it was nice having friends while it lasted,* I thought.

Taking one last look around at the group, I decided to head back into the house. They probably needed my help anyway. Turning, my stomach dropped further.

But then I felt Marcus grab my arm.

"Just give us a second to process," he said. "That's some pretty heavy stuff you're telling us. So...you're part witch, part werewolf?"

"It would seem so. I know for sure I inherited Mom's genes."

I looked over to the girls, trying to judge their feelings. Marcus must have seen me waiting for their response and answered for them.

"Well, I don't know about you, but *I'm* going to help clean up. You guys want to join, or are you going to head back to your house?" Marcus asked.

Izzie stepped forward and walked toward me. Coming close, she looked at me, squinting her eyes as though she was searching for something. Fighting the urge to look away, I felt myself shifting uneasily until her eyes finally softened. She smiled and, without words, reached out and grabbed my hand. We walked toward my family room together while her sisters and Marcus followed behind.

Walking into the family room, Aunt Cora and Uncle Roman stopped cleaning to examine the group that had assembled. Aunt Cora's eyes slipped in my direction and then down to where Izzie was holding my hand causing her to smile. Buddy jumped off the couch and walked over to the group then nuzzled next to my leg so I'd pet him.

"They came to help clean up," I said.

Uncle Roman stood taller at my statement. Buddy whined as he started nudging my leg again. I looked down at him and rubbed behind his ear, which seemed to appease him slightly. Although he stopped whining, he would not leave my side.

"They know what happened…everything that happened and are still here to help," I continued, looking at Uncle Roman.

"Well, that's just amazing. We have quite the mess in here and can use all the help we can get," Aunt Lilly chimed in as she watched Uncle Roman as well.

"Alyssa says the action was not just down here but throughout the house. They saw it from their house," I said.

"Hmm, maybe the girls and Cora can go upstairs? You boys and I tackle down here?" Aunt Lilly suggested.

Aunt Cora looked at her husband, who still maintained his firm stance. Eventually, and slowly, he nodded. But when I looked at him—really looked—I felt the hair on the back of my neck stand up. Buddy let out a low growl. I tried to calm him by petting him again, but he firmly positioned himself between Uncle Roman and myself.

A heaviness was within the room that had not been there before. I think Izzie picked up on it too because she squeezed my hand at Aunt Lilly's suggestion of splitting up. It caused me to break my stare at Uncle Roman to turn to her.

"There are only two rooms and a bathroom upstairs. One room is pretty empty, and the other one is mine, which is also pretty empty. You shouldn't be up there long," I said to her.

"Come on, girls. This will be a great bonding experience," Aunt Cora said to the sisters.

Aunt Lilly looked at Aunt Cora. "I'm not sure a bonding experience is the right phrase for this."

Aunt Cora smiled sweetly. "You know what I mean."

As she turned to head upstairs, Aunt Cora turned again to look at Uncle Roman with concern in her eyes. She seemed to examine him for an answer to an unspoken question between them. I wasn't sure what she was picking up on, but there was a definite change in him—a shift that I was having trouble putting my finger on.

Izzie looked at me with apprehension, and I tried to determine if it was it for me or herself and her sisters. Until I could completely determine what had changed, I would follow Aunt Lilly's lead.

"You'll be alright. I'm the one that set off the craziness, and I'll be down here," I told the girls.

"Come on, Izzie. The faster we get up there, the faster we can get everything cleaned," Zoe said.

She left the unspoken part about getting out of the house, but I think everyone knew what she was thinking. As the girls followed my aunt, I turned to look at my cleaning companions in the family room.

"Where do you want to start?" I asked them.

"Starting at the top and working my way down has always worked for me. Let's get these pictures back up on the walls too. Marcus, can you grab a broom and start sweeping? Roman, maybe straighten the blinds and furniture?"

Uncle Roman had not moved since we came into the house. At that moment, he nodded slowly before turning toward the curtains.

"Uh, sure. Where do you keep your cleaning stuff?" Marcus asked.

I pointed to the kitchen. "It's in the pantry next to the fridge."

"I really suck at taking directions. How about you show me?"

Marcus made his eyes widen a bit as he motioned toward the kitchen for me to follow. Before I could say another word, he had grabbed my shirt and began dragging me. Uncle Roman watched us while Aunt Lilly watched my uncle.

Once we were around the corner, Marcus pulled me close and whispered in a semi-frantic tone.

"What is going on? Your uncle has my spooky meter going off the charts. Buddy is not helping calm it either. Look, I don't know your uncle very well, but I *do* know that's not him out there."

"I know. I'm also trying to figure out what's going on. I'm just following your aunt at this point."

"Look, let's just get this place cleaned and get out of here. Do you think the girls are okay upstairs?" Marcus asked.

"Yeah. Aunt Cora seems herself. Shaken up but herself," I answered.

I looked up the stairs and tried to imagine what was going on. Turning my attention back to the family room, I stared at Uncle Roman, who was now cleaning again. He had always been very approachable—the pillar in each of the communities we have lived in. This was so out of character for him.

I could feel a knot forming in my core. As though he could sense me staring, Uncle Roman stopped moving and stood up tall. He turned to look back at me like he was an automaton. Buddy growled again, the hair on his neck standing up, something he had never done before.

Aunt Lilly stopped cleaning to watch. She then turned to look at me, visibly shaken by the way my uncle was moving.

"Okay. I feel like I just walked into a *Terminator* movie, and your uncle is the T-1000. Where is Arnold Schwarzenegger when you need him?" Marcus whispered.

"Maybe it's just everything that had happened today that has him on edge. Add in that the secret's out. All the kids on our block know who and what we are now. He'll be fine soon," I finished hopefully.

Marcus seemed to take in my suggestion. He hesitantly agreed with my assessment as we rummaged through the pantry for supplies. All the while, I continued to watch Uncle Roman in the family room. Grabbing a broom, window cleaner, furniture cleaner, and rags, Marcus and I cautiously headed back.

Both Aunt Lilly and Uncle Roman were busy cleaning once again. The air of agitation he had been giving off seemed to have abated somewhat. I glanced at Marcus, who shrugged after making the same determination I had.

We moved into the room and began working on our assigned tasks in relative silence. Soon, the house was presentable again. Around the same time, the girls came down from upstairs. They, too, seemed less stressed than when they had gone upstairs.

"It looks great down here! I may need to have Jace whip up a windstorm more often," Aunt Cora teased.

I laughed uncomfortably and looked at Izzie, who gave Aunt Cora a wide-eyed look.

"I think we've done as much as we can right now. Kids, you must have worked up an appetite. How about I take you all for some ice cream?" Aunt Lilly asked and the group of teens lit up.

Seeing a way to get a breather from the heaviness of the morning, I was ready to head out for a break of any sort as well. It seemed I was not the only one in agreement.

"Will you be okay if I take them out for a few hours?" Aunt Lilly asked Aunt Cora, purposely turning her back on Uncle Roman.

Aunt Cora regarded Uncle Roman, who appeared to be morphing back into his alter ego again. She nodded and said, "I think a chance to relax would be welcome. Are you okay going without us, Jace?"

Attempting to judge the validity of the question, I debated my answer. Appraising the group of teens in front of me and seeing their mounting apprehension in staying in the house any longer, I quickly said, "I think we could all use some ice cream. Is it okay if I go?"

"Be back before six, and don't ruin your appetite," Uncle Roman said, seeming to be back to himself again finally.

Reaching into his back pocket, he pulled out a black leather wallet and opened it. He rummaged through the items within and then pulled out some money and handed it to me.

"Please, let this be my treat. You all helped so much over here, and we genuinely appreciate it," Uncle Roman said.

"Thank you!" I spoke.

"Wonderful, let's get a move on. Girls, call your parents to let them know where we are going. I'll ask Mary if she wants to head out with us. Her car would fit everyone, anyway," Aunt Lilly said.

Zoe pulled her phone out and punched away on the screen. Within a few minutes, the phone chimed in response.

"Mom says it's okay. She and Dad are still at the café and will be back later tonight."

I walked over and gave my aunt a kiss on the cheek. When I hugged my uncle, though, I received a slow but firm hug in response. As we released each other, I investigated his face, trying to determine if everything was okay. He must have sensed my concern and smiled before he said, "I'm fine. Go have some fun."

Before rejoining the rest of the group, I said, "I'll talk with you when we get back. I love you, guys." I was looking pointedly at Uncle Roman as I said it.

Aunt Cora smiled and put her hand on my shoulder reassuringly. "Go out and fill up on ice cream. We love you too and will see you later."

As we walked to the front door, Buddy followed closely. He was whimpering and kept looking back and forth.

I turned to Aunt Lilly, who seemed to have read my mind.

"How about we keep him by our house while we're out?" she suggested.

I felt she had lifted a million pounds off my shoulders.

"Thank you. Let me just grab a few things for him."

Walking back into the family room, I saw Aunt Cora was touching Uncle Roman's face, who seemed distant again. It was as though he was a shell of himself.

"Is he okay?" I asked.

"Yes, sweetie. Go have fun with your friends."

She looked at the bundle of dog items in my hand.

"That's a good idea. I think we need some quiet for a bit."

I nodded before turning to head back to the group that had assembled outside the door. Putting Buddy on the leash, we walked to Marcus's house in relative silence. Across the court, Mrs. Hunter was standing next to her minivan, keys in hand.

"I told you this car would come in handy," Mrs. Hunter teased as we approached.

Aunt Lilly rolled her eyes at her sister and motioned for everyone to climb in as she took the leash and walked Buddy into their house. Izzie and her sisters climbed in first and moved to the back row, allowing Marcus and me the captain's chairs in the center row.

Seeing how tight the leg space was in the back row, I was eternally grateful for their choice of seating. Mrs. Hunter entered the car and scanned the occupants before turning to Aunt Lilly.

"Okay. Where to?" she asked.

"Anywhere other than here," Aunt Lilly whispered.

Mrs. Hunter's face dropped, and her eyebrows furrowed.

"Head toward Eddie's. I promised the kids ice cream. I'll tell you there," her sister said.

Being so close to the front seat, I overheard most of the conversation. There was a tugging sensation at my core. As we pulled out of the driveway, I looked over toward the house and wondered if leaving was a good idea. It felt as though I was abandoning my aunt and uncle. However, I think I needed the break as much as they did.

We completed the car ride mostly in silence. I found the gentle hum of the engine coupled with the rhythmic swaying of the car was enough to lull me to sleep. Everything outside Main Street requires a twenty- to thirty-minute car ride. So I allowed myself the chance to regain some of my energy with a small catnap.

I woke as we were entering a town. Small businesses speckled the side of the road. Passing by a handful of stores, I saw the brightly lit ice-cream parlor on the left. It was painted in pastel colors, and a large swirl cone adorned the top of the building. Along the perimeter were multiple seating areas.

A closer look revealed a seating area inside the building and an arcade just behind that. The bright colors and lights of the game room brought my inner child back to life, causing me to sit up straighter in my chair.

Aunt Lilly noticed my movement and smiled. "All the kids love this place. Come to think of it, all the adults do too, but don't tell anyone." Her eyes twinkled as she winked at me.

Mrs. Hunter pulled up to a spot right in front and our group piled out of the car and headed toward the building. We were now a buzz of excitement.

The inside was just as brightly colored as the outside had been. It had a feel of something straight out of a fairy tale, possibly *Hansel and Gretel*—minus the evil witch.

The decor looked like a gingerbread house, complete with gingerbread logs and icing oozing from between them. Behind the counter were large, intricately decorated gingerbread houses. On their doors were exposed spigots for the soft-serve ice cream.

Across the ceiling were small twinkling lights that added to the ambience. In the room's corner was a life-size gingerbread man. He was holding a sign in one hand that pointed to the game room and a tray of cookies in the other. The building brought me back to simpler times and a sense of peace washed over me.

As I marveled at the splendor in front of me, I felt multiple eyes watching me and turned to look at my friends.

"This place does that to everyone who sees it for the first time," Marcus said.

Walking to the counter, I investigated the contents below the slanted windows. Pooled in multicolored buckets were various flavored ice cream. I felt my mouth water as I tried to decide which to choose.

Seeing me analyzing my choices, Mrs. Hunter walked up and motioned to the signs that hung above the ice-cream houses.

"Perhaps a combo would be better?" she suggested.

Above the counter was a roof of gingerbread shingles that held three large signs. Inscribed on them were various combinations of ice cream, ranging from *Mikey's Mighty Mix* to *Sweet and Sour Sunshine*. After careful consideration, I decided on *Night at the Movies*. That one was buttered popcorn ice cream with chocolate candies and peanuts.

I paid and grabbed my confection before heading to the back room with Marcus. Aunt Lilly and Mrs. Hunter had found two booths that were positioned next to each other with a small wall partition between them. One side could hold two people while the other could easily seat six. They took up the smaller of the two stalls.

In the bigger booth, Izzie and Zoe sat on one side while Alyssa sat on the other. Seeing us approach, Zoe stood up and moved to sit next to Alyssa.

"I think I'll sit here. I can see the game room better on this side," she said as she moved.

I looked at Zoe, confused by the abrupt change in seats. Marcus, being in front of me, made his way to sit next to Izzie. Immediately, Zoe shot up out of her seat, startling everyone.

"I thought you would want to sit on this side too. We can strategize which games to play when we're done," Zoe said.

Marcus, now midway into a seated position, stopped and stared at Zoe. He then slowly stood up and went to sit on the opposite side next to her.

"If you say so…but I can see the game room better ov—" He winced as he was finishing the last of his sentence. Zoe's eyes became the size of saucers as she glared at him causing him to stop speaking immediately.

Seeing that my only option for seating was now next to Izzie, I quickly realized what Zoe's game of musical chairs had been all about. I looked at Izzie whose cheeks were flushed as she scowled at her sister. Alyssa smiled and chuckled as she watched us.

"Ah, to be young again," Aunt Lilly teased from their booth. "Jace, take a seat before your ice cream melts."

I sat down cautiously next to Izzie, who blushingly looked over at me.

"What did you get?" she asked.

"*Night at the Movies*. I'm not really sure about it, but it looked interesting."

"I've always wanted to try it but couldn't imagine how they could get ice cream to taste like popcorn," Izzie said.

"Do you want to try some?" I asked.

I realized the implications of the offer too late, and it made me want to pull the words back into my mouth immediately. She hesitated for a second, and then took her spoon, and swiped a scoop off the top.

"Oh wow! It really *does* taste like popcorn!" she exclaimed.

Enjoying her reaction, I took a bite myself and instantly fell in love. She was right. It somehow tasted like popcorn while retaining the creamy consistency of ice cream.

Diving into my new vice, I looked around the table.

"What did everyone else get?" I asked.

"*Sweet and Sour Sunshine*, and it's also amazing! If sunshine had a flavor, I would think this is what it would taste like," Izzie said.

I felt a small smile cross my face seeing her reaction to the ice cream.

"I was thinking of that one too but opted for this," I said.

"Do you want to try some of mine?" she asked shyly.

I felt my cheeks flush, and my pulse quicken at the question. She had already eaten some, and I had used my spoon. *What is the etiquette in this situation?* was all I could think.

"Just take a bite, Jace," Alyssa teased.

"She wouldn't have offered if it was a big deal," Zoe chimed in.

Before I could react, Marcus's spoon zipped past my face and sank into Izzie's ice cream. As the spoon entered his mouth, he closed his eyes as though reveling in the flavor. As he opened them again, he just grinned as we all stared at him.

With a mouthful of ice cream, he said, "What? She *offered!*"

"You're incorrigible, Marcus!" Aunt Lilly laughed.

Feeling relief at Marcus taking some, I lifted my spoon and nodded toward her bowl. She smiled and nudged it closer. I took a small scoop from the top and ate it. I could see what Izzie had been saying. There was a hint of citrus balanced perfectly with a velvety sweet consistency, as though the sun itself had kissed it.

"This is some of the best ice cream I have ever had," I said while still savoring the taste.

"Eddie has a few 'tricks' up his sleeve," Aunt Lilly said, putting air quotes around the word tricks.

Looking at my perplexed expression, Mrs. Hunter smiled and said, "He's fae."

Momentarily stunned, I had to remind myself there were things I had not taken seriously prior to this morning. Looking at the confections on the table, I decided only magic could have made this ice cream possible. Everyone at the table must have come to the same conclusion.

"Is he here now?" Zoe asked.

Aunt Lilly looked toward the counter and frowned.

"I don't see him back there, but if the store is open, he should be around somewhere. Children are a powerful draw for the fae because they are full of energy and life, which power them. Fortunately, most don't eat children anymore."

Her last statement caught me by surprise, and I felt a peanut get stuck in my throat, which prompted a coughing fit. Izzie, panicking, hit me on the back. Mrs. Hunter partially stood from her seat, looking as though she may lunge forward. Seeing her reaction, I raised a hand to stop her.

Taking a second or two more, I successfully dislodged the peanut. As it began to traverse down the correct tube, I stopped coughing.

"Sorry. I wasn't expecting that," I said with a husky voice, still recovering.

Aunt Lilly smiled and nodded in understanding.

"It's not really something they want to broadcast. Business may suffer. You know what I mean?"

Mrs. Hunter rolled her eyes at her sister and tried to change the subject.

"Eddie has been in business for over fifty years, and no children have ever gone missing. I think he's found another way to power himself."

She looked at the group of teens, who all had various faces of horror on them.

"Are you going to try your hand at some games?" Mrs. Hunter asked, still trying to change the subject.

"Of course," Marcus answered with sarcasm and indignation in his voice.

Aunt Lilly laughed. "Then finish up and get out there."

Marcus and I quickened our pace. We finished only to realize that the girls were still eating. Marcus stood up to head toward the game room and motioned for me to follow.

"We'll meet you in there?" I asked the girls but focusing on Izzie.

Alyssa waved her hand at us. "Go on. We'll be there in a few minutes."

Given a pass, Marcus grabbed my arm and half dragged me toward the gaming room. Opening the doors, a cacophony of sounds and flashing lights hit us. I soaked it in as I looked around. In the far corner, I could see a ticket system that allowed you to win prizes of various sizes.

Marcus motioned to follow him toward a large black machine, and I followed. I watched as he changed his cash for a cup full of bronze coins that had a cone on one side and Eddie's face on the other.

"Where do you want to start? I found Skee-Ball gives the most tickets," Marcus said.

"How many tickets do you have?"

Pulling out his wallet, he rummaged through a multitude of small pieces of paper till he came to the one he was looking for.

He said, "6,792. I'm trying to save up 10,000 for the virtual reality goggles," while pointing to a box behind the counter.

"How long have you been saving the tickets?" I asked in amazement, knowing that anything over 100 tickets in a visit to these establishments was impressive.

Marcus's face beamed with pride. "This is just from the past three or four visits."

Then his face dropped as he looked back over his shoulder to where his aunt and mom were sitting.

"Aunt Lilly always brings me here. Knowing what I do now, I wonder if she was helping?"

I looked in the same direction and then back to him. "If she did, it's just an added benefit to having one of the coolest aunts."

The corner of his lip lifted, and he motioned toward the Skee-Ball lanes. We chose two lanes next to each other and inserted our tokens to start the play. Deeming that our initial game was only a warm-up, we both separated a bit while we practiced.

After three rounds each of play, we joined back at neighboring lanes to start the competition. It was around this time that Izzie and her sisters joined. Feeling the stakes go up a notch with Izzie watching, I felt my competitive side emerge. We each dropped a token in our machine, and Zoe took on the role of referee.

"On your mark, get set...GO!" she said.

I quickly grabbed the first ball and launched it down the lane. It went off to the corner to land a 100 tube. Izzie cheered next to me, and I felt a smile cross my face. As I grabbed for the next ball, Marcus's side gave a cheer. He had also sunk a 100.

Launching my next ball, my aim was off by just a bit, and I landed a 50. Alyssa cheered for Marcus as he sank another 100, and Izzie gave a slight gasp. The next six balls had us neck and neck with each other. Our score became 780 for Marcus and 760 for me. Each one of us had one more ball.

Grinning, Marcus turned toward me and extended his hand. I looked down and cocked an eyebrow at him.

"Good game. Sorry I have to finish whupping you, though."

I squeezed his hand but said, "It's not over yet!"

Marcus smiled. "How about this? I'll shoot first, and then you can go. Anything over 80, I'll win automatically, though."

I looked at the lanes and nodded, "You're on!"

Marcus picked up his last ball and balanced it in his hand. He then shifted his weight back and forth before completing a few practice swings. When it looked as though he would throw it, he stood back and examined the ball again.

"Today, Marcus!" Izzie said.

"Patience, patience. I want to savor this! My man over here can summon hurricanes, but I'm the Skee-Ball champ."

His words hit me hard, and the game took on a new meaning. Leaning down again, he swung his arm and launched the ball. His throw was off, and it looked like he would not hit a corner 100 pocket. The most he could hope for was a 50. As the ball popped up, we all watched with bated breath. It seemed to linger in the air unnaturally long before landing in the 50.

"I hit my hand on the edge. Otherwise, it would have been in the 100," Marcus said.

Knowing that he never hit the ball off the edge, I still nodded.

"That's still an impressive score," I said.

"What is the max you can get in this game?" Izzie asked.

I smiled. "Nine hundred."

Izzie's eyes grew wide. "You almost had a perfect score!"

Marcus smiled and lifted his fingers to his mouth. He blew on them and then rubbed them on his shirt.

"Yeah. It was impressive. Let's see if Jace can beat an 830."

Izzie, visibly doing the math in her head, said, "You need to get 100 to win!"

I smiled and leaned down to grab my last ball. I looked toward Marcus and then down my lane. Taking a deep breath, I launched my ball. We all watched as it headed along the outside of the lane and toward the 100. As it hit the ramp, the ball lifted and flew in the proper direction.

Anticipation grew, and Izzie grabbed onto my arm, hiding her face behind it. I looked down at her and put my hand over hers, feeling a tenderness rise in me. Looking back at the lane, I watched just as the ball hit the corner of the 100 tube. It bounced left and back toward us, ultimately landing in the 40 tube. I felt Izzie's shoulders drop as the final score posted was 810.

Marcus jumped up. "Yes! I won!"

I smiled as I watched Marcus and then looked down at Izzie. "I think we both did."

"Huh?" Marcus said.

Then looking at me, he playfully punched me in the shoulder.

Izzie blushed and looked down then pulled frantically on my arm. It caused me to look at our feet where a small mountain of tickets had accumulated.

Marcus smiled. "I told you Skee-Ball was the best!"

I collected my mound of tickets and looked around, trying to determine what to do with them. Izzie reached out to grab the cache. She walked me to a different black machine in the room.

"There's a ticket counter over here. I'll go exchange them for you."

Smiling, I handed my winnings to her. Marcus cleared his throat, which caused us to all look at him. He lifted his hoard of tickets toward Izzie and playfully batted his eyes. Seeing that Izzie was already struggling with the mound I gave her, Zoe reached up and grabbed Marcus's tickets.

"I'll help you with that while you two keep playing."

The three girls walked toward the ticket counter, leaving us to determine our next move.

"You didn't lose on purpose, did you?" he asked, his eyes narrowing in suspicion.

Stunned by his question, I swung my head around to look at him.

"I swear to you, I didn't."

Marcus studied me carefully and seemed to believe what I had said. He nodded.

"Okay, where to next?" he asked.

"I'll follow you," I told him.

After another hour of playing and with our cheerleaders collecting our winnings for us, we had accumulated 1,959 tickets for Marcus and 1,567 tickets for me.

"I didn't think it was possible to accumulate that many tickets in one stop!" Zoe exclaimed.

Mentally tallying the totals, I looked at Marcus.

"With my tickets, you'll have enough to get the VR," I said.

"I can't take your tickets."

"There's nothing here that really appeals to me. Please take them," I said.

Izzie, also doing the math, looked at us perplexed.

"Guys, you need 10,000, and you only have 3,526. You're still 6,474 tickets shy."

Marcus smiled and pulled his wallet out. He opened it and revealed his other 6,792 tickets.

Zoe hit him playfully on the back. "Look at you!"

Walking back to the table, we found Aunt Lilly and Mrs. Hunter tightly engaged in a serious conversation. I felt guilty for interrupting. However, Aunt Lilly saw us approaching first. Her eyes lit up when she saw Marcus holding the VR over his head.

"Wonderful! You got it!" she exclaimed.

Mrs. Hunter turned and smiled as Marcus knelt next to her. He was extending the VR out as though it was a priceless artifact.

"Your grace," he said to his mom.

"More electronics? You're going to need to clean that room so you don't kill yourself in there playing with this."

"My room is clean!" he said indignantly.

Izzie and I both laughed, and he turned on us. "What? It is."

"That seriously depends on what your definition of clean is!" Izzie teased.

He seemed to ponder her words before answering.

"Okay. It may need a light cleaning before I play this."

Mrs. Hunter shook her head before standing and motioning for all of us to head back to the car. As we all piled into the minivan, Marcus sat staring at his prize. A broad smile was plastered to his face. Over his shoulder, I saw Izzie watching me watch him, and I felt the corner of my lip turn up.

CHAPTER 17

Running from the Pack

"Man, I really owe you for this! You can come over whenever you want to play," Marcus said as he looked at his trophy.

I smiled at the thought of having VR sleepovers and then felt reality hit me like a ton of bricks. My entire life had been running from danger. Now that danger was back, and it knew exactly where we were. Thinking back to Uncle Roman's reaction before we had left caused my heart to sink even more. *He* had known we were going to leave but didn't know how to tell me.

A mixture of emotions rose to the forefront of my mind as that realization became crystal clear. I listened as my friends laughed and teased Marcus about his win. They talked about all the games and adventures he could join in using his new VR set. I felt a pang of remorse and sadness at knowing that I was going to miss it all. *Would they remember me when I'm gone?* I thought to myself.

"Are you okay, Jace?" Marcus asked.

I tried to force a smile as I looked at the group, who were now closely watching me.

"I won't set off a hurricane if that is what you're thinking."

Marcus chuckled. "That's good to know, but not what I meant."

"I'm just thinking about all the ways I can win back my title of best gamer," I lied.

"It says there is a way to have a two-person game. When we get back, I'm challenging you to a match!" His eyes lit up with excitement.

I laughed. "You're on!"

"Are we allowed to watch this epic showdown, or is it a boy's only club?" Izzie asked.

"*You* can hang out with them. *I* plan on talking with Brian when we get back," Zoe said.

"Yeah, and I have some work to get done for school, so you're on your own," Alyssa added.

"I guess it'd just be me…if that's okay?" she said.

Smiling, I answered, "May the best man, or woman, win."

I felt my attention trail off once more as I listened to Marcus and the girls talking. No matter how much I didn't want it to be true, I knew in my core what was going to happen. *Where will we go now? Will I need to change my name? Can I even talk to them again?* The more I thought of what tomorrow would bring, the more my heart hurt.

"Whoa! What is going on?" Marcus asked.

It brought my attention back to the present. That was when I saw the flashing lights reflected in the night sky but could not fully make out where they were located. A pit started to form in my stomach as I prayed that it was not on Crystal Court. Unfortunately, deep down, I knew it was.

"Slow down, Mary." Concern was apparent in Aunt Lilly's voice.

"Pull down Mulberry and turn off the lights," she continued.

"Do you think it's Powell?" Mrs. Hunter asked Aunt Lilly in a low whisper as she pulled up in front of an empty house on the street.

Aunt Lilly looked over her shoulder at me and then at the rest of the passengers.

"If I had to take a guess, yes."

Mulberry Road was roughly two streets from ours and on the opposite side. It was also a street unto itself since it did not cross to our side. This allowed us relatively easy access, and we could see the commotion without being seen ourselves.

Aunt Lilly sat and watched as two more police cruisers flew past our current location.

"Well, I guess that answers that question," Aunt Lilly finally said.

"What do we do?" asked Mrs. Hunter.

"I'm thinking," Aunt Lilly answered curtly.

Mrs. Hunter scowled back at her sister, then looked in her rear-view mirror. She met my eyes, and her features softened.

"I'm sure everything is okay, Jace."

As the words left her mouth, my pulse quickened. I was just now realizing the danger that Aunt Cora and Uncle Roman could be in.

"We have to go help them!" I exclaimed, feeling the panic rising in my voice.

"No!" Mrs. Hunter and Aunt Lilly shouted simultaneously.

"He wants me. He'll hurt them!" I burst out.

"He won't hurt them. On the contrary, he's likely having trouble finding them, which is why so much backup is being called in," Aunt Lilly said calmly.

Another cruiser flew past us.

Aunt Lilly looked around the car and then back at her sister.

"They're Astrial and Solarian. I'm guessing they shed their glamor and left."

"Who's a what and a what?" Marcus asked.

"A sun fairy and moon fairy?" Alyssa answered from the back seat.

The whole of the car turned to look at her, causing her to shrink slightly in her seat.

"We learned about it in English last year. I'm not sure how close their descriptions in literature are to the real thing. But if that's the case, fairies use 'glamour' which is sort of a camouflage. If they drop their glamour, they can make themselves very tiny and almost impossible to find."

"Yes, that is true. I'm not terribly well versed in their kind either. But they are known to be able to hide themselves very well," Aunt Lilly said before looking at me.

"*You*, unfortunately, cannot hide so easily," Aunt Lilly said. She looked at her sister, and they had an unspoken conversation with their eyes before Mrs. Hunter spoke.

"You can't take this car. He's in law enforcement and can track it," Mrs. Hunter started.

"I have to get him back to his parents before Powell gets him!" Aunt Lilly said.

The weight of the situation left me feeling helpless. I looked at the six other people stuck with me wondering what their fate would be if they continued to harbor me. Possibilities ran through my head, but all lead back to the same problem—escape.

"Got it!" Zoe announced, causing all those in the van to spin and look at her.

"I was going to meet up with Brian anyway. We can take his car."

"Sweetheart, that is a very generous offer, but I'm not sure if that is such a good idea. Jace's mom is not in the state," Mrs. Hunter answered.

"Oh yeah. I already took care of that too. We're all spending the night at 'Melinda's house,'" Zoe said, accentuating her statement with air quotes.

A silence grew over the car as everyone stared at her.

"What? While all of you were watching the action, I was putting a plan into motion."

Aunt Lilly and Mrs. Hunter exchanged looks, contemplating the offer.

"Sometimes I could kiss you!" Alyssa answered.

"He's going to meet us at the back entrance of the complex. It will be easier if we go on foot. It's only a few blocks from here," Zoe said.

"I see you've done this a time or two?" Aunt Lilly asked.

"I plead the fifth on that one," she countered.

"I don't know that I feel comfortable just letting you kids run from the police right now," Mrs. Hunter said.

Ignoring her sister, Aunt Lilly stared at the group for a long while and then back toward the lights.

"This could work. *We* can act as a diversion. By now, they have to think that we are all together."

Mrs. Hunter turned to her sister, about to argue when Aunt Lilly touched her hand.

"Mary, this is his best chance. Roman and Cora have hidden him from everyone, including his parents. For twelve years, they have kept him away from the very person Powell will bring him to. If that happens, the last twelve years will have been for nothing!"

Mrs. Hunter seemed to ponder it for a few moments before nodding in approval.

"Do you have your phones on you?" Aunt Lilly asked.

We all nodded.

"Okay. We will try to keep them away from that entrance. Once we can, we will call you to find out where you are," Aunt Lilly said.

Pulling out her purse, Aunt Lilly grabbed a debit card and a wad of cash and handed both to Marcus.

"In case we can't meet back up right away, this will help."

Marcus looked at the money and quickly leaned forward to pull both his aunt and mom into a hug. Mrs. Hunter was wiping tears away when he sat back.

Seeing his mother's reaction, he gave her another hug and a kiss on the cheek.

"I love you, Mom. We'll be okay," he said to her.

"Please be careful!" Mrs. Hunter said as she opened the side door for us to exit.

As it was Marcus's door that opened, he left the van first. He placed his coveted VR on the seat and began helping everyone out of the car. Izzie was the last out. Before he could fully close the door, another cruiser sped past. A second later, it was heard skidding to a stop.

"Gotta go!" Marcus shouted as he banged on the side of the car.

"Scatter! Scatter!" he exclaimed.

Izzie stood motionless, staring toward the flashing lights that were quickly backing up. Realizing we were quickly losing options, I grabbed her hand and pulled her in the direction of the others, running toward the side of the house Mrs. Hunter had parked in front of. My heart was pounding in my ears, muffling all other sounds. I could feel the burn in my lungs as I quickly tried to suck in enough air to keep me going.

As we reached the corner of the house, I could see the flashing lights getting brighter behind us. I heard a car skidding away and turned briefly to see Mrs. Hunter trying to block the officers. Seeing her actions, dread washed over me as I realized the situation we now found ourselves. In order to help me, my friends were putting themselves and their futures in serious danger. Would Mrs. Hunter lose her job? Would my friends get expelled from school or even be able to get into college? Were Aunt Cora and Uncle Roman safe or captured somewhere? I felt myself slow and loosed my grip on Izzie as I looked over my shoulder.

"Don't even think it!" Izzie snapped at me.

She grabbed my hand tighter, and our roles reversed, with her now dragging me. In the distance, I could make out the silhouettes of her sisters and Marcus in the moonlight running through a clearing behind the houses. They were heading toward a wall of trees that surrounded the complex.

"There!" Izzie pointed.

I nodded as we picked up our pace to catch up with the group. Behind us, I could hear shouting and heavy footfalls. Then I saw a beam of light swaying wildly back and forth from behind us.

"They're chasing us!" Izzie cried.

"I know! Run faster!" I huffed.

From behind us, I could hear a male voice yelling, "Freeze!"

My heart felt as though it was going to burst out of my chest. Not trusting myself to look over my shoulder without running straight into a tree, I kept my head straight with Izzie keeping pace next to me.

Seeing our destination getting closer, I could hear the voice of an officer—no, wait. I hear two voices now, behind us getting louder and more demanding.

"Stop, now! We need backup in here."

Just inside the timberline, Alyssa, Zoe, and Marcus had crouched down low. Once in sight, they motioned for us to come to them, causing me to pick up my pace.

"We need to split up. I don't think they saw all of us. Just you and Izzie!" Alyssa said.

"Do you see the path up there?" Zoe pointed to one a few hundred feet ahead of us.

"Yeah, I see it!" I said.

"Good, turn right onto it and follow it. It will literally spit you out at Brian," Zoe said.

"Wait! You're not coming with us?" Izzie screeched in a panicked voice.

"Alyssa and I know these woods really well. If any of us can get out of here and home, it's us. Besides, they're looking for *two* people, not three. Wait till we are out of sight and then run."

Izzie hugged Zoe and then Alyssa before they ran off. Her sisters were making as much noise as possible as they ran to attract the approaching officers, who seemed to have stopped before entering the wooded area.

Within seconds, a beam of light shot out toward the right, following Alyssa and Zoe. I lifted a finger to tell Izzie and Marcus to wait, pointing to the light. Once the officers had fully turned to head in that direction, we slowly stood up. We began cautiously walking toward the path, trying not to make any noise. The track was well-beaten. Even so, in the gloom of the forest, someone could easily miss it if they were not looking for it. When I finally saw it, I felt a new appreciation for Zoe.

The path was very narrow and could only have us following in a single file. I took the lead with Izzie behind me while Marcus followed her. Fortunately, the ground was fairly level, allowing us to make excellent time.

Once we felt we were out of earshot, we took off running again. Within a few minutes, we could see the density of the forest lessening. Realizing that the road must be getting close, we began to look for Brian's car.

"What does he drive?" I asked over my shoulder.

"A new Honda Accord. Gray," Izzie answered.

Just outside the tree line was a road. I slowed my pace, leaning out slightly to look for the car. He must have seen us first because I saw the lights of a gray car flash, and it rolled forward.

We made a run for it, praying that we were racing for the right car. As we approached, I could see Brian in the driver's seat and felt a wave of relief. I opened the back door, and Marcus dived in, followed by Izzie. Once they were in, I opened the front door and sat down to face Brian's icy stare.

"Uh, where's Zoe?" he asked.

"They ran back to the house as a diversion," Izzie answered.

Brian looked over his shoulder at Izzie, contemplating her answer before turning back to the road and driving away. After a beat, he asked, "A diversion for what?"

"Um, the police?" Marcus answered.

Brian shot around in the seat, which was impressive considering how little space there was for him to move. Then he glared at me, saying, "What does he mean?"

I ran through scenarios of what I could tell Brian that would not shock him and leave us stranded on the side of the road. Not knowing what else or how else to say it, I just blurted out the first thing that came to mind. "So I just found out that my parents are actually alive. It seems I have been in a sort of witness protection program for the past twelve years. Powell knows the person who my aunt and uncle have been hiding me from and is trying to catch me to take me there himself. So I now have to get to my parents who can protect me."

Brian stared at me wide-eyed with his mouth slightly agape. Finally, he managed to say, "I have *so* many questions! But for now, Izzie, is he for real?"

Izzie nodded. "We have to go. They will be down here soon. Please, Brian. You're his only chance to get home."

He stared at Izzie and then turned to look back at me.

"Okay... Where are we going then?" Brian asked.

The question hit me hard. *Where do I have to go?* I thought. As though someone else was listening in, the answer hit me.

"Pennsylvania!" I blurted out.

CHAPTER 18

Danger in the Shadows

"Are you freaking serious? That's about seven states away! What the hell is in Pennsylvania?" Brian exclaimed.

"My parents?" I said in a low voice.

Brian gawked at me for an uncomfortably long time, especially for someone driving a car. He only broke his stare to return his eyes to the task at hand when I said, "Road?"

After a few minutes of driving in silence, he finally spoke, "I'll take you to the interstate. Then we'll regroup."

"How far away is that?" I asked.

"This road will take us right to it. It's up by Gainesville, about thirty miles away."

I looked at the clock on his dash, which read 7:20 p.m. I felt a heaviness in my chest. *We would be sitting down to eat dinner now*, I thought.

As we drove further from the only family I have ever known, an overwhelming sense of homesickness washed over me. The next twenty minutes passed in silence as I watched the scattered ranges of farmland and cattle mingling between the trees. My phone going off interrupted my thoughts. I jumped at the noise before pulling it out. I read the cryptic message from the unknown number and then stared at it, unsure what to think.

Don't stop!

"Who is it?" Marcus asked, watching my reaction to the text.

"I don't recognize the number," I told him.

"Read the number out. Maybe one of us knows it," Brian suggested.

I looked at my phone again and read the number. Izzie and Brian answered simultaneously, "Zoe!"

"What did she say?" Brian asked.

"Don't stop!" I answered.

"Well, that's not ominous at all," Marcus moaned.

"Should I call or text back?" I asked.

Marcus leaned forward and smacked the phone out of my hands. Watching it as it hit the floor of the car, I looked back at Marcus in horror.

"Have you not seen a *CSI* show before? Come on! They can track it!"

Realizing the logic in what he was saying, I picked up my phone and looked at it for a second. Then without thinking, I opened my window and threw it out.

"What the hell did you do that for?" Brian demanded.

"They can track the phone even if it's not being used. They're looking for *me* and will follow *my* phone. Better to drop it."

About to argue with me again, Brian leaned back in his seat. Then he closed his mouth as if finally understanding my point.

"What *is* the plan?" Izzie asked.

"The hell if I know!" Brian started. "Zoe asked me to pick her and some others up. She neglected to mention I was taking y'all to Pennsylvania, running from the police, and that she wouldn't be part of the group!"

"True...and for that, we are very grateful...," Izzie started.

After a few moments, she continued, "So *will you* help us get him to his parents?"

Brian looked at Izzie through the rearview mirror. He sighed heavily before he spoke, "Where do they live...in Pennsylvania?" Brian asked.

"I-I'm not exactly sure. I figured when I got closer, I would try to figure that out."

"What in the actual hell! Are you fucking serious?" Brian bellowed, hitting his hand against the steering wheel.

"So we just drive north blindly? Until what? Your spidey senses kick in?" he asked, not unfairly.

"Funny you should say that...," Marcus started, which caused me to turn to look at him. Staring back, he lifted his shoulders in a defeated motion. Brian was watching Marcus in the rearview mirror. His breathing had intensified.

"We're almost at I-75. I'm going to pull off in the first place I can. You're going to give a much better story about what the hell you have gotten me into!" Brian said, a vein bulging in his forehead as he spoke.

I had seen the same sign he must have, showing that I-75 was three miles ahead. It also indicated a series of fast-food establishments were located somewhere near the on-ramp. Counting down the mile markers, I suddenly felt a pang of uneasiness hit me in the solar plexus. It grew in intensity as we came closer to the interstate. Unsure about what I was feeling, I just knew that we could not get on it.

When I thought the pain was about to hit its peak, I saw a turnoff.

"Turn left here! Now!" I yelled.

Startled by my yelling, Brian swerved a little before getting into the left-hand turning lane. It merged onto a side street, next to the interstate. Fortunately, it was far enough away, making it difficult to see us. But it was close enough for us to see a hoard of flashing lights at the entrance to I-75.

"Holy shit! There was a checkpoint. How did you know that?" Brian asked.

"I-I don't know. I more felt it than saw or knew it."

Brian looked over at me, brows knitted, trying to determine what I had meant by that last statement.

"There's an on-ramp further up. I'm thinking we may need to stick to side roads for a few miles, just to be safe," he said.

"You know this area better than me," I replied.

About ten miles up, the next on-ramp to the interstate came into view.

"How are those spidey senses doing?" Brian asked.

"Quiet… I think we're ok to enter here," I answered.

As we came close to the on-ramp, we cautiously looked for unmarked vehicles or anything suspicious. Not seeing anything concerning, we all agreed it was safe to proceed.

"Use the GPS to find out how to get to Pennsylvania from here," Brian said, pointing to the dashboard.

Nodding, I flipped through a handful of screens till I landed on the proper one. I entered our closest approximate destination and hit calculate. I watched as the little hourglass spun on the screen. Within a few seconds, the map highlighted a few suggested routes. Brian glanced at the screen and frowned.

"Pick the fastest," Brian said.

Flipping through the options, I winced.

"What now?" Brian asked in an agitated voice.

"The shortest route is still fifteen hours, thirty minutes."

"We're going almost ten states away. Did you think it was going to be an hour-long trip?" Brian asked.

"No. The problem is, we're also going the wrong way. I-75 takes us up toward the panhandle, but we need to be on the eastern part of the state."

"Of course, we are. You're just a ball of good news, aren't you?" Brian said, exacerbated.

"It looks like a relatively quick course correction up ahead. In about fifteen miles, we have to transfer over to I-10, which will bring us to I-95. Then it's just a straight run."

Brian's sighed heavily.

"Just let me know when we need to turn."

With our destination now entered, we followed the GPS, eventually making our way onto I-95 and headed north. The tension in the car was palpable as the miles accumulated. Unsurprisingly, it finally hit a boiling point. As though the realization of what I had told him finally hit, Brian gripped the wheel tighter and pursed his lips.

"I cannot drive for fifteen hours straight. Who else has a license?"

Marcus awkwardly raised his hand. "I have a permit but can drive as long as I am with a licensed driver."

Dropping his head back against the headrest, Brian looked up to the sky before bringing his eyes back to the road.

"This trip just gets better and better." Then he looked at Izzie in the rearview mirror. "Remind me not to do your sister anymore favors."

After having been on the road for nearly ninety minutes, a sign for the Georgia border came into sight. It was followed by another that indicated *Yulee Rest Stop* just before the border. Looking at the car's gauges, Brian flipped on his turn signal. He made his way toward the rest stop, causing me to sit up in my seat. Brian must have noted my movements and shot back a response before I could even speak.

"The car needs gas. I need food and a bathroom."

"I think a reassessment of our situation would make sense too," Izzie agreed.

"And I'm liking the food and bathroom suggestion," Marcus chimed in.

As the car merged into the rest stop lane, I looked at the dashboard's clock, which showed 9:30 p.m. I felt a lurch in my stomach. I wanted, no…I needed to find out what was happening in Williston. Instinctively, I reached into my pocket to pull out my cell phone and frowned, remembering its fate a few hours earlier.

"Has anybody received a text or call?" I asked, hopeful for something other than radio silence.

Each person looked at their device, all with the same response—no contact. Slowing as we approached the gas station, Brian pulled out his wallet.

"No, man. My aunt gave me money." Marcus stopped him.

Brian eyed him before nodding.

"Normally, I don't care, but I'll gladly take the kickback this time."

Reaching into the back seat, Brian grabbed the money Marcus was offering before quickly leaving the car and walking into the building to pay for the gas. I looked over the seat to Izzie and Marcus. Izzie was leaning on her hand and looking out her window. Her shoulders were hunched, and her face was drawn. Seeing her distress only added to mine, knowing that I had brought it on.

Next, I looked to Marcus, who gave the flicker of a smile. He was attempting to mask the stress of the day.

"Are you guys okay?" I asked.

Marcus looked at Izzie and then back at me.

"As well as can be expected, under the circumstances," Marcus replied.

"Izzie?" I asked.

Without turning to look, she whispered, "I've never been this far from my family before. I'm okay... I'm just...processing."

Marcus reached over and rubbed her knee, which caused her to look back at him. The movement also illuminated her face for a fraction of a second, revealing the tears. As though hit by an electric current, I threw my door open and swung around to hers. Opening the door, I visibly startled Izzie who gasped, then jumped closer to Marcus.

Instantly, I realized how stupid my actions were.

"I'm sorry. I just saw you were crying. I didn't mean to scare you."

Her posture softened, and she moved closer to where she had been sitting.

"It's okay. But you were...," she trailed off.

"Fast!" Marcus helped.

The driver's side door opened, and Brian looked in. Seeing me by the back seat, his eyebrows rose.

"Everything okay? Or is there some other new piece of information y'all are about to drop on me?" he asked, his hazel eyes glinting in the station's glow.

"I promise, there's nothing new to add," I said.

"I'm not sure what we will find open at this hour, so I'd recommend grabbing some snacks from inside. The clerk says the bathrooms are around the outside of the building. After I pump the gas, I'll park us closer. I don't want Izzie going in by herself, so one of us will check and then stand guard," Brian said.

As Izzie was about to protest, Brian's eyebrows shot up, and he pointed to her.

"Not on my watch."

Her shoulders slumped slightly, but she nodded. I could see the displeasure in her attitude, but Marcus spoke up first.

"Izzie, we're in the middle of nowhere. Technically, we're also running from the police, and you are the only girl with three guys. Safety first."

She looked over to Marcus and squeezed his hand. Izzie smiled, holding his eyes for a few seconds. Then she turned to me and did the same. Brian finished pumping the gas and moved toward the driver's seat. Seeing him approach the car, I resumed my position in the front seat. We pulled away from the pump and parked on the side of the building. The spot he chose placed us between the bathrooms and the front of the building so both were visible.

Together, the four of us walked back into the store to buy snacks for the trip. As we entered, I had to squint. The stark contrast of the fluorescent bulbs to the outside night left my retinas burning. We split up in the store and ended up picking up a small cooler, reusable ice packs, some sodas, chips, and sandwiches before heading to the front of the store to pay. With our horde purchased and bagged, we made our way back out to the car, where Izzie began putting the cooler together. While she worked, we each took turns going to the bathroom, making sure that one of us was always with Izzie.

After she had packed the cooler, it was her turn to use the facilities. But as she stepped out of the car, there was a slight pause. The three of us stared at each other, determining who would accompany her. Izzie quickly realized it and threw her hands up in the air as she walked away.

Being the closest to her and the bathroom, I looked back and shrugged before turning back to follow her. At the door, I grabbed her arm to stop her.

"We'll go in together. I'll look around. If no one else is in there, I'll leave."

"You're serious?" she said incredulously.

"Izzie, we're in a rest stop gas station in the middle of nowhere at night. Be reasonable."

I opened the door and motioned for her to enter. She rolled her eyes at me and walked into the bathroom.

As we entered, the noxious smell of urine mixed with bleach hit my nose, and I had to fight back a gag. When I looked at Izzie, she seemed to experience the same sensation. Although there was a strong smell of cleaner in the room, it appeared they had not scrubbed it in an exceedingly long time. "Perhaps they sprayed the room in a vain hope that the cleaners would come to life and do the job of scrubbing for them like the commercials suggested?" Izzie giggled as she nodded.

It was a single toilet bathroom in a wide-open room. There were no closets or other locations where someone could hide. Feeling comfortable leaving her alone, I made my way to the door.

"I'm just outside, okay?"

"I'm fine, Jace… But don't hang out too close to the door. The acoustics are superb here. I may develop a shy bladder knowing you're right there."

Feeling a smile form at the corner of my mouth, I nodded as I left the room. Being sure that I heard the door lock engage, I stepped outside the wall which partially obscured the bathroom from the parking lot.

I looked at the wall and thought about its odd placement, from a safety standpoint. As I considered this, I felt the hairs on the back of my neck stand up. I looked toward the car and could see Marcus and Brian talking to each other. They were both casually leaning against the car and had their arms crossed in front of them. Turning toward the more wooded area behind the building, I strained to see if there was something tripping my alarms. However, I could only make out the blackness and the outline of the trees.

I kept looking back and forth. The sense of uneasiness grew inside me, and I had an overwhelming urge to get in the car. Realizing that I could not leave my position until Izzie was out of the bathroom, I stood my ground and kept my eyes on whatever was in the trees. Just when I felt as though I couldn't take it anymore, Izzie opened the door and saw me staring at something behind the building. She poked her head around the enclosure to see what it was, but I waved her back. She stood erect and glared at me.

I said, "Walk back to the car, slowly. I'm following behind you but don't want to give it my back."

"It!" she exclaimed in a strangled whisper.

"I can't see it, but I feel it staring at me. Just get in the car… slowly. Tell Brian and Marcus to do the same."

I could hear Izzie pick up her pace as we neared the car and whispering for the other two to do the same. Neither seemed to object because I heard three car doors close in near unison. That left only me to get in. At a slow pace, I made my way to the car while walking backward, and I sent up a silent prayer that I wouldn't trip.

I could feel my heart hammering in my chest as I inched ever closer to the door. Feeling with my left hand, I grasped the door's handle and pulled it open wide enough to allow me to make my way in. Once I had enough clearance, I jumped in and slammed the door shut. With all passengers inside, Brian locked the doors and turned on the car.

As the engine engaged, the headlights automatically activated and illuminated the area where we had just been standing. Initially, it appeared just like a normal wooded area. Then without warning, the foliage moved, and an exceptionally large dark object lifted its head and turned to move deeper into the brush.

Spotting the movement, we all jumped, and Marcus let out a yelp.

"Holy shit, that is the biggest damn animal I have ever seen! What the hell is it?" Brian asked.

"Who cares. It's leaving, and so are we. Let's not give it a reason to turn around and attack!" Izzie demanded.

CHAPTER 19

Road Trip

I felt inclined to agree with Izzie's train of thought. I was completely unnerved by the size of…whatever it had been. Brian threw the car in reverse and peeled out of the spot. Changing gears, he caused the tires to squeal again as we drove out of the rest stop and back onto the interstate.

"What the hell do you think that was?" Brian said.

"It was the size of a bear!" Marcus added.

"But it looked like a dog," Izzie said.

Her words hung in the air, and I wondered if it *was* a type of dog—or more likely a werewolf! And if it had been, was it following us, or did we just cross paths coincidentally? Unsure whether this piece of information would help settle Brian's nerves or not, I decided to keep it to myself.

Fully fueled and with all our vital needs addressed, we made our way back onto the interstate. As we entered the roadway, I looked at the clock, which read 10:10 p.m. The GPS had us arriving in Pennsylvania at 11:20 a.m. tomorrow, barring any stops. I looked over toward Brian to judge his ability to make the straight run through the night. On the surface, he appeared alert and capable. However, I knew that thirteen hours of nonstop driving would be difficult.

I glanced in the back seat where both Marcus and Izzie were staring out the window.

"Hey, man. How about you try to get some sleep? I'm sure Brian's going to need a break soon enough," I addressed.

Marcus, who nodded, started adjusting himself in the seat, trying to get comfortable.

Izzie turned to look over at Marcus struggling to find a comfortable position and frowned.

"Here, put your head on my lap," she offered.

Although I knew the option was a logical one, I felt anger at the suggestion and wanted to turn around to stop it. I took a few deep breaths instead and closed my eyes to rebalance myself. Brian had noticed my agitation and was looking at me.

"You gonna puke?" he asked with concern in his eyes.

Startled by the question, I opened my eyes and looked at him.

"No. I'm good. Just thinking."

Brian squinted at me and nodded slowly.

"Okay…but if you feel like you're going to be sick, you need to let me know."

"Deal," I said, reclosing my eyes.

At some point, the movement of the car had lulled me to sleep. When I woke up, I overheard Brian and Izzie talking. Not wanting to interrupt the conversation, I kept quiet while I listened.

"I'm not sure why your sister hasn't texted yet, but I think keeping quiet may be the best for now. If she needed to get in touch with us, she would have."

"I know. I'm just nervous that she's texting Jace's phone, and well—"

"Yeah. I'm still not sure if that was a good idea or not."

There was a brief pause in the conversation, and I contemplated moving when Brian started speaking again.

"So what *is* the deal with you and this one? He is crazy protective over you but not overbearing. I can't tell if you two are dating or what…"

Silence came from the back seat, and I felt my heart stop while I waited to hear Izzie's response.

"It's more complicated than that. I really like him as a person. But I don't really know him that well. The last time I got myself into a situation like this, it…well, we know how *that* turned out."

"True, but if I remember correctly, *he* helped you out of that situation. You have no feelings for him?"

"I do, but there is a lot going on…for both of us right now."

After a long pause, she spoke again.

"His family…his real family is in Pennsylvania. *I* don't live in Pennsylvania."

My heart dropped at the thought. With all the rushing to get to my parents, I didn't take into consideration the people I would be leaving behind. And at the top of that list were Izzie and Marcus. I suddenly felt a wave of anxiety rush me and an overwhelming need to make every minute last with them overtook it.

To keep from looking like I was eavesdropping, I waited for what I thought to be a reasonable period before shifting in my seat. I did an obvious stretch, so both Brian and Izzie would be aware that I was awake.

"Where are we?" I said in midstretch.

"Almost out of Georgia."

Instinctively, I looked to the dash to see what time it was—12:02 a.m.

"How are you holding up? Do you need a break?" I asked.

Brian also looked down at the dash and then yawned a deep jaw-cracking yawn.

"Yeah. I guess I do. We'll stop at the first exit in South Carolina that looks like it has life. I'm not looking for a repeat of the Yulee rest stop."

I heard movement from the back and glanced over my shoulder. Marcus had still been asleep on Izzie's lap but was now shifting into a more erect position.

Brian looked in his rearview mirror at Marcus.

"Mornin', sunshine. You feelin' up to drive yet?" he asked.

Marcus smiled sleepily and gave a thumbs-up.

Brian, seeing the gesture, rolled his eyes and frowned.

"We'll get some coffee in ya before we get moving."

In front of us rose a sign, saying, "Welcome to South Carolina."

"Check the map to see the next place we can stop," Brian asked me.

Moving the map around, I examined our options.

"Looks like Hardeeville. There are a few places for food, and if needed, a few places to sleep too," I hinted.

Brian looked at me and then over his shoulder at Izzie. He narrowed his eyes. "Let's see how sleeping beauty back there is feeling when we stop," Brian said.

Marcus, as though on cue, yawned loud and large. After an exaggerated stretch, again, he smiled and gave another thumbs up.

"You're not really filling me with positive vibes, Hunter," Brian retorted.

Looking back at me, "Do we even have a way to pay for a room?" he asked.

"Yes. His aunt gave us money and her debit card when we split up," I answered.

Seeming to contemplate our next move, Brian looked in the back seat again. When he gave an agitated sigh, it made me look. Although sitting upright, Marcus's head was lolling backward. With his eyes closed, he was now emitting low snores.

Seeing him made me chuckle. Then I found it harder to keep myself from going into a full-on laughing fit. Trying desperately to regain control, I felt myself bouncing in the seat with the suppressed laughter. Brian watched me and a smile crawled across his face too. It was soon followed by a small laugh.

"I'm sorry. I have no idea what is making me laugh so hard," I said.

"We all need a good laugh after the past few hours," Brian said.

"Not that I want to break the laugh-fest up there, but how far away is the next stop?" Izzie asked.

Slowly regaining my composure and wiping away a tear that had formed, I looked at the GPS.

"It looks like we're about five miles away," I said.

We rode in silence for the next ten minutes with only the radio and Marcus's ever-increasing snore to break the silence. Pulling off the road had helped to wake all of us up, and we began to look for the nearest areas to eat. Going left seemed to have the most options for both food and lodging. Cracker Barrel, Wendy's, and a Chicken Licken were all closed, though. Fortunately, there was a Waffle House open.

Brian pulled up to the yellow-and-brown building, and looking in, we could see that there were only two other patrons inside. Deciding that they did not appear to be a threat, we stepped out of the car and headed in. The smell of food on a griddle instantly hit me as we opened the door, and my stomach immediately started making itself known. Feeling the pangs of hunger, I tried to remember the last time I ate an actual meal and realized it had not been since the night of the grotto.

A petite middle-aged woman in a dark blue button-down shirt and navy-blue tie, with the logo emblazoned on her sleeve, approached our group. She sported a forced and weary smile.

"Welcome to Waffle House. My name is Abey. Would y'all like the counter or a booth?"

"A booth would be just fine," Brian said, tipping his baseball cap toward her.

Abey seemed to light up at the gesture and smiled more warmly as her cheeks began to flush.

"Right this way. I'll keep you close to your car," she said.

"Thank you!" Brian said, smiling at her.

Izzie sat down first, and Brian sat next to her, looking at me in a challenge. I moved into the seat across her, allowing room for Marcus to sit down next. I glanced over at Izzie and made eye contact briefly. I dropped my gaze when I saw Brian looking over. Marcus appeared only mildly more awake in the restaurant than he had been in the car. The thought of him being a handoff to allow Brian a break seemed more and more unlikely.

"Can I get y'all something to drink?" Abey asked while handing us menus.

"You can get this one the strongest coffee you have in here." Brian pointed at Marcus.

Abey looked to Marcus and chuckled.

"Next shift, I guess?" she asked.

"That's what we're hoping," Brian said.

"I'll have a cola," he continued.

"Sprite, please," Izzie said.

"Sprite too, please," I said.

"Be right back."

As Abey walked away, we all picked up the menus. By this point, my stomach was screaming at me, and if I could have, I would have ordered everything. I looked around the table to see if everyone else had made their selections.

"What is everyone thinking?" I asked.

"Well, you can't come to *Waffle* House and not get waffles. So I'll get that with some hash browns," Izzie said.

"I'll have a Texas Angus Patty Melt," Brian answered.

"I'm feeling a chicken hash brown bowl," Marcus said.

"I'm famished, and the All-Star Special is calling my name," I replied.

"Soda and breakfast. You two are a special kind of weird," Brian said.

"We're covering for dinner and breakfast," Izzie said with a laugh and smiled at me.

Walking back with our drinks, Abey looked around at our small group of misfits.

"Where are y'all headed? You seem a bit young to be taking on a road trip by yourselves."

An uneasiness came across the table at her question. I felt my stomach bunch up in knots, leaving me questioning food again.

"We're heading back to college in Virginia. We're all from the same town in Georgia and took a road trip for the holiday weekend," Brian said so convincingly that I questioned if that was, in fact, what we were doing.

"Which school do you go to?" Abey asked.

"Virginia State in Petersburgh," Brian answered with no hesitation.

"Don't mind me. Hazard of the profession, small talk," Abey said.

Seeing the honesty in her answer and wanting to hug Brian for his quick answers, I felt a few of the kinks release in my stomach.

"Are you guys ready?" Abey asked.

After we had given her our order, we watched as Abey walked away to deliver it to the cook. As I looked back to the table, I found Izzie staring at Brian with hurt in her eyes.

"You're really going, aren't you?" she finally asked him.

Brian dropped his gaze to his drink.

"That's really a conversation better suited to Zoe and me," Brian said.

"She thought you were going together?"

"I haven't figured out what I am doing yet. But VSU is a definite possibility. If I'm accepted this year, I don't want to wait."

Izzie looked as though he was leaving her and not her sister.

Brian winced. "Izzie, please. We have bigger things to deal with right now. I promise I will talk to Zoe when I get home. Scratch that. I will *have* to talk to Zoe when I get home because I know you three talk about everything."

Our group went quiet, not knowing what exactly to say. As if on cue, Abey walked up to the table with our food. As she passed out our orders, she looked us over and frowned. "Y'all look exhausted. Tomorrow, well, actually today, is Columbus Day. Y'all should be off, right?"

Unsure where she was going with her line of questioning, we all nodded. However, we continued to stare at her. She said, "Y'all look as though you were drug under the door. There's a Super 8 and Econo Lodge just up the road. Nice and cheap. At least you can recharge for a few hours."

She looked at Marcus and frowned.

"I can't see this one being ready to drive a Tonka truck, let alone a car tonight. Go get some sleep when y'all leave here."

"Thank you. We'll think about it while we eat this delicious-looking meal," Brian answered.

Abey smiled and walked back to the counter as we all started eating.

With each bite, the pangs of hunger lessened, but the waves of exhaustion increased. Judging by the appearance of my car-mates, the food was having a similar reaction on them. Shoveling the last of his food into his mouth, Brian sat back and stared at Marcus, as though he was contemplating his next step.

"Do you think we have enough money to stop?" Brian finally asked.

Realizing the question, Marcus sat up and pulled his wallet out. He began leafing through the money his aunt had given him. Surrounded by $15 in singles and two $20 bills were four $100 bills. Marcus's eyes went wide at the find.

"Yeah...I think we're good," he answered.

Seeing Marcus's face, Brian leaned over the table to see how much Marcus had just found.

"I guess that answers it. We'll go to whichever motel we pass first," Brian said.

At the completion of the meal, Marcus paid, and we piled back into the car. Now that we were actively looking for a place to stay, we could see a Super8 motel across the street. The Econo Lodge was about three streets away.

"Super8 it is!" Brian said.

Pulling out of the parking spot, Brian began moving toward the exit. A set of headlights turned on behind us, which momentarily distracted me. I looked back into the Waffle House. I no longer saw any other patrons within the restaurant. Thinking it was likely just another weary passenger heading to their future destination, I didn't give it another thought.

As we pulled out onto the road, we were hit from behind with immense force. It sent the car careening forward into the divider. As we hit it, there was a loud pop. My sight exploded into white while my face began burning, and I was having difficulty hearing anything.

Trying to focus made me feel as though I was watching a movie that was skipping scenes. I reached down and tried to open my seat belt and found that I was having difficulty maneuvering my fingers to get it to release. Just as frustration started to mount, I felt myself lapse in time. When I came to, I felt as though I was floating. I looked around, trying to determine what was happening.

Multiple bodies were standing around our car. There was also a van next to it. It was around this time that my brain started working enough for me to realize that I was, in fact, floating or, more accurately, being carried by two large men toward the van. Fear set in, and I tried to fight the duo.

I peeked in through the van's open door and saw Izzie lying on her side. Fear flooded my system. Realizing that I was about to be unceremoniously thrown in, I tried to brace myself so as not to land on her. As they released me, I quickly rolled toward the opposite wall of the van. Sitting up, I looked around and saw Brian and Marcus struggling as someone was tying them up. Feeling anger building, I leaped toward them. Then I felt a searing pain in the back of my head, and my vision went dark.

CHAPTER 20

Powers Revealed

With the light spray of mist hitting my face and the wonderful aroma of the sea, I looked over the railing at the crystal blue water with the colorful buildings of the island in front of us. I felt a hand on my shoulder, and I turned to see Uncle Roman.

"It's amazing, isn't it?" he asked.

"It looks like something out of a fairy tale. When can we go see it?" I asked.

Leaning slightly over the railing, he turned to look at me.

"We should dock soon. Hold on. It may be a bit bumpy as we do," he said with a smile.

"Where is Aunt Cora?"

He looked around the deck and shrugged good-naturedly.

"Around somewhere, I suppose. You know your aunt."

Uncle Roman looked over the railing again at the bow of the ship and frowned.

"Here we go. Are you holding on?"

I could see the dock and realized that we were moving far too quickly to dock safely. Panic rose as we rapidly moved closer. Uncle Roman was still watching the bow but had gripped the railing tighter. I instinctively tried to do the same but found that someone had tied my hands behind my back. My heart pounded in my chest as I struggled to release my numb limbs before we collided with the dock. But the more I struggled, the stronger the bond seemed to become.

"Uncle Roman, they tied my hands! Help me!"

Looking back at me, he adjusted his head to see the bonds and then gave a disapproving smile.

"You shouldn't have left. Now look what happened."

Shock waves ran through me at his words.

"I-I didn't leave you. You knew I was going to find them. *You* told me to find them!"

"We all have decisions to make, and then we have to deal with the consequences."

Feeling the burn of tears forming in my eyes, I looked to the man who had been my father. As the buildings in the distance grew, I felt the boat lurch forward as it hit the dock. Watching in horror, I could see the disappointment in Uncle Roman as the boat exploded into shrapnel of debris around him. Unsure how to avoid the destruction, I tucked my legs and head into my abdomen and awaited my demise. Hearing the boards breaking and splintering around me, I could feel the warm water from the sea below splashing up onto my face. *Did I fall through to an area lower down?* A disembodied voice came from somewhere, and I could feel someone touching my face. The tension in my back and shoulders loosened as I listened more intently to the voice and realized that it was Izzie. *How is she here?* Unsure how to answer, I listened closer and could hear her whispering in my ear.

"Jace! Please, Jace. Wake up. I'm scared."

Slowly coming back to the surface of my thoughts, I blinked my eyes open and looked around. I was in a vehicle of some sort, which was moving. Realizing my head was being cradled, I looked down to realize I was resting on Izzie's lap and she was leaning forward trying to comfort me, tears dropping from her eyes onto my face. Across us, along the rear of the boxed-in area, were Brian and Marcus. Their hands were also bound behind their backs and positioned next to each other, concern in both their eyes. I attempted to sit up, but the motion of the van caused me to fall back into my original position, Izzie letting out an "oof" as I hit her lap again.

"Sorry," I said.

"Oh, Jace! Thank God! I thought you were dead!" Izzie cried.

"I'm okay. I think. Where are we?"

"In a van, heading somewhere. We've only been driving a few minutes, but you were dead weight after the big guy hit you in the head. We all thought he might have killed you," Brian said.

Trying to lift myself, I lost my balance and landed on Izzie's lap again with a similar "oof."

"Let me try to help you," she suggested.

"Shift up more on my leg, and I will try to push you up."

Nodding, I maneuvered my body so that my shoulder was resting on her leg. Pulling her leg up toward her torso, she gave me enough lift to allow me to pull myself up the rest of the way. Shifting till I was in a kneeling position, I glanced back to Izzie and could see blood across her lap and shirt.

"What happened? You're hurt!" I exclaimed.

"Shhh!"

"But you're covered in blood!" I exclaimed.

She winced. "It's not mine."

Realization set in as I remembered the searing pain in the back of my head. I nodded and looked to Brian and Marcus.

"Are you two okay?" I asked.

Brian's face ran through a myriad of expressions.

"Not sure, Northall. This is quite the conundrum we're in. Do you have *any idea* what the hell is going on?" he asked in frustration.

"I heard them talking, and they mentioned meeting up with a different den and a man named Dillon… Dragon… Damien? I couldn't really hear," Izzie said.

My heart dropped as I realized immediately who we would see.

"Daegen," I said solemnly.

"Yeah! That's it."

Seeing my face, her expression changed, and she frowned.

"Who is Daegen, and why do you look like we're going to meet Lucifer himself?" Brian asked in an irritated tone.

"*He* is the person they were hiding me from. All the time away. All the years lost…for nothing. He's still going to get me."

Anger coursed through my veins, and I felt the tension in my arms as I pulled on the bindings, trying to free myself. I may not prevent coming face-to-face with him, but I would be damned if I

251

would do it bound. The more anger I felt, the harder I struggled till I heard a snap and felt the bindings loosen. With more force, I could feel its death grip ease. The bindings finally burst into a bundle of frayed material behind me. Pulling my hands forward, I rubbed at my wrists, and as I did, I could see the intensity of the red streaks and tears on my skin fading as though it was healing in front of me. *How is that possible?*

"How the hell did you do that?" Brian demanded.

He stared at me with venom in his eyes. Realizing we'd never explained the details of who I really was, I decided now was as good a time as any, seeing that no one was going anywhere. Moving to untie Izzie first, Brian moved forward.

"Don't touch her!" he growled.

I looked from Izzie to Brian, and she nodded toward Brian.

"Him first. He'll feel better," she said.

I shifted toward Brian, causing him to back up slightly at the movement.

"I come in peace," I said with a small smile on my face.

Brian narrowed his eyes at me before finally turning enough for me to see his bindings. Working on loosening the knots, I tried to explain all that I knew up till this point, with Izzie periodically adding in information that I may have missed. She shocked me by how much she had been paying attention and knew the story of my life. I smiled at her and felt my heart warm when I saw her turn away shyly. Within a few minutes, I had Brian free. Turning to Marcus, I realized he had been, uncharacteristically, quiet through all this.

"You okay, man?" I asked.

Marcus looked to both of us with a distant look in his eyes and nodded slowly, then stopped and then shook his head.

"Talk to us, big guy," Brian said.

Marcus's face almost seemed to crack before he spoke.

"I'm scared," he said in half matter-of-fact, half exacerbated manner.

My heart broke at his words, knowing that his helping me put him into this position. Brian put his hand on Marcus's shoulder for reassurance, and Marcus looked over at him, blankly.

"I know. We all are. Let's get you untied, okay?" Brian suggested.

Marcus nodded, still looking distant and dazed.

"I'll get him. You get her," Brian said, nodding toward Izzie.

Izzie was tight against a wheel well inside the van and needed to move forward enough before I could release her.

"I'm going to lift you a bit to get better access to the rope, okay?"

She nodded. Placing my hands along her sides, I carefully lifted and shifted her slightly into an ideal position. As I pulled away from her, I could see a blush cross her cheeks as she smiled and looked down.

"Okay, you two. We have bigger issues right now," Brian said from across the van.

"Are you sure he's not your big brother?" I asked.

"Yes, but I wonder sometimes." She chuckled.

Getting back to the task at hand, I positioned myself behind her and worked on her ties. Within a few minutes, I loosened her bindings, and she pulled her arms around toward the front of her, rubbing at her wrists. Lifting her hands into mine, I looked at her wrists and could see the chafing and burns to her delicate skin and felt the anger well up again. She must have seen it and touched my hand.

"It's just scrapes. They will heal," she said.

She looked to my wrists and saw that there was no sign of them being bound and then looked up at me, wide-eyed.

"H-How? I saw your wrists. They were raw and bleeding. Those men were unnecessarily aggressive with you!"

I chuckled. "Fast healer, I guess."

Looking from her wrists to Brian and Marcus's, it hit me.

"I wonder…" I looked at Izzie. "Do you trust me?"

"I-I think so," she said in a small voice while narrowing her eyes.

Taking her hands and wrists in my hands, I closed my eyes and imagined her skin in its perfect condition prior to the bindings. Feeling a sense of peace wash over me, I could see a blue light form in my chest, getting brighter and brighter until I willed it to travel down my arms and onto her. It was a warm sensation as it focused around her wrists. I did not feel her pull away from me, so I continued with my experiment. Within a few minutes, I felt the warmth dissipate and travel back up my arms, and once it was back in my chest, I opened my eyes to look at Izzie. Her eyes were the size of saucers. Looking down at her wrists, I could see that the trauma inflicted on her wrists had vanished.

"That was amazing! Everything, not just my wrists, feels better," she said, still wide-eyed.

"Holy fucking shit... If I had not just watched that, I never would have believed it," Brian said. "What the hell did you just do?" he demanded.

"I'm not exactly sure. I sent her some health is the best way I could describe it."

Watching Brian, I tried to gauge my next move.

"Do *you* want help?" I asked him.

Brian looked at his wrists and then back to Marcus, who was still not looking very well.

"Maybe him first."

Nodding, I moved over to Marcus and knelt in front of him.

"Hey, man. You okay with me trying to help you?" I asked, extending my hand out to him.

As though being brought back from another reality, he looked at me and then down at my hand quizzically.

"Sure," he said, voice distant.

Realizing that he needed more than surface healing, I tried to pull on something deeper to help him. *Can I give him courage? Strength?* Slowly, I grasped his hands and closed my eyes the same way I did with Izzie. Digging deeper, I pulled on something, asking to give Marcus what he needed to feel safe and comfortable again. As before, I felt a warmth start in my chest, but this time, it was more like a swirling motion, as though multiple things were being brought forward. As they swirled within my core, I felt them separate into distinct entities, each of a different color. I watched as they moved again out of me and into Marcus. Initially, he gasped and pulled back slightly, but I tightened my grip on him, calling the colors back to me.

"I won't hurt you. Please, trust me."

He stared at me with concern in his eyes before nodding. Trying again, I focused on the waves of colors. In my mind's eye, I could see each emotion as a different color and tried to focus on the ones that he would need the most.

The first strand I noticed glowed the color of teal sea glass, and I knew it was calm. I tried to push that through to him initially, and as it did, I felt a sense of relaxation grow within him. It was working.

Next, I looked for courage and found it glowing red. I gave just enough to give him the comfort he needed. The last thing we needed, right now, was an enraged teen in the back. Additionally, I sent strength, which glowed as bright yellow. I watched as Marcus appeared to sit more erect and less timid. Finally, I sent him health, which shone as a brilliant blue color. As we sat there, hand in hand, I allowed the magic to enter his body and decide the dose of each he needed then waited until I felt the warmth retreat up my arms and back within me. Opening my eyes, I looked at Marcus who appeared to be back to his normal quirky self. He was smiling and looking at his hands, then looked back at me with wonder.

"That was amazing. I feel like I could conquer the world right now. How did you do that?" he asked.

"I'm kinda winging it here, but it's working, so I'm going with it." I chuckled.

Looking to Brian, I nodded to his wrists. He hesitated and then looked to Izzie and Marcus for approval.

"It doesn't hurt. It's like getting into a warm comfy bed on a frosty night. It just wraps you up and you feel totally at peace. It's amazing!" Izzie said.

Somewhat stunned by her description, I stared at her.

"What? It did!" she answered to my stare.

"Okay. I'm game," Brian answered, sticking his hands out quickly to me and turning his head. I laughed at his reaction.

Reaching out, I grabbed his hands and told him to relax. Opening his right eye to look at me, he slowly turned his head forward and relaxed his arms. Following the same strategy, I allowed my inner self to send Brian what he needed to feel whole again. Once more, courage, strength, and health were given. Feeling the powers dissipate, I opened my eyes to see Brian smiling, relaxed, and comfortable.

"Izzie is right. That was amazing."

As though hit with a second thought, he looked back to me with his brows furrowed.

"How are *you*? You see this stuff in the movies, and it usually drains the person giving the power," Brian said.

Sitting back on my heels, I contemplated what he'd said and tried to do an internal evaluation. Oddly enough, not only did I not feel drained, but I felt energized.

"Actually, I feel great. Is that weird?"

"Your guess is as good as mine on this one. I am so far out of my neck of the woods here I can't even understand what is happening," Brian said.

"Shhh! The van is stopping. Should we get back into our previous positions?" Izzie asked.

"No. I want the ability to fight when those doors open," Brian said.

Hearing the brakes squealing to a stop and the van jostling as its front seat passengers exited, the three of us braced ourselves in the door with Izzie behind. Unable to hear anything happening outside, I realized the van must be soundproofed. As we waited for the doors to open, I could feel my heart racing and felt Marcus place his hand on my shoulder.

"We got this," he said, nodding firmly.

Glancing over my left shoulder, I nodded to him. I next looked over my right shoulder to Brian, who was in a similar position, ready to lunge at whoever was unfortunate to open the door. Seeing me look, he nodded. Turning back to the door, we heard the handle engage and release.

Bracing myself, I waited for the door to slide open and was momentarily blinded by a flashlight. I could still make out the three men's shadows and dived out of the truck as though we had practiced it one hundred times. Completely surprised by the attack, the men flew backward and began wrestling with the three of us. As easily as it had been for them to take us the first time, they were struggling this time. The only thing that broke up the fighting was a high-pitched whistle that caused all of us to stop and grab our ears. Looking for the source, I saw a large man holding Izzie by the upper arm as she kicked and thrashed. Instinct took over, and I jumped up. Instantly, the man grabbed her by the throat, and she let out a strangled yelp. Realizing that they'd caught us again, I stood down and waited for what was to happen next.

CHAPTER 21

Millstone Landing

We were standing in front of a large modern wooden three-story cabin with a wide front yard. There were multiple cars parked in front and roughly a dozen men of various sizes and ethnicities present and watching the melee on the grass. The front door to the cabin opened, and a large burly man emerged who could have been the inspiration for the Brawny paper towels mascot, down to the red plaid shirt and dark tousled hair and beard.

"Now, boys, I'm sure that you are not manhandling our guests," the man said.

Looking to Marcus and Brian, I could see that each had their assailant pinned tightly under them, as did I. So if anyone was manhandling anyone, it was not them.

"Mitchell, let go of that girl. Kyle, Kelly, and Morgan…go get cleaned up. You're embarrassing yourselves. Three teenagers, really?" he said, glaring at the men.

"Get off me!" The man I had pinned grumbled.

"After *he* lets go of her." I motioned to the man holding Izzie.

"Mitchell! Let her go before I come over and make you!" Brawny man bellowed.

"I almost want to watch this all day, but I'll let her go. For you, George," the man holding Izzie said.

Once he released her, I immediately stood and rushed to her side, followed shortly by Brian and Marcus, forming a shield around her. The man in the door saw our positioning and laughed a deep laugh that seemed to make the trees shake.

"Seriously, boys. You can relax now. Welcome to Millstone Landing!" he said.

Looking to George, I felt a pit in my stomach forming.

"Sorry if your offer doesn't fill us with a warm and squishy sensation. The thought of entering a strange place after being kidnapped doesn't really scream 'good idea,'" Brian said.

The large man seemed to consider the statement before responding.

"It seems these fools were a bit harsh in their escorting you back to our humble abode. You see, we have a common friend that has been looking for you, and I offered my assistance in the matter."

The large man walked up to us and we each tensed, ready for a fight. The large man grinned as though he were seeing a group of puppies performing a trick.

"My name is George Barlow, the leader of this den."

Looking at each of us, he narrowed his eyes, examining each closely.

"What I am trying to figure out is…which one of you is Christian."

The three of us relaxed slightly and looked at each other. Finally, Brian spoke up, "None of us are named Christian."

George stood back to take us all in and laughed that boisterous laugh again. Behind me, I felt Izzie touch my shirt. Looking over my shoulder, to be sure she was okay, I saw the concern on her face. I tried to ease her fears by mustering up a smile. I hoped that it would be. Seeing my response, her shoulders seemed to relax slightly, but her face was creased with concern. I instantly wanted to turn to her and hold and tell her that everything was going to be all right, but I was unsure if that was true. The best way to protect her, right now, was to deal with this man and his questions. Fortunately, Brian and Marcus were working with me to keep this group as confused as I was.

"Of course not! How naive of me," George said, interrupting my thought.

Returning to his previous scrutinization of each of us, he started pacing back and forth. Periodically, he would stop and stare at one of us, only to shake his head and keep moving. Finally, he raised his eyebrows and gave a shrug with a long sigh. Stepping back to look at the three of us collectively, he said, "I know that one of you was taken twelve years ago. I have been trying to figure out who, but you all seem to be equal in the likelihood, no matter how much I try to work it out."

"I think it's the big guy," Mitchell hollered from the doorway of the house.

George looked over his shoulder toward Mitchell, then turned back to us, nodding as he did. Walking back to stand in front of Brian, he considered Mitchell's statement before he spoke, gently stroking his beard. "I, too, thought the big one would make the most sense."

Turning next to Marcus, he continued, "But I was thinking perhaps they would not want him to be so obvious in stature. Let people think of him as the underdog."

Marcus looked to Brian and then down at himself. "Gee, thanks," he muttered.

His reaction took me off guard, and I chuckled at his response. Unfortunately, it also brought George's attention to me. While standing in front of Marcus, he turned his head to look at me and smiled. Not breaking eye contact, he walked toward me till we were practically nose to nose.

"Then there is you. The clean-cut, nonassuming teen."

The corner of his lip went up as he looked me up and down.

"I heard you gave my boys quite the fight in Hardeeville. They told me they had to give you quite the blow to take you down."

He leaned around to the back of my head, noting the dried blood, and made a wincing noise as he came back around to look me in the eye.

"No matter, we have someone coming that will help clear things up."

He looked to his watch, then clapped his hands together, creating a thunderous sound.

"Wonderful! He should be here in about two hours. Let's bring our *new friends* and settle them in the guest room."

As George walked back to the house, he hollered over his shoulder, as if it was a second thought, "And no more hurting our guests today, okay?"

Groans across the yard as a group of men made their way toward us. I pulled Izzie next to me and wrapped my arm tightly around her. Brian positioning himself behind us, with Marcus tucking up close to her on the other side. I could feel her shivering and looked down at her.

"Are you cold?"

"Honestly, I don't know what I am right now."

I tugged her in tighter to me as we walked toward the door of the cabin. This "cabin," however, was massive and imposing. As I took in its three-story facade, I realized that under different circumstances I may have been jealous of the man cave this group had created.

Jutting out of the front of the house was a large covered entrance that was the height of two stories and gave the house more of a resort feel rather than a home. Ornately detailed oak doors, which seemed far older than the actual house, opened to a large foyer with two sets of wooden staircases flanking its sides. The whole of the interior was wood. A small babbling brook running through the center was all that was needed to complete the outdoors brought inside feel.

Just beyond the foyer was a large sitting room with floor-to-ceiling windows that were just as wide as they were tall. Imagining the sunlight washing across the room in the morning made me partially long to see the effect for myself. This room seemed to be the heart of the house with multiple gathering areas within it, including a mahogany bar and matching pool table to the right. Along the left wall was a colossal fireplace made of large river rock with a large flat-screen TV strategically positioned above it, allowing the best vantage point. Surrounding the hearth were multiple reclining leather couches. Uncle Roman would have likely abandoned his poor La-Z-Boy for one of these!

As we walked closer to the sitting room, I could see there were two hallways that seemed to jut off this key area in the house. The left hallway, behind the fireplace, seemed to be bedrooms while to the right, behind the bar area, was a kitchen.

Pointing to the left, Mitchell directed us to what I assumed was going to be the guest room. After passing four other rooms, he opened the last door on the left and stepped aside to let us in. The room seemed to be an unassuming bedroom with two queen beds, a couch, and a TV on the wall. Unsure if I felt comfortable being locked in a room with no way out, I hesitated before entering.

"We can always lock you back up in the van," Mitchell said with a smile.

"She looks pretty cold. We would keep her warm for you." He flicked his eyebrows at Izzie, and my blood ran hot.

A growl rose from deep within, and I pulled Izzie closer to me. A smirk crossed Mitchell's face, along with a quick lift of an eyebrow. Guiding her into the room, I heard Marcus and Brian follow behind before the door shut and a latch engaged. Still holding Izzie close to me, I could fully appreciate how badly her body was shaking. I pulled her away from me enough to look at her.

"What's wrong?" I asked.

She laughed. "Seriously?"

Realizing the stupidity of the question, I asked again, "What's wrong, besides the obvious?"

She chuckled, and I saw a single tear roll down her cheek. Taking my thumb, I brushed it away and saw Brian and Marcus move closer to her.

"I-I think I'm just scared. I mean, I know it scared me outside, but what that guy just said...*that* terrified me." Her voice broke.

I pulled her close to me and held her tight.

"We won't let anyone hurt you," Brian said.

Holding her close, I could feel the flood of tears and emotions she must have been holding back release. Unsure what else to do now, I held her close as I listened to the sobs of fear and pain wash out. Once she seemed more relaxed, I pulled her away from me so I could look at her again. Using my thumbs, I wiped away the tears from her eyes as she turned to look away. I moved my head to look at her face and she shyly met my eyes.

"I look horrible right now," she said.

"You could never look horrible," I said with a smile.

"Ugh! Get a room you two—oh, wait!" Marcus threw his arms up.

Izzie giggled through her tears. "Thank you," she whispered.

He looked back and smiled. "Just trying to save us from the nauseating lovebird stuff."

Walking away from us, he dropped onto the bed and quickly jumped up off. He looked around the headboard and then tried to move it.

"Guys, come look at this," Marcus called.

Walking toward him, I could see that he was now trying to lift the side table between the beds.

"None of the furniture moves. It's like it was all built as part of the house. Why would you do that?"

"Because they put very strong things in here," Brian said.

I could see that he was scrutinizing the wall around the window that overlooked the front yard.

"Why do you say that?" I asked.

"If I didn't know any better, this looks like claw marks...*big* claw marks."

Moving closer, I looked at the marks on the walls and felt my breath catch at their size.

"It looks like a bear tore into this wall," Brian said. "Why would they keep bears inside a house?" Concern mounting in his eyes.

"It's not for bears," Izzie said as she lifted from the bed.

The realization hit me as well.

"It's for werewolves," I said.

Brian stood up and patted me on the back.

"You know. Had you said that just twenty-four hours ago, I would have been convinced you were one fry shy of a happy meal. Today, however, that is a totally normal statement."

Izzie chuckled at Brian's response and hugged him. As she pulled away, she let out a large yawn.

"I think I got the most sleep this trip, and all of you look exhausted. How about you guys lie down and I'll sit watch?" Marcus suggested.

The offer was extremely tempting until I looked to the beds and tried to work out the logistics. Brian followed my gaze and cringed. As we tried to determine how we would set up the sleeping arrangements, Izzie lay down across the far bed.

"One takes this bed, and the other takes that bed. Or both of you lay down on that bed. There are only so many computations you can come up with," she said.

Looking back to each other, we continued the contemplative stare while Marcus watched us from the chair.

"As entertaining as this is, let me—" Marcus interjected. "Just based on Brian's size, he should take the bed by himself."

Brian raised his eyebrows. "What does that mean?"

"Look at the size of you. No one else would fit. Jace and Izzie are going to have difficulty sharing that bed."

"That's what I'm concerned about," Brian said.

Marcus rolled his eyes. "There are four of us in this room, in a hostage situation. Do you honestly think any hanky-panky will happen?"

Opening his mouth to speak, Brian seemed to consider Marcus's words and closed it. Moving to his designated bed, he looked back to Izzie, who was already under the covers.

"No, under the covers, Jace," he said.

Nodding, I lay down on the bed facing the ceiling. Within seconds, it was obvious that position would not be possible for long as I could feel myself sliding off. I contemplated which direction would be best for me to turn. As I looked to Izzie on my right, I wondered if it would be too forward. Looking left, I met Brian's eyes boring down on me... Left side it is. Purposely turning away from her, I felt myself drift off to sleep.

I awoke to Marcus shaking me and whispering in my ear.

"Jace, wake up. Someone just pulled in."

Sitting up, I looked over to see Izzie was still asleep. Not wanting to disturb her unnecessarily, I let her rest. Looking to Brian's bed,

I could see he was also sleeping, later confirmed by the low hum of a snore. Lifting myself off the bed as carefully as possible, I walked to the window to see who the visitor was, trying to stay hidden.

"Hey, those creeper skills totally came in handy!" Marcus teased.

Slowly, I rolled my eyes as I looked at him. "Seriously?"

"Hey, just calling it like I see it," he teased.

Playfully punching him in the arm, I looked out the window. As was the case when we arrived, there were several cars in the front yard, but the van we'd arrived in was blocking the view of any newcomer to the house.

"I can't see anything past that damn van," I said.

Marcus moved to the door to listen for any noise.

"Jace, whoever it is, sounds like they're already in the house."

Moving away from the window, I motioned for Marcus to wake Brian while I moved to Izzie. Sleeping, she finally seemed relaxed and calm. Her hair spilled around her face in small ringlets, and she slept with her lips slightly parted. Although she was breathing quietly, I could detect the slightest snore that made her even more adorable. Watching her, my heart ached knowing that I would need to ruin that, and I hesitated to wake her. But I did not want her surprised by whoever was coming, so I gently rocked her shoulder.

"Izzie, they're here. You need to wake up."

Slowly, she blinked and then stretched with a smile on her face.

"Who's here?" she asked, still asleep.

"We're still not sure, but you really need to wake up."

Opening her eyes more, she looked more closely at her surroundings, and her eyes went wide as she shot up like a cannon.

"Whoa. It's okay. No one came in yet. I just wanted you up when they did."

Looking over, I could see Brian was up with his feet on the ground and his head in his hands as he tried to wipe the sleep out of his eyes. Marcus was sitting on the bed next to him, looking at Izzie and me.

"How are you doing over there?" I asked Brian.

"I could have used about twenty more hours of sleep, but it was better than nothing."

Across the room, I heard the lock on the door disengage and everyone in the room shot to attention, looking in its direction. Swinging it wide, Mitchell walked in and looked at each of us before hollering back into the hallway.

"They were asleep. You owe me twenty dollars, Kelly."

Heading back to the hallway with the door open, I considered making a break for it but knew I wouldn't get far. Besides, I would never leave my friends to fend for themselves. Before any other escape plans could come to mind, another man walked into the room. Although he was in blue jeans and a black button-up shirt with a matching black hat, Sheriff Powell was impossible to mistake. Feeling my heart sink, I watched as he looked at each of the inhabitants of the room before zooming in on me.

"That one," he said, pointing me out.

Stepping out of the doorway, he made room for a mass of men that rushed in, and Izzie screamed, "No!"

I pulled her behind me, trying to calm her with a look before turning to see Marcus and Brian stepping in front of the approaching men, ready to fight. Not wanting them hurt, I yelled, "Don't!"

To my surprise, all in the room stopped momentarily, the men looking back to Powell for guidance. The sheriff looked equally shocked by my response and the reaction of the men.

"Until we know what he is fully capable of, I want him restrained."

"Sir, he broke through the rope already," a man with blond hair and medium build stated.

Realizing that they may decide to incapacitate me with another hit to the head, I offered a bargain. "If I will come willingly with you and not try anything stupid, will you leave the others alone?"

Sheriff Powell considered my proposition and then looked around the room.

"This is the cell room, right?" Powell asked Mitchell.

"Yeah. They're not getting out of here." Mitchell looked back to us and smiled before running through the room's specifications." Steel bar cage wrapped in concrete surrounds the room with a wood frame for the walls. Bulletproof glass. An additional ten-inch concrete ceiling and floor, and a door, that besides capable of being used in a bank vault, would lead them right out to us. I think you can rest easy. We only needed to know, for sure, which one he wanted."

As Mitchell rattled off the specs, I felt Izzie grabbing tighter onto my arm. Powell seemed to contemplate what he had been told and seemed satisfied with the answer.

"Good. You can stay here, unchained…for now. Daegen will be here at 10:00 a.m., and he is never late. That gives you about seven hours of sleep. I would use it," Powell said as he turned to walk out the door.

"Good night, children. Pleasant dreams," Mitchell said as he closed the door again.

As I heard the heavy lock engage to the impenetrable door, I felt a sinking feeling in my chest. Marcus turned to look at me with concern in his eye.

"You okay, man?" he asked.

"I'm not sure right now. I feel like I was just given a stay of execution."

Brian paced the room, looking at the walls with a newfound appreciation of the architecture. Finally, he stopped and looked at each of us.

"There is nowhere to go and nowhere to hide in this room. I'm not sure why they would need something this reinforced but decorated so nicely. It's almost ironic," Brian said.

Looking around the room, I pondered what he had said and thought through the details of the past day. When I remembered the large animal in Yulee, everything seemed to fall into place.

"They're all werewolves," I said.

CHAPTER 22

Playing with Power

The group turned to look at me in unison. Seeing the shocked look on their faces, I continued to explain my theory. "Someone has been following us and likely giving our location. Remember that enormous animal we saw at the rest stop?"

The group nodded in unison, recognizing the logic I was following.

"I think that was a werewolf. Think of the size of it! Now I can understand why they would have this place locked down tighter than Fort Knox. You would probably *need* Fort Knox to keep something that big contained if it got angry."

"Okay…why would they lock *us* up in a room like this, though?" Izzie asked.

"They locked *me* up in a room like this. They put Brian and Marcus in here too because they didn't initially know who the werewolf was."

Brian held his hand up and dropped his head. Feeling a twitch of my lip, I waited for him to compose the question I knew he was about to ask.

"Again…I know this should not be a surprise to me at this point, but you're a what now?"

Finding it hard not to chuckle, I answered, "I'm not even sure I am. I know my father is, though. But as far as I know, I have never grown fur or changed into anything like that."

Izzie contemplated my answer, her brows furrowed deeply as though the weight of the world was on her shoulders.

"What's the matter?" I asked.

"I think you may be able to...to change," she said.

I felt my smile wash away instantly. "Why do you think that?" I asked.

"You growl like an animal when your mad or threatened and your eyes...glow," Marcus answered.

Shocked, I turned to look at him.

"Thank God I'm not the only one who noticed it!" Izzie sighed.

"I noticed it but kinda brushed it off that I was hearing things or seeing things. This kinda changes that," Marcus said, swinging his hand around in a circle.

"No, I saw the eye thing too. But I thought it was a trick of the lights in the car," Brian said.

"What color are they when they change?" I asked.

"I have seen two different colors. Golden seems the most consistent, but when you are really mad, like you were in the grotto, they're...red." Izzie said, dropping her voice at the end.

Remembering her sinking to the floor and not leaving the room, I felt a sense of relief and panic mixed in one.

"That's why you wouldn't leave," I said.

"I-I didn't know what you would do to him. I was scared for him, for me, for you, for everyone," Izzie said with a slight shake in her voice.

"Do you think I would hurt you now?" I asked.

"No. I know you would never willingly hurt any of us." The flush of her cheeks shone.

Looking back around the room, she frowned again.

"Why did they put *me* in here?" Izzie asked.

Brian laughed. "That's easy. Because they didn't want to risk someone going berserk if you were out of our sight. Now that they see how protective he is over you, they will be extra cautious about touching you. That's a good thing, though."

Izzie listened to Brian but looked up at me. I caught her gaze out of the corner of my eye and smiled down at her. She was still tightly hugging my arm but no longer shaking.

"I know in real life, things are not like the movies, but aren't werewolves supposed to have a superb sense of smell? You know... pick out their own?" she asked.

"I guess. This is all new to me, and just like I didn't follow movie protocol in the van, they may not follow it either," I answered.

"Or maybe they couldn't tell the difference, even *with* their sense of smell," Marcus mumbled nonchalantly.

"What do you mean?" I asked.

Marcus looked around the room, almost pleading for help.

"Is no one else feeling it?" he asked.

"Feeling what?" Brian asked.

"I can't fully explain it, but you did something to me in the van."

Realizing the absurdity of the statement, he rolled his eyes and shook his head.

"No. I mean more than just that."

Again, Marcus looked to Brian and Izzie for backup, but they both stood staring at him blankly.

"Seriously, nothing? I guess it's just me then."

Closing his eyes, he took an exaggerated deep breath, lifting his arms while bringing his middle fingers and thumbs together in front of him and drawing them down as he exhaled. Finally, he looked up, staring at me.

"Okay. I know it has only been a few hours, but every time you get upset, I can feel it. It's like an electric shock runs through me. The more upset, the stronger the jolt. It took me a bit before I could place where it was coming from, but it is, without a doubt, linked to you and your emotions," Marcus said.

Brian frowned and looked down as though analyzing what he said.

"Now that you say it, I think I see what you are saying. But I seem to pick up on your anger. It almost energizes me. I just thought that I was getting amped up watching you, but he's right. It is like an electric charge running through me."

We all looked to Izzie.

"Are you feeling anything different?" Marcus asked.

Izzie let go of my arm to sit on the bed and seemed to analyze her inner self. After a pregnant pause, she looked up.

"I'm not sure. I guess, I just feel more…protective over him, but I want his protection as well. Is that weird?" she asked.

Shocked by the revelation, I looked to my hands and then back to the group.

"After the van?" I asked in a whisper.

"Yeah, I think so," Brian said.

"Jace, I felt like I was drowning before you helped me. I'm not sure what you did, and I'm not arguing with it! I just wish I knew what had happened and if it will last," Marcus implored.

"What *did* you do?" Izzie asked.

I sat on the end of the bed she was sitting on and put my head in my hands.

"I only wanted to help," I whispered.

"You did." I felt Izzie kneel on the bed behind me, putting her arms around my neck and resting her head on my shoulder. I felt her cheek pressed against mine, and I placed my hand on her arm, squeezing reassuringly.

"We're not angry… We're just trying to understand it," Marcus said.

Sitting on the chair across from the bed, Brian leaned forward, resting his arms on his thighs, and looked at me.

"Walk us through what you felt or did. Maybe we can figure it out together," Brian said.

"The best way I can explain it was that I asked, whatever it was inside me, what you needed at the time to feel safe and whole, and I gave it to you."

The group contemplated what I said before Marcus spoke. "*What* did you give us?"

"I wasn't even sure I could do anything when I helped Izzie. Her being first, I only gave her health. Marcus…well, you needed more."

Digging deeper into my mind, I tried to remember what I had sent and felt my brows furrow as I did.

"To be honest, I sent both you and Brian the same, courage, strength, and health. I only added in calm for Marcus."

Izzie nodded. "It must have bonded you with us."

"I-I didn't mean to—"

Brian put his hand up to stop my thought.

"So we are sure that we are each linked to you, or at least your emotions. But are you linked to us? Or even more interesting, are we linked to each other as well? Kind of like using Jace as a conduit."

"I'm not sure. You seem to only be picking up what *I* feel. Not what I'm thinking," I said.

"Well, we never tried it out," Marcus said.

I shuddered at the thought of them reading my mind. Then shuddered anew, thinking of the possibility that I could read any of their thoughts. The room seemed in agreement with that sentiment as we all looked at each other uneasily.

"How do we figure this out?" Marcus asked.

"We have to be scientific about it. Otherwise, we won't know for sure," Brian said.

The group turned to look at him, all equally shocked by his previous statement.

"What? Under this tough exterior is a smart guy," Brian said.

"Okay, smart guy, how do you want to do this?" I asked.

Brian thought about it for a minute before coming up with an idea.

"We know it links us to you and causes us to respond to you. Let's first see if you're linked back to us."

Looking between Izzie and Marcus, Brian gestured for Marcus to come closer.

"How come I have a feeling I will *not* like this?" Marcus said.

"I won't hurt you...bad," Brian said with an up curve of his lip.

"That's what I was afraid of. Okay. In the name of scientific research." Marcus shrugged as he moved closer.

"Okay, Jace. Turn around. I am going to touch Marcus some-where, and I want to see if you pick it up. If not, I will try something stronger."

Sitting on the bed facing the wall, I closed my eyes and tried to focus on Marcus. Initially, I felt nothing, but then there might have been a tingling sensation in my left arm.

"Are you touching his upper left arm?"

Silence fell on the room.

"Well, I guess that answers that first part."

I turned around to see Brian's hand on Marcus's upper arm. A smile crossed my face. Brian looked to Izzie and motioned for her to come closer. I watched as she walked to stand where Marcus had been when I turned back to my original position. Refocusing my attention on Izzie, I waited.

"I feel nothing," I said.

Marcus giggled. "I think Brian is having difficulty figuring out where to touch her."

"Okay, okay... I got it. Focus again."

Slightly laughing myself, I focused again. Within a few seconds, I felt a tingle in my right hand.

"Are you...holding her hand?" I asked incredulously.

"Yes. I didn't know where else to touch that wasn't question-able!" Brian said, agitated.

"Which hand?" Izzie asked.

"Your right hand."

"He's good," she answered.

"This is amazing," Marcus said.

Nodding, Brian paced the room for a bit while he contemplated the next part of his experiment.

"Now to see if you can read our thoughts."

Pausing momentarily, he looked to the ceiling and sighed heavily.

"Yet another phrase I never thought that I would say and not be joking about it."

He looked toward me and made eye contact, smiling.

"Okay, we'll try first to see if you can just read them, regardless of if we let you. Or if you need us to let you," Brian said.

"Who's first?" Marcus asked.

"I'd rather sit back for this one till last. If that's okay?" Izzie said.

"I went first last time," Marcus said.

"I guess that leaves me," Brian said.

Pacing the floor, he contemplated how to execute this next part.

"There's no paper in here, right?" he asked.

"Not that I've seen. Even if there was, there are no pens," Izzie answered.

"Marcus, come here. I'm going to whisper it to you."

I turned around to reassume my previous position and tried to make my brain go blank.

"Okay. Did you get anything?" Brian asked.

I tried to focus my attention on Brian. There was nothing that seemed to come to the forefront. As I was about to give up and turn around, Izzie suddenly grabbed at her head and jumped up off the bed.

"*I* heard it! And you are not the strongest man alive," she said.

The room fell silent as I turned to look at her.

"Well, *that* was not what I expected," Marcus said.

"Is that what you were thinking?" I asked Brian.

Mouth slightly agape, he nodded in silence.

"I guess that answers another question. We can pick up on each other. At least Izzie can," Marcus said.

"Maybe try to send me a thought directly?" I asked.

Brian looked to Izzie and then back to me before nodding.

"I'm not exactly sure how to do that, but I'll try."

"When I have been picking up on you guys, I try to focus on you. Maybe do the same but in the other direction?"

"Okay, I'll try, but give me a second to think of something."

After a few moments, his face lit up, and he motioned for Marcus. As he was whispering into Marcus's ear, I turned to look away, waiting to receive his message. Feeling Izzie sit down next to me, I opened my right eye to glance at her, unsure if she would have another epiphany moment and effectively scare the life out of me again. Reassured that she appeared to be comfortable and not ready to jump out of her skin, I closed my eye again and concentrated.

My focus turned to Brian's face and was shocked when I noticed a halo of light pulsating around him. Initially, it was hard to see, but the more I concentrated, I could make it out better—it had a certain color. As I tried to encourage the aura to come forward to me, it became more apparent and shone with a deep golden hue as though the sun was rising behind and cascading its warm rays around him.

Fascinated by the brilliant, gilded movement, I beckoned it to me. Seeming to be freed for the first time, it was reluctant to my call, but as I tugged on it, it released and did as I asked. The illumination danced forward, and I watched the choreography in delight. As it approached, I could hear a whisper. Bringing it closer to my ear, I tried to listen more intently as the waves of light passed by. I became frustrated as only some words were coming through but not a full sentence. *Zoe, love, need.* Catching the gist of his thought, I tried harder to get the words to form more clearly. Rapidly, the words enhanced, and I could decipher the message. *I miss you, Zoe. God, I really love her.* I opened my eyes and turned around to look at Brian, who was smirking at me.

"I got something, but I'm going to bet it's not what you told Marcus," I said.

Brian's smile faded. "Jeez. What?"

"I think it is more of what you are feeling deep down as opposed to what you are saying, out loud."

Walking closer to me, he leaned down. "Whisper it," he said.

Relaying the message, Brian immediately shot to attention and stared at me.

"I've been thinking about her since I saw Powell. I want to know that she is okay," Brian murmured.

"Zoe?" Izzie asked as she walked to him, placing her hand on his arm.

"Yeah. This sucks! Not knowing where she is if she got away. I have so many what-if scenarios running through my head and I can't stop thinking."

"If anyone was going to be okay, it's Zoe. She is too hardheaded to not get her way," Izzie said.

Brian looked down at her and smiled. "You're right. Besides, I'm sure we'll be out of this mess soon. I mean, how much worse can it get?"

The group moaned in unison as Marcus jumped on Brian's back, playfully hitting him and driving him to the floor.

Standing, I walked over to the window to look out into the wilderness. The memory of what Uncle Roman had said the last werewolf-witch combination had been called—an abomination. Remembering my friends could now tune in to my emotions, I tried to keep them in check. My mind pulled in a myriad of directions but most of all wondering who Daegen was and what was his ultimate plan for me. Looking back into the room at the trio blowing off steam play fighting, I wondered what was going to happen to them after Daegen had me. *How much worse could it get?* If that wasn't the question of the year.

"What time do you think it is?" I asked the group.

Marcus sat up and looked out the window.

"It had been close to 3:00 a.m. the last time they were in here. It doesn't look like the sun is ready to come up, so I would say four or five."

"He'll be here in about five hours then," I said with a solemn tone.

As I thought about all that Daegen's arrival would bring, I felt my heart sink more. Flashbacks of my aunt and uncle came to the forefront of my mind, and I wondered where they were now. Thinking about Daegen also made me think about my own parents. Uncle Roman had said that Daegen was my dad's alpha. Would he still be alpha, and if he were, would he keep my dad in the dark about me being found?

Pondering my father left me imagining both of my parents and the life I would have had flashed in my mind. Anger and frustration tore at my core. Everything that was sacrificed was about to be for nothing. Feeling the anger swell, I punched the wall next to the window and turned to walk back toward the door.

"Jesus! You broke the wood!" Brian exclaimed.

Shocked by his words, I turned to look back and saw Marcus and Brian bending to the spot I just struck. Examining it closer, I could see that the wood had splintered and caved in the center of the punch. Knowing the construction under the walls, I was fairly sure that the wall would not be made of faux wood but likely a strong hardwood. Izzie rose from her seated position and walked to the wall. Frowning, she turned to grab my hand and examined it closer.

"It's not even red, let alone cut up. A hit on solid wood should have broken your hand!" she said.

"Not a werewolf, my ass! You have *something* powerful running through you," Brian retorted.

Still holding my hand, Izzie lifted her head till her eyes met mine. I could see the concern mounting.

"You look exhausted," she said.

Chuckling, I admitted, "I am."

"Is there anything we can do before he gets here?"

"I don't know... I don't think so."

"Then lie down and rest. You're going to need your strength in a few hours."

I opened my mouth to protest, and she immediately twisted her features to look more like a mother warning her progeny of their next fatal move. The change in her appearance brought a smile to my face, and I lifted my arms in defeat. Slowly, I moved toward the bed to lie down. Marcus, having seen the exchange, patted me on the back with a knowing stare as I walked past him.

"She's right. Get some sleep. We'll take turns monitoring things."

"We'll wake you when he's here," Brian said.

Looking back at the three best friends I have in this world, I couldn't help but smile as I lay my head on the pillow and closed my eyes.

CHAPTER 23

The Showdown

I woke to a sense of impending doom that seemed to intensify as the minutes passed. Opening my eyes, I frantically looked around the room, only to find Izzie and Marcus looking out the window and Brian by the door.

"He's here!" I announced, startling the three of them simultaneously.

"Yeah, they just pulled up a few minutes ago. We weren't sure who, but the time of day seems to match when he was expected to arrive," Brian said.

"What do you two see out there?" I asked as I stood to walk closer to them.

"A car pulled up about five minutes ago, and there has been more movement in and out of the house. Just like with Powell, the stupid van is blocking most of the view, so I'm not sure who or how many people came," Marcus said.

"Brian was hoping to hear something in the house, but the door is too thick," Izzie said.

I walked to Brian and, about halfway across the room, felt a jolt of pain rush through my back and up to my head.

"Brian, get away from the door. He's there!" I demanded.

His face went blank as he backed away and toward Marcus and Izzie. I could hear the heavy lock disengaging and braced for the man who had ruined my life. Assuming a somewhat crouched position, I could feel a growl coming from the depths of my chest. I imagined myself the victor, willing it out to the universe, hoping for some retribution from the upheaval my life has gone through. Behind me, I could sense my three companions assuming positions protectively behind the bed and was happy to know that Marcus and Brian would be there to protect Izzie if I no longer could.

As the door opened, a lone man became visible in the entrance. I felt the corner of my lip turn upward. *He came alone.* The man in front of me was tall and muscular, with tattoos up and down his arms. His dark hair appeared to need a trim although it was styled and had a similar-colored close-cut beard with strands of auburn highlighting it. He appeared to be in his late twenties or early thirties, which seemed an impossible age, considering his status and the length of time he has been trailing me. He was wearing a gray T-shirt with cut-up jeans and appeared to be going out for a quick errand as opposed to coming to finish a decade's worth of damage. His deep chocolate-brown eyes met mine, and a stare-off began.

The corner of Daegen's lip went up as he watched me from the doorway.

"You have been a very hard person to find," Daegen said unassumingly. As he looked around me, his smile grew.

"Aah. I see how it is. Who does she belong to?" he asked.

Realizing he was referring to Izzie immediately amplified my hate for him. Seeing my reaction, he looked back at me and readjusted his footing slightly. I could see a ring of amber forming around his irises. There was a shift in the room's energy. Unsure what was going to happen, I willed my friends to stay hidden, for fear they would get hurt.

"She doesn't belong to anyone," I said, acid in my tone.

"You seem pretty protective over her. Over all of them, actually."

"You don't have friends?" I growled back.

"Of course. Just not, well…," he trailed off as he motioned in their direction.

"Well, in my experience, they are better friends than yours."

Daegen laughed and looked back toward the doorway to find Powell standing there.

"You're sure it's the right kid?" Daegen asked.

"He's the right age, being raised by fairies, and has the characteristics we would expect," Powell answered.

"I don't know what you want with me, but I'm not going with you."

"I don't think you're going to have much say in the matter here," Powell said.

Remembering my last interaction with the sheriff brought my ire up a notch and I could feel my breathing intensify. Powell's eyes widen slightly. "You need to calm down. You're bound to get hurt if you don't," he said.

Ignoring Powell, I stared at Daegen, trying to expect his next move. He was no longer smiling, and his eyes were nearly all amber at this point. Powell looked at Daegen and then back at me. For an instant, he appeared to be showing genuine concern, but for who? *For me?*

"Kid, I'm serious. Back down!" Powell demanded.

Continuing to stare down Daegen, I could hear a deep growl coming from somewhere else in the room and realized it was Daegen. Powell immediately looked at him and then around me toward the far end of the room. Not breaking eye contact with Daegen, I tried to watch Powell out of the corner of my eye.

"Daegen, he's just a kid. He's never dealt with this or us before."

Realizing he would not convince Daegen, he turned to me next.

"Jace! Stop staring him down, damn it! Do you have a death wish?"

At this, Daegen crouched further, and I could hear the ripping of fabric.

"Oh shit! Kids, get over here, now!" Powell yelled as he made his way toward my friends with his arm outstretched.

His sudden movement toward them was the only thing that broke my concentration. A sudden surge of energy rushed through me as I felt a large gust of wind swirling around the room. As the storm intensified inside me, so did the gusts of the wind. Soon, I felt myself lifting off the ground and watched as Powell stood terrified in the center of the room, caught between me and Daegen.

He was still trying to coax my friends to come to him. With a twist of my wrist, I imagined the wind as a force with mass and willed it to grab Powell. What appeared to be a hand formed from within the wind, mimicking the movements of my left hand. Watching in amazement, I made a few motions and watched the wind hand match them. Looking back to Powell, I could see the fear in his eyes as he watched as well. I felt the corner of my lips turn up. Reaching forward, I grabbed Powell and lifted him off the floor, watching as he struggled, his legs dangling.

"Watch out, Jace!" I heard Izzie scream from behind me.

Turning to look back, I saw Daegen running toward me, and I shot my right hand out, causing a tremendous gust that blew him backward into the opposing wall. In the doorway, George and Mitchell appeared. They each looked around the room, horrified by the scene.

"Go get her. Now!" Daegen yelled.

The duo looked at each other as though trying to comprehend what Daegen had said. Without warning, George burst into the room as Mitchell turned and ran out of the door. Throwing my arms out wide, I caused a shield of wind to form behind me. Centering my attention on George, a quick flick of the wrist had him flipped upside down and suspended by one leg. Daegen stood up slowly, looking at George and Powell, then back at me before speaking.

"My god, where have you been?" Daegen asked.

"Hiding from YOU!" I exclaimed.

Daegen furrowed his eyebrows and drew his head back slightly. As he walked forward, I reached out another tentacle that grabbed ahold of him and tightened. Stunned by the strength of it, he planted his feet and began pulling back, stretching the blast as he did. Not wanting to lose control of him, I tighten my grip further, watching his face grow red and the veins in his neck bulge. I found myself balancing on the edge, enjoying the struggle for life slowly draining from Daegen. From somewhere, I could make out a faint voice. Partially trying to ignore it, the voice came through intelligible within my head.

"Christian, it's okay. You are okay."

The voice caused me to weaken my hold on the group of men momentarily, but I quickly had to regain the same grasp as they instantly tried to advance. Fear and anger were washing over me in waves, and I felt as though I would just as easily kill the three of them and force my way out of the rest of the house. As though the disembodied voice was reading my thoughts, it came again—this time much firmer and truly clear.

"Christian, release them! They will not hurt you. I won't let them."

Immediately, I felt all the energy release, and the wind stopped, dropping the three men like rag dolls. Realizing who was speaking to me, I could feel the tears flow as I spoke, "Mom?"

Daegen seeing the lull in the torrent of wind looked back at the door where Kelly now stood. In between catching his breath, he nodded to Kelly. Stunned, I watched as the man motioned for someone to come, and the anger swelled again. *He's playing tricks with me!* I thought.

Once again, I called on the power, but this time, I reached out, grabbing each man by the neck and lifting them. Just as their feet left the floor, the frame of a petite woman with blond hair and striking blue eyes slammed into the doorframe, out of breath. She glanced at the men and then rushed in past them and grabbed me by the arms, causing me to descend. Looking down, I stared into the face of the only person who could have caused me to break my hold on my captors. Releasing the three men again, I heard the loud thuds as each dropped mercilessly to the floor. In disbelief, I felt my legs go weak, bringing me to my knees. I grabbed her around the waist as she cradled me against her.

"Mom."

CHAPTER 24

Reunited

"Fuck! Remind me *never* to get on that boy's bad side!" George growled as he pulled himself up off the floor.

"Christ almighty! I knew I had the right one!" Powell said.

Half listening to the men complaining in the background, my attention was on the woman in front of me. Standing, I looked down at her and could see a thousand emotions running through her as she analyzed the face they had prevented her from seeing for twelve years.

Reaching her hands forward toward me, she hesitated for a moment as though trying to gain the courage to touch something that may vanish. Seeing her indecision, I pulled her hands toward my face, allowing her to cup my cheeks. I watched as a single tear rolled down her cheek, and I pulled her into an embrace that seemed to last forever. Pulling away, I could see the tears now falling freely from her eyes.

"I knew we would find you again. Even when they told me it was hopeless, I knew you were still out there," she sobbed.

"I always felt like you were both with me, even when I thought you were…dead."

I whispered the last word, afraid that it may bring it to fruition.

"I will never forgive them for what they did," someone spoke from the doorway.

Lifting my head, I saw a man slightly taller than me with salt-and-pepper hair and my face looking back at me. My mom followed my gaze and smiled, motioning to the newcomer. "He's home, Luca. He's really home," she said.

The man looked to my mom and then, with tears in his eyes, rushed over and pulled me into the tightest hug, cradling my head in his hand and sobbing on my shoulder. As the shock slowly lifted, I felt my arms lift and wrap him in the hug as well. Pulling me back, he looked me up and down, smiling and laughing between tears, then patting me on the shoulder and gently shaking me, before pulling me back into an embrace.

"My god! You're so big! Almost as big as me! In my mind, I still see you as that pudgy little boy playing pirates with me."

"You loved that game." My mother's voice caught as she spoke.

"That was the memory I had when this all started," I said.

My mother's smile faded, and her eyebrows furrowed in thought.

"How did you get away?" she asked hesitantly, glancing at my father.

Her question sent waves of confusion through me. Pulling out of the embrace, I looked around at the room and then back to her.

"I really didn't. We tried to get to you first, but they still caught me. The last twelve years were for nothing. We tried to get to you without Daegen finding me. I failed you."

As the words came out, the emotions of the past two days culminated, and the tears flowed uncontrollably again. My father's eyes grew wide, and he looked to Daegen who dropped his head.

"What did they tell you?" Luca asked in a low menacing whisper.

Confused, I investigated my father's face and was at a loss for words. As I fumbled to form a coherent sentence, a small voice answered from behind me.

"They told him y'all had an agreement to hide Jace from Daegen. That Daegen wanted Jace because he was going to take advantage of his powers," Izzie answered.

My dad, stunned by the movement, diverted his gaze from me to where Izzie, Brian, and Marcus were still hiding. He then turned to look at Daegen, who, once again, dropped his eyes away from my father, which seemed to be contrary to every werewolf movie I had ever seen. *Isn't the alpha able to hold eye contact with anyone?* I thought.

"Jace?" my father asked.

Hearing my name, I looked back at him and realized that they would not know that name—the name I had known most of my life, the name I would likely have to change. My stomach turned at the thought, but I kept myself upright.

"That's the name I have had for the past twelve years… Jace… Jace Northall."

"Mmm-hmm," he answered simply with his lips pursed tightly.

I extended a hand for my friends to join us. Slowly, they stood and walked toward us. Izzie reached us first, and my mom extended her hand out to Izzie, who willingly gave it. Once they touched, Izzie gasped slightly, and I felt my back stiffen. My father put his hand on my shoulder, which instantly calmed me. *How did he do that?* I thought. Seeming to know what I was thinking, he smiled warmly.

"You and your mom seem to have a gift of touch. Sometimes it comes out unexpectedly. She isn't hurting her," he said.

"I'm sorry if I shocked you," my mom said to Izzie, smiling sweetly. "Thank you for taking such good care of my boy and bringing him back to me."

In the corner of the room, George was still brushing himself off while watching the interactions happening in front of him.

"I'm glad to see you have recovered although judging by the back of my son's head, you likely deserved what you had coming."

George lowered his head. "I'm sorry, Luca. Two of my wolves got a little carried away with themselves last night."

"Do you think he is safe to come out of the cage now?" my father asked with bitterness in his tone.

"Yes, Luca. I'll have them prepare food for them now."

Luca's eyebrows shot up. "You assaulted him, abducted him, caged him, and didn't think to feed him knowing who he was to me?"

George lifted his eyes to meet mine and then quickly dropped them again. His appearance resembled that of a child that had just been caught and was about to be punished. The fear emanating from him was profound, and as I watched the encounter, I actually felt bad for him.

"It's not as bad as it seems. We had just finished eating before...," I trailed off, unsure what to say as I didn't want to make the situation worse.

My father looked back at me and narrowed his eyes slightly.

"Regardless, the aggressiveness in which they handled you was completely unnecessary."

My mother made her way around to my back to see the damage my father had just described. Surprisingly, she kept her composure very well, considering the amount of blood she was likely seeing. "Do you perhaps have a shower they can use before breakfast? Maybe some fresh clothes?" she suggested.

As though seeing both an escape and a way to rectify the harm from last night, George lit up at my mother's question. Immediately, he walked to the door and motioned for someone to come to him. My guess was Mitchell, who seemed to be his second in command.

"Yes. I believe we have clothes for the boys. I'm not sure about the girl though," George answered.

My mom shifted her gaze to Izzie and then down to herself.

"I think we're about the same size. Let me grab something from my bag."

Izzie smiled as my mom took her by the hand and guided her out the door. As she was about to leave, she hesitated slightly.

"It's okay. He'll be right behind us. You all need a bit of cleaning up and food," my mother said as she took Izzie by the hand and led her out of the room.

Within a few minutes, Mitchell arrived with the requested items for each of us, plus towels, washcloths, a toothbrush, and a fresh bar of soap. George led us to different bathrooms throughout the house, mine being the last stop.

It was upstairs and enormous, attached to an equally large bedroom. The room encompassed most of the third floor and had exceptionally large wooden planks along the walls and vaulted ceilings with exposed wood beams. In the center of the far wall was a king-size bed with an oversize chandelier made of antlers hanging above it. For a moment, I imagined Gaston from *Beauty and the Beast* kicking his feet up on the bed. On the wall opposite the bed was an immense window that extended from the floor nearly to the ceiling with ornate detailing to the top of the arch of the window. I wondered if it was an extension of the window from the first floor. Outside, was a breathtaking scene of wilderness caught in the transformation of fall and seemed more like a green screen effect from a Bob Ross painting.

The decor inside the room was in deep burgundies and greens and screamed head man cave area. The bathroom was comprised of river rock walls that extended across the floor with a large claw-foot bathtub sitting on top. Behind the tub was a waterfall feature that emptied somewhere behind the tub. I looked under the footing, trying to determine where the water was draining and how the room was not flooding but could not decipher how they had created the illusion. Above the tub was a large skylight that encompassed a large part of the room. Next to the tub was a glass enclosure with multiple spigots extending out of various positions from the remaining three walls. George followed my glance to the shower and smiled.

"Infinity shower. Cleans everything squeaky clean. If it's too much for you, then just stick with the rain showerhead."

Above us, I could see a large sheet of glass covering the enclosure with small openings within it, where the water would run out of.

"You can set it to be light, like a mist or full force, like a torrential downpour. I'm more of a fan of somewhere in between," George said.

Placing my new clothes and toiletries on the sink, he pulled out a fresh bottle of shampoo and conditioner and placed them on the counter. Leaning into the shower, he showed me briefly how to work it before finally stepping out.

Once I was alone, I stood in the middle of the bathroom, unable to move. As the weight of all that had happened culminated, I was finding it hard to move or breathe. Looking at my reflection in the mirror, I could see just how bad I appeared. Blood matted the back of my hair, streaking down and around my neck. But other than the blood, there were no other obvious signs of trauma, which was amazing to me. With each layer that came off, I would anticipate a bruise or cut, but there was nothing. If not for the blood, you may have never known there had been such a violent physical altercation.

Stepping into the shower, I followed George's instructions and played with the settings until I found one that was comfortable and didn't make me feel as though I was caught between two firehoses on at full blast.

The water was relaxing, and I felt a sense of peace as I watched it turn from a rust color to clear again. It made me feel as though I was reborn with all my troubles being washed away along with the dirt and blood from the day before.

After the shower, I toweled off and walked to the sink to brush my teeth. Along the wall, there was a fresh brush and a variety of hair care products for styling needs. Although my hair was not short, it luckily fell into order on its own and required only brushing to bring it into submission.

On the counter rested a pile of clothes. A pair of jeans with various holes in the knees, apparently for style, a plain black T-shirt and a gray pullover sweatshirt with "Millstone Landing" on the front. Under the cabinet were a pair of Puma sneakers with a green stripe running down the side and a bag of new crew cut socks.

These guys think of everything here, I thought as I admired my new outfit in the mirror on the back of the door.

I cringed at the heap of blood-soaked clothes on the floor as I wondered what I should do with them. Folding each, I stacked everything up and brought it with me. Approaching the stairs, I could hear voices mixed with laughter coming from two floors below. With a deep breath, I descended the stairs and ran into Mitchell when I got to the first landing. I stiffened at the sight of him, and he dropped his head slightly and frowned.

"No hard feelings. I wasn't sure you were who we were looking for. I had to protect who was here. You understand, right?"

Unsure what to say, I stood stock-still listening to him speak. When he finished, there was an uncomfortable silence before he noticed the clothes and lit up with a logical change of topic.

"Here, I'll take those from you. They're waiting for you in the kitchen," Mitchell said, nodding his head in that direction.

I handed the clothes to him and listened to the laughter and chatter, wondering what I would say when I entered. Mitchell was watching me.

"They thought you were dead as well. Over the years, there had been so many false hopes, and they had about given up on ever finding you again. Go. They need to see you as much as you need to see them," Mitchell whispered.

CHAPTER 25

Explanations

His words stunned me and left me with more questions than answers. Clearly, he could see it in my face and smile.

"They can tell you the rest. Go," he said as he gently elbowed my arm in the direction of the voices.

As I walked from the foyer, I could see a group of men sitting in the living area, cheering loudly as they stared up at the television. Walking past, I looked up to see a baseball game playing. One man noticed me looking and smiled.

"It's the World Series. Two of the most unlikely teams are playing. Mets versus Orioles."

Smiling because I had no idea what he was talking about, I turned right, inching closer to my destination and the answers to over a decade's worth of questions. As I passed through the large wood frame, I could see a long wooden table with about fourteen seats surrounding it. At the head of the table, with his back to me, was my father and my mother sitting next to him. On the opposite end was George. Across the table was Brian, sitting closest to my dad, Izzie, and Marcus. There were five others sitting around the table, including our initial kidnappers, Kyle, Kelly, and Morgan. George, who was facing the doorway, saw me enter first and stood up. The entire table turned at once to me.

So much for a subtle entrance, I thought.

My mother pushed her chair back and shooed Kelly, who had been sitting next to her. Shifting her seat over, she made room for me to sit between her and my father. As I approached the table, my father stood and patted me on the shoulder, smiling.

"Words cannot express how happy I am to have you with us again."

Sitting between them, my mother grabbed my hand and squeezed it. I glanced down at our now-joined hands and then back to her face and smiled.

Feeling awkward and on full display for the room, I looked at my friends who were watching me just as intently. Marcus was in a similar style of pants and was wearing a T-shirt with a pyramid and a rainbow coming from it with a Pink Floyd logo underneath. Seeing the T-shirt, I chuckled, knowing that Marcus would never go out without a large sweatshirt to cover himself up. Noticing my reaction, he smiled. "Pretty good look for me. I may have to change up my wardrobe when I get home."

They'd dressed Brian in relaxed-fit jeans, a plain white T-shirt, and a red flannel button-up over the top. Izzie was wearing a large gray wool sweater and jeans. Around her neck was a heart-shaped charm with a ruby red gem in the center. I stared at the charm, trying to remember if I had seen her wearing it before. Seeing me stare, she grasped at the charm.

"Your mom gave it to me. She said it was a thank you for helping you."

I felt a smile brush my face as my mother squeezed my hand.

"We were just talking to your friends about your adventure getting here," my father said with a softness in his eyes.

"Adventure… Yeah, I guess that is one way to put it." I chuckled.

I looked to my friends and then back to my mom and dad.

"It's crazy. I have so many questions but can't even think about what to ask first."

"It's not crazy. We're feeling the same way," my mom said.

"Maybe start with the beginning," Izzie suggested.

"I guess that is as good a place as any." My father nodded.

"Who should go first?" I asked.

"I may be overstepping my bounds here, but maybe getting Jace's version first may be better. You can then fill in the gaps for him," Brian answered.

My father seemed to ponder Brian's suggestion, then nodded. So for the next few minutes, I tried to summarize the last twelve years of my life. Feeling as though I was walking a tightrope trying to spare everyone's emotions, I felt myself on high alert, monitoring their reaction for anything that may cause them distress. At times, I detected my father's jaw tighten and, at others, heard my mom scoff or wipe a tear. By the end, my father had pulled himself up from the table and was pacing. As he paced, I watched the others in the room and saw that they all seemed to cower as he became more upset. My friends seem to notice it too, and Marcus was finally the one to speak up.

"So up till about, oh, I don't know, forty-eight hours ago—give or take an hour—werewolves, witches, and fairies were all a part of the movies. With that being said, most of my reference points are coming from those movies. Cora and Roman told us *you* were submissive, but I'm watching everyone around here, and they all seem to react off you—almost cower. Either my understanding of werewolves is wrong, or they lied."

My father immediately stopped pacing, and the tension in the room grew exponentially. Marcus instantly appeared to regret his question and dropped his head. Now standing behind my mother, my father's eyebrows were almost touching his hairline as he stared at Marcus.

"Okay. They lied. Totally get that now. Sorry, sir," Marcus blurted out.

My mother, watching the exchange, laughed at Marcus's reaction, which caused my father's posture to relax. Coming to sit back at the table, he looked over to Marcus.

"Yes, they lied," he answered calmly.

"Luca is not only the alpha of his own pack, but he is also the head of the eastern seaboard and probably of all the North American wolves," George said.

My jaw dropped at the statement, and I looked from my father to the far corner of the room where Daegen sat on a stool, away from the table, looking out the window.

"So who is Daegen in all this?" I asked.

"My second. But also the one that was guarding the house that night," my father answered.

"He made it a personal mission to find you," added my mother.

Seeing the man, quietly huddled in the corner, as though on patrol, I found that I had a new respect and understanding for him. As though sensing me staring, he shifted his gaze briefly to me and nodded. Returning the gesture, he resumed his initial pose, staring outside.

"But wait a second. He looked like he was going to attack Jace earlier," Brian said.

"Sheriff Powell was trying to get you to stop looking at him and get us out of the room," Izzie continued.

George smiled before he answered.

"Your friend is a Nova, Ms. Izzie, and they can be *very* unpredictable. If Daegen had not shifted, Daegen would be a dead man walking."

George turned to look at me.

"You were challenging him by staring him down. Daegen was protecting you, himself, hell, the whole damn house!"

"I thought he was the enemy. I was protecting..."

"You were protecting *your* pack," Daegen interjected from his corner.

"M-My pack?" I asked, just as stunned as the teens across the table from me.

"You claimed them as yours. I'm not sure how or when you did it, but you are all connected. I knew that as soon as I entered the room," George answered.

My father sat next to me and put his hand on my shoulder.

"You did nothing wrong, and it would have never happened by force, so it was mutual. I sensed it too but was going to wait before I brought it up."

"What happened? Do you know how you did it?" my mother asked.

I felt a sense of regret mixed with awe at this new piece of information. How was that possible? Was that how we were able to all communicate and sense each other? We had only begun to scratch the surface of those abilities, and I wondered what the ramifications of the connection now meant for all of us. My *pack* also seemed to be running through the implications in their heads as well.

"We were kinda figuring it out before Daegen got here. Marcus picked up on it first," I said.

"He helped us…healed us…when we were in the van," Izzie said.

My father's eyes flashed amber as he turned to Kelly and Kyle. Instantly, they dropped their gaze away, and I almost thought I made out a whimper from them. George, watching the interaction, tried to step up for them.

"I punished them for their stupidity, but I understand if you would like to ask them more questions," George answered.

My father stood and walked around the table to sit next to Marcus, which also positioned himself in front of Kyle and Kelly. Marcus shifted uncomfortably, his eyes wide and the color draining from his face. Seeing his fear, I smiled at him and tried to send him calm. Within seconds, the color in Marcus's face returned, and he appeared more in control. Out of the corner of my eye, I could see my mother, who was beaming. She squeezed my hand, and I could hear her in my thoughts.

You're an Empath too.

Her voice took me by surprise, and I looked in her direction, unsure of what I had experienced. She continued to smile at me before turning to watch my father.

"Gentlemen, please, tell me about last night." My father sat upright in his chair, looking back and forth from Kelly to Kyle.

"We were hungry, so we went to get some food. Kelly has a thing for the waitress that is there, which is why we choose it," Kyle started.

"I do not!" Kelly interjected.

"I don't care if you do or you don't. Get on with the story." My father's tone was menacing, amber flashing across his eyes.

Kyle appeared to gulp, looking from Kelly to my father and then to George before continuing.

"As we were eating, we noticed a car with Florida plates pull in and a bunch of teens getting out of the car. It was odd, considering the time of night, but we were more interested in eating at that point, so we didn't think anymore on it."

"Till they sat down, and I smelled it," Kelly said.

"It?" Brian asked.

"Wolf."

"We all have a scent that can be picked up by others," my dad clarified.

"We both caught it and knew that one of you was wolf, but we couldn't determine which one. It was around that time that George had sent the text to look out for a group of teen wolves that may come through the area," Kyle continued.

"Knowing that we had the kids they were looking for, we finished eating and tried to contact the house, but no one was answering," Kelly interjected.

"Finally, we were able to get ahold of Morgan. He wasn't sure why George wanted them but thought they had done something wrong and told us to bring them back."

My father's eyes slowly panned toward Morgan.

"And why were they considered a threat?" he asked in a normal tone, which was somehow more terrifying.

Morgan's face paled as he swallowed audibly before trying to speak.

"I didn't know if they were a threat or not. I just assumed they were because George was told not to let them get away."

My father nodded for Kyle to continue.

"We left the restaurant and moved our car so we could follow them. You know, in case they left before Morgan got there with help," Kyle said.

"We watched as they got in the car and pulled out of the spot and stopped at the roadway. We weren't sure what they were waiting for and thought they were considering which way to go. Morgan wasn't there yet, and I was afraid I was going to lose them… So I…" Kelly's voice trailed off.

"They slammed into the back of my car so hard that they threw us across two lanes of traffic and into a barrier wall," Brian said with hostility in his tone.

My father spun to look at Brian and then whirled back on the two men. Somehow, he had gone from a sitting position to a standing one and was now leaning across the table, dangerously close to the men. The speed of his actions scared Marcus, who had also jumped up and was now practically sitting in Izzie's lap.

"Think *very hard* about what happened next!" my father growled.

Both men exchanged glances, and Kelly nodded for Kyle to continue. Kyle narrowed his eyes and pursed his lips before taking a deep breath.

"As soon as we hit, we knew it was wrong. We could see the air-bags go off and none of the kids were moving. We got out of our car and walked over to theirs to see if they were okay. It was around this time that Morgan showed up with the van," Kyle said, then looked for Morgan to continue.

"When I pulled up, I thought they had tried to escape, so I told Kyle and Kelly to put them in the back of the van. Those three were easy to get in, seein' the accident had knocked them out and all. It was *your* boy that put up the fight. Kyle and Kelly were bringing him to the van when he started comin' to. Before they could get him in the van, he just went nuts. Kelly tossed him in, and blondie almost landed on the girl."

My father snarled, "He has a name!"

Morgan shifted uncomfortably in his seat. "Yes, sir. But I'm not too sure what to call him. You call him Christian, and they call him Jace. We had called them big boy, blondie, and red that night, so I stuck with it."

Glaring at Morgan, the realization about what to call me seemed to also hit my father. He glanced back at me, studying my face before returning to the trio on trial, decisively saying, "Jace. Call him Jace."

"Yes, sir. Well, Jace here came to life something fierce when he saw her, and I kinda gathered he was our Nova. He charged for me, and Kelly hit him in the back, which stopped him."

My father immediately turned to Kelly, whose eyes went wide. "*What* did you hit him with?"

"Sir, I didn't know who he was. I was just—"

"I don't care about that. What did you knock my son out with?"

Dropping his head, he mumbled, "The buckle from the U-line ratchet tie down."

A sound rumbled from my father that was not human, and I felt my skin go cold. My mother must have sensed it too because she quickly said, "Luca, he's here, and he's fine!"

My father looked back to me, and his face and shoulders tempered before he returned to Kelly and Kyle.

"Continue," he said through gritted teeth.

"We bound them up. I felt bad about his head, but we had nothing soft in the van. Since he was close to the girl, I sat her up and put his head on her lap," Kyle answered.

"After we closed the doors, we tried to figure out what to do next. We tied the car to the back of the van and towed it home with us," Kelly said.

Pushing off the table to stand fully once more, my father paced behind the seat he had just been sitting in.

"Why was he in the cage, George?"

Now it was George's turn to cower.

"The boys attacked my wolves and had them pinned on my front lawn. I didn't know which one was the Nova and questioned if all three were. It was for everyone's protection," George answered.

"Why was the girl put in then?"

"Pardon me saying, but your boy is *extremely* protective over her. If anyone so much as looked at her, he began growling. The other two were protective as well, but Jace was the reason we put her in with them!" George said.

My father turned to look at me, and then Izzie, who was watching the exchange, wide-eyed. Walking around the table, my father stepped behind me. I felt my heart rate pick up, not knowing what to expect, and my mother squeezed my hand in reassurance.

"I'm going to check your head, okay?"

"Yes, sir," I said.

He patted me on the shoulder reassuringly before moving his fingers through my hair. They probed, in vain, looking for the gash that should have been there.

"It already healed in the van," Izzie said.

My father stopped rummaging through my hair and turned to regard her. Izzie's eyes enlarged, but she kept her eye contact going.

"What happened *in* the van?" he asked her.

She finally dropped her eyes from him, thinking back on the events. Then she relayed them with complete accuracy. Listening to her recollection of my life was still fascinating for me. *She knows me. Really knows me*, I thought. Watching her recount the past few days, I felt the smile cross my face, which grew after she looked at me and smiled back.

"I'm grateful to know what happened to us, but we are all still in the dark about what happened twelve years ago," Brian interrupted.

"You're right," my father answered as he sat back in his seat at the head of the table.

Leaning back, he gave a deep sigh before shifting forward.

"We met Nick and Sophia about eighteen years ago," my father started.

Marcus awkwardly raised his hand, which seemed to catch my dad off guard.

"Yes?" he asked.

"Perhaps a stupid question, but who are Nick and Sophia?"

"I think you called them Cora and Roman?" he asked me.

I nodded and waited for him to continue.

"When we first met them, we didn't know that they were fae. Your mother and I had just started dating and were at an Irish street fair in Bethlehem. I had wandered into one of the vendor's tents and was admiring a Celtic sword. As I went to reach for it, someone else grabbed for it at the same time. Soon, we were all laughing and joking with each other as though we had known each other for years.

For the rest of the day, we hung out. It was clear we had forged a great friendship."

"A few years later, when your father asked me to marry him, it was a simple decision who to ask to be the maid of honor and best man. After the wedding, we moved into a large house in hopeful anticipation of a house full of children. One night, Sophia came to us and told us they were in trouble and needed a place to stay. Being best friends, we immediately opened our house to them," my mom added.

"What sort of trouble?" Izzie asked.

"We knew they were both fae, but it wasn't something that would have caused us concern, considering who we were ourselves. Apparently, they had a dispute with fairy royalty and were banished," my father answered.

"We never really found out what the falling out was over, but it seemed to have devastated Sophia," my mom answered.

Thinking of my aunt, my heart sank at the thought. Our family was her number one priority while I had been growing up. Then I remembered my aunt had stolen me from my parents, and I felt a strange mixture of emotions.

"After trying, unsuccessfully, to have children, we were told that we could not conceive. Seeing that our situation was…unique, we searched out other more worldly sources for help. That was when we were told that at no time in history had a witch-werewolf been successful at reproducing. Nick didn't believe that and dug deep into history. He found that it *had* happened once before and with the help of the fae," my father continued.

Beside me, my mother closed her eyes and dropped her head, a tear streaming down her cheek.

"After multiple miscarriages, we were getting desperate. Nick had suggested the assistance of his friends at court. In my heart, I knew asking for help from the fae was a dangerous proposition, but I wanted to hear their offer at least. So Nick contacted someone from the high fae court and brought us to see them."

"They promised us a baby within the year. While we were elated at the news, I was hesitant too. I asked what they wanted in return."

My father slammed his fist on the table, remembering the encounter.

Continuing, he said, "They wanted full access to the power of the child. Unsure what that meant, I asked for them to clarify their demand. They told us they would allow the child to stay with us. However, they would visit every year to collect its power. That would allow him or her to remain *normal* and us to have the child we'd always wanted."

"We asked to have time to think on it and that we'd give them an answer within the week. Later, at home, we discussed what that offer would mean. Realizing that our powers were part of who we are, we couldn't imagine someone taking them away from our child. That night, we decided that if it were a decision of having no children or having a child that would, in essence, be mined for its power, we would go without," my mother said.

"Later that week, we respectfully declined the offer and set our minds to living a life without children. But to our surprise, around three months later, we realized that your mother was pregnant again. We were apprehensive and anxiously awaited to see if there'd be another miscarriage. We had been told that our child would never make it to full term. Month after month passed, and you were still there, holding on."

"And fifteen years ago, today, at 11:10 a.m., you came into this world kicking and screaming!"

My mother's words hit me like a punch. I looked at my friends, who were equally shocked.

"Wait, what day is it?" I asked.

"October 9, and looking at that clock, 11:15 a.m., happy birthday, my handsome young man!"

"Hey, you can get your permit now and help with the driving!" Marcus chimed in, which caused the four teens in the room to laugh.

My father watched each of us with a smile on his lips but confusion in his eyes.

"It was a *long* drive, and only two people could do it. One drove while the other had an exceptionally tough time staying awake," I said.

His face took on a look of understanding, and he smiled, grabbing hold of my shoulder again.

"If someone had told me a year ago I would be with you for your fifteenth birthday, I would have punched them. We have come across so many people who thought they had seen you. But all the leads were dead ends!" My dad's eyes dropped, and this time, it was my turn to grab ahold of his arm in reassurance.

"So what happened after he was born?" Izzie asked.

"Nothing exceptional. It was exactly what you would expect for the first three years," my father answered.

"You were such a happy baby and toddler. No matter where you went, you would light up the room. I remember one time that we went out to eat with you. On the way out of the restaurant, you stopped at each table we passed, asking if the people liked what they had ordered. It was the cutest and funniest thing to watch. Everyone loved it!"

"If anyone came to the house, you were right there asking to play with them. Your dad, being who he was, had wolves coming from all over when they had problems. You would help calm them down and make them feel comfortable. The first three years were the happiest times of my life. Then came the Harvest Moon Festival Dance." Her voice trailed off as she spoke.

"Nick and Sophia were going to watch you that night so that we could go to the dance. Everything was completely normal. We had no way of knowing that we would never see you again after we left!" My dad's voice began breaking at the last words.

From the corner, Daegen spoke, which took everyone by surprise.

"I was patrolling the perimeter, as I always did. Around ten thirty that night, Sophia brought me some hot chocolate since it was an exceptionally brisk night. She had done that for me a thousand times in the past, so I thought nothing of it. That night was different, though. She had drugged the drink, and I had passed out, completely unaware of what was happening."

He sighed deeply before continuing, "When I woke, the entire house was aflame! Initially, I thought the three of you were in it and tried to get in. But the fire was too out of control. I looked around the property and had a sinking feeling that Nick, Sophia, and you had perished. The thought was so devastating, that I contemplated throwing myself into the fire as well."

"The next morning, when the fire was out, we anxiously searched the debris. We found three bodies, including a toddler, in the house. The fire department deemed it an electric fire. For years, I believed I had fallen asleep at my post, allowing you to die. Only much later did I remember Sophia bringing me that cup of hot chocolate."

"The only thing that gave us any hope was Daegen remembering that drink two years later. By that time, we could not have determined who the people in the house had been. My heart still breaks for the mother of that young child!" my mother said.

I sat back in my chair, trying to process all the information that I had just received. The two people who had cared for me, protected me, and loved me were horrible monsters. They had stolen me away from my parents and destroyed countless lives in the process. My aunt Cora's smile and laugh rang in my memory, along with my uncle Roman's demeanor—our recent talks. How could this possibly be true?

I felt the tears building in my core before they made it to my eyes, and I fought to keep them from falling. I was left mourning the two people who had cared for me for the past twelve years and left wondering if I would ever see them again. But right beside that emotion was a newfound hatred for the people who stole me—Nick and Sophia Tucker.

The people at the table sat and watched me. I sensed they were waiting for me to speak because I could feel all their eyes bearing down.

"I need some air. If that's okay?" I asked.

My mother nodded, her eyes reddened from the obvious attempt to hold the tears back for my sake. I looked around the room for an exit when I saw Daegen stand and open a door behind him. Standing too, I walked toward it and met his eyes before walking outside.

The backyard was immense and open with no boundary lines other than a perimeter of deciduous trees. The center was wide open with a large pool to the left side of the yard that was now closed for the season. The air outside was crisp and clean. I took several deep breaths and began to process all the information from the past few days.

How had everything become so crazy? I thought.

It felt as though my insides were being torn into two. Part of me was excited and relieved to be with my parents. But the other part of me longed for the life I had had with Aunt Cora and Uncle Roman. I knew my parents were picking up on how confused I was as I tried to reconcile both parts of my life into one cohesive whole. Would I ever be able to do it, or would I remain forever damaged and confused?

In the distance, I watched as a small bird flew to the opposite side of the yard, happily chirping as it did so. At that moment, I wondered where Aunt Cora and Uncle Roman were now and remembered that Sheriff Powell was still here. Quickly turning to the house, I rushed back in through the door. I nearly knocked Daegen off his stool as I raced back inside and past the group assembled in the kitchen. Barging into the main seating area, I found Sheriff Powell watching the World Series with a few other guys from the house.

"What happened in Williston?" I demanded.

The sheriff seemed stunned by my question and glanced left and right as though looking for backup.

"Regarding what?" he asked.

"Everything! Where are my aunt—where are Sophia and Nick? What happened to Mrs. Hunter and Aunt Lilly? Izzie's sisters? Everything!" I asked, my voice bordering on explosive.

With each question, my voice grew, as did the number of people filtering in from the kitchen and other areas of the house to watch the encounter.

Sheriff Powell scanned the faces in the room and then, standing up, looked at me. "I know nothing about Izzie's sisters. As far as I knew, they were at home this whole time. Mrs. Hunter and Aunt Lilly were brought in for questioning and eventually released. The last I heard, they were home too. The Northalls? We don't know where they are at this point in time."

From the corner of my eye, I could see Marcus, Izzie, and Brian all turned to talk to George. After a few words, they each walked back into the kitchen and disappeared. I narrowed my eyes on the sheriff. This man had been cruel to my aunt and uncle before he had known who or what they were. Now I needed to know what had happened and had no intention of being gentle with him.

"Why were there so many police cars going to my house that night?"

Powell's eyes narrowed dangerously. He was apparently not used to being the one on trial. "I could smell you from a mile away. Ethan had pegged you for a wolf, but it wasn't until I entered that house that I knew for sure. After meeting your aunt and uncle, I realized they were fae. Everyone on the Eastern Shore has heard about Luca Volk's boy, and this was checking off every box for me!"

"So why didn't you confront them there and then?" I demanded.

"You didn't think that was a confrontation?" he hmphed and continued.

"Well, I guess you've shown what *your* idea of a confrontation is!" Powell snapped back.

"Watch it, Powell!" my father growled from the doorway.

"No offense meant. I think I had made my point abundantly clear that I was not impressed with your uncle during that encounter."

"Oh, you were an absolute asshole during the encounter!" I retorted.

"Watch it, kid!" Powell sneered.

My father approached and stood behind me.

"I will not remind you again, Powell."

As the tension between my father and Powell mounted, Marcus burst through the door.

"My mom and Aunt Lilly are not at the house. I called my aunt's job, and they haven't seen her in a few days! I called to listen to my voice mail after that. They never called me. Something is wrong."

My father turned from Marcus to look at the sheriff.

"Would you like to rethink your previous statements? Where are the people my son just asked about?"

Powell looked visibly shaken but stood his ground.

"I told you already."

Within a few minutes, Izzie and Brian came into the room. Izzie's eyes were wide.

"They're not home. No one is home, and no one is answering their cell phones. I'm scared!"

"Buddy," I whispered.

"What?" my father asked.

"My dog. He was at Marcus's house. He's alone."

He searched my face and grabbed my shoulder.

"We'll get him."

I felt relief wash over me. My dad seemed to sense it before he turned his attention back toward Powell, his eyebrows narrowing.

My father stepped in front of me, partially blocking my view of the sheriff. He nodded toward two of the men sitting with Powell, who quickly stood and grabbed him, wrestling Powell to his knees. Once subdued, my father ambled closer with his arms crossed in front of him. He was glaring down on the sheriff as though he was reprimanding a small child.

"It appears you are no longer in a position to lie to me. My suggestion would be to change your story now and do it quickly."

My father's eyes tightened, as though contemplating how to devour his prey. Just as he was about to say more, Powell's entire demeanor and facial expression changed. One minute he was avoiding eye contact and cowering slightly. The next minute, without warning, his face had twisted into a maniacal smile. My blood ran cold at the sight of him, and I instinctively backed away. I heard my mother gasp, "Elashor, no!" as she ran to me. As quick as she had been, Powell was quicker. In an instant, there was a bright light, and the large bulking man had disappeared, replaced by a small ball of illumination. It caused the two men holding him to collapse forward onto each other, slightly cracking their skulls against each other's as they did.

Meanwhile, the ball slowly lifted and appeared to be turning slowly as it appraised the room from its new vantage point, hovering over the two men. I felt compelled to look closer at this new being in the room and stood in a state of wonder as I watched it rotate and morph into an ill-defined fiery eye.

Although I tried to focus more on what it actually was, I realized the entity was beckoning me, and I was unable to ignore its pull. As I approached, the surrounding sounds became muffled, leaving me feeling as though I was in a scene from an action movie where destruction and debris were flying all around the main character, but they seemed to be unharmed and moving in slow motion. To my left, I could see my father screaming in my direction but was unable to break the hold the floating eye had on me. I watched as my father desperately swung his head back and forth between me and the new curiosity in the room. To the right, my mother crouched down, making dramatic gestures with her hands. This seemed to bring forth swirls of glowing wind, which she sent forth toward the little ball, knocking me back as they hit their intended target.

As I fell backward, I felt the trancelike state end and could finally hear my father.

"Christian, RUN!"

Stunned by the change in Powell and no longer hypnotized by the small floating eye, his booming words brought my legs to life. I turned to run toward the only area not blocked with people—the foyer. Running for all I was worth, I flicked my wrist, causing the front door to fly open. Behind me, I could hear screaming, glass shattering, and furniture breaking, but I refused to turn back. Already halfway across the driveway, I began contemplating if a car was my best option when I felt an intense warmth on my back. Within seconds, the warmth spread, and I watched helplessly as the world around me dissolve into bright light.

Chapter 26

Elashor

I woke with what seemed like a jackhammer going off inside my head, and my mouth felt as though it was stuffed with cotton. I opened my eyes and looked in vain for something to drink. But was shocked by my surroundings which appeared to be some sort of prison.

What the hell just happened? I thought.

When I attempted to stand, I felt my head sway and had to grab the wall to keep myself from falling over. Getting up slowly from the floor, I could feel my fury mounting with each passing minute. In less than two hours, I had found my parents, only to have Powell take me away again. *But away to where?*

Still fighting to stand, I finally brought myself to an erect position, which allowed me to better survey the room. Slowly analyzing my surroundings, I felt myself go numb. The room looked like something out of a medieval movie scene. It was circular with a small window about six feet off the ground, which measured roughly two feet wide and three feet long. I took a turn in the room, searching for a door but could not find one.

How do I get out of here? Better question, how did I get in here?

Standing on my toes, I tried to look out the window, but its dimensions drastically restricted what I could see. The only thing I knew for sure was that I was high up. Straining, I could see the stone architecture replicated on the building outside, which had high walls and possibly a turret to my left. At the base of the wall was a canvas of large oak trees. Their foliage created a thick blanket, covering the ground below it and anything past it. Along the wall were small beings in chain mail meandering back and forth and appeared to be on patrol.

Are you serious right now? I was kidnapped…again! By another fairy and placed in the middle of a freaking fairy tale.

The more I thought of my predicament, the angrier I found myself. My heart was pounding wildly in my chest. I clenched my fist, pacing furiously around the room pointlessly until the electricity running through me slowed a bit. Feeling more in control of myself, I stood in the center of the room and tried to focus. Recognizing there had to be a way out, I searched the room again with more rational eyes.

The room's walls were constructed of heavy stone with a very tall vaulted ceiling, made of what looked like wood. Below, the stone appeared to continue to the floor and had hay strewn across it. I stood dumbfounded and felt a laugh emerge. Initially, it was more of a giggle. However, as I stood there, I bounced harder as I tried to restrain the laughter until it finally exploded into complete hysterics.

"I'm in the tallest tower of a castle. I guess this makes *me* the damsel in distress?"

I glanced toward the window and thought, "Too bad I don't have long hair."

The thought sent me into another fit of laughter, which caused me to back up. I felt my back hit the wall, and I slid down in defeat. My knees were tucked up tight to my chest, where the laughter dissolved into a well of despair. The emotional roller coaster of the past few days had arrived at its stop, causing me to let loose a deluge of tears, which I allowed to fall to their completion.

As I looked back up to the thatched roof, I extended my legs and felt my foot kick something hard, which caused me to jump slightly. Using the sleeve of my sweater, I wiped the remnants of my breakdown away as I hastily shifted to my knees. I was blindly swiping my hands through the hay until I found what my foot had hit.

There, in the center of the floor was a large heavy circular object. It rocked on a hinge and felt like an old door handle. After clearing most of the hay off it, I realized I'd found a large, old wooden trap-door with a large iron hoop and a skeleton key lock in the center.

What's the worst that can happen at this point? I thought, smiling as I remembered Brian's words while we were in the cage.

I straddled the door and bent down to grasp the hoop, pulling with all the strength that I had. I could feel the flex of the muscles in my back and arms as I strained against the substantial weight of my current foe. Finally, I released the handle as I felt the blood pooling in my head, causing the room to sway slightly. Still bent over the door, I attempted to catch my breath before resuming my grip. As I prepared to pull on the handle again, I heard the lock engage. Shocked by the sound, I immediately dropped the ring and backed up, accidentally tripping over a stone on the floor and falling backward into the bed of hay behind me.

Surprised by the fall, I shook its effects off and jumped back against the wall. Frantically, I began looking around for something to pummel whoever would pop up through the door. Then I remembered *I* was a weapon.

As the door opened, I prepared to unleash a hurricane of wind onto them but was stunned into immobility by who had surfaced. In the doorway's frame was a young girl, about eight or nine, looking around the room like a small gopher. I watched in fixed fascination as she turned till she located me and smiled. I stood there bewildered, unsure what to say or do. Just as fast as she had appeared, the girl dropped back down into the doorway, causing me to jump slightly.

I approached cautiously to see where she had gone when she suddenly popped up like a jack-in-the-box holding a tray of food. I jumped back, tripping over the same stupid brick, and fell back into the hay. Watching me, she giggled to herself as though I was a clown there for her amusement.

"Elashor says you will be hungry. When you finish, I will bring you to him."

I stared at her, trying to form a sentence but could only nod slowly. She grabbed the hook on her side and pulled the door.

"Wait!" I said, just as she was about to close the door over.

Pushing the door back open, she stared at me quizzically.

"Yes?"

"W-Where am I?"

She giggled again, and I found the hairs on the back of my neck standing on end.

"Iabriaria. You're silly. Elashor said you were silly!"

A million questions ran through my head. Before I could ask anything else, she had pulled the door closed behind her. It shut with a deafening boom and I was alone in the room with a tray of mystery food and the knowledge that I was in a place called Iabri…

Oh god! I forgot the stupid name already, I thought.

Trying to keep the panic down, I took a few deep breaths and thought back to what she had said.

Ia-bri-aria, I repeated the name a few times in my head to get it to stick. Yet I wasn't sure how I was going to tell anyone where I was.

I knelt next to the tray to inspect what she had left me. The tray was like one you would see in a school cafeteria. There were three sections for each of the food items to sit in without touching each other. The problem was that each section looked exactly the same—a pale-green-gray color with the consistency of a pudding.

Taking the wooden spoon she had provided, I carefully prodded at the mass and watched as it gave a small jiggle and felt a twinge of bile climb the back of my throat. Coaxing the noxious liquid back down to my stomach, I decided the food had not attacked me. So I dipped my spoon carefully into the mixture, listening to the slurp as I retrieved a spoonful. Slowly, I brought it to my lips and carefully licked a small piece of the gruel. Smacking it around inside my mouth, I tried to place where I had tasted it before.

"Apple pie? It tastes just like apple pie!" I exclaimed to the empty room.

I dipped my spoon into a different section and tasted. This time, it was roast beef and gravy. I looked at the spoon in disbelief and then back at the tray.

How is this possible? I asked myself.

Dipping into the last section, I tasted creamed corn.

It's an entire meal!

Realizing how hungry I was, I ate my fairy meal, savoring the flavors. At its completion, I found myself amazed. Although there were only a few spoonfuls of mush on the tray, after I had finished, I felt as though I had just finished a ten-course meal. Then I noticed a small wooden cup in the tray's corner. I lifted it to examine its contents and found a clear liquid that appeared to be water. Carefully, I brought it to my nose and sniffed and picked up a hint of fruit. When I took a cautious sip, the taste of fruit punch elated me. I quickly drained the cup before placing it back onto the tray, looking over the empty contents again.

That's an interesting trick.

Satiated, I sat back and took stock of the tiny room again as my brain filtered through various explanations for my capture. Unfortunately, I didn't last long before I felt the powerful tug of sleep. As I began steadily dropping into slumber, the sound of the lock engaging startled me awake.

Standing to prepare for my intruder, I saw the same gopher girl from earlier pop her head up through the door. Again, she scanned the room until she had spotted me.

"There you are. He's ready to see you now," she said before quickly dropping back into the hole.

I looked over the edge of the door, trying to see where she had disappeared off to. The only thing visible, though, was the top of a ladder. The area below it was pitch black, making it appear as though she disappeared into an abyss.

"Hello?" I hollered down into the hole apprehensively before waiting for a response. There wasn't any.

I was instantly gripped by a strong desire to stay where I was. *Maybe he can come here?* I thought.

As I contemplated my options, the gopher girl popped her head back up and glared at me, visibly irritated by my not following her instructions.

"He does not like to wait!"

Slightly taken aback by her tone, I stared at her and then at the hole behind her. Seeing me looking over her shoulder, she glanced in the same direction and then back at me.

"We can go down together if you like?"

"How? You barely fit by yourself."

She giggled as she climbed all the way into the room and stood in front of me with her hand outstretched.

"I won't bite...hard." Her face seemed to morph into some bizarre beast at that last word for a brief second before returning to that of a child, causing me to withdraw quickly from her.

"WHAT?" I shrieked.

"I'm teasing. Now hold my hand, and I will have us to the great hall in a flash."

I looked back down the hole and then at her, wondering which was the worse option. Then I took a deep breath and reached out, grabbing hold of her tiny hand. As our skin touched, a bright flash of light went off again, and I was ripped wildly through multiple corridors till we stopped at our destination.

Somewhere along the roller-coaster ride from hell, I had closed my eyes. When I felt the motion cease, we stopped, I cautiously opened them again to find I was now in a large chamber that could double as a cave or a palace room. The walls were constructed of large boulder-type rocks while the ceiling seemed to sparkle and dance. Looking closer, I could see a multitude of small jewels suspended from tiny threads, each reflecting light like a thousand tiny mirrors. Amazingly, they somehow illuminated the entire room.

Children of various ages, but none older than ten, lined the center walkway. Others bustled around the room involved in various tasks. In the center of the space was a large throne with a chubby child sitting in it.

Am I in a castle or something else? I thought.

"Something else!" the fat child on the throne bellowed.

Stunned that he had answered the question in my mind, I halted my forward progression and stared.

The girl that had brought me to the room turned and seemed to get nervous by my stopping.

"Keep moving. We cannot have him waiting!" she whispered impatiently.

I moved forward again, watching the boy on the throne. He was also about eight years old but far too heavy for his size and was breathing heavily. His clothes were something out of a renaissance fair. He even sat in a reclined pose while eating the classic turkey leg.

Cliché much? I thought.

"This is my kingdom, and I can experience it however I want."

He had again answered the thought in my head, which left me unsure about how to proceed.

"Why did you bring me here?" I asked as I approached.

"Because you belong to me," he announced boisterously.

"How do you figure that?"

"Your parents agreed to the contract when they bore you using my magic."

I felt my feet stop moving as I took in what he had said.

"But they didn't use your magic! They told me themselves."

He laughed a far deeper laugh than a child of his age or size should have been able to do.

"What are you laughing at? This isn't funny!" I yelled.

Continuing his laughter, he pointed toward a door to his left. Following his finger, I could make out the outline of a female figure. I strained to see who or what it was when the figure began moving closer to me, and I could see it was flying.

Once it was within a few feet, I could see that it was a female and stood roughly nine inches tall, which was much larger than the tinker bell reference I had grown up with. Her hair was held back with multiple braids that framed her face and tied it back into a long plat in the back of her head. Her outfit was a lavender-blue color with her shoulders mostly uncovered. It flowed down into a modest box-shaped neckline with a snug fit that put the focus on her top but gracefully. The sleeves covered her arms to just below her elbows in a simple yet elegant design—a perfect combination of grace and style.

Her waist was broad, but it looked like it was a comfortable fit. A small elegant belt accentuated it without being too much. Below, she wore leggings that covered midway to her calf and a skirt of similar color with a matching ballet-slipper type of shoes. Transfixed by her beauty and her size, I had nearly missed the almost-invisible

313

wings, which were only discernable when the light hit them at certain angles.

As she moved even closer, I felt my breath catch. Her features were that of Aunt Cora's.

I felt like someone had just punched me in the gut, and I found it hard to breathe. Seeing my distress, she shifted quickly to the Aunt Cora I had known and rushed to my side. When she was within arm's reach, I extended my hand to stop her.

"Jace, I-I'm sorry. I thought we could fix it!"

"What did you do!" I roared.

"*She* is the reason you are here," Elashor said.

I looked at him and then my aunt, who dropped her head.

"How is she responsible for this?" I demanded.

Elashor laughed again as he repositioned himself into an upright position so he could watch the encounter from a better angle.

"Callista was going to be an amazing mom...," my aunt started to say.

Stunned that she would have the audacity to bring up my parents, I turned on her.

"You never gave her the chance!" I was screaming and could feel a vein in my neck pulsing. The ferocity of my voice caused her to step away from me. Her head hung low, and I instantly felt guilt at my outburst although I did not dare move from where I stood. At least not until I knew what was happening and if I could trust her.

"I was with her when she lost the baby before you. It was the sixth one! They were both devastated and desperate..." Her voice trailing off as she spoke.

"She told me! They came to see him, but he wanted to take my power, so they declined the offer."

Aunt Cora smiled brightly. "You found her... Oh, sweetie..." Her face lit up as she took a step closer in a motion to hug me.

Stepping away from her, I yelled, "Don't!"

Aunt Cora dropped her head and turned to Elashor, who was now lying on his stomach with his legs up in the air. His feet were kicking back and forth, and his face was propped up on his hands.

He looked more like he was a child at a sleepover than a fairy king, and it made me wonder about how strong he could really be.

"They did reject the offer, but Elashor gave me the vial. I thought that if *I* gave it to her without her knowing, the deal would be void. After that last miscarriage, I couldn't bear to watch her go through it again. Each pregnancy would go further than the previous one. It was almost like fate was taunting them!"

"How did you do it?" I asked in a whisper, trying to keep my temper in check.

Aunt Cora studied my face, hers almost unreadable before she answered.

"She liked tea, and I would brew it for her once a week till you were born. When Elashor stayed away, we hoped he did not know about you…"

"But I did know!" His voice boomed through the cavern, causing her to cower.

He stood on his throne, laughing and jumping up and down like a kid on a sugar high. By this point, I wanted nothing more than to tie him to that stupid chair and gag him.

"The night we took you…we received a call from a fellow Astrial warning us. We hoped we could hide you long enough to devise a way out of this and get you back to them."

"Why should I believe you? Why didn't you say this the first time? Why wouldn't you tell them?" I spat. My blood was boiling. I was so mad at her.

"We didn't know how you would react, and I needed to get you back to them."

Realizing that she was alone, I searched for Uncle Roman.

The impish child, reading my mind again, danced on his throne and spoke in a taunting voice.

"He's not here! He was a bad boy and needed a time-out."

Aunt Cora's face looked distressed. A pang of anguish hit me, seeing her anguish and knowing Uncle Roman was in trouble.

She dropped her eyes to the floor.

"I don't know where he is," she said in a hushed tone. "I can still feel him, so I know he's still alive, but I don't know where."

Anger was building in me, and I was getting sick and tired of feeling helpless. I spun on the impudent little brat of a king and demanded to know where Uncle Roman was. He only laughed harder at my reaction. Feeling the power in me building, I looked up, encouraging it to rise.

"No! He wants you to do that!" Aunt Cora screamed, crashing into me and knocking me to the floor.

"Asteria! You're going to ruin all the fun!" Elashor chided with his lower lip puffed out.

"By you using your power here, especially on him, you'll give him a chance to remove it from you!" Aunt Cora cried.

I thought about it and wondered what the downside could be. I had lived my life as a normal kid until this point…more or less. If it lets me live with my parents with no threat hanging over our heads, then so be it. Aunt Cora watched me and must have recognized the conclusion I was coming to because she said, "He will take *all* your power, including your life force. He will kill you! He says you have linked your power to others. They would die as well!"

Her words hit me in the solar plexus, causing me to lean forward, and I instantly wanted to throw up. While I tried to regain my composure, I felt her come to my side and rub my back.

"You know, friends are such an amazing asset in life. I'm so glad that you found some to share yourself with," she said.

I stood up and stared at her as though she had lost her mind. I was about to die and possibly take my friends with me. And there she was, feeling all mushy-gushy that I had finally made friends.

"Especially Marcus," she continued to croon. "He's a *really* powerful friend. You two have such a tight *bond*."

I narrowed my eyes at her when I finally understood what she was implying. I immediately called on my link with Marcus while continuing to watch her, hoping that could keep Elashor out of my head long enough to make the connection. She grabbed my hand and nodded very subtly, acknowledging that she knew I got her message. I only hoped that she had some way to keep the psycho on the dais away from me until help arrived.

I took a deep breath and narrowed my eyes as much as I could without actually closing them and called for Marcus. Initially, I felt nothing, but soon, I felt a tug of recognition. My eyes widened slightly. She saw it and nodded again.

Help me, Marcus. I'm with Elashor in Iabriaria, I sent the thought to my friend, praying that he would hear it and cursing that we never checked if it would work when we were in the room.

Feeling panic rise at the thought of being stuck here forever, I felt Aunt Cora squeeze my hand reassuringly. I looked into her eyes and knew that she wouldn't let anything happen to me if she could help it.

Just as I was about to try to reach out to him again, I felt a rush of power come through me, and I could hear Marcus saying, *"We're here. Hold on a little longer."*

They're here? How are they here? Where is here? I thought.

Hoping that I wasn't hallucinating, I checked Elashor. He seemed to be examining me as though I was his newest present for Christmas. I turned back to Aunt Cora and whispered, "Does he ever move from there?"

"No. I don't think he has left it in a few centuries!"

"What? How does he sleep or go to the bathroom? Wait! On second thought, I don't want to know."

Without warning, Elashor stood back up on his throne and started jumping up and down. He had begun yelling and was throwing a full-on temper tantrum.

"You are in *my* kingdom! No secrets!" he thundered.

Hadn't he just been reading my mind a few minutes before? Unsure, if he was being truthful or not, I tested him.

Your kingdom is small and insignificant, I thought at him, then waited for the explosion. None came.

I stood there, watching him for any change in his demeanor. He was still stomping his feet and yelling incoherently like a toddler. It was unnerving to watch as he would scream at ear-piercing levels and suddenly stop to stare at us as though trying to discern our thoughts again. Confused by the change, I turned to look at Aunt Cora, who seemed to be concentrating strongly on something and would not turn in my direction.

Trying to determine my next move, I thought I saw a very slight nod from her. I realized she was creating a barrier between the imp and myself.

He's out of my head!

I felt a sense of relief wash over me as I tried to check on the bonds with my friends once more. Casually, I closed my eyes, hoping that the plump tyrant would not understand what I was doing. Pulling deep from within myself, I allowed the anchoring sensation of the white blanket to engulf me, creating a cocoon of safety. Feeling balanced, I began focusing my attention on each of their faces. Initially, I found the task difficult, and a sense of despair washed over me, causing my cocoon to drop briefly.

I need to help them help me. Focus, Jace! I thought.

I opened my eyes briefly to be sure nothing had changed and turned my energy inward again. The warmth of my white bubble wrapped up my legs and surrounded me. I allowed it to strengthen before I brought all my attention to Marcus. I imagined every detail of his face, from the shaggy auburn hair to the chestnut eyes. I began to feel a strong rhythm of force from deep within me. A sense of relief followed as I realized our link was still intact and glowing brightly as though it was energizing by my searching for him. Next to his chord, I could see two more and realized there was pulsating energy heading toward me from each.

That's Brian and Izzie. They're all giving me power!

It was then that I noticed two more strands that crisscrossed at my chest. I touched them and felt a powerful jolt course through, causing me to shift slightly. *These were my parents.* The pulse felt intense and near, and I felt my heart lift. They were close by and coming for me.

I opened my eyes to see Aunt Cora, who had concern in her eyes.

"How can they get in?" I whispered.

"They're here?" she mouthed.

"Yes. But I don't know where *here* is or how to guide them!"

"I will try to find them and bring them here, but I will have to leave. Remember, you cannot use your powers. Under any circumstances."

"I don't like this game! You are too far away, and I can't hear you!" Elashor scolded.

Aunt Cora turned and bowed to him as she backed away from me.

"I have tried to encourage him to play, but he will not. Maybe you can try with Ghrian. He always had a stronger relationship with my mate."

Elashor narrowed his eyes at her. Wanting to take the charade further, I scowled at my aunt.

"She pulled me from my family and had set me up for death before I was even born. I want nothing to do with her!"

Although I didn't mean what I was saying, a pang of guilt hit me as I watched her. Aunt Cora's face seemed to shatter at the words. Elashor also saw it and seemed to delight in her misery because he began dancing again and clapped cheerfully. His face twisted into a maniacal smile, like the one I had seen on Sheriff Powell before he had transformed. I saw her eyes go wide, and she lifted her hands as though blocking something. *He was going to do something to her. Oh my god, he was going to hurt her*, I thought.

I saw Elashor lift his hand, and I moved only to have her turn to look at me.

"I always loved you."

As she spoke, the room exploded in light so bright that it momentarily blinded me. When things returned to normal, I looked around, but my aunt was no longer there.

"What did you do?" I demanded, tears forming in my eyes.

Elashor sat down and frowned at me.

"I thought you wanted nothing to do with her. I only helped that happen. Astrials don't do well in bright light, considering they are formed from the moon. It's a pity too because she knew quite a few fun tricks."

The spot where Aunt Cora had been standing was now scarred with a shadow, like the ones seen after they dropped the atomic bombs on Nagasaki and Hiroshima. My heart sank, and I felt my knees go weak. I fell to the ground as I reached out for the remnants of the woman who may have made many mistakes but only out of love.

My heart shattered into a million pieces, and I longed to make everything right—to bring her back and give her the hug she tried to get from me moments earlier, to forgive her for being a friend to my parents, to hear her tell me everything would be alright. As I wallowed in my despair, I heard struggling from behind me and turned to see what was causing the commotion. There, I saw my uncle, bound at the wrists and ankles with an additional tie going around his neck. They had dressed him in rags. His hair was long, as were his beard and mustache. The contrast to his normal well-kept appearance was startling. Compounded with what I had just seen Elashor do to Aunt Cora, I thought my heart would break. Uncle Roman desperately searched the room, and when his eyes met mine, he went wild against his restraints. The three guards accompanying him fought to get him under control.

Meanwhile, Elashor sat on his throne, smiling as he watched.

"Ghrian! I am so glad you came to join us. Asteria was not willing to play, so I sent her away. I hope *you* will help me, though. She promised you would before she…left." He made a sweeping motion toward the floor to indicate how.

Uncle Roman's eyes widened when he noticed the spot I was kneeling next to. He dropped in the guard's arms, sobbing. I had never seen my uncle cry before. Right then, I felt severe pain in my chest as I watched his response.

Bent over, he took a deep breath, slowly lifting his torso, and looking skyward before screaming so loud I thought my ears might burst. Instinctively, I covered them and hunched into a ball, looking at him from around my arms. His skin glowed brightly, and I could feel the heat radiating off him. The louder his screams grew, the warmer and brighter he and the room became.

Elashor, for a brief moment, appeared worried.

"Ghrian! Calm yourself. We still need you, as does the boy. If you keep going, you will kill him as well," Elashor said.

His words hit me hard, and I felt dizzy at his nonchalance and my uncle's apparent disregard for them. When an even brighter flash of light and heat seared into existence, I pulled myself tighter into a ball on the floor and prayed that I would survive *this* blast. When it had dissipated, I opened my eyes and realized that I was whole although still hunched over. Slowly, I looked behind me to see my uncle standing there. His guards had been knocked backward, and the shackles were strewn around the floor at his feet. He pulled his hands in front of his body while around him was a warm glow, light like an all-body halo.

When it had gone, he was no longer the broken prisoner he had been a few minutes before. A younger-looking version of the man I had known stood in his place. He wore an older style white shirt, a loose tie at the neck, and decorative lavender bands at the edges near the wrists that would have matched Aunt Cora's outfit. Covering this was a leather jacket that extended to midthigh and had a narrow V-neck, which revealed a portion of the noble shirt worn below it. The jacket cinched at the waist with a big leather belt, bound by a small brass buckle. His pants were simple and a little narrow, reaching down to a matching pair of weathered leather boots of a basic design.

I stared at him in disbelief. Although I had known that he was fae, seeing him like this was still shocking. Behind me, I could hear Elashor jumping up and down and cheering once again, and I felt the rage flow through my veins like a freight train running loose.

"You came to play! You came to play! Let's start!" Elashor rubbed his hands together. A twisted grin decorated his face as he looked around the room, searching for something.

I really hated that fairy and would have loved nothing more than to pull his wings off and shove them down his fat throat.

With effort, I turned back to my uncle instead, and I watched as he walked past me, not even acknowledging my existence. A wave of pain hit me, and I wanted to cry out to him. However, I knew I had to trust in his movements and pray he would loop me in on them at some point.

"You have killed my mate! There is no playing anymore, Elashor!" his voice was loud and booming.

"She went against the Lunar Codex. How was I supposed to let her live?" he whined, puffing out his lower lip.

"On what grounds?"

"On ALL grounds!" Elashor's voice rose and was matching the intensity of Uncle Roman's.

"The child was born from the actions of a lunar spirit and under a lunar sign. He is a true Libra Moon Child and part of the prophecy. His life force will bring us immense power, brother. You only need to finish what she could not. Bring me his power, and I can restore Asteria to you."

Still kneeling, I saw Uncle Roman turn to me, his face expressionless. My heart dropped. *Was he about to kill me?* The man who had practiced as a physician for the past twelve years. The one who would rock me to sleep and kiss my cuts and scrapes. He was about to snuff out the past twelve years in an instant. I stared at him, pleading.

"Uncle Roman, please. Don't do this!" I cried out.

"Tonight is his first full moon, which will bring on his first change. When that happens, he will have less control of his power, and we can take it from him. With that power, I can raise us back to the glory we once had. We will no longer have to hide in the shadows of humans. We can rule them from above again!" Elashor exalted.

Uncle Roman listened while staring at me and nodding through the entire rant.

"You *are* the key to the codex," he said to me after Elashor was done.

I felt my eyes go wide. *Oh my god, he was actually going to do it. He was going to kill me!* I frantically looked around for help, but all I could see was the child faces of the Fairy Court watching this without moving or trying to help. *Where was the door? I have to get out of here!* Suddenly, I realized I had not seen Uncle Roman enter through a door and wondered if you needed fairy magic to enter or leave.

As panic mounted, I glimpsed a quick movement in the far corner of the room, behind Elashor's throne. I could only make out some of it, and it looked like the root of a large tree. A second later,

I saw a small servant child walk out from behind the throne. *I had to get back there, but how?*

I looked back to Uncle Roman, who was still watching me, a vacant look in his eye.

"Uncle Roman, please! It's me. It's Jace."

He continued to stare at me, his mouth moving as though he was speaking but at a nearly inaudible level.

Slowly, I lifted myself from the crouched position, straining to hear what he was saying.

"What? What are you trying to say? I can't hear you!"

Elashor sat watching the exchange, stuffing his face again.

Great. Now dinner and a movie, I thought.

Returning my attention to Uncle Roman, I was hopeful when I saw he had shifted his gaze down to the shadow on the floor while still speaking. For a moment, his face seemed to break at the sight. Without warning, though, he looked skyward, which caused Elashor and me to follow his gaze. Suddenly, the room darkened as though someone were sucking the light from it. I felt the hair on my neck come to attention and wondered if it was something he was doing or if it was already night outside.

Elashor clapped his hands as though trying to get everyone in the room's attention, pointing at me.

"The fun is about to start! It's almost time," he said.

What *fun* is he talking about now? That was when I remembered what Elashor had said.

He would have his first change.

He had meant me. What change was I going to undergo? My blood ran cold, and I felt sick to my stomach. Fear engulfed me and I could feel my body vibrating like a hot wire as the adrenaline kicked up to its max. All I wanted was the safety net of my uncle's arms to be around me and to know he would protect me. Unfortunately, he was still mumbling incoherently with his voice too low for me to hear.

A mixture of emotions bubbled up in me as I watched the shell of the man I knew. Resolutely, I stood up, getting in his face, and began shoving him.

ANNIE O'CONNELL

"You said you would be there for me! That you are the same person, you always were! That person would never leave me or allow someone else to hurt me. Why are you doing this?"

My voice broke at this last part. I could feel the tears forming, but I fought to regain control. I felt utterly alone and defeated although nothing had happened…yet.

I lifted my head and stood eye to eye with the man who had raised me. There was a blankness in his face as he continued to recite the same thing over and over. Sniffling, I leaned in closer to hear what he was saying. It was so low. *Why won't he speak up?*

I was about to give up and turn away when my uncle's eyes went wide. He gasped and finally spoke loud enough for everyone in the room to hear him.

> "As soon as the darkness rises once more,
> A sudden death shall mark an age of bliss,
> Bringing a change of leadership.
> It shall be then when the sun doesn't rise,
> A marked child shall bring the ascent of hope
> And the return of monsters."

I stared at him, utterly stunned by what he said.

"Am I the marked child? Is it my sudden death?"

He stared vacantly at me for a long while, but I thought, briefly, that I saw a small smile show like the ones he would give when he was proud of something I had done or said. But that glimmer of hope disappeared just as fast as I had seen it, and he resumed his robot-like stance, once more repeating the words at his original volume. This time, though, he slowly backed away from me. He raised his eyes to the ceiling, which was almost black, and I wondered if the stars had been absorbed into a chasm.

"Of course, you are the marked child!" Elashor answered my question.

"The first full moon rises in your fifteenth year on the night of All Hallows Eve. She timed it so perfectly." He continued shifting his feet back and forth in a demented jig while he clapped.

"All Hallows Eve? You mean Halloween? It's Halloween?" I demanded.

I felt as though the air had been sucked out of my lungs. I quickly did the math in my head, and my heart sank. That means I had been missing for three weeks! I turned on my heel to face Elashor.

"How has it been three weeks? I just got here today!"

His smile was nauseating as he answered in a soft voice.

"It is my realm, and I enjoy my kingdom how I want to enjoy it."

He sat on his chair and crossed his right leg over his left and stared at me. His actions were that of an adult and looked bizarre on a childlike visage. I wanted to say something to him, but as I was about to speak, I felt an immense searing pain start in my back and travel up my spine. It left me blinded momentarily, and I dropped to my knees.

Turning to Uncle Roman, unsure what the pain was, I extended my hand. I was begging for his help, his comfort, but he stepped back and looked at Elashor.

"It has started."

Unbelievable pain came in increasing waves of intensity. It felt as though my body was being pulled apart from the inside out, and I shrieked in agony as I dropped to my hands and knees. Within seconds, sweat was dripping off me as I fought for control. Trying to breathe, my body arched in spasms, and I felt my shoulders breaking.

I searched the room to determine who or what was causing the pain. From somewhere behind, I could hear the fabric of my shirt ripping, bones breaking, and my skin tearing. I tried to reach up for my uncle but could not extend my arms or use my hands. Realizing that my upper body was failing me, I tried to get to my feet. I saw the door behind Elashor again. *Could I make it? Would he stop me?*

I tried to pull myself up onto my knees, but as I placed pressure on them, I felt them swell and then buckle. Again, I heard the shattering of more osseous matter, and I forced myself to look toward Elashor, who was still sitting on his throne. At that moment, though, he was leaning forward with his elbows on his knees and his face propped in his hands, staring at me. I was on display...a circus side-show attraction, and he was enjoying watching me die.

I wanted to scream out at him, but as I opened my mouth to speak, I felt my face explode with pain, causing me to drop to the floor again. Fear washed over me in waves, and I tried to open my eyes to gauge who was around me but was flooded with a more intense wave of terror when I realized I could not see. *Oh my god, I'm blind! He's killing me, and I can't even see what is happening!*

I wanted to pull myself into a ball and just let the pain take me away when I felt something that was not pain rush over me. Not wanting to hurt anymore, I tried to focus on the unfamiliar sensation. It started small but seemed to grow stronger with each breath.

"We're coming, Jace! Please don't give up. I feel you. We all feel you!"

Marcus's words were strong in my head. It comforted me momentarily. They were trying to save me, but Elashor had broken too much of me. *How could they save me now?* I closed my eyes and relaxed as best I could. For a moment, it felt as though all the pain had stopped, and I took a deep breath. Immediately after, it felt as though a bolt of lightning had hit me. My body arched and spasmed violently one last time before I collapsed into a shattered heap on the floor as I slipped into unconsciousness.

CHAPTER 27

The Change

I woke to Elashor standing over me, his eyes wide, and I felt my stomach turn at his face being so close to mine. Instinctively, I tried to retreat from him, but my muscles lay flaccid as I tried fruitlessly to coax them to respond to my desperate need to leave this place. Realizing that I could not move, I felt my pulse quicken as I desperately scanned the room for help, and I quickly noted I was still in the same spot I had been when the pain took over, and that meant Elashor had left his throne to come to me.

"Amazing!" he said in fascination.

Not wanting him so close to me, I tried to move again. Someone put a hand on my back, but the feel of it was wrong. It moved up and down my back but had the uncomfortable sensation of a stranger running their hands through my hair. Struggling against gravity, I forced my head up. I glanced to my right where Uncle Roman was kneeling. *Was he petting me? Or had it been Elashor?*

I tried to get away from them both and felt dizzy, dropping back onto my side. Not wanting them near me, I tried to speak, but my voice came out as a growl. I stopped, startled by the sound. While still trying to regain my composure, I saw the young girl, who had collected me from my room earlier, approaching.

"Silly doggy. You should not growl at Elashor," she declared, wagging her finger at me.

I felt my breath catch, and my eyes widened. *Doggy?* When I lifted myself up off my side, I could feel the hand of my uncle helping me. I looked over at him and pulled away slightly, then stopped. Looking down, where I would have expected my hands to have been, I now saw large white paws.

Oh my god! Oh my god! Oh my god! Where are my hands? was all I could think.

Jumping up the rest of the way, I felt pain rush across my body, and I nearly collapsed again. Uncle Roman steadied me, earning him a quick nip at his hand followed by a growl. He must have understood the underlying meaning because he pulled his hand away. Still monitoring his position, I was hit with a thought that sent all others out of my head. "He will have less control of his power, and we can take it from him."

Well, I was pretty out of control at this point! I also knew that my situation had just gone from bad to worse. I attempted to walk and stumbled a bit as I tried to get used to walking on four legs as opposed to two. I felt a surge of heat thrashing through my veins, and I backed away from Elashor and Uncle Roman, as I lowered my head in as menacing a pose as I could muster.

A multitude of emotions ran through my head, and the more I tried to calm myself, the more I wanted to rip someone's throat out. This change was something I should have experienced with my father, who could have guided me. Yet another first that I missed out on with him because of my uncle.

My father...

Instantly, I recalled the connection that I had felt when I was calling for Marcus. I looked at Uncle Roman and Elashor and knew that I needed to hide any signs of weakness while I tried to connect with my dad. Standing again, I felt my legs wobble under me. When I tried to steady myself, I saw Uncle Roman reach out a hand in my direction. My eyes narrowed at him, unsure of what his intentions were anymore.

Continuing to back away from them, I growled as deep and threatening as I could as a sign of warning for all to stay away from me. Elashor seemed to enjoy my new stance and clapped cheerily.

"That's it. You are doing wonderfully. What a great pet you are going to make!"

My head shot up to look at him, and my growl intensified ten-fold.

There is no way I was going to be anyone's pet, I thought.

I tried to focus on my father but was having trouble concentrating on him while also having to watch Elashor.

I have to get out of here, if I am going to survive, I thought.

Elashor watched my every move and stood taller, smiling. He looked to his left and snapped his fingers at a young boy who looked to be about five years old. He appeared unkempt and was wearing ill-fitting clothes with holes scattered throughout and seemed to have not bathed in some time. At Elashor's snap, the child came to life and leaned down to grab something.

It was a small wooden box with a picture of a wolf on it. My heart sank as I saw the boy bring it forward. It was the box I had kept all my memories from my parents in when I was growing up. On seeing it, I felt the hair on my haunches rise, causing me to let out another growl.

Uncle Roman turned to look at the item the boy had just brought and appeared to have a moment of recollection.

Does he recognize it?

Elashor took the box from the boy and snapped his fingers again, pointing to the spot he had just run over from. With a small bow, the child turned and returned to his original spot, where he assumed the same stiff posture as though refrozen in time.

Holding the box close, Elashor rubbed the top of it and watched me. I wanted to lunge at him and rip his throat out. I bet I could probably do so if I had better control of my new body.

Smiling, he opened the box and touched the side of his face in wonder. His eyes had opened wide as though they fell on the most amazing thing he had ever seen. Unsure what I had in there that would bring this monster such entertainment, I just watched him. Slowly, he pulled something small out of the box and held it between his fingers then lifted it in the air like a trophy for all to see. It was my father's ring.

Instinctively, I looked down to my finger where the ring should have been. *Had it been there before the change? When did he take it?*

While I was trying to figure this out, Elashor stood there smiling as he observed my reaction.

"Watch this, little pup!" he said.

Putting the box down, he held the ring between the fingers of both hands and appeared to pull on it. Initially, nothing happened, but then it seemed to get larger. I watched, transfixed, and unsure of what he was planning to do with it. Again, I looked toward Uncle Roman, who was also observing the ring. I decided it was now or never and desperately tried to connect with my father.

Closing my eyes, I turned inward to find the connection. I could still see the pulsations coming from Marcus, Izzie, and Brian. We were still connected, but I was now struggling to grab onto my parents. I examined the two tethers coming from my chest and realized that they split at the ends to form two additional strands.

Initially, I did not understand what this would be. Then I realized the extra strands represented my *other* mother and father. A moment of clarity had hit me, and I felt my heart warm at the thought. I had always had two sets of parents. Whether that was by chance or by force, they were all there.

But right now, I needed to determine which one led to my biological father. Looking closer, I could see that one strand was thick and robust with an orange-gold color while the other was soft and equally strong but a deep violet. I touched each of them and concentrated on my father. An overlap was present between both strands, but I still found myself drawn toward the orange-gold strand. Dropping the purple one, I focused all my energy on the other.

"Dad. I don't know where you are, but I could really use your help right about now!"

I anchored my attention onto the strand and willed the message to send, unsure if it would make it to its desired destination.

When I opened my eyes, Elashor was holding a large ring-shaped object over his head. Even though it looked like my father's ring, it was large enough to be worn as a belt now. Bringing it down to eye level, he handed it to Uncle Roman and nodded toward me.

"Once we attach this, he will be ours forever," Elashor boasted.

My uncle examined the ring and then turned to me. Elashor's face lit up, and a mischievous smile crept across it.

"Ghrian, you can have the honors of securing his leash!"

My eyes went wide, and I backed away from my uncle. Realizing that time was quickly running out, I also increased the pleading in my head, which was now at a near fever pitch.

"Please, hurry, Dad! I'm in real trouble."

Uncle Roman took the ring and turned it in his hands, examining it. Then he pushed one of the rubies, and the ring popped open. I felt the adrenaline running laps through my body as I quickly worked to gain complete control over my new physique. Watching my uncle, I prayed that he would snap out of it, realizing that if he attached the ring to me, I would never see my family or friends ever again. I hunched lower, growling and snarling at him, ready to pounce.

He walked toward me, seemingly unfazed by my stance and ready to attach this leash around my neck. Backing away, I suddenly felt my hind end hit into something hard, and I quickly turned to see what it was. The wall that had been at least a few hundred feet away a few minutes ago was now right behind me, eliminating any chance of escape. With my uncle approaching quickly, holding my potential demise in his hands, I felt my heart hammering in my chest.

I quickly scanned the room for a way out before turning back to my uncle who was still advancing on me. At that moment, I understood it was going to have to be him or me. I sent a last plea out to my father and hoped it would get to him in time.

"I love you! I have always loved you, and I will always love you."

My uncle's hands were now within feet of my neck. I said a last goodbye and lunged at him. It was as though my legs had been tightening in a corkscrew. When I released, the kinetic energy my muscles had amassed allowed me to fly at him with the force of a runaway bull. With just a second to react, Uncle Roman twisted his body violently to the right to avoid the impact. While still in midjump, I realized I was now on a collision course with the impishly annoying Elashor, who stood in place wide-eyed and mouth agape.

Seeing the fear in his face gave me all the satisfaction I needed as I opened my jaw in anticipation to exact my revenge. But just as I was about to grab his throat, I was broadsided and sent hurtling across the room. Looking back, I saw Uncle Roman standing there, glancing between Elashor and me, still holding the ring.

"Enough of this!" Elashor roared.

Pulling himself up, he snapped his fingers, and the automaton-like children seemed to come to life.

"Seize him!" he yelled, causing the room to vibrate and forcing me to drop and cover my ears.

Raising my head, I could now see that I had more than just my uncle to contend with. The room was alive with children advancing on me with evil in their eyes but smiles on their faces. Scanning the room again, I saw the small boy from earlier standing off-center, flanked by a few children of equal height. I backed up a few paces and tried to judge the height needed to clear their heads when something caught my eye. The girl to the left of the child and the boy to his right looked like child versions of Izzie's parents. The resemblance was unmistakable. How had they come to be here? Remembering the panic in Izzie's voice at her family not answering, I wanted to fix the anomaly I was seeing in front of me but logic and self-preservation won out at the moment as I prepared to launch over the advancing children.

Waiting a few more paces for them to get closer, I took a giant leap, which caused the young boy in the center to drop slightly. Landing victoriously on the other side and in one piece, I took off running, my snout aimed at the door behind the throne. From all corners of the room, I could hear juvenile screeching and laughter as the children turned and started to run behind me as though I had just initiated the largest game of catch.

"Stop playing and get him! Stop him now!" Elashor was screaming as he jumped up and down. I sneaked a backward glance and decided he resembled a toddler more than a leader.

Watching my trajectory, comprehension shone in Elashor's face as he surmised the direction I was running. His eyes narrowed as he took off running toward the door as well. Within a few strides, I noticed that the room had started shaking with such ferocity that I had to slow down so as not to lose my footing. Still heading toward the door, I rounded the throne where a monstrous creature, that stood almost as tall as the room, was now blocking my exit. Immediately, I knew it was Elashor.

Attempting to stop myself, I nearly slid into it. My heart froze as I looked up to see the large being smiling down at me. Scrambling back, I tried to get away. Glancing over my shoulder, I could see that he now stood roughly fifteen feet tall. His almost yellow-green speckled skin was potted with dark marks that seemed to ooze a viscous material. He now had a large bulbous nose and horribly misshapen teeth that had a goopy green slime-like thread of drool dripping from the corners of his mouth. If I had to imagine a troll, he would fit that description.

Deciding that an alternate route to the door was needed, I began running in the opposite direction. I was plowing through small children and sending them flying in either direction as I barreled my way through the room. My attempt to stay alive long enough to escape was something Elashor seemed to enjoy. He laughed and jumped in delight, causing the room to shake as though a bomb had just detonated inside. Above us, the small gems came loose and began dropping like missiles from the ceiling causing the children to now scream and run in various directions.

As I rounded the room, I could see Uncle Roman standing in the center of the pandemonium looking around, bewildered. Surprisingly, he was still holding the ring, though.

Is he serious right now? I thought, trying to determine the best path around him.

Elashor stopped his celebration to scan the room. He homed in on me and pointed his gnarled finger.

"Ghrian! Do it, you fool! Put the collar on him now!"

My uncle spun to look at me, bracing himself. Frantically, I tried to course-correct, so I'd avoid a direct impact with him. Within a few feet of a head-on collision, the young girl from earlier crossed suddenly in front of us. I jumped up, kicking her in the side toward my uncle. Using that momentum, I ran in the opposite direction, briefly glancing over my shoulder to watch the girl and my uncle collide.

As they struck, Uncle Roman was knocked off-balance, and the ring fell, skittering across the floor into the melee of children. Elashor roared and lifted his foot over Uncle Roman as though he was about to step on him. I felt my heart stop in that moment. Changing my trajectory yet again, I ran full force at my uncle. I slammed into him, throwing him out of the way but sliding with him across the floor into the swarm of screaming children.

When we came to a stop, we were facing each other with the ring within arm's reach of him. He looked at it and then at me.

"Go! I'll distract him."

Unsure if I had heard him correctly, I stared at him, cocking my head to the side.

"You heard me. Now go!" he yelled and shoved me.

Not wanting to wait to see if he would change his mind, I jumped up. Elashor was standing over us, trying to look through the throng of little bodies, jumping over and around us. Surprised by my sudden movement, he flew to attention. Leaping out of the ruckus, I watched in horror as he lifted his foot, preparing to stomp again. Unwilling to be on its receiving end, I ran between his legs, which left him looking like a demented green flamingo.

Elashor advanced and slammed his foot down, narrowly missing me. He looked over his shoulder to see where I had gone. Finally, behind the throne, I could see my exit and ran as fast as I could for it. Just as I was about to reach the door, I saw a shadow fall on me and a second later, the throne exploded into a million pieces, blocking my exit.

I dropped and slid into the debris, yelping as my side hit a sharp piece of splintered material. It caused an explosive searing pain in my side, instantly making it difficult to breathe.

Elashor was towering over me, holding the ring between his bulbous fingers. I felt my blood run cold as I desperately scanned the room for Uncle Roman. In the distance, I saw him facedown on the floor. My heart stuttered. Pulling myself up, I tried to run between

Elashor's legs again. However, he was too quick this time and blocked my movement.

He laughed, holding the ring in his hand.

"That was a fun game, pup, but now it is time to finish this."

Without warning, his once clumsy hand shot down at lighting speed and pinned me to the floor. Immediately, I started fighting to get free, but Elashor held tighter. I heard a snap and felt a jolt of electricity run through my body as the pain in my side intensified. I now found it almost impossible to breathe.

With his other hand, he brought the ring closer to my neck. I fought with all the strength I had left but could not break the impenetrable hold he had on me. I watched in horror as the ring I had once held so dear inched closer to me. With the worsening pain in my side and the increasing difficulty to breathe, I found my vision flickered. As my reality came in and out of focus, I retreated into my mind, and I pictured all the faces of all those that I would miss.

Wishing that I could have more time to make amends with Izzie and to see Brian standing over her shoulder protectively, throwing sarcastic remarks my way. I dreamed about getting to have that VR sleepover with Marcus and see which of us really was the gaming master. I wanted to have just one more day with my parents and to tell them how much I loved them and always have. To be able to bring Aunt Cora back and apologize for my words and actions just before she died to save me. To run to Uncle Roman and hold him, the way he used to when I was hurt. Would I even remember them after this? Realizing that my options were limited and my demise was close at hand, I closed my eyes and tried to keep my loved ones' faces in the forefront of my mind. But just as I became resigned to my fate, the wall behind me exploded.

A multitude of large dark shapes flew into the room over me. Elashor dropped the ring and me as he backed away. He began howling in pain as the group attacked, ripping him apart and dropping him to the ground. As the fight continued in the distance, one of the large creatures turned and came to me. It was an enormous gray-and-tan wolf with a black stripe that ran down its back. The streak culminated in a large black spot on the tip of his tail, which was currently low as it whimpered. Looking at me as it began nudging and nuzzling against my face.

I was so weak, but I tried to get up and immediately collapsed down again. The wolf circled to my side and then came back to my face, concern in its face. I looked into its eyes, and the realization finally hit me.

Dad. I knew you would come! I thought.

The wolf sneezed and then nuzzled my face again, periodically turning to see the other wolves continuing their assault of Elashor. Panic rushed over me as I remembered that Uncle Roman had been lying hurt there and needed help. When I tried to stand, my dad pushed me down and growled. I looked over his shoulder, and dread flooded me. Elashor was on the ground, thrashing about roughly where Uncle Roman had been.

Help him. Uncle R.... Nick is over there, I thought.

My dad looked back at the group and growled at me again.

I know, but he saved me, and now he's hurt. Please!

He stared at me, contemplating the worth of saving the man who destroyed his life and had stolen his son. Unable to think straight anymore, I returned his glance with pleading eyes. Seeming resigned with the more important decision in keeping me happy, he ran toward the fight.

I watched, helplessly as he circled the perimeter of the group until he seemed to find something. Narrowly avoiding being brought into the fight, he grabbed and dragged it out from under Elashor's large frame. It was the body of a man, and it wasn't moving. I felt my heart stop at the thought of losing both Aunt Cora and Uncle Roman on the same day.

Seeming satisfied that he had pulled the body a safe distance away, my dad turned and jumped onto Elashor's chest. His jaws clamped down on his throat, ripping till there was a shower of red that bathed most of the room. As my vision seemed to dim, I felt something rush up behind me and gasp. Instantly, I knew who it was and tried to lift my head and comfort her. But I found that my head was too heavy and instantly dropped it again.

Am I dying? I thought as I felt my mother approach.

"Not today, you aren't!" she yelled at me through her tears.

Surprised, I opened my eyes and looked at her. She was crouched next to my side and doing something. I felt as though I was boiling and freezing at the same time. The sensation caused me to begin panting, which hurt…a lot! I wanted to stop the rapid breaths, but my body kept picking up where it left off. Then to add insult to injury, my body began to shake violently and uncontrollably.

Looking up into my mother's face, I could see a stream of tears falling, and I wanted to comfort her. To her rear, a group of men was walking in our direction. Each was covered in blood and…naked? I tried to avert my eyes but stopped at the sight of my father supporting Uncle Roman. They, too, were walking toward us although Uncle Roman appeared to have a limp. Seeing the two of them upright and alive gave me a bit of strength, and I tried to shift my position.

"Stop moving, Christian! You're hurt and losing blood. I think your lung might be injured too," my mom scolded while holding me down.

"Callista, please let me try to help. I know I don't deserve to ask you for anything, but please! Allow me this," Uncle Roman pleaded.

She turned and stared at him for what seemed to be an eternity. I felt my breath catch and a gush of warm liquid run down my side. I knew it was blood. My mom looked at the wound with horror in her eyes before turning back to Uncle Roman. Standing up, she walked to him pointing her finger into his chest and acid in her tone from between gritted teeth, saying, "If you hurt him, I will kill you right here where you stand."

"Agreed." Nodding, my uncle, knelt next to me.

He scanned my body before putting his hand on my head and gently scratching behind my left ear. I closed my eyes, relaxed by his touch and the knowledge that he was alive and alright.

"You may feel some warmth, but it won't hurt, okay?" he asked me.

I lifted my head and dropped it, trying my best to show I understood and agreed with him.

Repositioning himself next to me about midway down, he looked up to the ceiling and opened his arms. As he did, the light in the room slowly increased until it was almost blinding. When it could not possibly get any brighter, my uncle pulled his arms to himself. The light seemed to concentrate into a small ball of energy the size of a softball in front of him and he began moving his hands in a "wax on, wax off" motion.

I felt small waves of heat run through me and relaxed as he did so. With each stroke, his movements increased in speed. Gradually, I felt that my breathing improve. Touching my side, he encouraged me to roll onto my stomach, where he continued working on what I assumed was a broken rib—maybe two—from when Elashor had pinned me. As my uncle moved, I could feel the heat concentrate on that spot. Then I heard two quick pops from my chest, and my breathing quickly returned to normal.

Immediately, I was able to take a deep breath that I had not realized I desperately needed and stood up.

My mother let out a deep breath too, and my father hugged her.

Behind us, I could hear movement. I turned to see Marcus, Izzie, and Brian climbing through the wreckage in the wall. Once at the bottom of the rubble heap, Marcus tossed a duffel bag he had been carrying to one man near my father. The guy immediately opened it and started divvying up the clothes from within. I turned to look at Marcus, who stood wide-eyed as he took in the room's appearance.

"This looks like a scene out of Jason meets Munchkinland! What happened?"

Continuing his scan of the room, Marcus glanced at me. Then he did a double take. Slowly walking toward me, he said, "Jace?"

Unable to speak, I did the next best thing and nodded.

"H-hey, man...when I said you were a lone wolf, you didn't have to go all literal on me!" he teased.

I heard my mother chuckle behind me. Izzie stood next to Marcus just as flabbergasted with her hand over her mouth. Brian walked toward me and knelt, so we were eye to eye before he spoke.

"I hope you understand the years of therapy I will need after all this!" he said with a lopsided smile on his face.

Unsure of what else to do, I nodded again. Behind him, Izzie slowly moved close to me and stood behind Brian. Her face seemed guarded, and I felt a pang in my chest and let out a whimper. Brian, seeing my reaction, turned to see Izzie and frowned.

"Izzie, he looks different, but it's still him. You can feel that it's him, right?"

Kneeling next to Brian, she kept her head lowered unable to look me in the eye. I lowered mine and inched closer before dropping to the floor. I rested my head on her lap while looking up. She sat motionless, watching my movements before letting out a small chuckle. It dislodged a single tear from her eye. I lifted my head, which had me level with her face, and nuzzled her cheek with my snout. Initially, she did not move, but slowly, I felt her relax. She turned her face toward mine before lifting a hand and rubbing my cheek and ear. Then she wrapped me in a tight embrace with her arms around my neck.

"I think we just got him breathing again. Maybe loosen up the death grip?" Marcus teased.

Pulling away, she laughed slightly as she wiped away the tears that were flowing unhindered at this point.

"I didn't think I would ever see you again. You just disappeared. I thought you were dead!" she said as she looked me in the eye.

"Right after Elashor took you, your connection with us just vanished. It wasn't until about five days ago that I heard you again. Nearly scared the life out of me!" Marcus added.

Izzie laughed as she looked from Marcus to me.

"We all picked up on it, but Marcus heard you first. He seemed to be the only one who could get through, though."

I felt a hand running up my back, which sent a shiver down my spine. Turning, I saw my mother, who said, "My handsome boy, go to your father. He will help you."

She kissed my nose before pointing toward my dad who was now dressed and standing there in his human form, smiling warmly at me. Ambling toward him, I noted who else was in the room. To his left George and Mitchell, and to his right was Sheriff Powell. On seeing the sheriff, I stopped and began to growl. My dad said, smiling, "He's one of the good guys. Elashor was impersonating him."

Seeing my distrust hadn't faded, Powell backed away from my dad, nodding to him. When I maintained my stance, my dad came to me. He bent down, so we were eye to eye.

"You did good, my boy. I knew you would."

He brushed his head against mine, and I nuzzled him as well.

"The next part will not be so much fun, but you are not alone," he said, motioning to everyone who had assembled to help me.

"I felt your change. Actually, I think we all did. But we are with you this time and will help you through it."

My blood ran cold at the thought of more pain.

Maybe being a wolf full-time isn't so bad? I thought.

My dad chuckled and dropped his head, saying, "I'd prefer to talk with you, human face to human face."

I tilted my head in confusion that he had answered my thought. My dad smiled warmly and pointed at his head.

"You're *here*. I *heard* you and will always hear you now. I tried to send you my strength, but I was too far away and knew that I needed to shift to help you. I'm so sorry I wasn't here sooner. But I will be here from now on. We will all help you this time."

I looked around at their faces and back at my dad before nodding.

"The change is hard to describe, but I guess it feels like you're falling and then like you're folding in on yourself. You need to focus on the end shape you are looking for. If it is the wolf, you think of that. If it is human, then focus there."

I nodded, closing my eyes and trying to imagine myself as a human again. I could hear laughter coming from behind my father, which caused me to open my eyes again.

"Boy, you look like your about to relieve yourself all over the place. Relax a bit!" George said.

Dad dropped his head, chuckled slightly, and looked over his shoulder.

"Interesting analogy, George, but let's try to be more encouraging and perhaps a bit less graphic."

"Yeah. Of course," he answered as his cheeks reddened.

My dad smiled at me again encouragingly.

"I'm going to help you with touch, okay?"

I nodded and closed my eyes as he placed his hand on my head.

"Let's try that again."

Instantly, I felt a warming sensation rush over me, followed by the drop he had pointed out. But I felt supported like my dad had caught me before I fully fell. At that moment, it seemed as though I was being suspended between two locations. I imagined myself as I had always been. This time, I felt tugging and pulling as opposed to explosions and tearing.

From behind me, I heard a gasp and ignored it, focusing on my dad and the task at hand. After it was all complete, I heard him say, "There you are!"

Cautiously, I allowed my eyes to open. In front of me, I saw my father smiling, who extended his hand to cup it around my face. My human face!

"You did good, kid. Probably the smoothest and fastest shift I have ever seen," Mitchell said.

"It didn't hurt. Why did it hurt so bad the first time? I seriously thought I was going to die."

"We all got a taste of it. Dropped the entire group to the floor!" George said.

My father gave him a warning look before returning his attention back to me. He reached into the duffel bag that was at his feet and handed me some clothes. I felt my cheeks flush, and I immediately glanced at Izzie. Thankfully, my little group of friends had averted their eyes and stayed that way to allow me to dress. My dad, following my gaze, gave me a half smile. Attempting to break up the awkwardness, he struggled to answer my question.

"I'm not exactly sure. Perhaps fear? You had been missing for so long. Anything could have caused it."

"About that. How has it been weeks? I only woke up a few hours ago."

My father exchanged a glance with my mother, trying to form a response. Uncle Roman, who had been quiet along the periphery of people, was the one who spoke.

"Fairy realms are very unpredictable and can speed up or slow down time. He wanted you at your first change because of the powers and a lack of control. Going through it alone can do both to a first-time shifter."

Recalling the first part of my ordeal in this room, I glared at him.

"You tried to help him. Why?" I felt the words get stuck in my throat.

Before I had time to register the motion, my father was grabbing Uncle Roman around the neck and lifting him. Understanding the severity of the situation, I jumped at my father, pulling on his shoulder, trying to get him to release my uncle. As though consumed by years of pent-up rage, I felt as though I was trying to pull a steel girder from its footprint in a building. My mother stepped in and touched my father's shoulder, which caused him to relax his grip and lower Uncle Roman to the floor.

"Perhaps we can hear him out first?" my mother suggested.

My father considered her, then me. Releasing my uncle, he glared at him threateningly. Uncle Roman dropped his head momentarily as he tried to think of a response. Lifting his head to look at me, he said, "He is a fairy lord and can control other fae as he desires. *You* broke through it. When you were calling your dad, I heard it too. I was fighting it from the inside the entire time, but it wasn't until you saved me that I was truly released from Elashor."

"Why was he using the ring?" I asked.

My dad looked at me questioningly.

"What ring?"

"Elashor turned your ring into this type of collar that would have bound me to him. That was what I was trying to get away from!" I explained.

My dad's eyebrows lifted, and he turned his attention to Uncle Roman.

"I think this is a *you* question, Nick."

Uncle Roman nodded. "By using something that had strong sentimental value, Elashor could attach himself to you completely. Jace has always had that ring and would spend hours looking at it and holding it. Elashor knew the significance and used it against him."

I felt my dad squeeze my shoulder as Uncle Roman spoke.

"What do we do with it now?" I asked.

"Better question. Where is it now, and who are all these people?" Brian asked.

Looking around the room, the children who had formed the court had all disappeared. Now there were adults and teens scattered around, lying motionless. A sickening feeling ran through me as I remembered the small children who had looked like Izzie's parents.

"Split up and find it!" my dad addressed everyone.

Marcus raised his hand sheepishly as everyone was about to move, which caused the group to stop. "Stupid question. What does it look like?" he asked with an embarrassed grin on his face.

His reaction caused me to laugh, which had my father doing so as well.

"It's the silver ring with Celtic knots and three rubies in it," I answered.

My father's eyebrows rose. "I thought it was lost in the fire. I loved that ring because it reminded me of the three of us. Although it upset me greatly all these years not having it, I'm glad that it was giving you the same happiness that it had given me."

I nodded but now felt a darker resentment toward the artifact as it would act as a leash for me, taking me away from my family forever. My mother noticed my shift in attitude and touched my arm saying, "Yes, it does have a different meaning now. Regardless, we need to find it. As long as it is with us, it cannot hurt you."

With a wave of my father's hand, we all fanned out to examine those fallen bodies and to search for the ring. From the far corner of the room, we heard Izzie scream, which caused all of us to look in her direction. I could see her running toward a group of bodies and knew for sure that I had seen her parents earlier. Running toward her, I prayed that her parents would have survived whatever magic had enchanted them. By the time I was within arm's reach, I had to stop as I could see her sobbing. She was hunched over the four bodies of her family members.

Marcus came to a stop near me, and on seeing Izzie, started looking around the room frantically.

"They're here too then! Help me find them," he cried out, half out of breath with fear.

"Who?" I asked.

"Mom and Aunt Lilly!" he shrieked with a glossy haze over his eyes.

I turned toward Izzie and struggled to swallow a large lump that had formed in my throat and then nodded to Marcus. Immediately, the group changed tactics and began looking for his family. Roughly twenty feet away, we found them holding onto each other and face-down. I felt the burn of tears in my eyes as I turned to look at Marcus, who stood motionless and wide-eyed.

The day had turned on a dime. I had gone from being an orphan to having my parents returned to me while my friends had lost theirs. At that moment, I wanted to fix it, and my gaze fell on Uncle Roman, who was already moving toward Mrs. Hunter and Aunt Lilly.

Kneeling next to them, he closed his eyes and ran his hands over their heads without making direct contact. Suddenly, he opened his eyes to say, "They're not dead!"

A sense of relief washed over me, but I wondered what that meant since I could see their lifeless bodies.

"It's almost like suspended animation. I would have expected it to release them once Elashor left, but that hasn't happened yet."

"Yet? So it can still happen? They're going to wake up?" Izzie said with hope in her eyes even as her voice cracked.

"I think it is for protection. We need to get them home first, or at least out of here," Uncle Roman said.

"Then as soon as we find the ring, we will leave here with them. Has anyone found it?" my father asked.

Everyone seemed to glance at each other, but no one spoke up.

"What does this mean?" I asked.

"Elashor took it," Uncle Roman said matter-of-factly.

"Elashor is dead!" my dad interjected.

"You killed a shell, but not the essence, which is Elashor. He likely jumped to another child form he had here before you finished this off." Uncle Roman motioned to the monster carcass behind us.

I felt my knees weaken as I grasped the knowledge that Elashor was not dead and had taken the ring with him. Uncle Roman saw my reaction and extended his hand to me before retracting it, looking at my parents as he did so. My mother moved to position herself on my left, and my father stood in front of both of us, blocking Uncle Roman from approaching me.

"Luca, Callista, please understand that Sophia had every good intention with her actions. We hoped Elashor would never find him, but when he did, we hoped to fix it and get him back to you as soon as possible. You are like family to us. I know asking for forgiveness is too much but perhaps understanding? I love him and am filled with joy that he is back with you."

There was a pregnant pause as the three key adults in my life deliberated my future and whether Uncle Roman would be allowed in it. Watching them left me feeling like a ship lost at sea trying to decide on two equally desirable ports. I understood that I should never be able to forgive him but found that I yearned with all my being to have him close as well. As the seconds dragged on, the anxiety of the decision coursed through my veins. I wanted to interject but was stopped when my father finally spoke up.

"You're right. I don't know how I will ever be able to forgive you for what you did. You didn't even give *us* the chance to fix this. You simply vanished with my son! You were like a brother to me and Sophia like a sister to Callista." My father scowled.

Uncle Roman dropped his head in acknowledgment of the statement.

"I understand if forgiveness is an impossibility at this time. If the shoe were on the other foot, I would likely feel the same way. So for now, I will go."

His words hit me hard, and I cried out without realizing it. "No!"

I felt my father's eyes immediately and dropped mine away. How unbelievably selfish could I be? My parents are trying to reconcile the past twelve years with my captor, and I cry out to him. The feeling of guilt was swift and just. But the pull for my other father was great. For a fraction of a second, I tempted fate and stole a glance at Uncle Roman. His face was softened by my cry, and I could discern the slight lift to the corner of his lip. In the quickest of movements, I noticed him nod in approval and understood that he appreciated my sentiment and reciprocated it before continuing to speak.

"I need to find Elashor and the ring. Until that time Jace—I mean Christian is still in danger."

Listening to the exchange, I felt as though my body was made of lead. I was unsure of what to say. As I watched Uncle Roman turn to leave, I found myself incapable of standing still and watching him leave without a proper goodbye. Before my brain had the opportunity to process my desire, my legs reacted, and I ran to him, grabbing him by the arm. He swung around, eyes wide until he saw it was me, and his features tempered. Words still escaping me, I pulled him into a hug until I felt him lift his arms and embrace me as well.

"I love you! I have always loved you, and I will always love you," I said.

He pulled away, and I could see the tears in his eyes as he touched the side of my face as he had done so many times in the past to comfort me. He then leaned in to kiss my forehead.

"I love you too and hope to see you soon, but I have unfinished business I must attend to."

"Where will you go?" I asked.

He smiled a sad smile before he answered, "Although we stopped him today, he still believes you are his. So he will return to claim you. I will track him and keep him away from you as best I can."

Fear ran through me like ice water. As I tried to speak, he grabbed my arm firmly and looked me in the eye.

"I told you I would protect you as long as I am able, and I still plan to continue with that promise. Now that you are with your parents, I can set about being on the offensive instead of always having to run."

He let go of my arm, and the area he was standing in began to glow brightly. When it had returned to normal, a small ball of light floated where my uncle had been. I watched and waved as it flew out of the room.

While I was still looking up, my parents had walked up to me. Looking at where my uncle had just been, my dad said, "Let's go home."

CHAPTER 28

New Beginnings

Shortly after Uncle Roman had left, I inspected the chamber we were standing in. It no longer looked like the throne room we had been in just moments before and had morphed into a normal cave. I felt my jaw open slightly, and I turned to my dad to ask about it but was cut off by Marcus, "What happened to creepy Munchkinland?"

"Iabriaria is a fairy realm controlled by the Fairy Court or someone in it. Elashor is one of the highest reigning beings, so he can bring forth Iabriaria wherever he needs it to be. Since he is no longer here, there is no need for it to be here either," my father answered.

We all stared at the now-barren rocks and the small opening in the wall leading down to a tunnel.

"I'm assuming it will be a much easier trip out than it was in?" Izzie asked, concern in her eyes.

"Yes. Since there is no more magic overlaying it, we should be able to leave with no problems right through the corridor there," my mother pointed to a fissure in the wall.

"What problems did you face?" I asked.

"Let's put it this way. Have you ever had one of those dreams where you walk through one door only to realize it's a dead end? You go to walk back through the previous door, and it opens to a completely different room?" Brian asked.

I nodded as I looked from face to face.

"Well, I wish it had been *that* easy!" Brian answered.

I felt my eyes widen as I imagined the frustration and fear they must have encountered while trying to get to me. Then I remembered Marcus saying that he heard me five days ago.

"So how long have we been in here?" I asked, unsure if I wanted the answer.

"It could have been hours, days, or even years. We'll know when we leave," my mom said.

"Let's gather up everyone and move out. How many captives were there?" my father asked.

We all looked to the back corner where they had been prior to the transformation, only to find empty areas of dirt.

"Where did they go?" Izzie asked with panic in her voice as she desperately swung her head back and forth, running around the room.

"I-I'm not sure!" my mother answered hesitantly.

Peace filled me as I heard my uncle from somewhere in the back of my mind. "I sent them home. As far as anyone knows, no time has passed. You will remember what happened, but they will not." A chuckle echoed inside my skull before he continued, "Glamor has its perks!"

As the voice faded, I lifted my head to see seven sets of eyes staring at me.

"Uncle Roman brought them home when he left. It will appear as though no time has passed, but we will remember what happened."

"How will that work? Will it be Halloween still or the beginning of October when we go back?" Izzie asked.

"I'm thinking Halloween," I answered.

"Wonderful! Three weeks' worth of memories that Zoe will have and I won't. I'm going to be in the doghouse till Christmas!" Brian exclaimed.

"All right, let's get moving. I'll take the lead," Sheriff Powell said.

Climbing the rubble at the head of the corridor, we watched for signs of collapse and shifting earth. With each person who passed over the mound of debris, Izzie shifted back and forth while wringing her hands.

"Are you okay?" I asked.

"You'll be okay. We know what to look for this time," Marcus said reassuringly.

Unsure of what he meant, I shot him a glance. He gave me a half smile. "The walkway collapsed in the tunnel, and Izzie almost fell through it. Your dad grabbed her and pulled her back before she could, but I think it left a lasting impression."

I felt my eyes widen as I turned to look at Izzie, whose eyebrows were still furrowed as she looked back at me. Seeing her fear, I extended my arm. She walked to where I was, and I wrapped her in my arms.

"I am so sorry you went through that. Stay close to me when we go through the tunnel. I see a bit better in the dark."

She wrapped her arms around my waist and squeezed before lifting her head to meet my eyes and nodded.

Looking toward the rubble, I saw my mother watching us, smiling in approval.

"Let's get going, you two!" my father said.

"Are you ready?" I asked.

"Yes," Izzie answered with hesitation still in her voice but more sure than before.

Marcus climbed up the heap and waited at the top with his hand extended, waiting for her to grab hold. I nodded my head toward the pile, holding her by the arm, and guided her as she started her ascent. Unsure if the rubble would support both our weights, I stayed on the bottom. I steered her footing as best I could till Marcus was able to grab hold of her hand and pull her up to him successfully. Then he supported her across the top and disappeared.

Within a second or two, Marcus popped his head back up over the hill with his hand extended again, waiting to pull me up. Placing my hands and feet strategically, I systematically scaled the small wall. Even then, I could feel the earth shifting below me. I looked toward the summit and could see Marcus there, watching me intently. I reached him, and just as I was about to make contact, I felt the boulder under my left foot shift and the ground underneath me spasmed violently.

I was grasping wildly for something to stop my fall when I felt two arms grab hold of each of my arms. When I looked up, they belonged to Izzie and Marcus.

"So who's the one with superpowers in this friendship? You know, with the number of times I've had to save *you!*" Marcus said between grunts as he pulled me up the wall.

As I cleared the precipice, I felt the corner of my lip lift.

"You know, you *do* make a good sidekick!" I teased back.

"How are you three doing up there?" I heard George call from the bottom of the pile, which was roughly twenty feet down.

Izzie spun her body around to a sitting position. She angled herself to slide down the remainder of the way. My father had positioned himself at the bottom to catch her when she got there. Watching as she pushed off the wall, I felt my heartbeat quicken until I saw her land safely in my father's arms.

"Who's next?" he called up.

"If I go, will you promise not to fall backward or disappear or do some other alternative universe stuff?" Marcus asked with a grin, his eyebrow raised.

"Yeah, I think I'll be okay." I rolled my eyes at him.

He turned to position himself much like Izzie had before he slid down into my father's arms. I spared one backward glance for the now-barren room where I had been held captive for three weeks. Then I swung my legs around and pushed off the hill. I slid down until I felt my father grab hold of my waist to stabilize me.

"You good?"

"Yes, sir."

Cupping the back of my head, he pulled me into a hug again before we joined the remainder of the group. They were standing at the opening of a tunnel just big enough for one person to pass through.

"It may get a bit tight in there, but we will fit," my dad said, watching my face.

George went in first, followed by Mitchell, Brian, and Marcus. My mother extended her hand to Izzie, and they entered the narrow cavern next. My dad put his hand on my shoulder and guided me toward the opening.

"I'll be right behind you," he said.

I nodded before turning sideways to enter the tight opening. As I shimmied through the tunnel, I could feel a wave of claustrophobia pass over as my back and stomach met a wall simultaneously.

"We're almost past it. Just keep moving," my father encouraged.

Unable to move my head to look back at him, I kept up at my current pace. By then, I was anxiously anticipating the end of this torment. Just when I thought that I wouldn't be able to take anymore, I felt the distance between the walls gape, and I could breathe in deeply again.

Within a few paces, I had exited the corridor and was able to turn and walk straight. Just ahead of me, I could see our small group convening and felt my pace quicken to catch up with them.

"We're almost to the entrance," my mother was saying, pointing at something on the wall.

"We made markings when we realized the caves were shifting. It was so we would know where we had been and if we were looping back on ourselves. This was the first one," Brian explained.

Continuing, I could feel a shift in the temperature of the cave and realized that there had been a chill before while there wasn't one now. A bit further, I saw the dimness of the cavern being replaced by the warm glow of a late fall day from the outside.

"I can see daylight!" Izzie exclaimed as she started to run toward it.

Within a few feet, she had cleared around a corner and was no longer visible. I felt as if my heart were being squeezed in a vice. My imagination brought to life a thousand possibilities of her demise causing me to scream out, "Izzie!" as I ran toward her last position.

Reaching the blind curve she had vanished in, I picked up my speed, which nearly matched my pulse. As I was just about to clear it, she suddenly popped back around the bend. Skidding on the gravel, she let out a yip as we nearly collided, causing her to jump back and grab at her chest.

"What?" she asked in an irritated voice.

"I-I didn't know where you were," I managed lamely.

Her face relaxed as a small smile tickled the corner of her lips. "I'm right here. The entrance is just around the corner, and we have a surprise for you!"

Confused, I felt my eyebrows lift as I considered what it could be.

"I'm not sure I'm a big fan of surprises anymore. I think I have had enough to last me a lifetime," I said.

"True…but follow me anyway."

Grabbing my hand, she half dragged me through the last part of the tunnel. As we exited, I felt the glow of the sun beating onto my face. I shielded my eyes from the sharp contrast of the light and tried to focus. I was blinking feverishly to force my pupils to adjust to the new surroundings when I heard, *Was that barking?*

Next to me, I heard Izzie making a kissing noise while she clapped her hands. As I squinted, I could see the large form of my German shepherd barreling toward me like a small missile. Realizing that the impact was imminent, I braced myself. I was still thrown backward onto the sandy floor when he hit me. My face was covered with dog drool within seconds, and my body battered as he pounced all over me.

"Buddy!" I exclaimed, in between the loving assault, trying to calm him and hug him at the same time.

"Where has he been?" I asked as I attempted to crawl out from below him and stand.

"With Kelly. He's been waiting for us," George answered as he walked over to Kelly and patted him on the shoulder.

"How long were we gone?" George asked him.

"About ten hours. Give or take," he answered.

"I guess Nick was right. There wasn't going to be much of a lag in time," My dad said.

Kelly's eyebrow raised as he appraised the faces of the group and asked, "How long did you *think* you were gone?" he asked.

"It depends on who you ask. Jace thought it was only a few hours, but we felt like it was almost a week," Mitchell answered.

I felt Izzie come up from behind and start brushing off dirt and debris from my back. Her actions prompted me to look around and determine where we were. A strange sense of *déjà vu* hit me when I saw the enormous wall and sandy walkway. In the distance, the remnants of a firepit and the dilapidated pieces of wood that had acted as parking barricades were present.

"Are we at the blue grotto?" I asked.

"Yes. It surprised us when your trail led us back here. After you disappeared, we came back to Williston to pick up clues. It was a bit ironic that this was our starting point," Sheriff Powell answered.

"So we're close to the houses?" I asked.

"Yes. I would *really* like to see my family and make sure they are all right," Izzie said anxiously.

"I have the vans over here, ready for you," Mitchell answered.

I narrowed my eyes at him, remembering the last time I was a passenger in his van. He laughed a deep belly laugh.

"These vans have seats!"

Parked in the distance, I saw two passenger vans with men that I did not recognize sitting in the driver's seats. As we approached, both men jumped out and rushed around to the side doors to open them for us.

"Thank you, Victor and Darryl," my father said as he shook each of their hands.

Turning back to the group that had formed, my father seemed to take us all in.

"This is where we will part ways. Victor will take Brian, Izzie, and Marcus back to Williston while Darryl will drop George, Kelly, and Mitchell off. Then he will drive us back to Emerald Creek."

It felt as though the ground was giving way and I would fall through it. As far as my father was concerned, there would be no long drawn-out goodbyes. We would part as what, acquaintances? A bond had been created here, and I couldn't just walk away from it so easily. This move felt like all the previous moves my aunt and uncle had put me through and I felt my anger mounting.

Out of the corner of my eye, I could see my mother touch my father's arm. She walked toward me and gently touching my arm too as she said, "This isn't goodbye. This is more of a see you later."

"You don't understand! This is all I have ever done! But this time, I have friends! Please don't do this! Please don't make me leave!"

My mother looked back at my father, whose face was resolute, before looking back at me.

"You have powers that are just blossoming. Emerald Creek is well-protected and will allow you to grow and learn what you are capable of without danger from outside forces. I promise you will see them all again." My mother's voice was melodic but sincere, which helped to calm me.

"Many people in Williston think your parents are dead, that you have been living with your aunt and uncle. How would you explain that?" Brian interjected.

I stared at him, understanding what he was saying, but not ready to say our send-offs. I felt the familiar burn in my eyes as I fought tears that were defiantly still forming. I felt someone gently touch my left arm. Looking down, I could see Izzie's knitted brows and her trembling chin.

Opening my mouth, I tried to speak, but no words came out. She threw her arms around my waist and squeezed tight. The feel of her head pressed gently against my chest felt like home, leaving me instantly relaxed and wanting to never let go. Wanting to pull her closer to me, I raised my arms to engulf her in an embrace as well. Loosening her grip, she looked up at me and lifted herself onto her toes till she was nearly eye to eye with me. Her pupils were dilated, and her breathing had picked up, which caused me alarm, till she leaned forward and kissed me gently on the lips. A second later, she pulled back, and I regretted not knowing her intention. Fearing that I had ruined the moment, I lifted my hand to cup her cheek and leaned down. This time, the kiss was deep and lingered as we reveled in each other, allowing all those around us to disappear. At that moment, it was just us and I was not ready to let it pass. It wasn't until I heard my father clear his throat that I was catapulted back to reality. As we parted, Izzie dropped her head but was smiling.

"Don't forget about me?" she whispered.

"I could never forget about you."

Her face softened as a smile glinted across it. As I stared at her, I felt a firm pat on the back.

"We have quite a few missions set up on *Castle Core*. We're going to need the expertise of a wizard," Marcus said as he walked around to face me.

I felt the corner of my lip lift as he spoke.

"What's a wizard next to a god?" I asked.

"Good question. Upon further consideration, I think you'll be an asset to the cohort, but I will still be its leader," he answered with a grin.

"I'm going to miss not seeing you on the block, but I'm glad we got to meet," he continued as he ran his hand through his hair.

"We never got to clean your garage," I reminded him, which made him wince.

"If you could send some magical wind down to clean it, I would be eternally grateful."

"I'll see what I can do!"

Over Marcus's shoulder, I saw Brian standing there with his arms crossed over his chest, staring at me.

"Quite the adventure you took me on. You know I'm going to have Zoe call *you* every time I forget something that she thinks happened."

I let out a small laugh as I extended a fist to him. He stared at it for a second before walking toward me. Pushing it out of the way, he wrapped his arms around my body, pinning my arms. He lifted me in a gigantic bear hug, slightly swinging my legs as he did. When my feet touched the floor, Marcus and Izzie walked over, and we all joined in a group hug.

I felt a stray tear fall from my eye and heard Marcus mumble something in my shirt.

"What?" I asked as I wiped away the tear quickly.

"So how far do you think our little mental radio signal will last?"

"I'm not sure," I answered as I looked at my parents.

"With practice, you likely could hear each other from virtually anywhere," said my mom.

"Wonderful. I'll get to hear Marcus at night playing Dungeons and Dragons," Brian said as he rolled his eyes.

Izzie, Marcus, and I all corrected him simultaneously, "*Castle Core!*"

"Whatever!" his mock annoyance quickly relaxed into a smile.

As we parted, Izzie, Marcus, and Brian walked toward Victor's van. I stood there watching them, wondering what the next few days and weeks would bring for me. Without turning my head, I felt my mom come up on my right and my dad on my left. We stood there, watching my three best friends in the world driving away. I watched as their rearview lights slowly faded before finally turning and disappearing.

Instinctively, I turned inward, *Can you hear me?* I thought and waited for a reply.

After standing there for what seemed to be an eternity, I felt my bonds tug.

"*Seriously? We just left!*" Marcus scoffed.

"*We all hear you!*" Izzie answered, chuckling at Marcus's answer.

"*Yay... Something that I can't turn off,*" Brian replied with a strong note of sarcasm in his tone.

I chuckled to myself and turned to my parents. At that moment, I understood that although my life was never going to be the same, it was still going to be okay. For the first time, I was going to have a home that I would never have to move from ever again. And that no matter where I was, I had three friends that I knew had my back completely and always would. Although I would no longer see Uncle Roman as I had for the past twelve years, the knowledge that he was out there and still watching over me gave me a sense of peace. But most importantly, my parents were alive and well and would always be with me from now on. As I counted my blessings in my head, I heard my dad.

"Are you ready to start your next adventure?" he asked.

"I am now," I said.

CPSIA information can be obtained
at www.ICGtesting.com
Printed in the USA
BVHW040905111122
651446BV00038B/731/J

9 781639 858361